# THE WEIGHT OF WORDS

## GEORGINA GUTHRIE

OMNIFIC PUBLISHING
LOS ANGELES

Omnific Publishing
1901 Avenue of the Stars, 2nd floor
Los Angeles, CA 90067
www.omnificpublishing.com

First Omnific eBook edition, November 2013
First Omnific trade paperback edition, November 2013

The characters and events in this book are fictitious.
Any similarity to real persons, living or dead,
is coincidental and not intended by the author.

Library of Congress Cataloguing-in-Publication Data

Guthrie, Georgina.
   The Weight of Words / Georgina Guthrie – 1st ed.
   ISBN: 978-1-623420-72-7
   1. Contemporary Romance — Fiction. 2. University — Fiction.
   3. Shakespeare — Fiction. 4. Forbidden Romance — Fiction. I. Title

10 9 8 7 6 5 4 3 2 1

Cover Design by Micha Stone and Amy Brokaw
Interior Book Design by Coreen Montagna

Printed in the United States of America

Titian (Tiziano Vecellio) (Italian, about 1487 – 1576)
*Venus and Adonis*, about 1555 – 1560, Oil on canvas
The J. Paul Getty Museum, Los Angeles

# Aubrey

# The Wise Man's Son

Journeys end in lovers meeting,
Every wise man's son doth know.
(*Twelfth Night*, Act ii, Scene 3)

Some people thrive on conflict, but I've never been a fan of it. Years of listening to my parents arguing in their bedroom taught me to flee at the first sign of any verbal altercation. So when the sound of a heated conversation drifted out from behind my boss's door one morning, I cringed. Unaccustomed to hearing the dean of Victoria College shouting, I distanced myself from the argument, crossing to the far side of the outer office where I started plucking dead leaves from a hanging plant. It was a wasted effort. The voices only got louder.

"You've got to be kidding me, Dad!" I heard from inside the office. "Do we really have to go over this again? Enough already!"

*Dad?*

I froze, a dried leaf crumbling in my hand. Dean Grant was arguing with his son? I considered escaping to the washroom down the hall, but before I could bolt I heard Dean Grant angrily directing his son to stop shouting. Both men dropped their voices until all I could hear were harsh murmurs.

I tiptoed back to my desk, prepared to dash out if things escalated again, but there were no more eruptions. The dean's door swung open a few moments later, and his son strode out, averting his face as he walked past my desk. I shuffled a few papers around, pretending to look busy, but I couldn't help taking a quick peek as he made his way to the door.

I'd never met this son — or any of Dean Grant's family members for that matter — but from what little I could see, this young man's appearance clashed entirely with that of his perpetually well-tailored, carefully-groomed father.

"Different as chalk and cheese," my mother would say. *A recipe for disaster.*

As Dean Grant's son crashed out of the office, his leather laptop bag banged against the door frame. Stray papers threatened to spill from the top flap, and he muttered, "Fucking damn it," while jamming them deeper into the bag and kicking the door closed with his foot.

I blushed, not because I was offended by colorful language — far from it — but because I was certain Dean Grant, a consummate gentleman in every way, was standing right behind me. Sure enough, when I turned around, he was in his office doorway, grimacing in the direction of his son's retreating figure.

"Sorry, Aubrey, I'm sure that was unpleasant for you," he said. "That's my son, Daniel. He's having a bad time of it at the moment, but there's no excuse for crass behavior. I apologize on his behalf." He handed me several manila folders. "Can you please file these?" he added before returning to his office and closing the door.

I wasn't sure if I was more embarrassed for myself or him. In the five months I'd worked in the office part-time, I'd never once seen the dean lose his shit or overreact, even though his position required him to deal with all manner of crappy student issues. Then again, it's the people we love most who have a knack for pushing our buttons. Hearing him lose his temper with his son didn't make me respect him any less. It simply allowed me to see a human side I hadn't been privy to before.

I glanced at the clock. Eleven twenty. Ten minutes left in my shift. I rounded my desk, filed the folders, and organized some other papers and documents. Then I knocked on Dean Grant's door.

"Yes?" he called.

I poked my head into his office. "I'm on my way, sir. I've left Gisele some notes for this afternoon so she knows what I didn't get around to finishing. I hope your day gets better."

"Thank you, Aubrey. I hope so, too. See you on Wednesday morning. Don't work too hard, now." He wagged his finger at me, and I smiled as I left.

We both knew I wasn't about to ease up simply because the end was in sight. I was eager to maintain my excellent GPA *and* my place on the dean's list, an honor which meant so much more given the admiration I had for the man who conferred it.

Belongings in hand, I locked up for the lunch hour. Outside, the wind buffeted me across the snow-covered quad and over to Jackman Hall. All was quiet inside the residence apartment, my roommates nowhere to be seen. I tripped over the boots and coat Matt had left in the middle of the hallway the night before. His door was closed. I tried to move quietly, imagining him inside and sleeping off a brutal frat party hangover. Joanna's bedroom door was wide open, but I didn't look for her. She had a full morning of classes.

In my own room, I changed out of my nicer work clothes and put on a pair of jeans and a long-sleeved T-shirt. I surveyed my face in the mirror. The February *blahs* had set in and, along with them, a pallid complexion that positively screamed for some sun. Some girls could carry off the pale skin associated with long Canadian winters, their eyes leaping out of the creamy landscapes of their faces. I was not one of those girls.

I grimaced at my reflection and rooted around for an elastic hair tie, noting as I combed my hair back that my warm streaks were looking less like honey and more like molasses. Yet another victim of this year's long winter. I needed some vitamin D in the worst way. I also needed to hurry the hell up and quit mooning at myself if I wanted to get across campus in time for my class at noon.

Dragging my coat on, I dashed out of the apartment and hiked across campus. The stinging wind urged me along the paths through Queen's Park and bit my ears. Why hadn't I worn a hat? And where the hell were my gloves? I picked up my pace, setting my sights on the other side of the park, all but jogging by the time I reached University College, the imposing gothic building where I'd attended countless English lectures and tutorials over the past four years. A wall of warm air greeted me as I vaulted inside. Sweet relief.

I made my way up to the second floor, full of anticipation for my new class. This wasn't any old course. I was on the brink of the final semester of my U of T undergraduate career. My four full-time classes had reached the mid-term point, but I was starting my second half-course of the year — Studies in Shakespeare — a full three months studying my favorite writer. To say I was excited was putting things mildly.

The room was already crowded, but I scouted out an empty aisle seat near a heating vent by the door and made myself comfortable. The air blasting from the heater smelled faintly of wet gym socks. I wrinkled my nose but stayed put, prepared to suck it up. I was way too cold to switch seats.

A flurry of movement at the front of the room signaled Professor Brown's arrival. I craned my neck around the people sitting in front of me and watched as he settled in behind the podium, smiling at the assembled students. I'd taken two of Professor Brown's courses in the past, and we'd always had an awesome rapport — a definite bonus. His smile always made me think of my grandfather — a combination of cheekiness and unquestionable wisdom. I couldn't think of a better way to round out my course load as I neared graduation.

"Good morning, ladies and gentlemen," he said, moving over to the oak door and peering at his watch. "Or should I say *good afternoon?* I gather you're all here because you have an immeasurable love for the Bard and his works, and if that's not true, best make a speedy retreat now. I'll close my eyes for thirty seconds so you can run for it."

He made a show of covering his eyes. The class laughed politely as he peeked through his fingers.

"No takers? Excellent!" He closed the door soundly. "My name is Martin Brown, and I'll be your guide as you pursue your own passionate inquiry into some facet of the great Master's work. We will read some of his plays and sonnets together, but you will also chart your own course, studying an aspect of this unparalleled dramatist's work which most appeals to you."

Around the room, many of my forty or so peers smiled and whispered to each other. During this brief interlude, we were interrupted when the door reopened and a young man with a now-familiar head of dark messy hair flew in and headed straight toward Professor Brown.

"So sorry I'm late, sir," he murmured, moving past the professor to drop his bag on the table at the front of the room.

Professor Brown turned back to the class with a warm smile and gestured toward the newcomer. "Ladies and gentlemen, I'd like to introduce you to my graduate teaching assistant, Daniel Grant."

At that point, Dean Grant's son turned around and I saw his face for the first time as he scanned the room. He had the most glorious blue eyes I'd ever seen.

*Shakespeare who?*

# Playing the Fool

The fool doth think he is wise,
but the wise man knows himself to be a fool.
(*As You Like It,* Act v, Scene 1)

Professor Brown motioned for Daniel to take a seat at the wide table at the front of the room and then continued his introduction to the course. He might as well have been speaking Egyptian for all I heard. I was completely distracted by the young man sitting behind the table, appraising the students before him. He seemed tense, probably still reeling from his earlier argument with his father.

I tried not to stare, but I couldn't drag my eyes away from his features. My first impression of him earlier that morning had been right on the money. Unlike his father, he had a complete disregard for his appearance. Half of his collar was tucked inside the neck of his shirt, and there was an enormous hole in the knee of his jeans. If he was going for the absent-minded professor look, he was on the right track. Yet despite his shoddy grooming, his glorious eyes, defined cheekbones, and full lips tipped the scales completely to the other side. Simply put, he was gorgeous.

As he tossed his head to flick the hair out his eyes, I found my-self mirroring his gesture, my own headshake an attempt to make myself focus on Professor Brown who was gesturing toward Daniel and suggesting he go through the tutorial process. Daniel stood and pulled his bag toward the podium.

"Yes, as Professor Brown said, I'll be the TA for this course. I'll attend classes along with you, and I'll be responsible for evaluating some of your term work," he explained. "You'll each participate in one tutorial a week. The class will be split into three fairly equal seminar groups, and part of your course mark will be a result of the effort you put into these tutorials. I'll post these sign-up sheets outside the seminar room downstairs tomorrow morning at quarter to nine."

He gestured to three crumpled sheets. Were those the papers he'd mashed into his bag earlier? I suppressed a smile. He really was a hot mess.

"It's up to you to get here early tomorrow to secure the tutorial spot you'd prefer, and the first session will be on Wednesday," he added, casting his eyes around the room. As his eyes flickered over mine, my stomach flipped.

*What the hell?*

"Are there any questions?" he asked. I saw movement in my pe-ripheral vision. "Yes? Go ahead, name first, please," Daniel said.

"Hi, I'm Cara. Cara Switzer."

I stifled a groan. Of course. When I leaned forward, I noticed her D-cups—her best asset—commanding the attention of all the males in her general vicinity. Even a couple of females looked suitably impressed. Having taken a couple of courses with Cara in the past, I remembered her inability to string together an intelligible phrase and braced myself.

"I was wondering," she said, her inflection going up at the end and making the statement sound like a question. "If we, like, need *extra* help, will you be available in your office to meet and stuff like that?"

Her inane question along with its suggestive undertone aroused a few muffled titters. I glanced at Daniel, interested in his reaction. A muscle in his jaw twitched before he looked at Professor Brown, who merely waved his hand at his TA as if to say, "You're on your own with this one."

"Well, I don't actually have an office of my own, but it's incumbent on me to be available at certain fixed times to discuss any questions or difficulties you might have," Daniel said. "Of course, you could make an appointment outside of those times as well."

I peered around at Cara who was making a show of nodding innocently, her *genuinely intelligent inquiry* answered. She didn't fool me. I was sure she was racking her brain to figure out what the word "incumbent" meant.

Daniel took his seat, and Professor Brown proceeded to deliver an introductory lecture, which I did my level best to pay attention to despite the epic distraction sitting at the front of the room. After a thirty-minute spiel, Professor Brown gathered his papers into a neat pile.

"Okay, folks, we'll leave it there for today," he said. "You know from your reading list that you're to have read *Hamlet* before Wednesday. It's a whopper to start with, but '*though this be madness, yet there's method in't.*'"

He looked around the room, one eyebrow raised. This was a challenge. Among those who took his classes, Professor Brown was known for quoting Shakespeare from time to time and expecting someone to be able to identify the play, the character, or the scene. He continued to look around, but no one was biting, perhaps not realizing what he was waiting for.

I raised my hand reluctantly.

"Miss Price! Nice to see you again. Taking a stab at it, are we?"

"Yes, sir." I saw Daniel lean forward at the front table, perching his chin on his clasped hands. "The speaker is Polonius in act two of *Hamlet*, reacting to the strange behavior of King Claudius's nephew," I said, confident in my knowledge of the play.

"Nicely done, Miss Price." Professor Brown's smile was complimentary. "I see you haven't lost your impeccable attention to detail. I'm eager to see what topic you select for study this semester." He nodded to indicate he was done for the day, and people began to gather their belongings and move toward the door.

I snuck a glance at Daniel. He'd relaxed back in his seat, rubbing his chin as he appraised me. I held his gaze boldly, and he tilted his head forward, as if to commend me for impressing Professor Brown. I averted my eyes, stomach somersaulting again.

*What, now I'm in grade nine?*

When I looked up again, Cara was flouncing past the table at the front of the room with one of her ditzy friends. "Have a good afternoon, *sir*," she purred, sashaying toward the door, and then giggling at her dopey girlfriend beside her, mouthing, "I know, right?" She wasn't even remotely discreet.

Daniel nodded at the two idiotic girls, remaining seated and busying himself with his wrinkly papers. I was pulled out of my reverie by a sudden noise behind me—a girl clambering down the aisle and then throwing her arms around my neck.

"Aub! It's so good to see you!"

"Julie? I'm so glad you're here!"

My enthusiastic greeting was entirely genuine. Julie Harper and I had taken several courses together over the last three years, hanging out between classes and sitting together at lectures. We'd been in touch on Facebook over the past few months, but we'd both been busy and struggled to find time to meet in person. I was happy to see we'd be able to rekindle our easy friendship.

"I didn't see you when I came in," I said. "Where were you sitting?"

"I was at the back. Normally I don't care if I can't see anything as long as I can hear, but I was kicking myself today," she added, her voice dropping to a lower register. "If you know what I'm sayin'."

She raised one eyebrow and gave her head a subtle bob toward the front of the room where Daniel was doing his best to iron out the three wrinkly papers. I put on a face of mock horror. "Julie Harper, I am shocked and appalled at what you're suggesting."

She laughed. "I've missed you, girl," she said. "We'll get caught up later, okay? I've gotta run. Rehearsal in fifteen minutes on the other side of campus."

"Rehearsal," I said, pointing to the tightly coiled blond bun perched on the top of her head. "That explains it."

"I know, right?" she said. "Super attractive. Look, let's grab a coffee or something after we sign up for the tutorial tomorrow."

"For sure."

She smiled and squeezed my arm before pulling on a striped toque and racing out the door. I gathered my belongings and made my way out into the corridor in time to see Daniel heading down the stairs. It was the second time in as many hours that I'd seen him walking away from me, and this time I checked out his ass. I cursed the wrinkly untucked shirt, but I must say, from what I could see—it was a very fine ass indeed.

At the bottom of the stairs, his phone rang. He fumbled in his pocket, answering as he walked.

"Penny!" he exclaimed. "What a coincidence. I was about to call you. How are you, love?"

*Love? Damn it!*

I clenched my teeth in disappointment, but really, what the hell was I thinking? I'd been aware of his existence for all of two hours and somehow I felt as if I had some claim? I scoffed at how ridiculous I was being. But did that stop me from following him?

Hell no.

On the contrary, I found myself listening in on yet another one of Daniel's private conversations, but whereas the first time I'd tried to remove myself, this time I did the opposite, picking up my pace so I could stay close behind him and eavesdrop. Though I couldn't hear the other side of the conversation, I could guess what the girl had told him based on his reply.

"Miss you? Ha! Completely inconsolable is more like it," he said.

We were almost at the exit when he stopped and leaned against the wall near the large double doors. Worried he'd turn and see me following him, I spun around to face the giant bulletin board on the wall, feigning interest in the flyers and ads attached to it as I listened.

"Well, rest assured, I'll be taking you out for a lovely meal on Valentine's Day, so prepare to be wined and dined," he said, laughing gently. "All right…I love you, too, Penn. Okay, I have a ton of shit to get done. I'll call you later?" After a brief pause he added, "Will do, love. Bye for now."

He hung up, quickly punched a number into his phone and waited. I stood, rooted to the spot, and listened to yet another one-sided conversation during which he spoke to someone named Geoffrey and made a dinner reservation for two for seven thirty on February fourteenth. The boy wasted no time.

At the end of the call, he jammed his phone into his pocket and strode toward the doors, completely oblivious to my existence.

After he left the building, I opened the door a crack. He was crossing King's College circle near a row of cars parked bumper to bumper on the other side of the street. I leaned against the building's stone entryway as he approached a spotless black BMW, unlocked the car, and threw his bag in the trunk. Within moments, he'd hopped in and was off toward University Avenue.

I let out a shaky breath which became a snort as I got a sudden objective view of my behavior. What in the living hell was I doing? I was like a junior high student following around my latest crush like a puppy dog, trying to figure out his class schedule so I could conveniently *appear out of nowhere* at the most opportune moment.

I'm not sure why I found him so fascinating, but one thing was certain: Any hope of a romantic liaison with Daniel Grant was futile. He had a girlfriend. Her name was Penny, he called her "love," and he missed her. No, scratch that—he was *completely inconsolable* without her.

*And* he was the TA of the course I was taking. Definitely a no-touching zone.

Period.

I shook my head, appalled by my invasion of his privacy. I'd had the gall to be all holier than thou while Cara was flirting shamelessly with Daniel, only to turn around and engage in creepy stalker-like behavior myself. Hypocrite.

I rested my head on the stone wall in front of me.

"You stupid fool," I sighed.

# CHAPTER 3

## True Love

The course of true love never did run smooth…
(*A Midsummer Night's Dream,* Act 1, Scene 1)

A blast of winter wind brought me back to my senses. I was standing outdoors in sub-zero temperatures, holding my coat in my hands. I dashed inside to bundle up before making the journey back across campus. I sniffed and gasped as the wind rushed at my face and into my mouth. Spring really couldn't come soon enough.

Inside the apartment, I quickly dropped my bag and coat, my runny nose sending me on a wild goose chase in search of tissues. With none to be found, I ended up in the bathroom, blowing my nose with toilet paper.

When I retraced my steps to the hallway to hang up my coat, I noticed Matt's jacket and boots lying right where I'd seen them earlier. His door was still closed. This wasn't like him. Even after a major booze fest, he rarely stayed in bed past noon, and it was almost one thirty—a perfectly logical scenario if his girlfriend had stayed over, but there was no sign of Sarah's stuff in the hallway and no *Do Not Disturb* sign on his door. I thought of the stories I'd heard about people choking on their own vomit and dying before anyone could help them. I pressed my ear to Matt's door. I couldn't hear anything so I tapped lightly. Still nothing.

I slowly turned the knob and squinted into the dimly lit room. He was lying on his side with his knees curled up, still wearing the clothes he'd gone out in the night before, and staring at the wall. He looked like hell, but he was alive. I breathed a sigh of relief.

"Matt?" I said. "Can I get you something? Water? Tylenol? A bucket?" I added, laughing gently.

His eyes made a lifeless sweep across the room. "I'm not hung over, Aub," he answered flatly.

He turned back to the wall, and my smile receded. Stepping into the room, I noticed balled up Kleenex all over the floor, the box clutched to his chest.

"Are you sick, dude? Do you want me to make you some chicken soup or something?"

He groaned and rolled onto his back. "Sarah dumped me," he said, bringing a hand up to cover his eyes.

"Oh, shit, Matt. I'm so sorry." I sat down beside him. "Do you want to talk about it?"

"No."

His tone was curt, but I knew he didn't mean to hurt me. I started to swing my legs back to the floor, figuring I'd leave him alone to marinate in his misery for a while, when he moved his arm away from his eyes.

"I thought she was *the one*, you know?" he said softly.

His expression was pained, his eyelids puffy. He'd been hardcore crying over this girl. Hell, he was working his way through a whole box of tissues over her.

"I didn't know you guys were headed in that direction," I said. "I knew you liked each other. Some nights I could tell you *really* liked each other." I rattled the headboard, and he shot me a poisonous glare. Okay, I totally deserved that. "I guess I didn't know things had gotten so serious."

He snorted cynically. "Yeah, she had no idea either. Or at least she pretended not to." He sat up and hugged his knees. "I don't know. When she invited me to her place in October to spend Thanksgiving with her family, I thought that seemed like a pretty solid sign.

Maybe she was trying to be nice, knowing I couldn't exactly head to Vancouver for the weekend." He exhaled heavily again. "But we'd been getting along so great. Well, *I* thought so, anyway. Stupid, right?"

He paused to blow his nose, tossing the tissue on the floor with the others. I leaned over, resting my head on his shoulder and rubbing his back. "She doesn't deserve you, sweet cheeks."

He shook his head slowly. "You're right." He leaned his forehead against mine. "I wish you and I weren't so grossed out by each other. We could've been great."

I smiled, remembering the night back in first year about two months after we'd met. We'd become fast friends during frosh week, and Matt was protective of me right out of the gate, but one night at a party, each of us having drunk our fair share of a keg, we found ourselves dancing among a group of gyrating freshmen. One thing led to another, and before we knew it, we were kissing up against a wall and then recoiling in horror, wiping our mouths off frantically. Even with our beer goggles on, we both felt like something akin to incest had occurred. It never happened again, and we remained the best of friends.

He'd become increasingly like a brother as the months went by. We often laughed about that fateful frat party, but whereas I'd always felt we could never be more than great friends, I'd caught him looking at me wistfully from time to time, as if he wished things could be different. That had all ended when he'd started dating Sarah the previous April. He'd fallen for her quickly. And hard.

"Believe me, Matt, there's someone wonderful out there who deserves you." I patted his back. "Shit, that sounds so trite. I'm sorry. I don't know what to say."

"It's okay, Aubs. Thanks for trying. You're an amazing friend." He took my hand and squeezed it.

"Ew, keep your snotty hands to yourself there, cowboy." I pushed myself off the bed and rubbed my stomach. "I'm starved. You interested in eating?"

He sighed in defeat. "Yeah, I guess so. I should shower, too. I've been lying here since midnight. I might need to burn these." He gestured to his rumpled clothes.

"You grab a shower, and I'll make some English muffin pizzas," I offered. "Pepperoni and tomato sound okay?"

"Perfect." He stood up and peeled off his long-sleeved T-shirt. "Now scram, before you get more than you bargained for," he threatened, pulling the top button of his jeans undone. "'Cause by the looks of things, you're finding my ripped abs mighty enticing."

He looked at my chest, cocking an eyebrow. I followed his gaze downward. The headlights were on full-beam.

"Don't flatter yourself." I laughed. "It's cold enough out there to freeze the brass nuts off a monkey. I'm still defrosting."

He snorted and mumbled something about my "sad state of denial" while I headed for the door, carefully navigating around the balled up Kleenex.

Two hours later, Matt was clean and almost human again. While we ate lunch, I'd offered to watch a pretentious film of his choice with him, and we were now curled on the couch watching Sergei Eisenstein's *Battleship Potempkin*. As a film major, Matt was a huge cinema buff. I'd learned a lot about film from him over the last few years, but sometimes I didn't get what all the fuss was about. This was one of those times. I found myself stifling yawns throughout most of the movie.

About half-way in, Matt paused the film. "Can I run something by you?" he asked solemnly.

"Of course." I shifted to face him.

"After I spent Thanksgiving at Sarah's, I guess I kinda got ahead of myself, thinking things were getting serious, and I made a reservation for Valentine's Day for Sarah and me at this restaurant downtown. It's called Canoe — ever heard of it?"

"Dude, are you kidding me? The owners are Oliver and Bonacini, right? They own Auberge du Pommier, too. Their menus are phenomenal. I can't believe you got a reservation!"

"Well, I made it four months in advance. Now I guess it was wasted effort. Unless…" He looked at me expectantly.

"Unless…?" Could he possibly be suggesting what I hoped to God he was suggesting?

"Would you want to come with me?" he blurted. "I know it'll be expensive, and I'll pay. I was going to treat Sarah anyway and, I don't know, maybe you've got plans with someone else, 'cause I don't know what's going on with you and stuff, but I'd love to do this for you, I mean *with* you…" He ran out of steam, trailing off.

I was touched by the sentiment and frankly pretty damn excited about the prospect of eating at Canoe, regardless of the circumstances. I'd always dreaded Valentine's Day and the way popular culture made single people feel crappy—as if we didn't already feel like losers every other day of the year.

"I would *love* to join you for dinner on Valentine's Day. I'll gladly pay for my own dinner, but promise me if you and Sarah get back together, or if you meet someone else you'd rather take, you won't be all freak show about it. Give it to me straight, okay?"

"It's only two weeks away. I think the odds of me meeting the girl of my dreams between now and then are slim to none. As for Sarah, well, she was very, um…*decisive*." His face twisted as he spoke, the previous night's events still too raw.

"You know what I mean," I said, squeezing his hand.

"Yeah."

"Now, I hate to pull the rip cord on our film festival, but I need to get some reading done before tomorrow. You gonna be okay?"

"Yeah, I'm fine. You go ahead," he said. "I might bail on the rest of the movie and take a nap anyway. I'm friggin' exhausted." He punctuated his words with a huge yawn and stretch.

Satisfied that he was all right, I grabbed my backpack, snagged some munchies from the kitchen, and retreated to my room where a giant pile of homework awaited me.

I changed into some cozy clothes and flopped onto my bed. I knew I should do some reading for my children's lit course, but I didn't. Instead, I found some mellow tunes on my iPod and flipped through my *Norton Anthology of Shakespeare* until I found *Hamlet*. I scanned the play, contemplating some of the important themes that might come up in the tutorial.

As soon as the idea of the impending tutorial began swirling in my mind, I completely lost focus. I saw Daniel holding court at the head of the table. I imagined him gazing at me in admiration, oblivious to the other students, as I made one incredibly insightful observation after another. Then the tutorial ended and the room emptied, leaving us alone. He closed the door and swept the table clear of all books and papers so he could lean me over it and have his way with me right then and there—

Crap! What was it about this man that had me feeling like a high school girl with her first crush? Here I was, twenty-three years old and mere months away from graduating from university. I normally wasn't prone to such idle daydreams. But as much as I tried to stop thinking about him and focus on reading, my mind continued to wander, replaying the events of the day.

What had he been arguing with his dad about? What had he been thinking about when he'd looked at me after the lecture? Was his relationship with this Penny woman serious? And did the man really not have access to an iron, razor, or hairbrush? I smiled against my hand.

Feeling more and more like an infatuated, hormone-riddled teenager with every passing moment, I balled up my fists and rubbed them against my eyes. My reading of *Hamlet* wasn't going well.

I slammed my anthology shut and crawled into bed with my copy of *Haroun and the Sea of Stories,* yet another book I was supposed to have finished reading by now. I struggled along for about an hour, but my bed was so comfy and warm and the music from my iPod dock so soothing that soon my eyes began to close.

My last thought before drifting into unconsciousness was the look on Daniel's face as he'd nodded at me, giving me silent kudos for identifying Professor Brown's *Hamlet* passage. I'd probably never know what he'd been thinking, but at least he'd noticed me. That was something, wasn't it?

# Some Must Watch

For some must watch, while some must sleep:
Thus runs the world away.
(*Hamlet*, Act III, Scene 2)

Y ou know when you have a hot dream about a guy, and then
you see him, and the dream rushes back to you and it feels so
real — more like a memory than a dream? That's what happened
when I walked toward the tutorial room at eight forty-five the next
morning. Daniel was standing in the open doorway, and the most
amazing series of risqué images flashed before my eyes. I quickly
ducked into an alcove to collect my thoughts or, more accurately, to
eagerly sift through the details of the dream.

Daniel had been watching me scan a bookshelf full of Shakespeare's works. One minute he'd been suggesting books that I might
like to borrow, and the next thing I knew, he was coming up behind
me and pushing me up against the bookcase, his hand in my hair,
his lips brushing my neck. I wasn't sure if I'd said anything, but his
voice had been hot and insistent at my ear as he slowly undressed me.

*"I can't stop thinking about you."*

*"Your skin is so soft."*

*"Please tell me you want me as much as I want you…"*

The memories sparked a hot flush. How could I walk down the hall and greet him without betraying my thoughts? On the other hand, how could I leave without seeing him? I was damned if I was going to pass up the opportunity to talk to him one on one.

I fanned my warm cheeks, took a quick cleansing breath, and then put my game face on, resuming my journey down the hall toward the seminar room. Daniel looked hotter than hell, still sporting yesterday's five o'clock shadow, but somehow he was even more gorgeous than the day before. He was leaning casually against the doorway, one hand propped against the frame, the other stuffed in the front pocket of an ancient-looking leather jacket.

*Holy hell, man. Could you be any more stunning?*

Three other students from the class were standing in front of the bulletin board, pens in hand, hemming and hawing, weighing their tutorial time options. Daniel watched them impassively. Was he always so miserable? Would it kill him to smile?

*I bet Penny makes him smile,* I thought dismally.

I stood behind my three indecisive classmates, waiting for them to finish and move the hell out of the way. As I peered impatiently over their shoulders, I noticed Daniel had taken the time to make new sign-up sheets. All three pages were crisp and clean, pinned to the cork board in a neat row.

The three stooges in front of me finally got their shit together, signed up for the Wednesday time slot, and moved away down the hall. I stepped forward, finding all fourteen spots on Friday available. A few keen people had already signed up for the Monday and Wednesday tutorials. I was beginning to wonder where Julie was and whether I should call or text her when Daniel moved from his post at the door, taking a few slow steps toward me.

"You're Miss Price, right?" His voice was smooth and silky.

"That's right. You have a good memory." I flashed what I hoped was a fabulous smile. "Aubrey Price," I said, and as I spoke—I had to do it—I reached out, offering a handshake.

He glanced at my outstretched hand, and I thought for a second he might refuse my gesture, but then his palm pressed warmly against mine. It sent a surge of heat through me—not a jolt like an electric shock or anything ridiculous like that—but more like a wave, a slow moving but eventually all-encompassing surge of warmth, which turned my brain, among other things, to jelly. An image of his fingers curling around mine as he pushed me against that bookshelf made my knees weak.

"Well, Miss Price, it's a pleasure to meet you," he said, reclaiming his hand and entirely ignoring my first name.

"You can call me Aubrey," I said.

"I don't think I've ever heard that name before. It's quite unique."

"I was named after my grandmother. It's a bit old-fashioned, I guess, but better than the alternative, which would have been way worse."

He cocked his head as if he expected me to explain myself. The chiseled perfection of his jaw up close obliterated my ability to think straight, but I stupidly barreled on anyway.

"Honeysuckle," I explained. "It's my mother's favorite plant. My dad swears she wanted to call me that. Honeysuckle Price. Sounds a bit like a stripper's name, right?"

I have no idea what possessed me to share this story or to ask him such a stupid question, but he nodded, seeming to give serious thought to the issue.

"I imagine it would have been an interesting name to endure."

I swallowed and shifted my weight, wondering if I should assure him that I wasn't a stripper and had no aspirations of ever becoming one. Luckily for me, he spoke first.

"So based on your exchange with Professor Brown yesterday, I gather you two are acquainted?" he said.

"Yes, this is my third time in his class. Not the same class of course—I passed the other two—which were two different courses and this one's different as well."

I realized with horror that I'd become as inarticulate as Cara Switzer. But in my defense, he was gazing at me with those fathomless blue eyes and speaking to me with those delicious full lips…

"You'll have to excuse me," I said. "I can't seem to think straight this morning. I didn't get much sleep, not because, you know…" *Oh my God!* "Well, I had a—well, rough night—and oh man, I need a coffee."

I clamped my mouth shut, figuring I'd better quit while I was ahead. But then the heavens opened and a choir of angels sang because he smiled at me, and he had these cute wrinkles around his eyes and the most gorgeous dimple puckered his right cheek. It was the most beautiful thing I'd ever seen.

"Don't worry," he assured me, leaning forward. "I feel your pain. I was in a rush to get here and missed my chance to grab coffee. I must look like I've been dragged through a hedge backwards."

I smiled at his choice of expressions, exactly the sort of thing Granddad Price used to say. I remembered Dean Grant once mentioning his wife's English background. Perhaps Daniel had an English grandfather who used silly expressions too.

"Hmm, well, it can be tricky getting into a routine at the beginning of a new semester," I said. "I'm sure you've got lots of intro stuff to deal with, right?"

"Yes, if it's not one thing it's another." He breathed out like he was preparing to end the conversation. I wasn't ready for the exchange to end, though, so I tried to think of something else to say. This was tricky. Because of my nosiness yesterday, I knew things about him I wasn't supposed to know. I couldn't exactly say, "And how is the Beemer? Did you wash it this morning? What about Penny, is she having any luck finding something to wear for Valentine's Day?"

Thankfully my synapses reconnected. "I work for your dad over at Vic College, by the way," I said as casually as possible.

His eyebrows shot up, and he pulled his head back sharply. Guess he didn't see that coming. That made two of us. "Really?" he asked, his voice rising at least an octave higher than normal. "In what capacity?"

"I guess you'd say I'm a liaison between your father and various student groups on campus—" I started to explain but was interrupted by my phone ringing. It was Julie.

"Excuse me for a sec. I need to grab this," I said, holding up my cell phone. He nodded, sauntering back over to the tutorial room doorway.

"Hey, girlfriend, I'm a loser," Julie groaned. "I just woke up. You're there, right? You're such a trooper. Is it crazy busy?"

"Yes, I'm here, and no, it's not too bad at all. I guess it's a class of slackers. Present company included, you lazy ass. But it's not quite nine yet. I figure the rush is on the way, so you'd better haul your skinny carcass out of bed."

"It's so cold out. I don't wanna get up," she whined. "Can you sign me up for the same day as you? I betcha Mr. Shmexy TA won't know I haven't signed up myself if you use a different pen and maybe change the writing a bit, right? I doubt he'd be that much of a tight ass to care, anyway."

I laughed at her apathy and her new moniker for Daniel. Mr. Shmexy summed him up quite nicely. "Well, since he's standing right here, that could be tricky, sweetness," I told her.

Daniel looked over, realizing he was the subject of our discussion.

"Hang on a minute, Jul." I turned to Daniel. "My friend wants to know if you'd care if I sign up on her behalf."

He smirked as he swung around to close and lock the seminar room door. "I sense you're the kind of person who'd do anything for a friend, Miss Price. Be careful, though," he said. "'*For some must watch, while some must sleep: thus runs the world away.*'"

He made a show of drinking an imaginary cup of something to indicate he was off in search of coffee. I have to say, Julie was right on the money with the term *tight ass*, although I was probably interpreting her expression in a slightly different way.

I took a few seconds to pull myself together. After all, it's not every day the guy you've had a hot sex dream about smirks at you while quoting Shakespeare's *Hamlet*. I finally remembered the phone in my hand and cut short my starry-eyed musings.

"Hey, Jul, I'm signing us up for Friday, okay?" I said, quickly filling our names in on the third sheet.

"Thanks so much. Listen, I can be at Hart House in fifteen minutes if you still want to grab a cup of coffee. I'll throw on some clothes, okay?"

"Sounds good." I was already making my way to the exit. "I'll go over now and see you when you get there."

"Thanks, Aubrey, you're the best. I won't be long," she promised.

I dashed from University College to the Hart House coffee shop and ordered a small mug of coffee and a blueberry muffin. I claimed a table for two away from the draft of the doors and settled in to enjoy my breakfast while waiting for Julie.

As I nibbled on the muffin, I wondered how Matt was feeling. The apartment had been dead quiet when I'd left, both he and Joanna still sleeping. I'd hated seeing him so distraught the day before. He'd get over it, but breaking up was never easy.

*Almost as bad as dealing with feelings that aren't reciprocated in the first place,* I mused, and before the thought had properly gelled in my mind, there he was, Mr. Unrequited himself, standing in line for his own hit of java. I turned away, hoping to escape his notice. I'd already made enough of a fool of myself for one day.

I sent Matt a good morning text, and as I twisted around to put my phone back in my pocket, Daniel walked past me. Sitting down at a nearby table with his back to me, he pulled a pile of papers and his laptop from his bag. He shrugged off his jacket, and when he turned to put it on the back of his chair our eyes met. He tilted his head to the side and smiled. Gosh, I loved that dimple. Picking up his coffee, he stood and sauntered over to my table.

"Are you following me?" I teased.

*Yeah, that's rich, Aubrey.*

"That would be challenging, Miss Price, since I left *first*," he replied, his cheek puckering tartly.

"Hmm. I suppose you have a point there," I said, trying not to pay too much attention to him licking his lips and rubbing his thumb along his jaw.

"So, mission accomplished?" he asked, tilting his head back toward University College.

"Yep. Friday it is," I said.

"Very good." He leaned over with his coffee mug, clinking it against mine. "Well, cheers. I'll see you tomorrow at the lecture."

He started to turn away, but before he could get too far, I said, "*'For some must watch, while some must sleep: thus runs the world away.'* *Hamlet,* act three, scene two. Hamlet's speaking to Horatio after confirming Claudius's guilt with the Mousetrap Play."

He looked at me quizzically. "I see you've regained the ability to articulate clearly, Miss Price. This must be damn good coffee." He offered me another wonderful smile and headed off to reclaim his seat, busying himself with his papers and leaving me utterly breathless.

## Friend or Foe

These are certain signs to know
Faithful friend from flattering foe.
(*Sonnets to Sundry Notes of Music*)

J ulie arrived at the coffee shop a few minutes later in all her bun-
headed glory.

"I'm sorry I'm late. I'm all kinds of fail this morning." She grimaced apologetically as she squeezed between the tables to reach me.

"No worries. You can buy me a second coffee to redeem yourself."
I grabbed my coat and backpack and waved my empty mug. "Do
you want to grab one to go and we can head upstairs to sit in the
library or something? It'll be more comfy."

Truthfully, staying in the coffee shop would have been fine under
normal circumstances, but knowing Daniel was four tables away
made me self-conscious. I wanted to get caught up with Julie without
being distracted by soulful blue eyes and dimpled smiles. Julie agreed,
leading the way back to the coffee bar.

As we approached the doors that led to the main floor hallway of
Hart House, I allowed myself one final glance across the café. Daniel

was typing away, completely engrossed in his work and oblivious to everything around him. I secretly wished he'd notice me leaving — my yoga pants did fabulous things for my ass and legs — but I sure as hell wasn't going to continue staring over my shoulder to see if my wish was granted.

Julie and I made our way to the second floor library — more appropriately termed a reading room — one of my favorite spots on campus. Red leather couches and wing-back chairs allowed plenty of people to sit in comfort around the room, and floor-to-ceiling bookshelves covered every wall.

Students frequented the library between classes to study, do homework, chat with friends, and sometimes nap on the couch in front of the fireplace. Since the first time I'd stepped inside the reading room, it had fed into my romantic sensibilities, transporting me to another era and conjuring thoughts of Jane Austen novels. Today, however, the rows of bookshelves elicited much naughtier images than Jane Austen would have dared put to paper.

I banished thoughts of Dream Daniel whispering provocatively in my ear and flopped down on a couch by one of the large bay windows.

"I was so happy when I heard your voice in class yesterday," Julie said, squeezing my hand warmly. "I've missed hanging out with you."

"I know! It's been a busy year, and I've been hard core with the school work, but that's no excuse. I'm glad we reconnected," I said. "Why didn't I know you were taking this course? I remember comparing classes with you in September."

"I switched out of a classics half-course at the last minute. My course load is brutal. I needed something a little more familiar. Although, when I heard Cara's annoying valley-twang yesterday, I seriously considered running to the English Department office to switch back to classics. I can't stand that girl *or* her giant boobs."

"That wouldn't be sour grapes, would it? No pun intended," I added, gesturing to Julie's rather flat chest. She was a dancer and one of those extremely athletic girls who exercises so much she loses her curves. All the more reason to be a couch potato, in my opinion. I wouldn't characterize myself as overweight by any stretch of the imagination, but fitness wasn't exactly my forte.

"Yeah, now that you mention it, I guess I wouldn't mind a little extra in the boobage department." She pouted playfully before changing the subject. "So what's your take on the class? You know Professor Brown, right? Is he decent? Fair?"

"Oh yeah, a bit old-fashioned. Not a fan of posting notes online, still stuck in the chalk-and-talk era, that sort of thing, but he's a good teacher and he's very kind. He genuinely wants people to do well."

"No online notes. That means no skipping lectures. Thanks for the heads up," she said, sipping her coffee. "Not that I think attending class will be a chore with Daniel sitting at the front of the room. Did you get a load of him? Fuck me sideways, he is one good-looking man!"

"Yeah, he's a long, hot drink of Saturday night sexin'. This morning he looked like he rolled a bum on Yonge Street and stole his clothes, though," I said, making light of my attraction to Daniel. "Weird thing is, I know his father."

"Really? Do they live in Oakville?"

"No, I don't know him from home. David Grant is the Dean of Students at Victoria College. I work for him."

"Right. I'd forgotten about your job. It stinks that you have to work. Fourth year is stressful enough as it is."

"I know, but what else can I do? Taking a year off to work full-time after high school helped, but that money couldn't last forever. My parents do what they can, but it's not nearly enough."

"I guess. So what's he like? Daniel's father? Is it a decent job?"

"It's perfect. I only work three mornings a week. Dean Grant is a great boss. He's a damn fine specimen of a man, too. The Grant DNA is *definitely* solid," I said.

"Is it too late to transfer from Trinity College to Vic? For some reason I feel inspired to make the dean's list." Julie laughed and then leaned forward, switching subjects again without missing a beat. "So, tell me about your family! What's going on with your mom? She and Rick are good?"

My mother had met her new husband Rick while the two of us were in Las Vegas the February before. They fell madly in lust, he paid for her to go down for the May long weekend, then again for two weeks in June, and the next thing I knew she was packing up the apartment and moving to Nevada.

"They're doing great, I guess. Mom loves Vegas, and they're having a blast together."

"That's kinda nuts," Julie said. "Do you like him?"

I shrugged. "Rick's fine. My mom's happy. She's kind of getting a second chance. It's nice for her."

"Nice for her, but shitty for you. With your dad in Calgary and now your mom gone too? I don't know what I'd do if I couldn't escape to Windsor once in a while to have my mom feed me and do all my laundry."

It was odd hearing Julie's take on my life. She was right—my situation was weird. I'd recently started stewing over the fact that soon Reading Week would be upon us, and everyone would go home or leave for a southern getaway. I didn't have a home anymore in the sense that everyone else did. Between flying to Vegas for Christmas and being a broke university student, I'd be staying in residence alone for Reading Week. Then, of course, there was the fact that after my summer residence lease was up, I'd have to move out and find something comparably priced in the real world. My lack of safety net was a constant worry.

The conversation turned to Julie, and she updated me on her family and the new dance company she'd hooked up with in Toronto. I listened as she moaned about her sketchy social life and nodded sympathetically at her even sketchier love life.

"I can relate," I said. "I've been holed up like a groundhog all winter. It sucks."

"Well, that's decided, then," she said. "I grabbed two tickets to an indie music revue next Thursday and was going to invite my roommate, but I think you should come with me instead."

"Seriously? It's been ages since I've been to a show. Remember all those concerts we used to go to in first year?"

"Those were so fun. It's been way too long. So what do you think?"

"Hell, yes! I'd love to."

"Perfect. It's a date."

I peeked at my watch. My first lecture of the day was looming. I drained the dregs of my coffee and stretched languidly. "Sorry, Jul, but I should get going. I have to head back across Queen's Park for my children's lit class."

"Yeah, I should get back too. I have so much homework. This has been nice, though. I love how we can always pick up where we left off," she said.

I smiled. "I'll see you tomorrow in class, okay? Grab me a seat if you get there before me."

"Same goes for you. And not too far back. I'd like to have a clear view of the, um, *proceedings*, shall we say?"

"Done."

As if I needed any extra motivation.

My lecture dragged, my fuzzy understanding of *Haroun and the Sea of Stories* making most of the content of the lesson incomprehensible. I'd tried to read the book the night before, but I'd had trouble focusing.

Daniel was already single-handedly threatening my academic success, and I'd only known him for a day and a half! I tried to banish him from my thoughts, but I caught myself checking the time at noon and doing a little jig in my seat to celebrate the fact that I'd be seeing him again in exactly twenty-four hours.

The lecture wrapped at ten to one, leaving me barely enough time to trek back to Victoria College for my two-hour French lecture. Snacks in hand, I dashed across St. Mike's quad, following the pathways joining the two colleges.

When I reached the top of the steps bringing me into Vic's quad, I spotted Dean Grant rushing through Victoria's Gatehouse, returning from what must have been an extended lunch break. Then, two paces behind him, Daniel emerged from under the archway. I'd just congratulated myself for going a full forty-five minutes without thinking of him, and there he was, rubbing salt in my wounded grade point average.

Their expressions were stormy — mirror images of anger. I wondered if Dean Grant and his son ever got along. Daniel turned and caught sight of me coming up the pathway, and although it didn't seem possible, his expression visibly darkened. He shook his head with what seemed like disgust before lightly jogging to catch up with his dad.

*What the hell? Bipolar much?*

I wished my arrival in the quad hadn't coincided with Daniel's. His pissy expression had ruined my memories of dimpled smiles and sparkling eyes. I stomped the rest of the way to my French class where I sulked through my lecture, making tons of notes I knew would make no sense when I tried to read them over later.

I was still fuming at three o'clock when I returned to residence, hoping like hell I'd find the apartment empty so I could mope in peace. No such luck. I was greeted by a blaring television and found Matt flaked out on the couch in sweats and a T-shirt, drinking a beer. Four empty bottles were lined up on the coffee table, and an almost empty bag of Doritos spilled out a few stray chips on the sofa cushion beside him. He glanced up as I walked in.

"Hey," he said, the very picture of world-weariness.

I kicked off my shoes, turned the volume of the TV down a little, and plopped on the couch beside him, collecting a few Dorito crumbs in my hand and dumping them on the coffee table.

"I see you've moved on to stage two of the program we unattached folk like to call *Being Single Sucks Ass.*"

He offered me a wry smile. I took that as an encouraging sign.

"It's the stage where you say, 'Screw the snotty Kleenex,' and skip your afternoon classes to watch *Maury Povich* while swilling beer and working on your Dorito mustache." I laughed and leaned over to wipe the tiny orange smudges off his upper lip with my thumb.

He grabbed my hand in mid-air.

"I don't think you want to do that, Aub." His words were slurred, and his voice was thick.

My smile froze. "Jesus, Matt, it's three in the afternoon! How drunk are you?" I asked, gently prying his fingers from my wrist.

"Enough to think I'm ready for stage three," he said, a dark undertone in his voice.

"And what might that be?"

"The stage where you see if your gorgeous, green-eyed roommate wants to try again. To see if there's any chance — "

I saw no other option than to interrupt him before he said too much.

"Okay, cowboy, you've had one too many wobbly pops. You're not thinking straight." I stood up to put some distance between us and continued to make light of the situation, even though the expression on his face suggested he wasn't joking in the slightest.

"Have you consumed every beer on the premises, or might I actually be able to join you?" I called out as I made my way to the kitchen.

"There's plenty left. Be my guest."

I grabbed one of the dozen and a half or so bottles remaining in the fridge and noticed two additional empty bottles on the counter. Talk about drinking with intent.

"Wowza," I said, heading back to the couch. "Beer at three in the afternoon. It's like being in first year all over again."

"Drink up," he encouraged. "You've got a lot of catching up to do to get to stage three."

I tilted my head to the side and frowned. "*Matt*," I said, trying my best to tell him I didn't want to go down this road again.

"I know," he groaned, rubbing his eyes with his fisted hands. "I'm sorry. Bear with me, okay? I'm a friggin' train wreck here."

*Oh, I know how you feel*, I wanted to say, but I held my tongue. The sting of my unrequited schoolgirl crush on Daniel wasn't remotely comparable to Matt's pain. So I sat with him, being his friend, drinking way too much beer and eating hideous junk food, all the while hoping he'd wake up in the morning with a rousing case of stage four—hung over as hell and swearing to never drink again but realizing there *must* be other fish in the proverbial sea.

CHAPTER 6

*Spurned*

Fair sir, you spet on me Wednesday last;
you spurn'd me such a day…
(*The Merchant Of Venice,* Act 1, Scene 3)

When my alarm screeched at seven o'clock the next morning, I strongly considered taking a sledgehammer to it. But that would have required effort, and I could hardly lift my head off the pillow as it was. What had possessed me to stay up until two in the morning drinking beer, eating crap, and watching Quentin Tarantino movies?

It hurt to move, but there was no getting around it. I had to be at work by eight thirty. I groaned and dragged myself out of bed, throwing on a pair of flannel PJ bottoms. Water. I needed water and I needed it now.

Stumbling out to the kitchen, I found Matt already up and sitting at the table with his head resting on his arms, three empty water bottles in front of him. By the time we'd finally decided to turn in the night before, he'd engaged in an eleven-hour beer-drinking marathon. He was virtually paralyzed by the time I helped him into bed and propped him on his side with pillows so he wouldn't roll over onto his back. No wonder he was dehydrated.

I felt a nagging unease in my stomach, thinking about what he'd said the day before. Were things going to be weird between us? What if agreeing to go to Canoe with him on Valentine's Day had sent him mixed signals?

*But that's ridiculous. We've gone out alone together many times over the years. Why should things be different now?*

"Dude, what are you doing up?" I croaked. I grabbed a bottle of water and took a long drink. He grunted and sat up, chugging back water like he'd been in the desert for a week.

"I had to get up. My brain was screaming for Advil," he groaned. "And I have the worst case of the zacklies."

"What the hell are the zacklies?"

"You know, when your mouth tastes zackly like your ass."

"Ew, that's disgusting!" I laughed, then grabbed my temples as pain seared through my brain. "Oh, no. No laughing. Not good. Not good at all." I downed the rest of my water and tossed the empty bottle into the recycling box. "I'm grabbing a shower. Hey, have you seen Jo?" I asked over my shoulder.

"Nah, she stayed at Stephen's again," he said, slumping forward onto his forearms with a moan.

I frowned as I made my way down the hall. Joanna and Stephen were spending a ton of time together, mostly at his off-campus apartment in the Annex. If her parents knew the residence room they were spending thousands of dollars on actually functioned as a walk-in closet and occasional study space, they'd be pissed. It wasn't easy for me watching money being wasted while I was working so hard to put myself through school and racking up a healthy student debt in the process, but as my parents were so fond of reminding me, once I'd earned my degree, I'd have no one but myself to thank for it.

Unfortunately, I also had myself to thank for the crazy-ass headache beating in my temples. I washed down two Tylenol with a handful of tap water and then took a gloriously long, hot shower.

Afterward, I stood in front of my closet, contemplating my wardrobe as I planned out my day. I'd been rushed on Monday, running home to change before class. It would make more sense to wear something appropriate for work but not too over the top for class so I could skip the trip home in between. I opted for dressy black jeans and a snug chenille sweater—a perfect compromise.

When I emerged from my room, Matt was leaning against the kitchen counter, eating plain toast. I grabbed some snacks and an extra bottle of water for good measure.

"Sorry about yesterday," he said. "I was out of line."

"Chill, Matt, it's not a big deal. I'm irresistible. It's a cross I have to bear." I smirked, purposely downplaying his concern. I pulled on my coat, remembering to grab mittens and a hat for later. After heaving my backpack onto my shoulder, I leaned around the corner to peer back into the kitchen, shaking my fist at him. "Do it again, though, and I'll punch you in the junk."

He smiled and shook his head. Thank goodness. We were cool.

"And get your ass to class today!" I yelled, pulling the door closed behind me.

My morning at work went by quickly. Dean Grant remained locked in his office, emerging only once to refill his coffee cup, while I dealt with a steady stream of walk-ins and caught up on unanswered emails. My stomach started to churn as I watched the hands of the clock creeping toward eleven thirty.

On Monday I'd been excited at the prospect of starting a new course, and this time yesterday I'd been eagerly anticipating seeing Daniel again, but after the dirty look he'd tossed my way the day before, I now felt ambivalent. Not that it mattered. Since there was no point pursuing him, it was best to get a grip and accept the reality of the situation.

Before knocking on Dean Grant's door to tell him I was leaving for the day, I took a moment to pat myself on the back for *finally* thinking rationally.

My trip to class was much calmer without the frantic detour home after work to change. I even had time to swing by the Hart House coffee shop to grab a cup to go. I arrived in the classroom to find Julie sitting in a spot on the opposite side of the room, two rows back, directly across from the desk where Daniel would presumably sit again. I slid between the rows of desks to claim the seat beside her.

"Hey, girlfriend, how's tricks?" Julie asked, helping me pull my coat off my arm and sliding it over the back of my chair for me as I juggled my coffee cup.

"Oh, I've had better days. Went on a bit of a bender last night," I admitted.

"On a Tuesday night? I love you, Aubrey."

"Not my usual Tuesday night ritual, believe me. Matt and his girlfriend broke up on Sunday night. He was drowning his sorrows and using me as a life raft. By midnight I think we both could have used some CPR."

"Oh, poor Matt. Is he still a hunk of burning love? Maybe I can help him forget his sorrows," she suggested, a wicked gleam in her eye.

"Yep, still as hunky as ever, but a self-professed train wreck at the moment. I wouldn't go near him with a ten-foot pole if I were you, Jul."

She laughed and then bobbed her head toward the door. Professor Brown and his trusty protégé, Mr. Grumpy, were walking in together.

"He looks like he stopped at the Salvation Army on the way here to pick up that outfit," Julie whispered, gawking at Daniel. "I'd still bang him in a heartbeat, though," she added dreamily.

It was true. Daniel seemed to be getting more unkempt with each passing day. His hair was actually a little greasy now, and I tried to convince myself that his lapses in hygiene made him completely repulsive, but Julie was right. His scruffiness wasn't a turnoff; in fact, I had a strange urge to take him home and give him a very hands-on sponge bath. Why was it that as soon as he was standing before me, any rational thought went straight out the window? Damn him!

He sat at the table and took out a notepad and pen while Professor Brown assumed his position behind the podium. I avoided making eye contact with Daniel, still reeling from the death stare he'd shot at me the day before. It turned out my efforts were completely unnecessary. He spent the whole time gazing blankly at the notepad in front of him. I couldn't believe this was the same person I'd laughed and joked with the day before. Maybe he *did* have bipolar disorder!

I focused on Professor Brown, and as he was winding down his lecture, he turned to Daniel, asking him if he was ready to introduce the upcoming assignment. Daniel stood stiffly, and he and Professor Brown switched places. I shifted in my seat, stifling a yawn. How I was going to make it through my evening lecture was a mystery.

Daniel cleared his throat. "Well, as Professor Brown suggested on Monday, there's a reason we've started our course reading with *Hamlet*." He reached into his bag and pulled out a theater playbill, holding it up for the class to see. "Next week there's a three-night run of a performance of *Hamlet* at the Hart House Theatre, and one of your first term assignments will be a comparative analysis of the text and this live performance of the play. It will be worth five percent of your term mark and my first assessment of your work."

He paused to take a breath, and before he could proceed, people started whispering and several hands shot up around the room.

"I'll take questions once I've explained how this is all going to work. If I don't address your concerns, you can ask at the end, okay?" he said. "So, the play runs Wednesday through Friday nights…"

Again the restless muttering kicked in. *What the hell, people? Let him finish.*

"What if you can't make to any of those performances?" a guy called out from the back.

"If you'd let me continue," Daniel said, a muscle in his jaw twitching. Professor Brown looked highly entertained. Julie arched her eyebrow, her mouth twisting in amusement.

"So, as I was saying," Daniel resumed, "the play runs from Wednesday to Friday, and although it's short notice, see what you can manage to arrange. However, if none of the three dates is an option, there is a performance of *Much Ado About Nothing* scheduled for later in the semester, and you can wait until then to do this assignment. You'll have advance notice for those dates. That's the alternative if next week doesn't work."

His explanation seemed to appease the grumblers.

"I have a block of tickets booked for each night, but I've been asked to confirm numbers with the box office and release the seats we won't need. Please check your schedules and let me know what your intentions are by Friday's lecture. Fair enough?" he asked, his eyebrows raised expectantly. "I'll stick around for a few minutes in case anyone has any further questions, but I'll be meeting with today's seminar group shortly, so I can't stay long."

He turned to Professor Brown to give him back the floor. Again, the lack of oxygen in my brain forced a huge yawn from me. I couldn't stifle this one. Beside me, Julie snickered.

"Ladies and gentlemen, this is an excellent opportunity Daniel has arranged for you," Professor Brown said. "I trust you'll do what you can to adjust your schedules accordingly. Have a good day."

He nodded his head conclusively, and people began packing up their bags. Julie turned to me with a bemused expression.

"Well, that was interesting," she said.

"Yeah, no kidding."

Behind us, a group of people griped about the timing of the performances. Above the garbled complaints, Cara Switzer's voice rang out shrilly.

"As if you're gonna go see a play for class on a Thursday. I mean, it's totally pub night all over campus. And there's that huge party at the Kappa house on Friday, right? This is *so* not working for me. How about you, Lindsay?"

"Totally. Not gonna happen," her idiotic sidekick agreed, examining her manicured fingernails.

Julie and I simultaneously rolled our eyes. "Do you want to try to go to the show together?" she asked.

"Sure. We'll have to go Friday, though. I have class Wednesday night, then there's the show at the Revival on Thursday, right?"

"Friday would work for me," she said. Then she leaned forward to whisper, "And a certain frat party is conveniently scheduled at the same time."

"Good point."

"Okay, it's a date." Julie pulled on her coat. "I guess we're supposed to wait to tell him on Friday." She nodded her head in Daniel's direction.

"I guess so," I said, shrugging on my own jacket. We moved toward the door, but before we could escape into the hall, Daniel called after us.

"Miss Price? Could I have a moment?" I glanced at him and then back at Julie with a sigh.

"I'll see you on Friday," she said, her eyes glinting mischievously as she moved through the door and started to pull it closed behind her.

"Leave the door, please," Daniel asked.

Julie obliged and disappeared down the hall. Daniel rubbed his temple and then brushed his hair back off his forehead, a wasted effort as it simply flopped back down. His hair needed a trim as well as a good wash. How was I supposed to properly admire his eyes when his hair was always in the way?

"I have a small request," he said.

"Fire away." I crossed my arms, waiting for him to continue. Would he smile beatifically or shoot daggers at me through his eyeballs? The suspense was killing me.

"I've given some thought to what you told me yesterday, about how you work for my father. You two have a close relationship?" he asked.

"I think highly of your father. He's a wonderful man."

"Well, I think it's probably in your best interest if you didn't tell him you're in this class," he said.

"That's a strange request."

"Not really," he said, resting his hands on his hips. "My having taken on this position as TA is stressing him out. He's inordinately concerned about how things are going. Maybe he thinks if I do badly it'll reflect on him or something. He takes a lot of pride in his reputation on campus. If you tell him you're in this class, you'll become his one-stop shop for information. He'll be quizzing you daily. He'll put you in an uncomfortable position, I can almost guarantee it."

"So you're trying to protect me from being pestered by your father—from becoming 'his informant?'"

"I suppose you could put it that way," he admitted. "I also don't want to open a can of worms. If my father discovers we're acquainted, he might discuss things with me that would breed familiarity between you and me, or share information about your performance at work, whether good or bad. I'd like to avoid anything that could undermine my objectivity." He looked down at the floor for a moment before bringing his eyes back up to search mine. "Can you do that for me?"

I considered asking him what the big deal was. Did he feel like he was losing objectivity with me? Or was he warning me about *my* behavior? Could he overreact more? Yeah, I was confused, but I nodded dumbly, feigning comprehension.

"Yeah, okay, I won't mention it."

"Thank you. Well, I'm sure everyone's waiting for me downstairs, so..."

"Right," I said, nodding vigorously.

He took two steps and then turned.

"Oh, and you might want to get some sleep in the next couple of days. I'm sure the tutorial will be interesting on Friday. I'd hate for you to nod off and miss all the fun."

*Ouch! You overly observant bastard!*

He turned on his heel again and briskly exited the room. And as amazing as it was to watch his perfect ass swaggering away, I couldn't help yawning once more.

Yeah, I was *that* tired.

## A Woman's Reason

I have no other but a woman's reason;
I think him so because I think him so.
(*The Two Gentlemen of Verona*, Act 1, Scene 2)

I spent virtually all of my time on Thursday attending classes and forcing myself to focus, dismissing all thoughts of Daniel Grant and his fabulous ass. On Friday morning I contemplated the day ahead, the tutorial in particular. I was intent on owning it, if for no other reason than to remind myself that my number one priority was still my academic record.

Of course, if I were to be completely honest with myself, I'd be forced to acknowledge the other reason I wanted to shine during tutorial: I wanted to impress the pants off Daniel—literally.

So much for banishing him from my mind.

I'd replayed the conversation we'd had on Wednesday several times over. I couldn't dismiss the suspicion that there was more behind Daniel's request that I not tell his father that I knew him than Daniel had let on. What if he'd been trying to let me know that my less than subtle eye-gropings were making him uncomfortable and I needed to cease and desist because I was making it difficult for him to do his job properly?

I imagined a conversation he and Penny would have in which he'd tell his girlfriend all about me, this bright but misguided girl in class who kept ogling him. How he'd tried to be pleasant, but I wasn't getting the message. Penny would laugh and kiss him, explaining that it was his own fault for being so damned gorgeous.

Gah! Stupid Penny!

I dragged myself out of bed and headed to the kitchen to grab a quick breakfast. Joanna and Matt were sitting on the couch in the living room, drinking coffee.

"Jo! Stranger! What's up?"

"Hey, Aubrey. Sorry I haven't been around. I'd been so busy with school. After Stephen and I have dinner each night and then do a few hours of homework, I can't be bothered to schlep back here. No offense, you guys," she said, looking back and forth between Matt and me.

"Hey, none taken," I said. "I'd take schtupping over schlepping any day if I had a choice."

*And how.*

Joanna rolled her eyes and blushed a little. Such a sweetie. I tried not to feel envious of her situation with Stephen. They were so happy together.

"Hey, say the word, Aub, I'd be happy to help you out with your unlucky streak," Matt offered.

"Jesus, Matt, is your memory that short? You wanna be able to reproduce one day?" I glanced down at his package and shook my fist at him.

"I'm just sayin'." He laughed, cupping his crotch with both hands.

Joanna narrowed her eyes. "Did I miss something?"

"Don't ask," I said, turning back to Matt. "So, dude, you seem to be in better spirits. Good sleep?"

"Oh yeah, even though twinkle toes here woke me up at midnight when she came crashing in." He gave Joanna a gentle shove.

"And you told Jo what happened?" I asked, dismayed by the thought of him having to repeat the story of his heartbreak again.

She nodded sympathetically. "He told me the whole story. It's pretty crummy."

*Pretty crummy.* So cute. The girl seriously wouldn't say "shit" if her mouth was full of it.

"Look, ladies," Matt said, kicking his feet up on the coffee table, "I'll bounce back. I appreciate your concern, though." He took a long swig of his coffee and then bobbed his head at me. "I didn't see you at all yesterday. What time did you come home?"

"I put in a four-hour marathon at the library after classes. When I got home at ten, you were out like a light on the couch. There's no way you were waking up," I told him.

What I *didn't* tell him was that seeing him curled up on the sofa the night before, all rosy-cheeked with the blanket pulled up under his chin, had completely tugged at my heart. I also didn't tell him I'd ruffled his hair as I'd tucked the blanket more tightly around him, wishing I could force myself to feel something other than sisterly affection for him.

No, I didn't tell him any of that.

If I thought I was going to have a leisurely Friday morning at work, I was sadly mistaken. I ran around the office like a maniac for three hours and was sweltering by the end of my shift. I briefly contemplated racing back to residence to change out of my black turtleneck, but a quick visit to the washroom after saying goodbye to Dean Grant changed my mind. My face was flushed, but the color did me good.

I repeated my new routine, swinging by the coffee shop to grab a snack before class. I still made it a good five minutes before the lecture was scheduled to start. Julie had reserved what were apparently going to be *our seats*. We humans are such creatures of habit.

"Hey, dollface. You look really nice! I love that sweater on you," she said. "Makes your boobs look awesome, but not in a trashy way."

"Thanks, I think." I laughed.

"Hey, I have that concert ticket," she said, pulling a small envelope from her pocket.

"Great. I'm so psyched. How much do I owe you?" I asked.

"Pfft, buy me a few beers at the show and we'll call it even."

"Cool, I can do that."

We settled into our seats, awaiting the arrival of the dynamic duo. Professor Brown and Daniel arrived together in the midst of what appeared to be a fascinating discussion. Daniel was waving his hands around, highly engaged in the topic. He looked adorable, making it difficult for me to continue being pissed off at him.

He reclaimed his position at the front table, and Professor Brown took out his lecture notes, spending the allotted time concluding our study of *Hamlet*. I snuck a few glances at Daniel, but he was busily writing away, so I ignored him.

When Julie leaned over to whisper, "I don't know what's outside, but check out Daniel's face," I looked up, and sure enough, he was staring fiercely out the window as if he wanted to kill whoever was on the other side. I scanned the quad. There was no one out there. "Wasn't he all smiley and happy half an hour ago?"

I shrugged and shook my head, retreating to the safety of my notes and beginning to wonder in earnest if he had some sort of mood disorder. As class drew to a close, Professor Brown assigned the reading of *The Taming of the Shrew* and explained to the class that Daniel would be staying around for a few minutes to confirm dates for the following week's viewing of *Hamlet,* but that his Friday tutorial group could proceed downstairs and provide our preferred dates during tutorial.

"That's us," I said to Julie, gritting my teeth and collecting my belongings.

She followed suit, and we went down the stairs to wait outside the seminar room. We both groaned as Cara and Lindsay strutted along the hall in our direction. Could this get any worse?

"Oh, crap," I groaned.

"Kill me now, Aubrey," Julie said.

Sure enough, they parked themselves beside us, talking inanely about how much they'd had to drink the night before, each one blaming the other for waiting too late to sign up and being forced to pick Friday's tutorial slot. After a few moments, there were thirteen or fourteen of us milling around outside the room. Daniel finally came down the stairs.

"Sorry about that, folks," he said as he opened the door and stood back to allow us to enter.

The expected jockeying for positions ensued as people insisted on sitting beside friends. Cara did her best impersonation of a speed bump, just standing and looking at the long table. Perhaps assuming that Daniel would sit at the head of the table, she took the seat at the corner beside the empty end chair. She and Lindsay exchanged a meaningful glance. Julie and I took that as our cue to sit at the opposite end of the table. I sat at the corner, and she plopped down beside me.

Once everyone had taken a seat, Daniel came in and closed the door. He looked at the fourteen of us, seven at each side of the long table, and hesitated before dropping his bag on the floor and sitting down at one end.

The one beside me.

Cara fixed me with an angry glare from across the room, and I looked blankly back at her. I wasn't thrilled with the prospect of navigating the next hour sitting that close to Daniel, but Cara's reaction made the situation bearable.

"Well, it seems the best way to start today would be with an ice breaker," Daniel said. "So take a moment to share your name and give a brief explanation of your area of study. Why don't we begin with you, Miss Price?"

He turned to me expectantly, and I took a deep breath. His proximity was making it difficult for me to remain unruffled.

"Sure," I answered with a small smile. "I'm Aubrey Price and I'll be graduating this year. I'm specializing in English with a minor in French lit, and I'm affiliated with Victoria College."

I sounded like a beauty pageant finalist introducing myself to the crowd. *And I'll be performing a baton routine.*

"Are you a commuter or are you in residence at Victoria?" Daniel asked.

"Residence. I live in Rowell Jackman Hall."

"Thank you, Miss Price," Daniel said matter-of-factly.

Again with the last name—obviously part of his MO. I wondered if we were expected to call him *Mr. Grant.* I'd never referred to a TA by his last name before, and Professor Brown had set a precedent, referring to him as "Daniel" from day one, but he seemed determined to avoid our first names. Was he being pretentious or overly professional? I opted for the former. Surely professionalism would extend to taking the time to wear clean clothes and groom his hair. At least his hair was washed today, I noted, although it was still hanging in his eyes. I longed to lean over and pull several stray pieces out of the way or, better yet, grab my nail scissors and make several carefully-chosen snips.

"Next?" Daniel asked, looking at Julie. I leaned back in my chair so he could see past me.

"I'm Julie Harper," she said. "I'm double majoring in English and art history. I live in residence at Trinity."

"Nice to meet you, Miss Harper," Daniel said.

He took notes as everyone around the table took a turn. A number of the people in the group were new to me, although I knew Shawn Ward from previous English classes. He was a good friend of Matt's from the frat house. I saw him at parties from time to time. Vince, the guy sitting beside him, was another fraternity acquaintance of Matt's.

Cara and Lindsay giggled their way through their introductions, batting their eyelashes at the frat boys. Did they honestly think guys were impressed by that sort of behavior? I took out my notebook, and after quickly jotting down everyone's first name, I turned the page in preparation for the beginning of our discussion.

The introductions over, Daniel dropped his pen and clasped his hands in front of him. "Well, the next order of business is a quick survey of your plans for next week's *Hamlet* performances—"

"Um, aren't you going to, like, tell us about yourself?" Cara interrupted.

And I never thought I'd say it, but I actually agreed with her. Some nods of agreement and murmurs around the table indicated we weren't alone in our curiosity. Daniel shifted in his seat.

"All right," he said. "Well, as you know, I'm Daniel Grant. I'm in the midst of writing my PhD thesis. I'm actually back in the city after a long stay abroad. I transferred here in September."

"Where did you transfer from?" asked the sweet-faced girl sitting opposite me. Mary, maybe?

Daniel cleared his throat uncomfortably. "As a matter of fact, I lived in England for the last eight or nine years. I did my undergrad and my master's degree at Oxford, and I started my PhD there before transferring here," he explained.

Well, you could have knocked me down with a feather, and judging by my peers' reactions, they were surprised too. Oxford? I was impressed. And I *had* noticed he occasionally said certain words with a slight lilt, a trace of an accent, but I hadn't given it a lot of thought, too distracted by his lips and jawline.

"And now," he said, cutting his introduction short, "I am privileged to be sitting here with all of you. I think we ought to get down to business, though, or we'll fall behind Wednesday's group."

Back to business it was. He canvassed the room to find out people's intentions for next week. Five people were taking a pass, claiming unavailability.

"It's a super busy time right now," Cara explained. "I'm sure April will be totally more convenient," she said, nodding confidently.

"Absolutely," Daniel said. "Why do today what you can put off until tomorrow? That's what I always say."

He spoke breezily, but his sardonic tone wasn't lost on me. I bit my lip to keep from laughing, and Julie tapped me under the table with her knee. So discerning that girl was.

"Thanks for being so understanding," Cara said, all seriousness.

I covered my mouth with my hand to stifle the guffaw building behind my lips.

"Are you all right, Miss Price?" Daniel asked me, steeliness flashing in his blue eyes.

"Yes, fine," I answered, clearing my throat and regaining my composure but feeling like a sixth grader who'd had her wrist slapped.

At the end of Daniel's survey, four people from our tutorial group were attending on Wednesday, three on Thursday, and it was just Julie and me on Friday. He told us we would pick up our tickets from him in the lobby before the show on our appointed night.

"I think you'll enjoy this interpretation," he said. "I've watched some rehearsals. It's quite edgy, with post-modern undertones. It'll be particularly interesting watching the play after having read it, and as you know, a play isn't fully realized until it reaches the stage."

I thought about that for a moment and couldn't help disagreeing. Of course, I couldn't keep my big mouth shut, could I? "I'm not sure I agree with you on that, *Daniel*," I said, trying out his name for the first time. He looked taken aback.

"Could you elaborate?" he asked, leaning forward with interest. My classmates were all ears too.

*Oh, shit.*

"Well." I tried to bring my opinion into focus. "If you say a play is only fully realized when it reaches the stage, doesn't that undermine the value of what was originally written on the page?"

I glanced around the room.

"Sure, having the visual is beneficial, but the author's original words are significant, too. You can't discount the *weight* of those words without the performance attached. They're two different mediums entirely. A reader's unmediated experience with a text is pretty important." I looked around again. A few people were jotting down my words. "I don't know. That's my opinion," I added, suddenly feeling self-conscious.

"You make some interesting observations, Miss Price," Daniel said, his voice measured and controlled. "Where Shakespeare's concerned, I'm not convinced I agree. In fact, I think I disagree entirely, but you've given us something to think about. Perhaps we'll have to set aside some time to discuss your opinion in a future tutorial."

There was an edge to his tone, as if he wasn't thrilled about being contradicted. "*In fact, I think I disagree entirely*"? I briefly considered pursuing the point, but I had no desire to instigate conflict, so I nodded and kept my mouth shut. Daniel forged onward.

"This is the assignment Professor Brown mentioned on Monday," he said, passing around a sheet outlining the term's independent study.

I was relieved to have a moment to breathe. My heart was racing.

"As you all know, one of the aspects of this course is the independent pursuit of a topic that interests you," Daniel explained. "I won't be evaluating this final product, but I'd be happy to assist if I can. I thought we'd take a moment to throw out some ideas and get the wheels turning. Anyone care to share?"

Shawn spoke up, sharing his interest in the role of magic and the supernatural in Shakespeare's work. Daniel recorded Shawn's preliminary ideas in his notebook.

"Good. Anyone else?"

Silence ensued. He looked at me pointedly, eyebrow raised. A challenge?

*Okay, Aubrey. Game on.*

"I'm quite interested in exploring feminist themes," I said, meeting his eyes. "Possibly misogyny. I imagine I would focus on *Hamlet, Othello, Cymbeline*, maybe *Macbeth*."

Daniel leaned back in his chair, narrowing his eyes and bringing his clasped hands under his chin. As he moved, his knee grazed mine under the table — an accident, of course — but he might as well have thrust his hand between my legs, considering the effect it had on me. My face began to burn.

"Great topic," he said. "I have some interesting books that I might be able to lend you."

He wanted to lend me books? Vivid memories of Dream Daniel's seductive whispers ghosted though my mind as visions of bookshelves appeared before my eyes.

"Let me ask you this," he said, leaning forward again, twirling his pen between his fingers. "Do you think Shakespeare himself had a hatred of women?"

I paused, unprepared to take a stand one way or the other, but eager to show him I wasn't a dimwit.

"I'm not sure. He certainly explores the motif a lot, but an interest in a subject doesn't mean one is a proponent of that ideology. Who knows, though? Maybe he was a misogynist and he felt safe spouting his views from behind the mask of his heroes' behavior. I suppose that'll be something I'll pursue in my paper."

"I see," he said, nodding meditatively.

I waited for him to say something else, but he merely looked at me. Was he preparing a rebuttal? Everyone else in the room seemed to be holding their breath. Julie came to the rescue, quickly breaking the uncomfortable silence.

"I've been thinking a lot about the use of non-secular themes in Shakespeare's plays," she said. "I'd love to take a closer look at the conflicting Elizabethan attitudes toward religion and how they play out in his work."

The tension eased almost immediately as everyone collectively let out a breath. I looked at her gratefully.

"Another worthwhile topic," Daniel said with a nod, surveying the faces around the table. "Anyone else, before we move on to talk about this week's *Hamlet* lectures?" he asked.

Apparently Cara felt the need to be heard, blurting out, "I totally want to look at the theme of love in Shakespeare's plays. Like *Romeo and Juliet*. It's so romantic." She punctuated her statement with a breathy sigh.

Daniel frowned. "Well, that's a rather…broad topic, but I'm sure with a little work we can narrow it down," he said, seeming to choose his words carefully.

Julie couldn't contain herself. She wrote on the corner of her page, "*Gah! Airhead!*"

I smiled and wrote on my notepad, "*I know! The wheel may be turning, but the hamster is DEAD!*" I angled my page so she could see my response, and she squeezed my hand under the table. Yeah, we were bitches, but Cara was too much.

We spent the remaining half hour talking through some of the questions Professor Brown had asked us to think about. I had to give him props—Daniel handled the rest of the tutorial masterfully. He validated people's opinions and dealt carefully with people whose comments were completely off-base.

By the time everyone was packing up at the end of the tutorial, my ass was getting sore from sitting on the fence where he was concerned. Cara clambered around the table, jutting out her boobs as she asked Daniel if he'd mind answering a few of her questions *privately*, looking over her shoulder to see everyone's reactions. As far as I could tell, no one was interested in her mindless flirtations.

"I, uh, sure, yes, that would be fine," he told her. But then he turned to me and said, "Actually, Miss Price, I need to speak with you once Miss Switzer has asked her questions. Could you stick around for a few minutes?"

Julie looked at me with an expression that said, "Again? What is going on with you two?"

I shrugged and mouthed, "No idea," before I told her I'd call her over the weekend and reclaimed my seat. Cara looked at me in aggravation.

"Well, can I make an appointment, then?" she asked Daniel. "I mean, I do need some help, *one on one*."

I rolled my eyes at the wall.

"Why don't you jot down some potential times, and we'll chat after class on Monday to see if we can figure out something mutually convenient?" Daniel suggested.

"Okay, thanks," Cara replied, bouncing up and down slightly before heading out of the room. Daniel turned to look at me from the doorway. I stood up, throwing my bag over my shoulder as I rose.

"What is it now?" I asked.

"Actually, never mind. It's nothing," he said, shaking his head with a frown. "Have a good weekend, Miss Price."

With that, he bolted from the doorway, leaving me standing in the seminar room, completely bewildered.

## The Lady Doth Protest

The lady doth protest too much, methinks.
(*Hamlet*, Act III, Scene 2)

*Oh, no you don't,* I thought, slamming the door and rushing down the hall after Daniel. I elbowed my way around the clusters of students as I tried to catch up, reaching him right before he pushed his way through the front doors. When I grabbed his jacket to pull him to a stop, he wheeled around and gaped at me, no doubt shocked to see that I'd not only followed him, but actually had the nerve to physically restrain him.

"What was *that* all about?" I asked, gesturing toward the tutorial room. "If there's something you want to say, go ahead and say it."

"I have no idea what you're talking about," he said, drawing his head back in surprise.

I laughed cynically. "You *can't* be serious."

"I'm dead serious."

"So, what — in the space of two minutes, something goes from important to inconsequential? That's absurd."

"You're blowing this completely out of proportion." He put his hands on his hips and looked around the hall distractedly. "I was going to tell you more about the books for your topic of study, but I think you need to flesh out your own thoughts before you muddy the waters with secondary sources. I changed my mind about the recommendations, that's all," he explained, his matter-of-fact tone blowing the wind out of my sails. "I'm sorry if you misunderstood."

"Oh. Well, you seemed kind of angry. If I've done something to offend you…" I trailed off, feeling small and ridiculous.

"You've in no way offended me," he said with an impatient sigh. "But if you'll excuse me, I don't have time to discuss this right now. Professor Brown is expecting me."

"Yes, of course."

I stepped aside so he could pass by. Three long strides and he was out the door. Once I was sure he'd made his escape, I stepped outside in time to see him climb into his car and speed off around King's College Circle. I plodded down the steps toward the sidewalk.

*I don't have time to discuss this right now.*

Translation: *You are of no significance to me. Please move along.*

After my embarrassing confrontation with Daniel, I wanted nothing more than to shut my brain off for a while. I had to stop fixating on him, so I contemplated my plans for the evening. Or should I say my *lack* of plans. As the year had progressed, I'd been secluding myself more and more, but I hadn't felt the ill effects of isolation for the majority of the year, being consumed by work and school and otherwise quite content to mooch around by myself. Now I was in dire need of distraction.

When Matt came home at five o'clock and I asked him if I could hit the frat party with him, he looked genuinely thrilled. "Wow, Aub, I'd love it if you came. Gotta admit I'm a little surprised. Last time you came to a kegger, you swore you were 'so fucking done with this.' Those *were* your words, right?"

I snickered. He was right — I had said that. Truth be told, a keg party was the last place I wanted to go, but I was prepared to put up with the drunken idiocy of frat boys if only to escape from my own whirling thoughts for a while. Simply put, I was desperate.

"Yeah, well, it's been about six months since someone's hurled down my back," I said, recalling the vile events of a party back in September. "I figure I'm due, ya know?"

"Aw, come on, you have to admit, it was freakin' hilarious."

"Maybe for you, but you didn't have some freshman's Chef Boyardee Beefaroni chunks in your hair."

"Yeah, you're right," he said. "It *was* gross. The look on your face, though? Absolute mint."

"All I know is I'm so glad Sarah was there. It takes a pretty special person to help you wash some pimply guy's puke out of your hair."

Matt's face clouded over.

"Oh, crap. I'm sorry. I shouldn't have dropped the S-word."

"Naw, it's okay." He rubbed my arm gently. "You can stop walking on egg shells. It's cool. Gets a little easier every day."

Out of nowhere, he pulled me into a giant hug, wrapping his arms tightly around my waist and burying his face in my hair. I should have pushed him away, or at least cut the embrace short, but after the week I'd had, it felt good to be held by someone who genuinely cared about me. I sighed contentedly. When he finally pulled away, he looked at me tenderly. I felt a pang of guilt. I shouldn't be sending him mixed signals. Luckily, he stepped back with a sad smile, retreating to his room and saving me the trouble of back pedaling.

At nine thirty, Matt and I were standing in the crowded Kap common room, beers in hand while loud music pumped through the giant floor speakers.

I had to concede, it felt good to be out socializing. I'd been taking myself way too seriously for too long. My determination to graduate with distinction didn't mean I couldn't have a life. I needed to take some time to unwind and blow off some steam once in a while. That was probably why I'd been so intense and reactionary, meeting Daniel and allowing him to occupy my thoughts exclusively. I was spending too much time in my own head.

I had a few drinks, but with Wednesday's hangover still fresh in my mind, I was reluctant to go overboard. A few people fawned over me excessively, claiming they'd thought I was dead. Charming. At one point, I bumped into Shawn Ward who high-fived me, saying my performance at tutorial that afternoon had been "fucking epic."

"Daniel's a bit arrogant, don't you think?" he said. "I mean what's with all the 'Mr. Ward, Miss Price' crap? I'm thinking, 'Dude…you're like four years older than me. Get over yourself.'"

Despite the humiliation I'd felt earlier, I had a strange compulsion to defend Daniel. Here I'd come to the party to get away from thoughts of him, but apparently there was no escape.

"I don't know; I think he's doing okay. It's probably his first time at this. He's trying to maintain a distance. It would be hard being a TA when you're so close in age to the students, don't you think?"

"Man, you're the last person I figured would stick up for him," he said. "Things got a little tense with you two today. Anyway, I don't care what you say. I still think he's an ass."

I shrugged and we both moved on, dancing, mingling, and stopping to chat with people here and there. By midnight, I was ready to bail. The witching hour was approaching. As everyone got drunker, the potential for projectile hurling would increase exponentially. I found Matt hanging with his friend Dustin and let him know I was leaving.

"Want me to walk you back?" he asked.

"No, I'll be fine," I assured him.

"Can you text me when you get home? If I don't hear from you in fifteen minutes, I'll send out a search party."

"You'll send one? You won't join it?" I asked playfully.

"Hey, the fun's about to start here," he said, looking around the room. "I don't want to miss anything!"

I laughed and punched his chest.

"I mean it, though, Aub. Text me," he repeated with a look of total seriousness.

"I will. See you tomorrow."

"I'll try not to wake you when I get home," he promised as he leaned over to kiss me on the cheek.

Yeah, I was totally missing the boat on this one. How I wished I wanted Matt sometimes. Life would be so much easier.

I actually felt something akin to cheerfulness as I crossed the quad on Monday morning, ready to tackle my three-hour shift. I had my school work well in hand, and I'd even taken some proactive steps to resuscitate my floundering social life. To top it off, I had a concert date with Julie to look forward to.

As I was arriving at the office, Dean Grant was pulling on his overcoat and making his way out.

"Good morning, Aubrey," he said. "I'll be back in an hour or so. I'm heading over to Wymilwood to grab a coffee with my son. You know, Daniel—the one who graced us with his ill-humor last Monday?"

"Yes, right, I remember," I said, cringing at my lie by omission. I didn't relish the idea of having to keep my in-class relationship with his son a secret, but I'd made a promise to Daniel and intended to keep it. I'd also promised myself not to continue obsessing about Daniel, but that didn't stop me from spending a good ten minutes mulling over why hadn't come to the office to visit his father as he had the previous week. Was he actively avoiding me?

I brought a decisive halt to my musings, renewing my vow to stop dissecting his every move, and spent the rest of my shift entirely focused on work. I even went as far as to arrive at my Shakespeare lecture early to secure two seats on the side of the classroom closest to the door. When Julie arrived, she frowned as she sat down, pouting theatrically. She wanted to stare at *Mr. Shmexy.*

"Sorry, Julie. I can't sit over there. It's hard to think straight," I whispered.

"You're telling me," she said, chuckling under her breath.

"I'm not talking about how gorgeous he is," I hissed. "I'm talking about his moodiness. He was so weird on Friday. I don't know what I've done to tick him off."

She tried to placate me by telling me she was sure Daniel's attitude wasn't personal. According to Julie, some men were wholly incapable of coping with smart women. In her opinion, Daniel found my intelligence threatening.

I shook my head and shrugged, trying to seem indifferent. I avoided sneaking looks at him for the entire class and felt damn near euphoric at the end of the lecture when I realized I'd successfully steered clear of making eye contact with him.

On Tuesday, I congratulated myself for managing to keep thoughts of Daniel at bay all day. Of course, the fact that I was swamped with reading and research was partially to blame for the limited space in my brain for wayward thoughts, but there was no need to admit that. I was quite enjoying patting myself on the back, thank you very much.

Back in class on Wednesday, Julie and I sat close to the door again. I focused entirely on Professor Brown's lecture, taking lots of notes that would support my use of *The Taming of the Shrew* in my independent study paper. As Julie and I packed up at the end of the class, my brain was still ticking over ideas for my essay when Daniel crossed the front of the room, heading down to the tutorial room for his Wednesday session. As he passed, he cast a pained smile in my direction. Although his gesture stopped me dead in my tracks, I gritted my teeth and willed myself to feel nothing.

*Rien.*

*Niente.*

*Nada.*

"*The lady doth protest too much, methinks.*"

What, even Hamlet's mother was talking to me now? *Shut up, Gertrude,* I thought. *Isn't there a poisoned chalice around here you'd like to take a swig of?*

I stormed out of class in a huff, wishing I could fast-forward to the concert with Julie on Thursday night.

# Expectation

Oft expectation fails, and most oft there
Where most it promises; and oft it hits
Where hope is coldest, and despair most fits.
(*All's Well That Ends Well*, Act II, Scene 1)

One time when I was a kid, I went to an amusement park with my parents. There was this cool ride, and I *had* to go on it. My parents advised me against it, but I refused to be dissuaded. Despite my efforts to be brave, within two minutes I wanted to scream, "Stop the ride! I want to get off!"

That's how I felt as I crossed the quad on Friday morning. I was completely overwhelmed. I didn't want to go to work, I didn't want to go to class, and most surprisingly of all, I did *not* want to go to see *Hamlet* that evening. I had the strangest feeling of lethargy and dread combined. I wanted off the ride.

I could almost hear my parents' voices. "You need to pace yourself or you're going to get run down," Mom would say. My dad would warn me against "burning the candle at both ends." But what could I do? I needed my nine weekly hours of employment. I couldn't make ends meet without the four hundred or so dollars a month those hours of work guaranteed me. There was no way I was about to start skipping classes either, not with the dean's list right there—a brass ring, ripe for the grabbing. As for my social life, I'd only started enjoying some "me time" after months of what had amounted to self-imposed exile. I'd have to plough through.

I dragged my ass into the office, trying to talk myself into facing my day. Dean Grant was holed up with his door closed when I arrived, so I grabbed a coffee and sat at my desk, resting my head on my folded arms and wondering what the heck was wrong with me. I'd been home from the concert and in bed by midnight the night before, dropping off to sleep easily. When Dean Grant popped out of his office to grab himself a coffee, I lifted my head to look at him wearily.

"Good grief, Aubrey!" He stopped in his tracks. "Are you feeling okay?"

"Oh, it's nothing. I'm a little tired." I tried to brighten my expression, turning to the computer and opening my student liaison email account. "Once I get rolling here, I'm sure I'll be fine."

"Are you looking after yourself?" he asked, his eyebrows drawn together with concern. "Eating properly, getting enough sleep?"

"I'm doing my best. I'm having one of those weeks where a few assignments are due at the same time. I went out with a friend last night, too. Probably overdoing it a little," I confessed.

"It's a good thing you only have one more week of classes before Reading Week. Make sure you get plenty of rest over the next few days," he advised.

"I will. Thank you, sir," I said with a grateful smile.

Was I PMS-ing or something? I honestly felt like I could cry. I was desperately in need of some parental love.

"If it's not too busy, put aside the inbox items for Gisele to work through this afternoon. Help the walk-ins, but take it easy, all right?" he said.

"I'll try to get a few things done, but I appreciate your concern."

He smiled in a warm, fatherly way and went into his office, closing the door. It must have been a gift from God because there were maybe half a dozen walk-ins just needing help with straightforward issues. When I wasn't helping those students at the counter, I stayed at my desk, sifting through emails, taking it easy, and trying not to feel guilty about leaving so many items in the "to-do" pile for Gisele.

I worked my way through a couple of cups of coffee, and by the time I left for University College I felt a little better.

Julie was sitting in our row when I arrived at the lecture. I flopped into the chair beside her, unable to disguise my lethargy.

"Wowza, you look like hell," she said.

"Thanks. I love you too."

"You're not hung over, are you? You didn't drink that much last night. I, on the other hand…" She grimaced and rubbed her temples.

"I'm so bagged, Jul. Everything's catching up with me, I guess."

"Yeah, I feel your pain. I'm pretty beat, myself. Think I'll catch a nap this afternoon before the play tonight."

"A nap is definitely in the cards," I said. "And you were full of win last night. You were turning heads like nobody's business."

"Oh, stop it," she said, waving her hands with a "carry on" gesture.

I laughed, thinking about the way the guys had been sizing her up at the concert. She'd been a dancing machine. "So, do you want to meet in the Hart House lobby tonight, say quarter to seven?" she asked.

"Sounds like a plan, sweetie." I stifled an enormous yawn.

When Professor Brown and Daniel arrived, I quickly made the very scholarly observation that Daniel's wrinkly navy blue button-down shirt did fantastic things for his eyes. I kicked my own ass for caring and slumped back in my seat to listen to Professor Brown's lecture. Within forty minutes, *The Taming of the Shrew* was put to bed. I had no doubt there would be a lively conversation about it during the tutorial, although I wasn't exactly feeling up to the challenge.

With Professor Brown's departure, I quickly pulled my things together and told Julie to hurry up. I was all for getting down to that tutorial room pronto so I could pick a choice spot. I planned to sit in the middle of one of the long sides, hopefully nowhere near Daniel. I leaned against the doorframe when I reached the room, ensuring I'd be the first one through.

Cara glared at me. She probably thought I was planning to stake out the same seat I'd sat in last week, hoping Daniel would sit beside me again.

*Well, you are all kinds of wrong, you tart.*

Finally, Daniel came sauntering down the hall. Yeah, Shawn might have a point. Daniel did have an air of arrogance. I'd been too intoxicated by his other qualities to pay any notice. As Daniel approached, he cleared his throat.

"Excuse me, Miss Price," he said, rousing me from my thoughts.

I moved away from the door enough for him to be able to unlock it. Clearly I was still hovering too closely because he was forced to clear his throat again. I took another step back, and he pulled the door open wide. I bolted through and walked halfway down the table, pulling out a chair four seats from the end. Julie sat beside me.

Cara gaped at me. I drew the swift conclusion that there was a potential career choice for her if all else failed—a kickass human fly-catcher. She sniffed with an affected air of superiority and pulled out the chair I'd sat in last Friday, "saving" the seat beside her for her dingbat best friend.

As everyone took their seats, Daniel had the option of sitting at the end of the table closest to the door or making a scene by squeezing past everyone to reach the other end. He opted for the first choice, subtly moving his chair toward the other corner, closer to sweet-faced Mary. Cara didn't notice. She was too busy looking around the table with a triumphant smile, although no one seemed the least bit interested in her so-called victory. She whipped her head around as Daniel began to speak.

"Well, I hope you've all had a good week," Daniel started, meeting my eyes briefly, along with everyone else's. "We've been enjoying the run of *Hamlet*, and I look forward to attending the show again tonight with those of you who have signed up for the final performance. However, I don't want to spend time talking about that. There's the risk of spoilers of course, and not everyone is even seeing the performance, so we'll leave that for now. First of all, does anyone have any questions?" he asked, finding an empty page in his notebook.

"Um, yes I have a question, *Daniel*. When we were out for coffee yesterday—" Cara leaned forward to suggest some shared intimacy "—you said something about Metrucio being a foil for Romeo in the love plot and stuff like that, and I was wondering if you could explain that for me again." She held her pen poised, ready to write.

I almost snapped my pencil in half. *Metrucio? You've got to be kidding!*

"Our meeting yesterday was specifically aimed at your independent study topic, Miss Switzer. I'd be happy to clarify the way in which *Mercutio* acts as a foil for Romeo, but this isn't the best time for that. We'll book another meeting during my next office hours, okay?"

I smiled, hearing the slight inflection in Daniel's voice as he corrected her pronunciation of the character's name.

"Oh, did you get an office?" she asked coyly.

"Uh, no—figure of speech," he explained. "But we'll speak about this later, yes?"

She nodded, almost conspiratorially. I could barely contain my disdain for the girl. I longed to smack her in the face so hard her whole family would feel it. Daniel interrupted my violent daydream by opening up a discussion about *The Taming of the Shrew*.

Debate centered around the sibling rivalry between the two main female characters and quickly veered toward the relationship between the shrewish Kate and her suitor-turned-husband, Petruchio, I clenched my teeth. There was so much I could say, but I didn't have the energy. I'd save my opinions for my essay.

As predicted, Petruchio was maligned by almost everyone. It was difficult not to react to the strongly anti-feminist themes in the play, and Petruchio was an easy target. But Mary, cherubic-faced Mary with her equally sweet voice, managed to capitalize on a lull in the discussion.

"I think Petruchio's a misunderstood character."

Daniel turned to her, a look of surprise on his face. "How so, Miss Langford?" he asked.

"Well," she said, taking a deep breath and steeling herself against the scrutiny of her peers, "I think he doesn't know how to show love, that's all. His instinct is aggression and violence. He doesn't realize he would get much further by showing Kate some kindness."

"An interesting observation," Daniel said.

Mary became more confident after Daniel's validation. "I don't think Kate was really a shrew either. She's always played second best to her sister," she said. "Once Kate and Petruchio were able to chip away at each other's pride and bravado, they both saw there was a wonderful person underneath."

Mary's words reverberated in my mind. Pride and bravado. Yep, she'd nailed it. But was I thinking about the play now, or was I transferring this analysis to my own life? I was becoming the poster child for pride and bravado. Crap, there went the PMS again! I wanted to throw my hands in front of my face and sob into them. What the hell was wrong with me?

"That's certainly a valid way of looking at things," Daniel said to Mary.

I could see him nodding in my peripheral vision. I resolutely kept my mouth shut, my arms crossed in front of me while my mind wandered. From time to time, I caught pieces of what people around the table were saying. Julie contributed her two cents' worth now and then. I noticed Daniel gazing at me, a confused expression on his face. I trained my eyes on my notebook, doodling idly and whiling away the passing minutes. I shouldn't have even gone to the tutorial. What was the point if I wasn't going to say anything?

When two o'clock finally arrived, I sighed with relief. We poured out of the room, and Julie and I walked down the hall together. Friday was definitely in the air, but I wasn't quite able to rise to the occasion. We shared a quick hug before separating at the front stairs, both of us looking forward to our afternoon naps.

That evening, as I was getting ready to head out to the Hart House Theatre, Matt was on the couch, eating pizza and drinking a beer, getting a head-start on the Kap party. I was beginning to worry about him. He'd purposefully moved into residence to escape from the constant binge drinking that went hand-in-hand with living in a frat house, but he seemed to be holding his own little frat party right here in our apartment several nights a week. I cursed Sarah for crushing his heart.

Watching him chug his beer made my stomach turn. Frankly, so did the smell of the pizza. Despite my nap, I still wasn't feeling back to normal. I grabbed my coat and mitts, hoping the fresh air would make me feel better.

"Hey, you," I said to Matt. "Don't drink too much tonight. We have a date in Swanksville tomorrow. I want you in fighting condition."

"Yeah, yeah. Don't be such a worry wart. Have fun at the *thee-ah-tah*," he added with a mock snooty British accent.

"Oh joy," I said. "See ya later, dude."

I ventured out into the darkness, breathing deeply as I walked, filling my lungs with what passed for fresh air in Toronto. Crossing to the other side of Queen's Park Crescent, I was approaching the front steps of Hart House when my phone vibrated in my coat pocket. Probably Matt checking to make sure I'd arrived safely. I made my way into the lobby, answering as I walked.

"Hi, Aubrey?"

It wasn't Matt after all. It was Julie.

"Hey, bun-head, you running late?"

"Ha! I wish. I'm not running anywhere except back and forth to the bathroom. I just puked my guts out."

"You're kidding! Are you okay?"

"I don't think it's anything serious. It came out of nowhere. It's like a flu bug or something. There's no way I'm gonna make it tonight. I'm really sorry."

"You don't have to apologize, Jul. I'm sorry you're not well. Thanks for letting me know, though. I hope you feel better soon," I added.

"Thanks. Can you tell Mr. Shmexy I'll do the make-up assignment in April?"

"For sure. Don't worry about that. You concentrate on getting better, okay?"

"Thanks, Aub. I'll try."

I switched my phone to vibrate and popped it back in my pocket, turning to scan the lobby again. I couldn't see anyone else from class. It was only six forty-five and the play wasn't starting for another fifteen minutes, but we'd been instructed to arrive ten to fifteen minutes early to get our tickets.

I sat glumly on a red velvet bench by the wall, toying with the idea of leaving and selecting the *Much Ado* option as well. In fact, I was standing up to cross to the door when Daniel walked through it, eliminating my opportunity to escape. He saw me at once and wandered over, hands in his coat pockets.

"Good evening, Miss Price," he said.

And I swear I've never used the word before, nor can I remember ever needing to, but he sounded suave. *Suave*, for Christ's sake.

"Hello, Daniel," I replied coolly.

"Where's your Miss Harper?" he asked, scanning the lobby as if she might materialize magically from thin air.

"She called to tell me she's not well. Probably a flu bug. She won't be coming."

An uncomfortable expression flitted across his face. "Oh, I see."

"Where's everybody else?" I asked.

"Miss Harper *was* everybody else," he said dryly.

"What? Only Julie and I were coming tonight?"

"It appears that most of your classmates had other plans for this evening," he explained. "A certain Kap party seems to have been the destination of choice."

I suddenly realized how my evening was about to play out.

The two of us.

Alone in a darkened theater.

This was not good.

"Well, here's your ticket," he said, handing it to me. "Did you want to check your coat?"

"Um, sure, I guess so."

I removed my jacket, retrieved my cellphone and the small notepad and pen I'd brought, and jammed my gloves into the empty pockets.

He held out his hand. "Let me take your coat for you."

"Thanks," I said, feeling a little off balance.

Why did he always have to contradict my expectations? When I expected him to be happy and lighthearted, he was miserable and surly. Now, when I assumed he would be abrupt and irritated, he was kind and considerate. He was beyond confusing.

I watched him approach the coat check. He hadn't changed out of his ratty jeans, but he was wearing a black, long-sleeved T-shirt instead of the wrinkly, button-down shirt he'd worn today. As he walked back to me, my eyes lingered momentarily over the hole in his jeans, right above his knee. I also noticed the way his shirt clung to his broad shoulders and chest. Lord, he was so hot. If there was a specific recipe for disaster, I felt certain the ingredients were currently lining themselves up quite nicely.

"Shall we?" he asked, gesturing for me to walk ahead of him into the theater.

I gave my ticket to the usher who handed me a program. We were sitting in the tenth row at the aisle. Daniel motioned for me to sit in the second seat, and he claimed the aisle seat. I did my best to angle myself away from him. As with last week's tutorial, the proximity was overwhelming. Sitting this close, I swore I could actually smell his soap. Or was it his cologne?

*Sandalwood.* There's a word I had been storing somewhere alongside "suave." What the hell was sandalwood anyway? In the dictionary beside the word, there would probably be a picture of me blissfully sniffing Daniel's neck.

I snuck a sideways glance at him. He was flipping through the program, his Adam's apple bobbing as he swallowed. It was the single most erotic thing I'd ever seen. Recipe for disaster, indeed.

People were gradually filling the seats around us, and we had to stand a couple of times to let people by. Once our row was full—with the exception of Julie's empty seat beside me—I tried to get comfortable, my left elbow bumping his right one in the process.

I apologized, feeling like a fumbling idiot.

"Not to worry," he said. Then he shifted in his seat to face me. "You were quiet in tutorial today, Miss Price. I was expecting you to have a lot to say."

I looked at him, and without missing a beat, I said, "Well, I've come to realize it's best not to have excessively high expectations. That way you're less likely to be disappointed."

I turned to scan my program, feigning fascination with its contents. I could see out of the corner of my eye that he was still looking at me. When the house lights dimmed and the stage lights came up, revealing a scantly lit scene which would introduce the ghost of Hamlet's dead father, Daniel cleared his throat and faced the stage.

I kept my body tilted to the right, making a conscious effort not to touch him with any part of my body, when all I really wanted to do was plunge my fingers into the hole in his jeans so I could feel the soft hairs on his leg. Okay, maybe I wanted to feel something more than that, but I would settle for the leg as a starting point.

Focusing on the action on the stage took a superhuman effort. I could practically feel heat radiating from Daniel. Or was that me? I didn't even know. After about forty minutes of trying to sit perfectly still and refrain from leaping onto his lap to straddle him, I began to feel even warmer. At one point, at the beginning of Act III, he leaned toward me to whisper, "This scene is phenomenal. Misogyny alert, Miss Price."

As his breath tickled my neck, I shivered involuntarily. Two inches…that's all it would have taken. If I'd turned my head *just so*, I would have been centimeters away from his divine lips. I tugged at the neck of my shirt and struggled to stay composed.

And then the nunnery scene unfolded. Hamlet hurled insults at Ophelia, and she cowered in fear. As he delivered his line, "I did love you once," he plunged his hand between the actress's legs, making her cry out.

*Holy hell.*

She whimpered her next line, and he threw her violently to the floor, scoffing at her for ever having believed in his love. Daniel was right; their performance was phenomenal. It was sexy and angry and sad and dangerous all at the same time. I sensed rather than saw Daniel turning toward me. I leaned over slightly.

"They're fucking incredible," I whispered. I immediately felt the blood rush to my face as I realized I'd dropped the F-bomb right out of left field. He smiled before looking back at the stage.

That's when I started to feel *really* warm. This time it wasn't a *girly-bits-afire-take-me-now* kind of warm. I was actually starting to feel clammy. Then I got a strange sensation in my throat and mouth. Oh my God—I was going to be sick! I stood up, covering my mouth with my hand and clambering across Daniel's legs to dash up the aisle. I ran to the washroom, making it into a stall with five seconds to spare before throwing up violently.

"Damn you, Julie," I moaned, steadying myself on the sides of the stall.

I pulled a long stream of toilet paper off the roll and cleaned myself up, hovering over the bowl as I waited for a second wave. When a few minutes passed without further incident, I left the stall and leaned over the sink, soaping up my hands and running them under the cold water. My reflection in the mirror peered back at me, deathly white. The door opened as I was smoothing my hair back, and the usher who had shown us to our seats rushed in.

"Are you all right?" she asked.

"Yeah, a little wobbly, but I'm okay. I don't think I left a mess," I said, gesturing behind me.

"Don't worry about that," she said. "Your boyfriend is outside. He seems pretty worried."

*My boyfriend? Sweet Lord.*

"He's not my boyfriend," I corrected her.

"Oh, well, do you want me to tell him you'll be out in a minute?"

I contemplated asking her if there was a back door, preferably one that led outside straight from the bathroom, but I only nodded weakly.

How mortifying. I dreaded facing him, but I had no choice. I rubbed my fingers under my eyes, trying to erase the black mascara smudges. No use. I looked like…what was it Daniel had said about himself that first day we'd chatted? *I look like I've been dragged through a hedge backwards.* I tried to pinch some color into my cheeks and swished my mouth out with tap water. Then I put on a brave face and returned to the lobby.

Daniel was leaning against the wall, one hand in his pocket, the other massaging his temple. I crossed to join him, not exactly steady on my feet. He pushed himself off the wall, meeting me in the middle of the lobby. "Are you okay? Jesus, that came out of nowhere!"

"Yeah, I'm fine. I guess that's what happened with Julie earlier. You might want to look for some hand sanitizer. I'd feel terrible if you got sick too. Oh, I feel kind of dizzy." I pressed my hand to my forehead.

"Here, come and sit down." He led me back to the red bench by the wall. "Lean forward. Put your head down between your knees." I did as he told me. "Is there someone you could call to come get you?" he asked. I squinted at the carpet. I couldn't think. "This is yours, right? You left it on your seat." He held out my phone and slipped it into my hand.

"I don't know how I'll get back to residence. I don't think I can walk that far right now."

I looked up at him. He was grinding his jaw muscles, casting his eyes around the lobby.

"I guess I could drive you home," he finally offered with an exasperated sigh.

"Don't trouble yourself," I snapped.

"It's no trouble, Miss Price," he said, trying to muster a gracious tone. "You probably shouldn't be alone, though. Is there someone home?"

Matt was at the Kap house. Joanna would be at Stephen's for the weekend. I scrolled through my contacts and was about to dial Matt's number when another wave of nausea hit me. I handed Daniel the phone. "Matt. Call Matthew Miller." I dashed back to the bathroom, my hand clasped over my mouth.

I dry heaved over the toilet bowl a couple of times, but nothing came up. I waited a few minutes, but the feeling passed. Again, I washed my hands and splashed my face before heading back out to the lobby. Daniel was sitting on the bench, staring vacantly at my phone.

"Did you get hold of him?" I asked.

"Yes. He was at a rather loud party."

"Kap house."

"Ah. Well, he sounded concerned and said he'd leave right away and meet you back at Jackman within fifteen minutes." He was quiet for a few seconds before adding, "Is he your boyfriend?"

"Roommate," I said. *Not that it's any of your business.*

"Do you think you'll be all right now? Will being in the car make you feel sick?"

"I think I'm okay," I said, trying not to snap at him again, certain he was worried I might hurl in his Beemer.

"All right, let's go." He handed me my coat, and I reluctantly pulled it on. I was boiling. "You should do up your zipper. You'll catch your death," he said, gesturing to the front of my coat.

*Okay, Mom,* I thought, but I zipped myself up anyway. We walked without speaking, crossing the paths to King's College Circle. I must have been visibly shaky, but he seemed to be in his own world, making no offer to support me or prop me up. His car was sitting along the curb near the spot he'd parked in last week when I'd watched him — no, scratch that — when I'd *followed* him after class.

He held the passenger side door open for me, and before joining me in the car, he looked around as if he thought he was being followed, like he'd robbed a bank and was trying to make a speedy getaway. Finally he climbed in and started the car. The interior was spotless. You could have eaten a meal off any surface with no qualms whatsoever. As the engine purred to life, he pulled swiftly out of the spot and drove toward University Avenue.

"Do you mind if I open the window?" I asked.

"Not at all." As I rolled it down, he flicked on the heat, turning it to full blast. "Are you sure you're all right?"

*Relax! I'm not gonna puke in your damn car!*

"I'm fine," I said, taking deep breaths of fresh air. Several quiet minutes later, we were traveling west on Charles Street. I saw Matt up ahead, jogging toward Jackman.

"That's Matt," I said, pointing out the window.

Daniel pulled up to the curb and quickly skirted the car to open the door for me.

"Matt!" I called out.

He turned and made his way toward us. "Aubs, what happened, sweetheart? Are you okay?" he asked, brushing my hair out of my face.

"I'm fine. I've picked up a stomach bug or something. I think I'm okay now. Daniel didn't think I should be alone, though. Oh, Daniel, this is Matt. Matt, this is my TA, Daniel Grant."

They shook hands, sizing each other up. *Why do men always have to do that?*

"Well, I see you're in capable hands, Miss Price," Daniel said. "I'll be off. I hope you feel better tomorrow."

"Thanks," I said, my voice sounding hollow and reedy.

Daniel gave us a tight smile, but his eyes remained distant. He raced off in the Beemer, and Matt put his arm around me, leading me to the lobby.

"Come on. Let's get you inside."

We took the elevator instead of the stairs, and Matt helped me to my room before disappearing to the kitchen. I undressed, threw my clothes in a heap on the floor, and pulled on a T-shirt and some pajama bottoms. Matt reappeared, setting a bottle of water on my night stand.

"Thanks, Matt," I said, crawling into bed with a groan, and then the tears that had been threatening all day finally spilled over.

"Hey," he said. "What's going on?"

He lay down on top of the blankets beside me, pulling my head onto his chest and letting me cry all over him. I didn't want to talk. Instead, I snuggled into his side and he rubbed my back, soothing me until I fell into a restless but puke-free sleep.

## Hungry

Other women cloy
The appetites they feed, but she makes hungry
Where most she satisfies...
(*Antony and Cleopatra*, Act II, Scene 2)

When I woke on Saturday morning, I was alone. Matt had managed to leave without rousing me. I rolled my eyes around. They were a bit achy, but not unbearable. My neck was stiff, and my throat hurt a little. I leaned over to grab the untouched bottle of water Matt had left for me, chugging the whole thing.

*Matt.* What a star he'd been last night. My personal knight in shining armor.

I stood up, testing my equilibrium. Not bad. My face, on the other hand, was a mess. I had a nasty snail trail of dried spit down the side of my chin. *Attractive.* I dabbed at my cheek with a tissue and glanced at the time—ten o'clock. Awesome sleep. I headed out to the living room where I found Matt on the couch, eating Captain Crunch and watching cartoons.

"What are you, nine years old?" I asked, leaning against the wall with my arms crossed.

"Well, I guess I don't need to ask how you're feeling this morning," he said. His tone was sarcastic, but he was smiling widely.

"Yeah, I'm feeling almost back to normal." I walked over to join him on the sofa.

"Gee, can't wait till you're a hundred percent."

"Oh, come on now, you love my razor sharp wit. Don't deny it."

"Yeah, yeah, it's definitely my favorite thing about you." He laughed. "Seriously, how are you feeling? We still gonna be able to hit Canoe tonight?"

"Oh, for sure. I guess I had a twenty-four-hour bug or something. I felt like crap all day yesterday, but I didn't know why. After I puked, I felt so much better."

"Last night was you feeling *better?* That's scary. I've never seen you cry like that, Aubs." He was looking at me with concern.

"Man, I don't know. I guess being sick kind of knocked me on my ass a bit, you know?" I said evasively. "Thanks for coming home and helping me. Sorry I dragged you away from the party."

"Are you kidding me? I wouldn't have missed your droolfest for a million bucks. Besides, it was Friday the thirteenth. Something had to wreck my night. No brainer."

I laughed. "Jesus, way to make me feel like shit. But sorry about the drool. I guess I was doing some mouth breathing."

"And snoring up a storm," he added.

I punched his arm. "I was not. I don't snore."

"Oh, you have no idea."

"Pfft. Whatever, cowboy."

Matt continued to snort with laughter as he took his dirty bowl to the kitchen, and then he was off, heading to the Kap house to help with the post-party clean-up and promising to be back by five. I had a quiet Saturday ahead of me once again.

I woke up from my afternoon nap slowly, straddling dream and reality. I knew I was on the couch in the living room, but I refused to open my eyes, determined to recall the details of my dream which were hovering around the edges of my consciousness.

I'd been lying on a red velvet sofa, and Daniel had been leaning over me, his eyes burning as he gazed at me and his lips deliciously close to brushing mine. His hair had fallen forward and tickled my face. I smiled, rolling from my back onto my side, trying to hang on to every nuance of this sweet dream. The rest of it was hazy at best. Gradually awakening, I opened my eyes, only to see Matt's face no more than two feet away from mine.

I gasped and jumped, shrinking back against the cushions. He was perched on the edge of the coffee table, clutching a bunch of flowers.

"Is that any way to look at your Valentine?" he asked.

"I'm sorry. You scared me."

He held the bouquet of pale yellow carnations out to me. "For you."

"Oh, Matt, that's so sweet. You didn't have to do that."

"I know, but I wanted to. I've been moping around here so much the last couple of weeks. I haven't been a very good friend, but I'd have to be blind not to notice you've been pretty down yourself. Last night kind of capped it off, you know? I'm sorry I've been so self-absorbed."

I took the flowers, touching the petals gently.

"They're really nice, Matt. Thank you. But, yeah, you've been a total pain in the ass to be around."

"Shit, really?" His face fell.

"I was kidding," I said. "You shouldn't have to apologize for being in a vile mood after what happened with Sarah. Joanna and I both understand. If you can't be yourself with your friends in the comfort of your own home, well, that would blow, right?"

"Thanks for understanding," he said. "But I don't want to mope tonight, okay? I want to have a kick-ass dinner with you, green-eyes. Deal?"

"Deal. What time is it, anyway?"

"Almost six."

Whoa! Time to start getting ready.

"I'm gonna grab a shower," Matt said. "You need in there before I do?"

"No, I had an awesome soak in the tub this afternoon. I'm good. I'll be in my room. Quarter to seven you said you wanted to leave, right?"

"Yeah, that should be good," he said, and he headed off for the bathroom.

I arranged the flowers in a vase on my desk, and then I took my time getting ready. As I hummed along to the music playing on my iPod, I leaned against the dresser, thinking about Daniel's angular jaw and full lips, imagining him smiling at me as he bobbed his head to move the hair out of his gorgeous blue eyes. After last night, I now had the sexy, long-sleeved, black T-shirt with tight chest muscles underneath to add to the repertoire of details for my fantasies.

I glanced at the flowers and then looked at myself critically in the mirror. What was my problem? Here I was, living with a handsome guy, someone sweet and kind. Despite our years of claiming to be grossed out by each other, it was becoming more and more obvious that Matt would be quite willing to give us another chance—and all I could do was moon over someone who was beyond my reach, not to mention completely uninterested in me.

With Matt, I always knew where I stood. He said what he thought, and he didn't play games. If he screwed up, he apologized, and he never made me feel like something he'd done wrong was my fault.

I was officially an idiot. I needed an attitude adjustment in the worst way. I set my mind on having a great night out with Matt. Mooning over Daniel was wasted energy.

Hair and makeup done, I slipped my dress on. Giving myself a once-over in my full-length mirror, I smiled at my reflection. This was one of those dresses that made me feel beautiful. I was having a good hair day too. Why did that always seem to seal the deal? Humming to myself, I pushed my feet into my black stilettos. Good thing we were taking a taxi. I'd be bleeding and crippled by the time we reached the restaurant if we were to take the subway.

I grabbed my clutch purse, some money, a lip gloss, and my ID. I was good to go. Matt was standing against the kitchen counter chugging a glass of water when I emerged. He lowered the glass slowly and whistled as I walked toward him.

"Hot damn, woman, you look *fine*," he hooted.

"Thanks." Suddenly self-conscious, I motioned toward his suit. "Looking pretty good yourself there, my friend," I admitted, leaning forward to straighten his tie.

"Shall we?" he asked, putting on his coat and then helping me with mine.

"I'm ready when you are."

After walking as briskly down to Bay Street as my shoes would allow, we managed to hail a cab. Traffic was heinous, and the cab smelled like a mixture of dirty socks and stale barf—not an aroma I needed to revisit, given last night's fiasco. I glanced at Matt and pinched my nostrils shut. He looked at me with a panicked expression and opened the window a crack. I leaned toward it gratefully. After the longest twelve minutes of my life, we pulled up to the Toronto Dominion Bank Tower. Matt quickly paid the driver, and we leapt out of the car, gasping for fresh air as we crossed the sidewalk to the building's entrance.

"I never thought I'd be happy to inhale smog and sewer stench," he groaned, taking several deep breaths. He took me by the hand and led me to the revolving doors. "This okay with you?" he asked, gesturing toward our clasped hands.

"I suppose since it's Valentine's Day and all, I'll let it go." I gave him a wry smile. "But don't get any ideas."

We rode the gleaming elevator to the fifty-fourth floor, and the doors opened to reveal the tastefully appointed lobby of Canoe. The restaurant itself was behind a set of glass doors. Matt held the door open for me, and we stepped inside.

"Can I help you?" the maître d' asked.

"Yes, I have a reservation for two for seven o'clock. It's under 'Miller,'" Matt said, looking at me and raising his eyebrows excitedly. He looked like a kid on Christmas morning.

"Yes, of course, Mr. Miller. May I take your coats?"

Matt took off his coat and helped me with mine, handing them both to the maître d' who passed them off to a girl manning a small room behind his desk.

"Allow me to show you to your table, Mr. Miller."

Matt led me by the elbow as we walked to the other side of the restaurant. A row of tables for two ran along the mirrored wall, flanked on one side by chairs and on the other by a padded leather bench. After holding the chair out for me and moving aside for Matt to maneuver into the bench seat, the maître d' took our starched white napkins and shook each one out, placing them gently on our laps.

"Have you dined with us before?" he asked.

"No, this is our first time here," I said, smiling at Matt.

"Well, allow me to be the first to welcome you. I hope you enjoy your evening. My name is Geoffrey, should you need anything."

"Thank you, Geoffrey," Matt said in a vaguely pretentious voice.

"You're welcome, sir. Enjoy your evening."

I smothered a laugh.

"Sorry, that was a little over the top. I couldn't help myself," Matt admitted as he scanned our surroundings. "So this is how the other half lives."

"I know. It's fucking incredible."

"Aubs, I'm pretty sure the other half doesn't drop F-bombs at the dinner table in a swanky restaurant."

"Then I'm not sure I want to be one of the other half. They sound pretty fucking boring."

Matt chuckled. We were interrupted by a different man in a dark suit who approached the table with several menus.

"Good evening. I'm Raymond and I'll be taking care of you while you are with us tonight. Here are your menus, and I'll leave the wine list here. The sommelier is on site should you have any questions. Now, would you care for a drink from the bar while you are perusing the menu?" he asked, looking back and forth between us.

I hesitated, wondering if I should play it safe, but decided to live a little.

"I'll have a vodka and soda, with lime and lemon please," I said.

"I'll have a Keith's," Matt said.

"Very good," Raymond said, taking a moment to lean over the table to light the floating votive candle before retreating to the bar to place our orders. A few moments later, he returned with our drinks before moving to a nearby table to refill their water glasses.

"Well, cheers." Matt lifted his glass. "Happy Valentine's Day. I'm glad you came with me tonight."

"Thanks, Matt. Me too." I gestured around the room. "I never dreamed I get a chance to eat here. I'm glad I'm sharing this with you."

He looked at me warmly, and I tried to take in his features objectively. How would he look to a woman meeting him for the first time? Sparkling eyes, awesome skin, dark wavy hair, and a gorgeous smile. His body was muscular too, which wasn't necessarily my thing; I preferred my men tall and lean, but Matt was certainly—what had Julie called him?—a hunk of burning love? I smiled and shook my head as I thought of Julie working the room on Thursday night.

"What are you grinning about?" Matt asked.

"Oh, just remembering Julie's antics the other night. She's such a hoot," I said.

"It's cool you two hooked up again, especially now that Joanna's pretty much moved in with Stephen. You need someone to talk to. I do my best with the girl-talk, but I'm not so good with the painting nails and braids."

"Maybe you need some practice. You can do my toes tomorrow," I said with a smile.

"Wow, that sounds like a blast," he deadpanned.

I handed him a menu, my tummy rumbling. "We should figure out what we're going to eat."

We scanned our menus. The prices were outrageous.

"Sweet Jesus." Matt whistled between his teeth, looking up over his menu, a dazed expression on his face.

"I know! Expensive, huh?"

"No, it's not that. Check it out, heading to that table on the other side of the room by the windows. That is one fine-looking woman."

I looked into the strip of mirrors along the wall over Matt's shoulder where I could see the tables on the other side of the restaurant. *Handy way to spy on people.*

I had to agree with him. She was gorgeous. Tall and curvy in all the right places, her ebony hair cascaded down her back in waves. Her dress was stunning—all black and incredibly close fitting with a slit up one leg that reached dangerously high up her thigh. She was the kind of woman the term "femme fatale" had been invented for. Geoffrey pulled her chair out for her, and then proceeded to help her with her napkin. They were smiling and chatting. *Probably a socialite who dines here often.* I looked back at Matt.

"Easy there, cowboy. Put your tongue back in your mouth."

She was sitting facing us, and I could easily imagine him getting caught ogling.

"Shit, sorry, Aubs, I've just never seen…"

He trailed off, still gazing at her in admiration. I looked down at my menu.

"Well, this is romantic," I said.

"Sorry." Matt cleared his throat. "You're right. My bad. Where were we?"

"Well, I don't know about you, but I'm checking out these appetizers. They look phenomenal."

"The entrées look impressive too." Matt flipped back and forth between the pages.

"Hmm, maybe I'll have an entrée and dessert. They have crème brûlée," I said, my mouth watering. I snapped my menu closed. "Okay, I know what I'm having."

"Yep, me too," Matt said. "Gotta do the prime rib."

He flipped his menu shut, and I looked around for Raymond, hoping to catch his eye. It was in that precise moment that the earth, which had previously been spinning quite nicely on its axis, came to a screeching halt.

Daniel.

He was here.

He was walking toward a table on the opposite side of the room.

The raven-haired beauty was standing up, throwing her arms around him and hugging him.

He was kissing her on both cheeks.

He was holding her chair out for her.

They were sitting down at the table.

Together.

*Together* together.

My heart fell into the pit of my stomach as I came to a swift and painful realization: This woman, this other-worldly beauty who'd just sent Matt into paroxysms of desire—*this* was Daniel's "love."

His Valentine's date.

Penny.

# The Green-Eyed Monster

O, beware, my lord, of jealousy;
It is the green-eyed monster which doth mock
The meat it feeds on…
(*Othello,* Act III, Scene 3)

B ile rose in my throat and my stomach knotted with jealously. I wanted to stand up and throw a bread roll at Penny's head. This was not a reasonable option. Doing so would likely put a teensy damper on our lovely dinner. And so I sat, seething in quiet desperation until Matt's insistent voice interrupted my vitriolic inner monologue.

"Aubrey? Yes or no? Hello?" He snapped his fingers in front of my eyes.

"Huh?"

Numbness was spreading across my face.

"Wine. Did you want to get a bottle of wine? There's a Pinot Gris called Burning Owl they're recommending here on the wine list. It's from B.C., so it's gotta be good," he said with a superior grin. "A little expensive, but I think that's to be expected tonight."

"Oh, yeah, sure," I said. "Whatever you want is fine with me."

It took supreme effort to maintain eye contact with Matt.

"Okay," he said hesitantly. "That was easy."

I picked up my drink and knocked back what was left in the glass. The vodka burned my throat, soothing me as its warmth spread through my chest. When Raymond reappeared, Matt quickly ordered the prime rib and I requested the Ahi tuna, suddenly feeling as if I might be incapable of chewing and swallowing meat. My throat constricted and my mouth felt dry. I took several large gulps of water while Matt took care of ordering the wine.

"Hey, Aubs, are you okay? You're a little pale. Are you feeling sick again?"

My eyes flickered over his shoulder briefly to look in the mirror. All I could see was the back of Daniel's head.

*Move along, Aubrey, nothing to see here.*

"Actually, I *am* feeling a little odd. I'm gonna head to the washroom for a minute, okay?"

I stood up, dropping my napkin on the table. Matt looked up at me worriedly.

"Do you want me to grab a waitress to go in with you?" he asked.

"No, it's okay, Matt. I need to splash some water on my face, that's all," I assured him.

*And pierce that bitch's eyeball with the heel of my stiletto. No worries. All in a day's work.*

I hurried off to the washroom, feeling Matt's eyes following me. Safely away from his scrutiny, I sat on the leather sofa in the outer room which adjoined the washroom area, breathing deeply through my nose. Once the pounding of my heart had settled, I made my way to the sinks, gritting my teeth as I ran my hands under the cold water.

I needed to pull myself together. Really, what was the big deal? I'd known since the first day I'd met him that Daniel had a girlfriend. Nevertheless, now that I'd seen her for myself in all her stunning, voluptuous glory, the reality of his unavailability was crushing. I could *not* compete with *that*.

I sighed and leaned against the counter, enjoying the solitude. The peace and quiet was not to last, however. Someone with a lively voice burst through the door, interrupting my tranquil moment. I turned to look at the person who was talking so animatedly, and there in front of me was the woman who was single-handedly dashing my hopes.

*Penny.* She was talking into a cell phone in a strong—and might I reluctantly add, very charming—English accent. She dropped onto the sofa I'd vacated.

"No, that's okay. I left Daniel at the table," she said to the person on the other end of the line. "I'm in the loo now, which is bigger than my mum and dad's front room at home, by the way." She ran her hand over the soft leather of the sofa as she listened. "What's that? Oh, absolutely, it's been hard. He's so busy, working all the time. He's knackered constantly…Oh, I know, it'll all be over soon. Once we're married, he said he'll try to cut back. Can you believe in six months I'll be Mrs. Penny Grant? I'm so bloody excited I can barely stand it."

*Married?* They were to be married in six months? She wasn't his girlfriend—she was his *fiancée!* I looked grimly into the mirror, my heart shriveling in my chest. Could it get any worse?

I weighed my options.

Shoe to the eyeball?

If I did it quickly, I could make a speedy exit, grab Matt, and jump in a cab. No one would be the wiser. I was being ridiculous, of course, but it was tempting. Penny was winding up her conversation, and I splashed around in the sink, trying to cover up my eavesdropping.

"Anyway, this is costing you a fortune. I should ring off," she said. "Give everyone my love, won't you? I'll drop you an email next week. Yes, of course I will…Cheers, Ronnie. Bye now."

She rose and joined me at the sinks, opening her purse. She removed a bottle of expensive perfume and sprayed herself liberally. I tried to busy myself with my purse too, rooting around for my lip gloss, but before I could apply any, her perfume went right up my nose. I sneezed several times.

"Oh, Jesus, sorry. That was bloody rude of me. Are you allergic?" she asked.

*Don't be nice to me, you bitch. I'm trying to hate you.*

"No, I'm not allergic. Not used to such *strong* perfume, I guess."

"Oh, I know. My fiancé bought this for me." She gestured to the bottle. "I think he reckoned I'd love it because it's so expensive. I wear it for him more than for myself," she said.

My eye was drawn to the giant diamond on her hand. That, too, looked to be expensive.

*God, don't look, Aubrey. And while you're at it, ignore her fabulous boobs. Seriously. You don't want to look.*

I stared at her blankly, at a loss for what to say and incapable of maintaining the charade a moment longer. She looked back at me uncomfortably.

"Well, listen to me rabbiting on at you," she said. "Sorry about that. I'm new in town, and don't have many girls to chat with. I tend to latch on to any friendly face I see these days. Sad, really."

*Friendly face? Was she on crack?*

I ignored her apology. "If you'll excuse me, I should get back to my date."

"Of course, love, don't let me keep you." She turned back to the mirror to reapply her lipstick. As I pulled the door open she called after me, "Oh, and happy Valentine's Day!"

*Oh, you too, Penny. Have fun steamrolling my heart, you bitch!*

I zipped up my clutch as I walked through the restaurant. Matt was scrolling through messages on his phone. When I reached the table, he put the phone away and stood up to hold the chair out for me.

"I was starting to get worried. You were in there for ages."

"Yeah, I needed a minute. I feel a lot better now, though," I said.

*Lies. All lies.*

The wine had arrived in my absence. A full glass was in front of me.

"How about a toast?" Matt said, lifting his wine.

"Allow me," I offered, trying my best to sound convincing. "Here's to putting the past to rest and focusing on new beginnings."

"I'll drink to that." He smiled warmly at me.

I moaned appreciatively as I took a large swallow of wine, thinking, *I'll drink to anything right about now...*

"Mmm, that *is* good." I licked my lips.

"At that price, it better be," Matt said with a chuckle.

Then his eyes drifted over my shoulder. In the mirror, I could see Penny returning to their table. Again, Matt was entranced. I watched Daniel stand and pull her chair out.

"Hey, isn't that—? Yeah, *it is!* That's your TA guy from last night. He's her date," he said, his eyes wide.

I feigned confusion. "What's that?" I glanced over my shoulder, as if noticing him for the first time. "Well, so it is. That's a coincidence, huh?"

"Lucky bastard," Matt muttered.

*Lucky bitch*, I thought.

"He must have some coin," Matt said. "That's one hell of a nice suit."

Matt was right. With his beautifully cut suit and the pale blue shirt open at the neck, Daniel looked impossibly hot. And lo and behold, he'd shaved and brushed his hair. Even from this distance, I could tell that when he shaved, his jawline was even more chiseled.

It occurred to me that not only did he have a Dr. Jekyll and Mr. Hyde thing going on with his behavior, but he was also sporting a similar split personality with his appearance. At school, TA Daniel looked like something the cat had dragged in, whereas in his private life he could double as a male runway model.

I decided to rename him. Henceforth, he would be Dr. Hobo, the shabbily dressed and hygienically challenged doctoral candidate who morphed into Mr. *GQ* when the sun went down. Either way, he was gorgeous. He'd probably be hot as hell wearing a potato sack, but *this* get-up? *This* was staggering.

Matt was swishing his wine around in his glass.

"You okay?" I asked.

"Yeah," he said with a tight smile. "Thinking."

*Oh, believe me, dude, I know.*

We drank our wine in companionable silence for a while, and though I tried not to, I glanced occasionally in the mirror at Daniel and Penny. They were laughing and having a grand old time. At one point, Daniel took her left hand in his and rubbed his thumb across the ring on her finger. The hardened pebble that had taken the place of my heart cracked in two.

Luckily our entrées arrived a few moments later, and I tried to focus on my dinner. The plates were works of art. There was a reason the meals were forty dollars a pop. I hoped the other reason had to do with the taste. Raymond refilled our wine, asked if there was anything we needed, and when we said we were fine he moved on.

My meal cheered me up somewhat. The tuna was exquisite. I assumed Matt's food was the same. He closed his eyes as he chewed, looking like he'd been transported to heaven.

"You have to try this," he said, cutting off a slice of his prime rib. He held his fork over to me and—I don't know why I did it—I gazed into his eyes, reached over to hold his hand in place, and seductively tugged the meat off the fork with my teeth, licking my lips slowly afterward.

Stunned, Matt watched my mouth as I chewed.

"Wanna try mine?" I asked, gazing up at him from under my lashes.

"Um, well, yeah, sure," he stammered.

I cut off a piece of tuna and leaned forward, holding out my fork. He mimicked my gesture, holding my hand while he took the tuna from the fork.

"Good, huh?" I asked.

"Incredible," he said, looking at me in wonder.

I smiled brilliantly and finished my second glass of wine.

"Want some more?" Matt held up the wine bottle.

"Absolutely." I stretched my leg out under the table and slipped the toe of my stiletto under the cuff of his pant leg.

The combination of wine-buzz and heartbreak was doing strange things to me, but Matt seemed to be enjoying it. He smiled and shook his head, continuing to eat zealously. About halfway through my meal, I pushed my plate aside and turned my attention to my wine glass, a warm glow enveloping me as I continued to drink. I picked up the bottle. There was a tiny splash left.

"Go ahead," Matt urged.

I emptied it into my glass and continued to sip at it while Matt finished his meal. Raymond walked by, and Matt stopped him to ask for some more water. "I have a feeling I'm going to need this," he said, gesturing to his water glass as he poured his remaining wine into my glass.

"Matt, are you trying to get me drunk?" I asked.

"Possibly," he said, smiling and raising one eyebrow suggestively.

He placed his knife and fork across his now empty plate.

"You ordering dessert?" I asked, my voice a little breathy.

"Hell no," he said, staring at my mouth.

"Wanna go?"

"Hell yes."

He got Raymond's attention and requested the bill. I worked my way through Matt's last glass of wine, and when Raymond returned, Matt put his credit card in the waiter's hand.

"No, Matt, that's not what we agreed on," I protested.

"Now, what kind of Valentine would I be if I didn't pay for my girl?" he said, flashing his white-toothed smile.

Raymond returned with Matt's credit card slip. "This isn't over," I said, gesturing to the bill as he signed it.

He stood up and held my chair out for me. "Whatever you say, Aubs."

As I turned around, I allowed myself one final glance at Daniel and Penny. They were eating their meals, chatting animatedly. Penny looked up as Matt rounded the corner of the table to place his hand gently on my lower back. She gave me a silent thumbs-up. I wanted to shout across the restaurant, telling her what she could do with that thumb. Before bending to that rather inappropriate compulsion, I moved quickly with Matt to reclaim our coats.

The ride down in the elevator was uncomfortable. I don't think Matt knew what to make of my behavior. Hell, *I* didn't even know what I was doing. I was buzzing, warmth spreading throughout my whole body. I wasn't sure the wine was completely to blame.

As we crossed the lobby to the revolving doors, Matt grabbed my hand like he'd done earlier. I squeezed it, and he rubbed his thumb along the top of my knuckles and smiled at me. Outside, we hailed a cab, and I was relieved to find that there was no vomit stench in this one. Matt gave the driver our address and leaned back in the seat, still holding my hand.

My heart was flipping around, more in panic than anything else. What the hell was I doing? I couldn't reason. I was tipsy, but I certainly wasn't drunk. I was completely aware of what was happening, but some force was dragging me along and I felt powerless to fight it.

Matt released my hand and brought his fingertips up to touch my cheek. Then he moved his face toward mine and kissed me tenderly. He pulled back to look at me, measuring my reaction. I closed my eyes and leaned into him, reciprocating his kiss with one of my own. It was sweet and lovely and gentle. He didn't stick his tongue down my throat or throw me back against the seat of the car. He just pressed his lips warmly against mine, and then moved back to his side of the seat.

We rode in silence like that, holding hands and gazing at each other from time to time. When we arrived back at Jackman, I pulled a twenty dollar bill from my purse and handed it to the driver. Matt helped me out of the cab, and we made our way upstairs. Inside the apartment, Matt flicked on a couple of lamps and helped me with my coat. He took off his suit jacket and draped it over the back of the chair before turning around and wrapping his arms around my waist. I put my arms around his neck and let him kiss me again, and this time he ran his tongue gently against my lips before tentatively sliding it in my mouth.

Now, don't get me wrong, I wasn't carried away in a wave of passion or anything, but it was a nice kiss and it was pretty wonderful feeling him exploring my tongue with his. He finally broke away from me, his breathing shallow and restrained. He took me by the hand and led me into my bedroom, pulling me onto the bed with him.

We kissed and he pressed himself against me, and there was something I never thought I'd feel — Matt's erection. And it was rubbing against my thigh. Unbidden images of Daniel played behind my eyes. I imagined this was his mouth, his tongue, his body pressed hard against me. Matt groaned against my lips but pulled away quickly, leaning his forehead on mine and whispering, "Aubrey, what are we doing?"

"I don't know," I whispered back. "I'm trying not to think."

He rolled onto his back and put his hands over his face. "You have no idea how much I want this right now," he said.

I pulled his hands away from his eyes. "Then what are you doing?"

"God, I don't know! Being the good guy, I guess." He looked at me, anguish in his eyes. "You know I love you, Aub. I always have. But if I've got some crazy rebound thing going on…well…I don't know. I'd hate myself if I hurt you. Can we give this some time? Maybe see how we feel after Reading Week?"

Wait, was he rejecting me? Oh my God, this couldn't be happening! I tried not to overreact.

"I thought this was what you wanted," I said, my voice strained.

"It *is*," he said tracing circles on my cheek with his thumb. "I'm just not sure about the timing. And there's something going on with you. I don't know what it is, but you're not yourself right now. I know we should *not* be doing this tonight."

"Maybe you're right." I sighed in resignation, flopping onto my back.

"We'll talk tomorrow, okay?" he said. He leaned over to kiss me tenderly once more. "I had a great time tonight."

"Me too," I whispered.

He crossed the room, stopping at the door. "Goodnight, Aub. Happy Valentine's Day."

"Yep. You too."

That's all I could manage before my throat tightened with restrained tears.

CHAPTER 12

## Heart on Sleeve

But I will wear my heart upon my sleeve
For daws to peck at: I am not what I am.
(*Othello*, Act 1, Scene 1)

When I woke up Sunday morning, the first thing I saw was my dress hanging over the chair in the corner. It would be going through the shredder. How could I ever allow the Double-Rejection Dress to touch my skin again? I wanted nothing to remind me of the events that had transpired the night before.

Lord, I was tired. I'd tossed and turned for three hours in the wake of Matt's magnanimous decision to cock block himself, and I didn't feel rested at all.

Glaring at the yellow carnations, I grabbed the entire bunch and dumped them unceremoniously into the garbage. I regretted the irrational impulse almost immediately, so I replaced them in the vase. I was being completely immature. Matt was right. If we'd gone any farther last night, we'd both be stewing in regret right now—probably for different reasons—but nevertheless, we'd both be sorry. I was lucky he'd had the self-control to pull the rip cord on the proceedings.

Why on earth had I behaved like that? Was I developing feelings for Matt beyond the easy friendship and sisterly love I'd felt for him for years? No, of course I wasn't. I'd been reeling from seeing Penny and Daniel together, from discovering their engagement. I was beside myself with envy, pure and simple. I'd sought an ego-boost, and I was prepared to use Matt to placate my own wounded pride. I needed to apologize and clear the air, and I needed to do it now.

I ventured out into the living room. All was silent. Matt's door was closed. On the kitchen counter beside the coffee maker, I found a note.

> Aubrey,
> I've gone to the gym to work out. Will probably
> hang at Kap for a bit after. See you later.
> We need to talk!
> -M

As much as I wanted to talk to him and hash things out, I was relieved he wasn't home. I could do with a few more hours to sort out my thoughts and bring things into focus. I'd have to tread carefully. I didn't want to hurt Matt's feelings or bruise his ego, and knowing my luck, now that I'd decided last night's events were a terrible mistake, he was probably thinking it was all a wonderful prelude to a short engagement and fall wedding.

I spent the afternoon at the library, using my homework as a salve for my gaping wounds. An afternoon of intensive study was exactly what I needed. After four hours of reading and note-taking, with a little research thrown in for good measure, I repacked my bag to head home, proud of what I'd accomplished.

I arrived back at the apartment, weary and hungry, and was pleasantly surprised to find Joanna in the kitchen, chopping vegetables for what appeared to be a stir fry.

"Hey," I said. "I thought you were going to see *The Sound of Music* with Stephen tonight."

"No, that was last night. Remember, it was my Valentine gift?"

I actually hadn't remembered. Jo was around so little, I wasn't exactly plugged into her social life. I bit back a snarky comment. There was no need to make her feel guilty for actually having a successful love life and a boyfriend who spoiled her rotten.

"Oh, I guess I got my dates mixed up."

"That's okay. How was dinner? You and Matt went out, right?"

She gave me a pointed look, as if she thought I'd have some cataclysmic news to share. I was in no mood to share cataclysms.

"We had a nice time. He's a good friend," I said, emphasizing the last word, while hoping the events of the night before hadn't completely ruined our friendship. "But I don't want to talk about my night. How was the show? Were the hills alive? How *did* they solve a problem like Maria?"

"It was amazing," she gushed. "The staging was incredible. I don't know how they pulled off the first scene on the mountain top. It was super cool."

I listened to her ramble on about *The Sound of Music* for a while, helping her slice veggies and prepare rice. It was nice to have her home. She was a breath of fresh air. She encouraged me to share dinner with her, and we ate together in front of the TV. We talked about inconsequential things, and as we chattered on about nothing in particular, I realized I was talking like this with *everyone*. A constant stream of trivialities and one-liners was all I seemed capable of sharing, confiding in no one. It couldn't be healthy.

I'd feel stupid divulging my feelings for Daniel to Joanna, though. She was a lovely girl, but she was so level-headed. If I went out on a limb and shared the inappropriate crush I was harboring on my TA, she'd disapprove and tell me to smarten up. And she'd be right on the mark.

After dinner, I sat on the floor while Joanna sat on the couch behind me, styling my hair, one of her favorite ways to relax. I loved it when people played with my hair, so I wasn't about to complain. Three different braid experiments, a couple of practice up-dos, and two hours of mind-numbing reality TV later, we were both partially brain dead and we called it a night. I curled up in bed to read some short stories for Wednesday night's class. I'd been reading for about an hour when there was a gentle tap on my door.

"Come in," I called out.

Matt entered, moving awkwardly to sit on the edge of the bed. He looked drained. I guessed he'd slept as badly as I had.

"Hey," he said.

"Hey, yourself."

I sat up, wrapping my arms around my knees.

"How was your day?" he asked.

"Okay, I guess. I went to the Metro Reference Library to get some work done. You went to the gym?"

"I did. Kind of needed to blow off some steam. Played pool at the frat house this aft. I needed to chill with the guys."

"Yeah, I get that. So...?" I said, not knowing how to begin. This was what I'd been afraid of. The awkward silence. The "how do we broach this topic" dance.

"Are we okay?" he asked.

His voice sounded so choked and tight, I thought he might actually cry. I held out my hand to him. "Come here," I said. He took my hand and crawled up to sit beside me.

"Last night was pretty crazy. I'm not gonna lie; I did *not* see that coming. I don't know what got into me, well, aside from a vodka and soda and three-quarters of a bottle of wine," I said.

This was only partially true. I knew exactly what had gotten into me, but I wasn't about to tell Matt I'd been using him to boost my own damaged ego, especially considering how soundly I'd failed.

"But I'm not blaming the wine for my behavior. Leading you on like that was wrong."

Matt tried to interrupt me, but I squeezed his hand and shook my head to stop him.

"Please, let me finish, I need to do this," I said. "Matt, you are an incredible guy. Every day I wonder if things could be different for us, but the truth is, I'm scared to death that if things didn't work out, I'd lose you. I'm not prepared to sacrifice our friendship for a little bump 'n' grind, you know?"

He snorted. "That's exactly what I was trying to tell you last night," he said. "Although I don't think I put it quite so eloquently." He laughed and kissed my forehead. "Aubrey. You're one in a million, you know?"

"So I've been told," I said, pressing my cheek to his shoulder.

"Hey, I mean it," he said. Then he delivered his zinger. "Whoever this guy is, if he can't see what a great woman you are, he doesn't deserve you."

"What—?" I said. "How—?"

He gently cradled my face in his hand. "This expression here? It's very familiar. I've been seeing it in the mirror every day for the past two weeks."

I gaped at him.

"Just say the word, sweetheart. I'll kick his ass." He pushed himself off the bed and moved to the door. "So, yes, we're okay?" he asked, his hand on the doorknob.

"We're awesome, cowboy," I assured him.

*You're awesome*, I thought. *I don't even come close to deserving you.*

Monday morning. Five more days until Reading Week. This was manageable. I could do this. Again I was out the door and off to work at eight twenty. I would not think about Daniel. Thoughts of him ultimately led to thoughts of him with Penny—and them walking down the aisle, dancing their first dance, feeding each other cake. I refused to contemplate the honeymoon.

When I arrived at the office, the lights were out and Dean Grant was nowhere to be seen. Maybe he'd met Daniel for coffee at Wymilwood again. The Monday morning meeting seemed to be part of their routine. Thank God they weren't meeting here. As the coffee brewed, I separated the mail, slipping Dean Grant's correspondence into the plastic inbox attached to the wall outside his office door. I was about to sign into the student requests email account when the phone rang.

"Good morning, Victoria College, Dean Grant's office, how can I help you?"

"Oh, thank goodness you're there, Aubrey!"

It was Dean Grant. He sounded winded and a bit panicky.

"Is everything okay? I was worried when I arrived and you weren't here. I hope you're not ill. There's a nasty bug going around."

"No, no, everything's fine. I do need your help, though. Do you have a pen and some paper?"

"Yes, go ahead. What can I do?" I wheeled my chair forward and leaned on the desk.

"Once we're off the phone, I'll need you to go into my office," he explained. "Grab the extra keys out of the filing cabinet."

"Okay," I said hesitantly, waiting for him to continue.

"The bottom right-hand drawer of my desk is a file drawer. I need you to find something for me."

"I don't know how comfortable I feel going through your desk. Isn't that a bit—"

"I wouldn't ask if it wasn't important, Aubrey. I trust you implicitly and I know you would never do anything to violate my trust. Will you help me?"

"Yes," I agreed, albeit reluctantly. "Carry on."

"Okay," he said. "In that drawer, you'll find alphabetized and color-coded files." I smiled. Of course they were color-coded. The man had a serious case of OCD. "You're looking for a file named 'Davis, Shannon.' I'm almost positive it's red. It should be close to the front. Got that?"

"Yes." I jotted the name down.

I knew all about Shannon Davis. She was a first-year Vic student whose family home had burned down over Christmas break. Her parents were struggling with the insurance company. Shannon's second semester tuition fees remained unpaid.

"Once you've got the file, I need you to fax me everything inside it."

I hastily wrote down the numbers he recited. "If you don't mind me asking, where are you, Dean Grant?"

"I'm at the Bursar's office. I was called along with the deans of all of the colleges on campus this morning and told to report directly here. Some funds were released to the university by the provincial government last night, and the bursar wants to earmark some awards right away. I think he's afraid the premier might change his mind," his said, chuckling darkly. "I'd like to get Shannon a bursary. The papers in that folder will help me to plead her case."

"That sounds like a wonderful idea," I said. I wasn't kissing his butt either. The man was so thoughtful.

"I'll call you when I've received everything, then you can lock up my office and go about your morning."

I agreed and hung up, using my keys to open the standing filing cabinet where Dean Grant's extra office keys were hidden. When I entered his office, my heart clenched. Even though I had his permission, being in there without him still felt wrong. I crossed the office and sat at his desk, noting how odd it was seeing the room from this perspective. I opened the bottom drawer and began to flip through the neatly labeled files.

Before I could get to Shannon's file, my eyes fell on one titled with large black printed letters: *Daniel's Court Case—Oxford*. My breathing halted. I pulled the file out of the drawer slightly, millions of questions racing through my mind. Court case? Why had Daniel had to go to court? Had he committed some terrible crime at Oxford?

Dean Grant's words echoed in my head. *I know you would never do anything to violate my trust.* Daniel's criminal past was none of my business and certainly not my problem. Penny was marrying the felon, not me. And Dean Grant *trusted* me. I gritted my teeth, replaced Daniel's file, and continued until I found the one with Shannon's name on top.

Inside it was a newspaper clipping, a record of Shannon's marks, and a letter written to the college from Shannon's parents dating back to early January. Satisfied that I'd accessed the correct file, I faxed the pages to Dean Grant. A few moments later, I slipped the file back into its rightful place in the drawer.

I was about to return to my desk to await Dean Grant's phone call when a small collection of family photos perched on the desk caught my attention. The largest one, a photo in a dark oak frame, showed Dean Grant and a lovely auburn-haired woman—his wife, I presumed—surrounded by three young men. One of them was Daniel. I guessed the other two must be his brothers.

The photo emphasized how alike Daniel and his father were—both tall and dark, broad-shouldered, and similarly handsome. One of the brothers was dark-haired like Daniel, but was taller with a dimple topping off both sides of his smile. The other brother was slighter and seemed to favor his mother's fair coloring and features. They were all fabulous looking—especially Daniel, of course. In the picture, he looked like he had on Saturday night: clean cut and well-dressed. Hot in the extreme. Mr. *GQ*.

*Gah! Screw off, Saturday night!* I did not want to think about Saturday night. Not ever again.

I returned the photo to its spot and glanced at the others. And there she was. Penny, the femme fatale. Mrs. Grant-to-be. But... *what the hell?* She was being embraced lovingly, not by Daniel, but by one of Daniel's brothers, the tall one. He was holding her hand out and facing the camera, showing off the engagement ring while she stared adoringly at him.

I fell back in the chair, the wind knocked out of my sails. *Wasn't she engaged to Daniel?* I was so shell-shocked, I must not have heard the outer door to the office open because suddenly there was Daniel himself, standing before me in all his Dr. Hobo glory, his face clouded with fury.

"What are you doing in my father's private office?" he demanded. "Why are you sitting at his desk?"

I grimaced, quickly sliding Dean Grant's file drawer closed. "This isn't what it looks like," I said calmly. "What I mean is, your father knows I'm in here. He wanted me to do something for him—"

"You can't seriously expect me to believe that? Do I look like an idiot to you?"

Now I was pissed. I stood up. "No, I definitely don't think you're an idiot, but I guess I *have* overestimated your ability to be a good judge of character!" I shot back.

He clenched and unclenched his fists for a moment before pulling his phone from his pocket and swiftly dialing a number. He turned on his heel with a dark backward glance over his shoulder and walked across the room to look out the window.

"Hi, Dad? Where are you?" His voice was tight and controlled.

I crossed my arms and tapped my foot impatiently.

"Did you forget we were meeting this morning at Wymilwood at eight thirty? Yeah, I figured as much. Well, I'm here at your office. I came looking for you." Daniel gave me another glare.

He listened to his father for a minute or so, and I watched as his eyebrows shot up, his lips straightening into a grim line. "Yes, she's right here, in fact. Hold on." He approached the desk, his hand outstretched to pass me the phone. "He wants to talk to you," he said sheepishly.

I took the phone, and Daniel slumped down onto one of the chairs in front of the desk. I resumed my seat behind the desk. "Dean Grant?"

"Hi, Aubrey. Thank you so much for taking care of that for me. Everything came through fine. You can re-file Shannon's information and lock up my office now. I'll be back within the hour," he said. "Oh, and this is all strictly fencepost, Aubrey. Shannon's already been through enough. No need to stir up the rumor mill."

"Fencepost" was Dean Grant's code word for "Top Secret." As a man who prized discretion above many other traits, "This is between you, me, and the fencepost" was one of his favorite expressions.

"Fencepost. Absolutely. See you shortly."

"Thanks so much. Tell Daniel I'll give him a call tonight to re-schedule our coffee meeting. See you soon."

I leaned across the desk, handing Daniel his phone. "He said he'd call you later."

Daniel gazed at me contritely. "He's told you about 'fencepost'?"

Of all the things I expected him to say in that moment, that was definitely not one of them. I couldn't help smiling. "Yes, among other things," I said.

"I see you've earned my father's respect and trust, two things he doesn't dole out to the undeserved," he said. "I think I owe you an apology."

Well, shit. My defiance faltered as a series of images and thoughts collided in my brain—the illicit dreams and idle fantasies he'd starred in, the way I'd shamelessly followed him after class that first day, the phone conversations I'd eavesdropped on, not to mention how close I'd been to ripping open the file in the drawer beside me to pour greedily over its contents. Now here he was apologizing to me for overreacting to what had appeared, for all intents and purposes, like an employee snooping through her employer's office.

"There's no need to apologize," I said. "Your reaction was perfectly understandable."

"You can't honestly be that gracious. Five minutes ago, you looked like you were going to spit bullets at me," he said, the right side of his mouth turning up in that one-dimpled grin that made my knees wobble.

"Well, I've decided to forgive you for your father's sake," I ex-plained, giving him a wry smile of my own.

"I see. That's kind of you." After a brief pause, he scanned my face. "By the way, how are you feeling? No aftereffects from Friday's illness, I hope?"

"No, I felt fine by Saturday morning. Thanks for asking, though, and thanks for…well, taking care of me and bringing me home."

He frowned, perhaps aware of the piss-poor job he'd done. I didn't want to review the events of Friday night, but I didn't want him to leave yet either, so I quickly leaned forward and picked up the family photo.

"I couldn't help noticing—this is your family, right?" I asked.

He leaned over to glance at the photo. "Yep, that's Mom and Dad, of course, and my brothers, Bradley and Jeremy."

"Hmm." I gestured to the photo beside it. "They make quite a couple."

He picked up the frame and looked at the picture, sitting back down as he gazed at it. "Penny and Brad? Yeah, they were made for each other. I've known Penny for years. Met her in my first year at Oxford."

He smiled nostalgically, leaning forward in his chair. "In fact, I met her within my first week at the university. I was new to the country, paralyzed with fear, all that sort of thing. She was a force of nature. Totally intimidating, ballsy and smart. I think she decided right away I needed help and took me under her wing. We've been great friends ever since. Brad came over to visit me two years ago—once I started my PhD, it got harder to come home for visits. He met Penny, and within ten minutes, it was pretty much a *fait accompli*. The rest is history." He replaced the photo beside the family portrait.

His affection for this Penny, despite his fortuitous lack of engagement to her, was obvious. I was intoxicated by the warmth in his voice as he talked about her, not to mention his apparent failure to remember that he was talking to me, one of the students from class: *She Who Must Never Be Spoken to As a Human Being with a First Name.*

I had hundreds of questions, but I didn't want to break the spell that had settled on the room—a spell that seemed to make him feel as if it was all right to finally wear a little piece of his heart on his sleeve.

"So Penny moved all the way here from England to be with Bradley?" I prodded.

"Yes, they got engaged over Christmas, but Brad's been in Chicago for six weeks on business. Thankfully he'll be home soon. They're both inconsolable without each other," he said, chuckling ruefully.

Isolated snippets of the phone conversation I'd overheard the first day I'd met him replayed in my mind: "*Miss you? Ha! Completely inconsolable is more like it.*" God, he'd been talking about Bradley all along!

And "love" was nothing more than a term of endearment for a dear friend and future sister-in-law. In the washroom at Canoe, Penny had told her friend on the phone that she was going to be

"Mrs. Grant," but she wasn't referring to Daniel. I thought about the way I'd tortured myself and almost speared Penny with my stiletto, all because of a non-existent engagement. Not to mention what had almost happened with Matt as a result of my wounded ego. Good God.

I snorted and shook my head, amazed at my own foolhardiness. Daniel misinterpreted my reaction.

"Yeah, it's nauseating watching them pine for each other, but Penny's been a great friend. She's been by my side through some pretty difficult times. I'm doing my best to return the favor," he explained.

*Of course, by taking your future sister-in-law out for dinner on Valentine's Day while her fiancé is away so she doesn't sit at home sulking.* This was all too good to be true.

"Well, I'd best be off," he announced, breaking the spell.

"Your dad said he'd be here shortly. If you wait for a few minutes, I'm sure…" What I really wanted to say was, "Please stay. You can help me pick out some books from the bookshelf!"

*Ah, the fantasy. Back in full-force. Oh, happy day!*

"No, I think I'll leave you to it. I'm sure you've got work to do, and I should probably take advantage of the time to review Professor Brown's lecture notes from Friday. I didn't get much done this weekend, what with the play on Friday and family commitments."

I cast my mind back to Friday again, and the roller coaster ride that had found me sitting beside Daniel in the dark auditorium one minute, then bending over a toilet puking while he stood outside waiting for me the next.

"So I'll see you in a few hours?" he asked, interrupting my thoughts and standing up.

"Absolutely." I followed him across the room. I closed the door behind us and locked it before returning the keys to the filing cabinet.

"I'd rather you didn't tell my father about my abysmal behavior here this morning," he said.

"Fencepost," I said, locking my lips with an imaginary key.

He bit his lower lip contemplatively and gave me a quick parting smile. Beaming like a thirteen-year-old who's been asked to her first school dance, I watched through the large front windows of the office as Daniel walked away. Heart thumping and knees wobbling, I dropped into the chair behind my desk.

In reality, not a lot had changed between us, although I certainly had a tiny bit more background information to go on. However, most importantly, one of the seemingly insurmountable obstacles I'd wrongly imagined between us had evaporated into thin air. Damn it, I couldn't help it—I giggled.

And I may or may not have clapped my hands.

## This Petty Pace

To-morrow, and to-morrow, and to-morrow,
Creeps in this petty pace from day to day,
To the last syllable of recorded time…
(*Macbeth*, Act v, Scene 5)

ater that afternoon when I was in class with Julie, Daniel sat at the front of the room, cool demeanor in full force. I refused to let myself scrutinize every expression that crossed his face. Besides, I was still busy mulling over the events of that morning. Daniel had been livid with me, which was definitely not without its strange appeal. Angry-Daniel was something to behold. But then he was Tail-Between-His-Legs-Daniel, followed shortly afterward by Tiny-Piece-of-Heart-on-His-Sleeve-Daniel. The episode was rounded out nicely by Dimpled-Smile-and-Lip-Biting Daniel. Smorgasbord, right? Was it too much to hope that we might begin working toward a comfortable friendship? Now if only I could get some *benefits* to go along with that friendship.

I tried not to let my over-active imagination amplify the significance of the court case file either. For all I knew, he might have challenged a speeding ticket or been arrested for being drunk and disorderly at Oxford. On second thought, that one was hard to believe, but the speeding ticket? Certainly plausible. Regardless, I pushed the whole issue to the farthest recesses of my mind, determined not to make a mountain out of a molehill.

My decision to stop overanalyzing everything made for a much more relaxing and productive week. I handed in a couple of English papers, wrote two tests, and delivered a seminar in my French class. Everything was going swimmingly.

By the time Friday's tutorial rolled around, everybody was in high spirits and anticipating the spring break. Now that we'd been in class for three weeks and spent several tutorial sessions together, we were bonding as a group. For the most part, we'd settled into the habit of reclaiming the same seats. On Friday, Julie and I were in "our" seats halfway down one side of the table, chatting about her plans for the break, when Daniel arrived.

"Well, ladies and gentlemen, I can see you're all excited to get started on your vacation," he said. "One more hour and you'll be free, so let's get to work and you'll be on your way before you know it." He pulled his copy of *Macbeth* out of his bag, along with a pen and some note paper. "I thought we'd try something a little different this week. I'd like everyone to take a few moments to flip through the play and jot down one of your favorite lines. Each of you will have a chance to share your line and explain why you like it or why it resonates for you."

Right away, everyone started scanning the play. I, on the other hand, wrote down the line from Act I that I'd always found to be a most poetic explanation for King Duncan's obtuseness. Finished, I leaned back to watch my peers.

Julie was scribbling frantically, but I resisted peeking at her page. As I looked around, my eyes met Daniel's. He glanced at my page, which of course he couldn't see, but I made a big show of covering it up protectively anyway, like a third grader trying to hide her answers on a spelling test. He smiled.

*Oh, how I love thee, one-dimpled smile.*

He cast his eyes around to see how everyone was progressing. Cara was chewing the end of her pencil like a gerbil. I actually found her less irritating since I'd decided to laugh at her stupidity rather than see it as some sort of personal affront.

Finally, Daniel rubbed his hands together and said it was time to share. He turned to his left. "Miss Langford, care to start?"

Sweet Mary. She was beginning to come out of her shell, but being the center of attention still pained her.

"You're going to laugh," she said, her neck already flushing with embarrassment. "Okay, my favorite line is in act three, when Banquo's ghost comes to haunt Macbeth at the banquet and Macbeth says to the ghost, '*Never shake thy gory locks at me.*' Every time I read that scene, it reminds me of Thanksgiving when I was twelve and my Uncle Bernard fell into the woodpile in the backyard after drinking too much Southern Comfort. We were waiting for him at the dining room table, and he came in with all this blood in his hair. My Aunt Joan almost had a coronary. She thought he'd chopped a limb off or something. He'd actually planned to cut wood for the fire. It was pretty funny."

Mary was right. We did laugh. Poor Uncle Bernard, but what a great cautionary tale. See, kids—never drink and chop wood. Danger lurks!

"Thank you, Miss Langford," Daniel said. "It never ceases to amaze me how Shakespeare's imagery can connect with the simplest things in our lives. Okay. Next? Any volunteers?"

He looked at Cara. She was still flipping madly through her book.

"Having some difficulty deciding, Miss Switzer?" Amusement danced at the edges of his eyes.

"Well, I can't find the one I want. It's, like, Lady Macbeth talking about sex and stuff. You know, when she's, like, talking about her breasts. God, where is it?" She was rifling around frantically.

"Surely you aren't referring to her 'unsex' me soliloquy in act one?" Daniel asked.

"Yeah, maybe…" Cara said uncertainly.

"Well, as you know, that speech is primarily Lady Macbeth railing against her gender. It's not really about sex. When she's talking about her breasts, she's calling out to evil to take away her womanly qualities, her maternal instincts, her femininity," Daniel explained.

All I heard was, "Blah blah blah *sex* blah blah *breasts* blah blah." Where was a good solid bookshelf when you needed one? My reaction was entirely immature, but hearing him uttering those words, even in a scholarly context? I may have lost the academic plot, but my girly bits were definitely taking notes.

I was pulled out of my erotic thrall by Julie piping up to share her line.

"Okay, you'll like mine, Cara," she was saying. "This one actually *is* about sex." She gave a saucy smile. "So you're going to think I'm all kinds of pervy for this, but my favorite line is from the porter's soliloquy."

I smiled at my notebook. Was she actually going there? *Oh, Julie, bring it, baby. I frickin' love you.*

"So you know when he's drunk and about to answer the door, how he's reflecting on the power of alcohol, and he says, '*Drink provoketh the desire, but takes away the performance*'? Well, to me, that line is stellar."

I laughed behind my hand. The guys looked sheepish, and Mary was bright red from the collar up. Daniel had his lips pursed, trying to remain composed. As per usual, Cara was confused.

"I don't get it," she said.

Daniel decided it would be appropriate to provide a visual, holding his pen at a forty-five degree angle.

"'*Drink provoketh the desire,*'" he said, enunciating carefully as if English was Cara's second language, "'*but takes away the performance.*'" As he said the end of the line, he allowed his pen to wilt through his fingers.

I couldn't believe my eyes. The poster child for decorum was actually being sexually suggestive. Loosen up those buttons, baby! A flagging pen-erection had never been so incredibly sexy.

Cara blinked, her face blank, and I kind of felt sorry for the dimwit. But then she had her light bulb moment. I loved it when you could actually *see* a person having an epiphany.

"Oh, I get it. God, that's so true," she mused.

"Steve Pollard," Lindsay said.

"I know, right?" Cara murmured, her eyes flickering over to the guys.

Shawn and Vince exchanged a horrified glance. Had Lindsay forgotten we were all there and perfectly capable of hearing her every word?

"Ah, TMI, ladies," Daniel said, clearing his throat. "Thank you, Miss Harper, for taking us straight to the gutter, but that's a good example of comic relief after a particularly tense and gruesome scene. Anyone have a favorite line that's *not* about sex?" He looked around the table. "Please, Miss Price, tell me you've written down something about a decapitation or multiple stab wounds."

"Nothing that gory, I'm afraid. One of my favorite lines belongs to King Duncan after he's discovered the treachery of the Thane of Cawdor. He says, '*There's no art to find the mind's construction in the face.*' I think that's such an eloquent observation about how difficult it can be to read people."

"I like that one too," Daniel said. "Do you see Duncan's lack of insight into character as a weakness?"

A few days ago, I'd accused *him* of being a bad judge of character. Was he remembering that now?

"I don't know about that," I admitted. "I think he saw what he wanted to see. He wanted to believe everyone was faithful to him. That simply wasn't the case. Of course, believing everyone capable of evil wouldn't have been helpful either. Paranoia isn't healthy. Sometimes all you can do is go with your gut instinct, but there's always a chance you'll be wrong."

Daniel looked at me for maybe a moment too long. A few people cleared their throats, and Daniel regained his focus, continuing around the table until everyone had shared.

Once we'd all had our say, Mary turned to Daniel and put him on the spot. "What's your favorite line, Daniel?"

His eyebrows shot up in surprise. "Well, I don't know. Let me think for a minute," he said, rubbing his temple with his fingers. "I suppose I'd have to say it's the speech Macbeth delivers after his wife is discovered dead. '*To-morrow, and to-morrow, and to-morrow, Creeps in this petty pace from day to day, To the last syllable of recorded time; And all our yesterdays have lighted fools; The way to dusty death.*'"

"Wow, you like that? I think that speech is so depressing," Mary said. "He sounds so hollow. At the end, when he says his life signifies nothing? I don't know; it makes me sad to see someone value his life so little."

"Yes, I suppose it's sad, but how can it not be? His reign is in shambles, his friends have deserted him, and his wife has died. No one trusts him anymore, and there's nothing he can do to make amends. Anyone who's so far from being able to redeem himself is bound to feel and say some pretty sad things. And you're probably going to become unrecognizable, even to yourself."

Daniel's eyes had taken on a lost, faraway look, like he'd moved beyond the confines of the play and was waxing philosophical about life in general. I wanted to climb over the table and hug him. Other things would surely follow, but first he definitely needed a good cuddle. He shook his head almost imperceptibly, and his eyes refocused before he checked his watch.

"Well, I don't think it'll hurt to finish a little early today," he said. Around the room, the fidgeting began. "Anyone doing anything exciting next week?" he asked.

Shawn and Vince said they were going to Fort Lauderdale, and Julie shared her excitement over her trip to the Dominican with some friends from the dance studio. Most people were heading home to visit family. With nothing interesting to share, I kept quiet.

"Well, remember your comparative paper on *Hamlet* will be due the Monday we return after the break. Have a great week off, everyone," he said as he packed up his bag.

The room emptied quickly. Hoots of excitement rang down the corridor. Julie and I walked down the hall together. She was excited but trying not to rub my nose in the fact that I was staying here on campus while she left to bask in the sun for a week.

"So what are your plans?" she asked.

"Oh, I don't know. Chill out, get ahead on some work, do the museum rounds. Maybe hit the art gallery."

"Oh, you should. If you go, say hi to the gallery for me. I haven't been in ages."

"Yeah, well, when you get down south, say hi to Mr. Sun for me, and tell him to get his sorry ass back up here. I'm so over this winter."

We hugged goodbye, and she headed to Trinity. I was standing on the steps of the building, feeling lost, when Daniel pushed his way through the doors. He stopped on the top step, leaning against the stone wall of the entrance.

"So, Miss Price, no big plans for the week, I take it?"

"Nope. Saving some coin for a summer trip to Europe before real life comes along and whisks me away. You?" I asked.

"I suppose I'll spend some time with my family. Unpack my condo. I moved in a few weeks ago, and it's a total tip right now. I might head to Ottawa for a few days. Nothing too exciting."

"Well, enjoy," I said.

*I'll miss you, Dr. Hobo.*

He headed down the steps, turning at the bottom to say, "Nice job today, by the way. You're quite perceptive—much more than you probably realize."

Then he strode across King's College Circle to his car. I tried to remember exactly what I'd said in tutorial. Again, I wondered if he was talking about my insight into the play or something more. At the end of the day, it didn't matter. I'd take the compliments where I could get them.

Daniel climbed into his spotless car and sped away. Yep—the court case? Definitely a speeding infraction.

I tried to be gracious as I watched Jo and Matt pile their packed bags in the front hall. Joanna and Stephen were going to Florida together, and Matt was heading home to British Columbia to spend the week with his family. Matt hugged me tightly before climbing into his taxi. Our relationship seemed to have changed, but not necessarily in a bad way. We still joked around and pushed each other's buttons, but there was a much deeper undercurrent of affection between us. Instead of making us uncomfortable around each other, the Valentine's Day experience seemed to have brought us closer.

He hadn't pursued his suspicion that I was harboring unrequited feelings for someone, and I didn't volunteer any information. It was enough to know that he cared and was in my corner whenever I needed someone to talk to.

I woke up on Saturday to absolute silence, certain I was the only person left in the entire building. Feeling mopey, I convinced myself I needed some retail therapy. Considering the state of my bank balance, this would prove difficult. In the end, I treated myself to a new Sarah Waters book and took a roundabout route back to Vic that brought me through St. Mike's quad.

As I approached the path leading to Victoria College, I saw Mary from my tutorial loading the trunk of a car with several knapsacks. The car was full of people—her mom and dad in the front, two little girls in the back. I called out to her and waved, wishing her a good week. She waved back, offering similar good wishes. Seeing Mary with her family underscored my own isolation. I tried not to mope, vowing to get the most out of my week.

Each day I planned a different outing, visiting the art gallery on Monday and the Royal Ontario Museum on Tuesday. On Wednesday, I was intending to visit the Gardiner Museum of Ceramics, which, like the ROM, was a five minute walk from Jackman and one of my favorite places to go when I needed a meditative escape from the bustle of campus life. In the end, the weather report made me change my plans. With the temperature finally above freezing, I decided I'd take the subway down to the St. Lawrence market and get some much needed fresh air.

I was all wrapped up and ready to go when my cell phone rang. I peeled off my mitts, pulled my phone out, and checked the display.

*David Grant.*

I panicked, instantly fearing something terrible had happened to Daniel. But that made no sense. Why would Dean Grant call me if that was the case?

"Dean Grant?"

"Aubrey, hi. How are you keeping?"

I relaxed. He sounded perfectly calm.

"I'm doing fine — having a quiet week but getting lots done. How was your long weekend in Nassau?"

"Gwen and I had a lovely time, thanks. We were chatting about you while we were there. She'd like to meet the young lady whose praises I'm constantly singing. That's actually the reason I'm calling. I told her you're all alone there this week, and she insisted I invite you over for a family dinner on Saturday."

Oh, shit. Family dinner? Of course I couldn't go. Daniel would have a conniption. I racked my brain for a suitable excuse.

"I don't know, sir. My roommates will be getting home that day and — "

"And they'll be exhausted and have unpacking and laundry to do. Please join us. Gwen will be so disappointed if I'm unable to convince you."

"Well…"

What could I say? If only I'd had time to prepare an answer.

"If you're worried about feeling overwhelmed by the family, there's nothing to be concerned about. Bradley and Jeremy are perfectly harmless. And Bradley's fiancée, Penny, would love some female companionship. She's recently moved here from England. Please say you'll come."

He hadn't mentioned Daniel. "What about your other son?" I asked, trying to sound vague.

"What, Daniel? No, he won't be joining us. He'll be in Ottawa for the weekend, so there'll be one less Grant to deal with."

Okay, that changed things. Daniel would probably be ticked off when he found out I'd been in his family's home, but he had to give me some leeway. I'd known his dad far longer than I'd known *him*. I could still maintain my promise not to tell Dean Grant about the fact that Daniel was my TA.

"Well, I suppose you're right. I can get caught up with Joanna and Matt on Sunday—"

"Perfect, I'll take that as a yes. Tell you what, I'll come down to Vic in the afternoon, get some things sorted out in the office, and then I'll pick you up at your building at four thirty. How does that sound?"

"That sounds great," I said.

After we'd hung up, I contemplated the fact that I was going to be inside Daniel's family home. Would I get to see his childhood bedroom? His school photos? I fell back into my chair, playing out an imaginary conversation with his mother.

"Aubrey, dear, have I told you about my son Daniel?" she'd ask.

"Why, no, you haven't, Mrs. Grant," I'd say, taking her hand and leading her to a comfortable chair. "Why don't you sit here and tell me *all* about him."

Hell yes. Dinner with the Grants? *This* I would enjoy.

# Breathing Life into a Stone

I have seen a medicine
That's able to breathe life into a stone...
(*All's Well That Ends Well*, Act ii, Scene i)

When Saturday finally arrived, my stomach was clenching with anticipation. There was something titillating about visiting the house of someone you're lusting after, especially if the person wasn't going to be home. It made me feel kind of naughty.

To while away the day, I spent a couple of hours brainstorming for my independent study. I also made a pot of spaghetti sauce so Matt and Jo would have something to eat when they got home. Then I cleaned up my week's worth of messes so they wouldn't have a shit fit when they walked through the door. I'd always had a tendency to be a bit of a slob. Dirt I'm not a fan of, but clutter? Meh, it's all good.

A relaxed and tanned Dean Grant picked me up at four thirty on the nose. We chatted about his week, and he spoke animatedly about his four-day trip to Nassau with his wife. He was excited about me meeting her, assuring me we'd get along famously. Driving through Forest Hill, I gawked out the window at the houses. What a treat to grow up in a neighborhood like this. My mother and I had shared a cramped two-bedroom apartment after my parents had split. Clearly I was out of my element. As Dean Grant pointed out landmarks along the way, I anticipated my arrival at the house. Would Penny remember me? It had been two weeks since Valentine's Day. It was hard to say.

When Dean Grant pulled into the circular driveway, I couldn't contain my gasp. The house was like something from a magazine spread—the ivy-covered walls and stone walkway surrounded by well-manicured shrubbery were everything I'd ever wanted in a dream house of my own. Dean Grant led the way to the front door, ushering me into the enormous front hallway. He locked the door behind him and took my coat, hanging it in the hall closet.

"Hello? I'm back! I've got Aubrey with me!"

His wife came out to the front hallway, wearing an apron over her tailored pants and blouse.

"Oh, Aubrey, it's so wonderful to finally meet you," she said, pulling me into a warm embrace.

"Yes, you too, Mrs. Grant," I said, embarrassed and shy. She was tiny but beautiful, her green eyes bright and full of vitality.

"Please call me Gwen, and you'll have to pardon my appearance," she said, plucking at the apron. "I'm at war with some meringue at the moment, and it's not cooperating. I've been on the phone all day, trying to wheedle cooking tips out of all my friends."

She moved to a door on the right hand side of the large foyer, and called out, "Bradley? Can you all come up here please? Dad's home with Aubrey!"

Footsteps crashed up the stairs, and then Bradley burst through the doorway. He was an older, slightly more solid version of Daniel. His handshake was hearty and his double-dimpled smile so warm it could melt the polar icecap.

"Hey, good to meet you, Aubrey," he said. "Dad talks about you all the time. This is my fiancée, Penny."

Penny stepped forward to shake my hand, and as soon as she looked at me, a flicker of recognition transformed her features.

"Oh, I don't believe it! It's you, the sneezing girl! Bradley, isn't that funny? I ran into Aubrey in the loo at Canoe when Daniel took me out to dinner there a couple of weeks ago. How are you?" she asked, pulling me into a hug. "See, I knew from the moment we met we were meant to be friends. There was something so friendly and open about you."

*Oh Penny,* I wanted to say, *that's so true. I have this uncontrollable urge to relieve all of my good friends of at least one of their eyeballs. Definitely one of my greatest BFF qualities.*

But since she seemed pleasant enough and was clearly not attached to Daniel, I would permit her to keep her sight. In both eyes.

"It's nice to see you again, Penny," I said warmly.

"And this," Gwen said, "is Jeremy."

Jeremy stepped around to shake my hand. Though his features were finer than Brad's, he was handsome as well, with the same amazing hazel-green eyes as his mother. Good God, what a stunning family. I was the proverbial ugly duckling in their presence.

"Why don't you give Aubrey a quick tour?" Gwen said. "I have to figure out who else I can call to get help with this blasted meringue!"

"I'll take my briefcase upstairs," Dean Grant said. "Back down in a minute."

Jeremy offered to take me on "the nickel tour" as he called it. Somehow, a nickel didn't seem like it would even come close.

"Well, the kitchen's back there. I say we avoid that part of the tour right now. Mom'll have us whipping up meringues in no time." Gesturing to the staircase, he said, "That's upstairs, obviously. Um, there's a washroom there." He pointed to a door off to the right. "Don't lock the door if you use the washroom, though. The lock's pooched. You'll get trapped inside." He then walked us down a hallway to a closed door. "This is the 'music room,'" he said, drawing quotations in the air with his fingers as he spoke.

He opened the door, and before me was one of the most beautiful rooms I'd ever seen. I felt like I'd walked into the pages of a Victorian novel.

"Oh my God," I said in a hushed voice. You have to speak quietly when you're in that kind of room.

There was a magnificent grand piano beside an enormous bay window. Three different guitars and another stringed instrument — I was guessing it was a cello, but I wasn't entirely sure — were on stands on the other side of the piano.

"Are you guys like the von Trapp family or something?" I asked.

Jeremy laughed. "Not exactly. Mom made us take music lessons when we were kids. We all play the guitar, and Daniel — my other brother, the one who's not here—he and I took piano lessons. We don't play much anymore, but Mom does."

"So Bradley didn't take piano lessons?"

"He tried, but he didn't get far. He plays the drums, though. Mom drew the line at having a drum kit in here."

I laughed, my hands clenched under my chin as I took in the bookcases lining the wall. They were extraordinary. The vaulted ceiling must have gone up about sixteen feet, and the dark cherry shelves went all the way to the ceiling on two sides of the room. The bookshelf had one of those sliding ladders attached to it, like the ones you see in movies. Behind us, a trio of brown, soft leather couches opened into a U-shape facing a large stone fireplace.

I walked around the piano to peek out the window.

"Your back yard is huge," I said.

"Yeah, it's a good size, I guess. There's not as much lawn as there used to be. Now it's mostly patio and garden. Mom's quite the gardener," he explained. "She hosts a lot of events out there."

"Wow, this is unreal," I said. "It must have been amazing growing up here."

"Yeah, it had its moments," Jeremy replied, looking a little wistful. "That's mostly it for the main floor. Brad and Penny are probably in the living room, if you wanna head back."

"Yeah, sure. Actually, do you mind if I hit the washroom?" I said.

"Go ahead. Don't forget about the door. The living room's right through there," he said, leading us back out to the front hallway and pointing to a set of closed French doors.

"Okay, thanks."

Heeding Jeremy's warning, I left the washroom door unlocked. I peered at myself in the mirror. The color of my cheeks screamed *anxiety*. Everyone was welcoming and kind, but the fact that I was in Daniel's family's house — no, scratch that, Daniel's family's *palatial mansion* — well, it was all a smidge overwhelming. I grabbed a handful of Kleenex and ran them under the cold tap and dabbed my warm face.

As I was holding the wad of cool tissues to my cheek, I heard the front door bell ring and Dean Grant call out, "I'll get it." His shoes clattered down the hardwood stairs, and then his surprised voice rang through the front hallway. "Daniel! What are you doing here?"

My reflection in the mirror morphed from anxious to horrified. *Daniel?*

Holy. Mother. Of. Crap.

Daniel was home?

Wasn't he supposed to be in Ottawa?

Oh, shit, shit, shit. This was not good!

I shifted my weight and chewed on my thumbnail, trying to decide what to do. Transfixed, I listened to the exchange in the front hallway.

"Sorry, Daniel," his father said. "I don't mean to make it sound like we're not happy to see you, but…"

"No, Dad, that's fine. I'm sure I'm the last person you expected to see," Daniel said. "I was trying to call, but the line's been busy for ages. I did leave a message. My plans in Ottawa fell through."

"Oh, that's unfortunate. I know you were looking forward to going. Well, regardless, it'll be great to have everyone together, especially now that Bradley is back. In fact, there's someone joining us for dinner who I'd like you to meet. You've already met her in passing, actually, a couple of weeks ago in the office. You remember Aubrey?"

"Aubrey? *What?* Not the Price girl," I heard Daniel say.

"Yes, that's her," his father replied. "Remember I told you I wanted you to meet her? She really is a lovely girl. Like I said before, I think you'd have a lot in common with her. She's hard-working, bright, and attractive—"

"God, Dad, what the hell are you thinking?" Daniel hissed.

My face was on fire now, and I leaned my forehead and hands against the bathroom door. Dean Grant had wanted me to meet Daniel? Half of me was thrilled at the thought, but the rest of me was plagued by the distress in Daniel's voice, not to mention my predicament. I couldn't stay in the bathroom indefinitely, but I couldn't walk out into the middle of their conversation either.

Their hushed voices neared the bathroom as they moved out of the vestibule and away from the kitchen and living room to speak in private, not realizing that rather than moving away from prying ears, they were actually moving closer to mine. They were right outside the door, and now I was *literally* trapped in the washroom.

"Daniel, let go of my arm," his father said. "I'm not sure what you're so upset about. She was alone for Reading Week, and I invited her over to join us for dinner. Not a big deal."

"She's in my class, Dad—in Martin's fourth year class. I'm her TA for Christ's sake—"

Daniel's hysterical whisper made me cringe. This was getting a little weird. He certainly seemed to be overreacting.

"What? Daniel, why didn't you tell me when I brought her name up before?" Dean Grant asked, equally alarmed.

"I don't know. I guess I thought you'd freak out, knowing you'd been talking about her and then finding out she was in the class. But it's irrelevant now, isn't it?"

Oh my God! So that's why he'd asked me not to tell his dad that he was my TA. His father had already planted a seed in his mind about me. No wonder he panicked when he connected all the dots.

"So what did she say when you invited her here?" Daniel asked his father.

"At first she was averse to the idea, but I wore her down," Dean Grant explained. "I told her you'd be in Ottawa this weekend, so brace yourself. She'll be surprised to see you."

"Well, maybe I should leave now, before Mom—" Daniel started, but he was interrupted by his mother's arrival in the vestibule.

"Daniel! My handsome boy, I just heard your message on the answering machine. How wonderful to have all my boys together under the same roof. Now what are you two whispering about? Come into the living room, there's someone we want you to meet!"

I heard the sound of the French doors opening and several voices echoed through the front hall, as Penny, Bradley, and Jeremy greeted Daniel. Everyone was speaking at once, and then I heard them moving off somewhere.

Holy shit! What had I gotten myself into? Obviously Daniel was appalled to find me here, and Dean Grant sounded just as distressed, but in all fairness, I'd thought Daniel was going to be away. I'd been genuinely looking forward to spending time with Dean Grant and his family, but now? Things couldn't possibly get more awkward. But one thing was certain: I couldn't stay in the powder room any longer.

I opened the door and made my way through the front hall, my heels clicking conspicuously on the wood floor as I neared the living room, in time to hear Gwen say, "She's using the powder room. I hope she's all right. Did you tell her about the lock, Jeremy? Oh, wait, yes, here she comes."

In the living room, Penny, Bradley, Jeremy, and Gwen were relaxed and completely at ease. On the other hand, Daniel and his father both looked like they'd been caught with their hands in the cookie jar, united in the realization that I'd heard their entire exchange from inside the bathroom. Gwen approached me and took my hand in hers, leading me to where Daniel was standing stiffly beside his father.

He was clean shaven and in full Mr. *GQ* mode today, not a single hobo in sight. I quickly took in his open-collared white shirt and tailored black pants. And was that the mystery sandalwood again?

"Aubrey, we have a surprise addition to dinner. This is my son, Daniel. His plans to visit a friend in Ottawa fell through, so he's joining us for dinner after all." She then turned to Daniel. "Aubrey works for your dad at Vic. She's your father's Girl Friday, by all accounts."

I smiled at Gwen and turned to Daniel to say something, but he beat me to the punch.

"Mom, we've actually met at the office," he explained, his eyes silently imploring me to allow his explanation of our knowledge of each other to stand.

"That's right," I said. "Dean Grant looks forward to Daniel's Monday morning visits." I inclined my head toward him. "It's nice to see you, Daniel."

"And you...*Aubrey*," he responded, looking me squarely in the eyes.

My heart thrummed as he said my name for the first time.

"Daniel, your dad tells me Aubrey is a literary aficionado. Apparently, she has quite an interest in Shakespeare. I'm sure you two will have *so* much to talk about," Gwen said with a meaningful glance at her son.

The rationale behind my invitation to dinner came quickly into focus. Dean Grant was "scouting" on behalf of his son, and he'd brought me home to meet his wife for a second opinion. And now that her son had actually arrived on the scene, she wasn't wasting any time. While her approval of me was comforting, the turn of events was causing Daniel grave discomfort. Before I could consider the situation any further, Bradley interrupted, clapping Daniel on the back.

"You're not going to start boring us all with your literature mumbo jumbo, are you, man? I was hoping we could play some pool or darts or something."

Gwen smiled at her sons. "I think that's a wonderful idea. Why don't you all take Aubrey down to the game room? There's plenty to drink in the wine chiller and the fridge. Dinner will be at five thirty, so you have a little while to relax. David, your help in the kitchen, if you please," she requested with a sly wink.

Dean Grant followed his wife, but not without shooting a worried glance at Daniel. Penny squeezed her way between the boys to link her arm through mine, walking with me to the basement stairs.

"Well, I must say, you're a busy girl," she said suggestively. "First charming the pants off David, and now Gwen's practically measuring you for the bridal gown. Nicely done, darling. All that *and* a dishy hunk wining and dining you on the side. I'm impressed," she said, smiling in a self-satisfied way.

*Matt.* She thought I was dating Matt.

Daniel cleared his throat uncomfortably behind us while Jeremy and Bradley argued over whether we would play pool or darts first. As we reached the bottom step, I took in the massive game room. It was every man's fantasy hangout. Pool table, dart board, foosball, ping pong, a huge flat-screen TV with gaming paraphernalia scattered about, and a fully stocked bar. Penny and I sat on stools while Bradley played bartender.

"Penny?" he asked, holding up a bottle of Shiraz.

"Mmm, that'd be bloody lovely," she said.

Bradley uncorked the wine and poured a healthy glass for his fiancée. "How about you, Aubrey?"

I thought about the wine debacle of Valentine's Day. Penny still had both her eyes, and I had a lot less motivation to deprive her of one of them, but hey, the night was still young.

"Um, do you have any beer?" I asked.

Bradley smiled broadly.

"Did you hear that, Daniel? Your lady friend wants to know if we have any beer!"

Your *lady friend.* Gah!

Daniel was turning ten shades of red and looking everywhere but at me. Bradley snorted, grabbing my hand and dragging me around the bar where he opened up a fridge. Inside, there were rows upon rows of different brands of beer, domestic and imported, cans and bottles, some lying down, some standing up. A beer hound's booty.

I peered in and made a quick decision. "I'll have a Stella," I said.

Bradley leaned in and grabbed two, uncapping both, handing one to me and taking a long drink of the other. "Glass?" he offered.

I shook my head and took a large gulp. I was in dire need of some liquid courage.

He smiled and said, "Atta girl," before handing Jeremy a Keith's.

Daniel made his way behind the bar, maneuvering past me in the small space and then bending to open the cupboards underneath. He stood with a can of Guinness in his hand and reached into the overhead cupboard for a beer glass. I returned to sit beside Penny, beer in hand.

"When are you gonna get over that shit?" Bradley asked, gesturing to the can as Daniel poured.

Daniel took a long drink and sighed in satisfaction. "To each his own, Bradley."

Penny smiled at Daniel before turning to me. "So how *is* that handsome friend of yours?" she asked. "You know, the one you were with on Valentine's Day?"

Daniel lowered his beer, his mouth dropping open as his glass made violent contact with the marble surface of the bar.

"What, Matt? Oh, he's fine. He's been in British Columbia all week. He's probably landing at Pearson right about now," I said, sneaking a peek at my watch before looking at Daniel again.

"Isn't that a coincidence, Daniel?" Penny said. "There you were the whole night sitting right across the restaurant from each other, and you didn't even know it."

"Wow, that's really something," Daniel said, the muscle in his jaw twitching. He downed half his beer before turning to Bradley and Jeremy. "So? We playing pool or what?"

"Yeah, let's grab a quick game before dinner," Bradley said. He moved over to the pool table to set up the balls.

"You guys go ahead," Jeremy said as he headed over to the TV and messed around with the batteries in the Wii remotes.

Penny slid off the barstool, offering Brad a quick pre-game kiss. Realizing this was the first real opportunity I'd had to speak to Daniel, I leaned over the bar and whispered, "I'm so sorry. I had no idea you were going to be here."

"I think it's safe to say this is about the last place I figured I'd find you, too," he said.

"I tried to decline. Your father was very persistent."

"Let's just get through the night, all right?"

"Are you going to tell them?" I bobbed my head across the room.

"Three of us are already mortified beyond words. No point dragging everyone else down with us," he said. "Whatever you do, don't tell my mother."

He swigged his beer and headed over to the pool table, grabbing a cue from the rack on the wall. *Mortified beyond words?* Is that how my presence made him feel? *Nice.*

Penny came back to sit with me. "Watch this. He's brilliant," she said.

"Who, Bradley?"

"Bloody hell, no, love. *Daniel,*" she said with a laugh.

I watched as Daniel unbuttoned and then rolled up his shirt sleeves. *He* may have been mortified, but I was too busy reining in my desire to run my fingers through the hair on his tightly muscled forearms to feel anything akin to mortification. With confident precision, he leaned over the table and smashed the white ball into the triangle of balls at the other end, scattering them all over the table. A purple striped ball rolled decisively into one of the corner pockets.

Penny raised her eyebrow as if to say, "See?"

"Right, I'm stripes then," he said, pacing for a moment to decide on his next shot. This time when he leaned over, he hitched his leg up as he positioned himself behind the white ball. I watched his left hand create a sturdy bridge for the pool cue. Once more, his shot was carefully planned and perfectly executed. The yellow striped ball dropped swiftly into the side pocket.

Daniel continued his domination of the game for a few minutes, but finally he missed a shot and it was Bradley's turn to begin working on the solid-colored balls. Daniel topped up Penny's wine, offered me another beer which I declined, and then poured himself another Guinness.

"Bloody Nora, Daniel. That's not even touching the sides, is it?" Penny observed as Daniel took a long swig.

"You have no idea how much I need this right now."

"I love your sayings, Penny," I said. "I've never heard that expression before. What does 'bloody Nora' mean?"

Penny shrugged.

"It's most likely an old Cockney expression that's evolved over the years as letters have dropped at the beginning and end of the words," Daniel explained.

"What are you, fucking Google-on-legs?" Bradley said with a snort. *"Sex-on-legs" is more like it.*

Before Daniel could answer, his father appeared at the top of the stairs. "Dinner's ready! Come on up, please."

"Thank Christ. I'm starved," Bradley said, tossing his pool cue on the table. "Coming, beauty?" He took Penny's hand. Jeremy, Daniel, and I followed, Daniel making short work of finishing his beer and depositing the empty glass on a table near the bottom of the stairs.

Dean Grant directed everyone to their seats and then helped Gwen bring the platters and bowls of food to the table. We were having turkey with all the fixings. Daniel's parents sat at opposite ends of the table. Penny was in the middle of one side flanked by Daniel and Bradley, and I settled opposite Daniel with Jeremy beside me.

"You'll say grace, dear?" David asked.

"Of course," Gwen replied, bowing her head and crossing her hands in front of her. Everyone did the same, and I followed their lead.

"Dear Lord, we thank you for your bounty and for bringing us together as a family today. We strive to be deserving of your grace. Amen," she said.

I sent up a silent prayer of my own. *And, dear God? Thank you for creating Daniel in all his sweet-ass hotness. That's probably sacrilege, but I mean it most sincerely. Amen.*

Once the hush that had accompanied grace was over, Bradley and Jeremy began fighting over various parts of the turkey. Gwen slapped their hands repeatedly, urging them to use the serving fork instead of their fingers to grab pieces of meat.

Dean Grant moved around the table, pouring everyone their wine of choice while Gwen looked dejectedly at her sons' appalling display of manners. "I honestly wonder why we spent all that money on private school, David. It doesn't seem to have made a stitch of difference in their comportment."

"We did what we could, dear," her husband said with a smirk. "Unfortunately I don't think UCC offers refunds."

"UCC. That's Upper Canada College, right?" I said, turning to Jeremy who was loading his plate with mashed potatoes. "Was it a good school?"

"Top-notch academically," he said. "Kinda stifling, though. After being there from kindergarten all the way through, it was a relief to finally graduate and have a change of scenery, you know?"

"No girls, though, huh? How was that?" I asked.

"It sucked," Bradley piped up, his mouth full of butternut squash. "Good thing all the Havergal and Bishop Strachan girls got their licenses and pretty cars for their sixteenth birthdays. It could've been worse." Penny slapped his arm. He blew her an air kiss, and Jeremy laughed. Daniel shook his head.

"Bradley," Gwen said, a note of warning in her voice. I can only imagine what a handful he must have been to raise.

"So do you work, or are you still going to school, Jeremy?" I asked, purposely avoiding Daniel's eyes. Jeremy was so conciliatory; it was hard not to take advantage of his willingness to share.

"Jeremy wanth to be a danthah," Bradley lisped.

Jeremy glared at his brother and threw a piece of roll at him.

"Boys, *please*," Gwen pleaded. "We have a guest. I'd appreciate it if you'd behave civilly."

She looked at me apologetically. I smiled back as if to say, "Oh, it's okay, boys will be boys." What I was thinking was, *Please carry on. This is entertaining as hell.*

"Actually, Aubrey, Jeremy is a freelance graphic artist," Penny said, coming to her future brother-in-law's defense. "He's working on an ad campaign for the National Ballet of Canada. He's brilliant."

"Wow, that sounds cool," I said.

"Yeah, it's a good gig. I'm still figuring things out. Up until about six months ago I was an A-and-R rep for Sony Canada, so this is a real learning curve," Jeremy explained.

"Why'd you leave Sony? I think it'd be amazing to do something like that. I love discovering new music."

"Yeah, it was a good job, but it was kind of sucking the joy out of music a bit, *having* to listen to new stuff, you know, making it feel like a chore?"

"Oh, I get that. I feel that way with reading a lot of the time." I tried to focus on my plate, figuring I'd monopolized enough of the conversation. Gwen wasn't having any of it, though.

"So, Aubrey, you're specializing in English, right?" she asked, shooting Daniel another meaningful look.

He rolled his eyes and looked back down at his mashed potatoes, studying them as if the Rosetta Stone had magically appeared under the gravy, offering him untold linguistic secrets. He was hardly eating anything. He was enjoying the hell out his red wine, though, refilling his glass frequently.

"Yes," I said. "I'll graduate with a specialist in English and a minor in French."

"French? How wonderful. Are you fluent?" she asked.

"I can't imagine studying French at university and *not* being fluent. I'd fail every course."

"The boys all speak French too. My family's always had a house in the south of France. It was important to us that everyone be bilingual."

Oh my, the plot was thickening. The picture forming in my mind of these young men was pretty damned impressive. Private-school educated, musically gifted, fluent in French, well-traveled. And absolutely gorgeous, all three of them.

"And, Daniel, how is Professor Brown's class going?" Gwen asked.

Daniel's fork fell with a clatter onto his plate. Beside him, Penny jumped.

"Sorry about that," he said, reclaiming the utensil and looking for all the world like he wished the ground would open up and swallow him.

*Mortified beyond words? I'll say.*

"Daniel is a TA for a senior English course," Gwen said to me by way of explanation.

*Well, you don't say.* Dean Grant looked at me, waiting for my response.

"I imagine that's quite challenging," I said vaguely.

"You did tell me it was a nice class the last time we talked," Gwen said to Daniel. "Is everything still going okay?"

"Some of the students are bright and quite a pleasure to work with," Daniel said.

I smiled at my potatoes.

"I gather you stayed in residence this week," Gwen said, turning her attention back to me. "I hope you weren't too bored. It must have been awfully quiet."

"It was a bit of a ghost town," I said. "It was nice, though. I went to the art gallery and the ROM. I was going to try to go to the Gardiner Museum too, but I didn't get around to it."

Gwen smiled at her husband.

"Oh, we adore the Gardiner, don't we, David? I have a couple of complimentary tickets. Remind me to give them to you before you go. There's a fabulous new exhibition in the main gallery."

"That would be lovely. Thank you. Maybe I'll try to go on Monday after class, before homework gets too crazy again."

The easy conversation continued. What a wonderful family Daniel had. I'd adored Dean Grant from the first day I met him, but they were all so awesome. By the time everyone else had finished eating, Daniel had still hardly touched his food. He'd worked his way through several glasses of red wine, though, and was certainly starting to look a little more relaxed.

Gwen served dessert, finally having mastered the meringue nests. Fresh fruit was nestled inside each little frothy blob. It was divine. After dinner, everyone helped clear the table, but then Gwen shooed us out of her perfectly appointed kitchen, insisting we head back down to the basement. Dean Grant told me to let him know when I was ready to leave, and he would take me home.

We all headed back downstairs, Bradley rubbing his belly and belching loudly. Luckily his mother didn't hear him.

"You feeling all right, love?" Penny asked Daniel, brushing his hair away from his eyes. "You hardly touched your dinner."

Oh, how I longed to run *my* fingers through his hair and call him "love."

"Yeah, I don't have much of an appetite, I guess," he said.

As Bradley and Penny took their after dinner drinks with them to the sofa, Jeremy and I sat on the stools. Daniel poured himself another Guinness and then opened the fridge, grabbing a Stella and a Keith's. He held them up, eyebrows raised in question.

"I'll have another. Thanks," I said.

"Cheers, bro," Jeremy said. He took a swig and then rested the bottle on the bar. "Okay, I know this is going to sound weird," Jeremy said, "but I swear I know you from somewhere. Like, I think we bumped into each other recently, but I can't think where."

"You've got to be kidding, Jer," Daniel said. "Is that the best you can do?"

Jeremy shot him an annoyed look. "I'm serious." He turned to me again. "You know what? Were you at the indie music revue a couple of weeks ago?"

"Yes, I was!" I exclaimed. "You were there?"

"Yeah, I went with a friend of mine who's a music reviewer." He snapped his fingers at me. "I knew I recognized you." He gave Daniel a smug look. I thought for a second he might stick his tongue out. "I have to be honest, though, it was your friend who caught my eye."

"Well, that's not insulting at all," Daniel said with a laugh.

"It's okay," I sighed, pretending to be deeply offended. "I'm used to playing second fiddle."

"I find that difficult to believe," Daniel said, looking at me over the rim of his glass as he took a long drink.

His voice was thick, and his words were beginning to run together. I picked at the label on my beer bottle, confused by this compliment, which came out of left field. Luckily Jeremy was now on a fact-finding expedition, and he filled what might have been an awkward silence by quizzing me about Julie.

"Is she single?" he asked.

"You're talking about the blond girl, right?" I asked him.

"Yeah, blond and cute as hell. I don't think she stopped singing along and dancing all night."

"Yes." I laughed. "That's Julie. And absolutely, she's very much single."

Daniel shot me a surprised look. *Yes, Daniel, that Julie*, my expression told him.

"Do you think it would be super creepy if I got her phone number from you?" Jeremy asked. "And maybe you could tell her about me? Put in a good word? I was kicking myself for not asking for her number that night."

Daniel snorted cynically.

"Hey, you should see this girl," Jeremy said.

*Well, actually…*Daniel must have been thinking. We shared another glance.

"She seemed feisty and cute and confident and sweet, all at the same time." Jeremy had a faraway look in his eyes. "I didn't even meet her, but there was something about her that struck a chord… that sounds bizarre, right?"

Daniel tilted his head pensively. "No, I think I know what you mean, Jer," he said, locking eyes with me.

I looked away, trying to convince myself that I was misreading the signals he was sending me. I was desperate to ask him what he was thinking, but it was neither the time nor the place. I focused instead on Jeremy's dilemma.

"Sorry, Jeremy, but I don't think it's a good idea for me to give you Julie's number. Not without her permission, anyway."

"Why don't you take Jeremy's number?" Daniel suggested. "You can pass it along to your friend and then the ball can be in her court."

I tried to read Daniel's expression. Was he really okay with the idea of his brother dating someone from Professor Brown's class? I sure hoped so. Jeremy was a great guy.

I gave Jeremy my phone so he could type in his information. Then he asked for my number. I saw no good reason not to provide it. Daniel gulped his beer as he watched our exchange. With my phone safely back in my purse and Jeremy suitably placated, he and Daniel wandered off to join Bradley while Penny returned to the bar to refill her wine glass. At the pool table, Brad must have said something hysterical under his breath because Daniel started giggling like a nine-year-old girl.

"My God, he's wankered," Penny said. I looked at her quizzically. "Drunk," she clarified.

"Right. Gotcha." It was as if she was speaking a different language sometimes.

"Daniel's awesome when he's drunk," she explained. "You know how some blokes get mean or angry? He gets silly. Listen to that laugh!" She smiled over at him affectionately.

It was true. He had the best laugh ever. I wanted to curl up in it and roll around.

"So, what do you think, love? You and Daniel?" Penny said, lifting her eyebrow and clicking her tongue inside her cheek.

"Oh, no, not at all," I protested. "I barely know him."

*Oh, the lies.* I was marinating in them. I could have been basted, turned over, and served at the next family dinner. My face burned as Daniel sauntered back over to the bar, grabbing himself yet *another* beer. I'd lost track of the number of times he'd replenished his drink, and believe me, I was watching his ass every time he bent down to open that cupboard.

"So then you *are* seeing the bloke from Canoe?" Penny persisted.

"No, it's not like that with him, either."

Daniel surveyed his glass. "Tell me, *Aubrey*, is there someone with whom it *is* like that?" A trace of a smile danced on his lips. God, he was unreal! Nobody uses "whom" properly. How the hell was he able to do it when he was half wasted?

"Not at the moment, although I do have a few irons in the fire," I replied.

"Really?" he said, his voice silky.

"How about you? Do you have any irons in the fire?" I asked.

"I don't think he does, Aubrey, but I'm guessing there's one fire he *wouldn't mind* putting his iron in," Penny said.

I quietly celebrated this confirmation of Daniel's single status while Penny laughed at her own crude joke then walked over to cajole Brad and Jeremy into playing a game of darts, leaving Daniel and me alone at the bar. Between turns at the dartboard, Penny and Bradley cuddled and kissed. Poor Jeremy was an unfortunate third wheel in the proceedings.

"Oy! You two, get a room!" Daniel yelled across the room.

"Sod off, wanker," Penny hurled back.

Daniel looked at me, the one-dimpled grin working its way to the surface. His face was flushed, and he looked like a vulnerable little boy. I returned his smile, but then I had to look away, certain that my face must be betraying every detail of the way I felt.

Instead, I watched Penny in action. The girl knew her way around a dart board. Daniel took the opportunity to mock his brother's lack of skill compared to Penny's command of the game.

"Jesus, you daft prat! You're not gonna let her walk all over you like that, are you?"

"Fuck yourself, Daniel," Bradley said good-naturedly.

"You couldn't hit the back of a bus with a banjo, bro," Daniel mocked.

There was something about being with Penny that brought back Daniel's accent and the accompanying lingo with a vengeance. It was unbelievably hot.

Suddenly he took my hand and said, "Come on, I'm going to teach you to play snooker." However, between his slurring and his emerging English accent, it sounded like, "C'mon, I'm gon'ta teachoo ta play snookah."

Delicious.

I adored drunk Daniel. Bring on the Guinness! It was dissolving his stony, carefully maintained exterior quite handily.

He led me to the pool table and put our drinks on the ledge. "Ever played before?" he asked.

"Um, no. I don't even know how to hold the cue properly," I confessed.

"Well, we can't have that now, can we?" he asked. "You've got to know how to hold it before you can do anything else, *Aubrey*."

My name, a husky sigh rather than a word, was rolling off his tongue so smoothly I wondered how he'd cope on Monday when he had to revert back to calling me "Miss Price."

He retrieved Bradley's discarded cue and grabbed a little blue square off the edge of the table. He was standing far too close to me, looking at me through lidded eyes. Everything seemed to be moving in slow motion.

With the cue in his left hand, one end on the floor and the tip up, he took the blue square between his fingers. "This is cue tip chalk. Before you begin, it's a good idea to rub some on the tip, but gently. Not too hard. If you get too much on the tip, you blow it off—like this."

His gentle breath fanned strands of my hair around my face. My knees turned to rubber as he spun me around to face the table.

"Take the cue in your left hand here and your right hand here. Now lean over the table."

I did as I was told. He leaned in behind me, wrapping his left arm around mine to help me plant my fingers on the table in a little bridge.

"Now take the cue and place the tip *right there*," he said, helping me balance it atop my left hand.

*Oh, I'll tell you where to place the tip, Mr. Shmexy.*

"With your right hand, grasp the *shaft* of the cue *firmly* up here."

I looked over my right shoulder. His face hovered beside my ear and his right hand wrapped around mine.

"How does that feel?" he asked, his voice so low I almost couldn't hear him.

"That feels good," I said, and then I brazenly shifted my position slightly so that I could feel his crotch pressing against my ass. "Wait... now *that*? *That's* perfect."

I looked over my shoulder again. He was grinning naughtily. And I never thought I'd say it, but Shakespeare was wrong. There was no "performance" being compromised by drink in this scenario.

"Now, slide the cue back and forth on your left hand to get a feel for it. Don't grasp it too tightly here." He loosened my right hand a little. "You need *exactly* the right amount of pressure to follow through properly. It's all about angle and speed. If you hit it too hard, you'll lose control; too softly and you might miss it entirely."

"I see. What about earlier, what was that you were doing with your leg?"

"Yes, well, sometimes you have to hitch your leg up a bit to give you better—"

"Friction?" I asked.

"No," he said, his tone becoming more and more seductive. "I was going to say *access*."

*Hitch your leg up to give you better access? Oh yes, I know exactly what you mean.*

"Daniel, are we still talking about pool?" I giggled.

He laughed softly too. "I'm not sure I was *ever* talking about pool."

*Oh, God!*

He gently trailed his left hand up mine before allowing it to come to rest on my wrist. He rubbed himself against my backside, and I moaned softly.

All of a sudden, Bradley broke the spell. "Dude, are you trying to teach her to play pool, or are you molesting the poor girl?"

Bradley laughed at his own joke, but Daniel froze behind me, quickly releasing my hands. Before I even had time to process what was happening, he'd pulled away, saying something about needing coffee and striding across the room to the stairs, his hands frantically raking his hair out of his eyes. The mood had changed in an instant.

*Bradley, you dink.*

"Well done, you silly bugger. He was starting to have fun then," Penny said.

*Yeah, so was I.* My girly bits were all aflutter.

"Yeah, idiot, I haven't seen him having that much fun since...well, in a long time," Jeremy added, clipping Bradley on the head with his hand.

"Aubrey?" Dean Grant's voice called out.

I walked over to the bottom of the stairs. "Yes?"

"I'm going to have to take Daniel home. He's in no shape to drive. I'll drop you off on the way. We'll leave in a few minutes."

"Um, okay," I said, grabbing my purse.

"Jeremy? Are you able to drop off Daniel's car for him tomorrow?" Dean Grant said.

"No, can't do it tomorrow," Jeremy called up to him. "I'm in Scarborough all day. Maybe Monday?"

"Okay, we'll figure something out."

Dean Grant retreated from the top of the stairs, and I threw my purse over my shoulder.

"Well, it was nice meeting you all," I said.

Penny hugged me warmly. "It was nice to meet you properly, lovey."

I was glad I'd left Penny's eyes intact. She was a great girl—a little rough around the edges, but hey, I wasn't one to judge on that score. Bradley gave me a wave.

"Take it easy, Aubrey. Maybe we'll see you soon?"

*Oh, I don't know about that, Bradley.* I imagined the fallout this day would surely have. Jeremy gestured to my purse.

"Don't forget about the phone number," he said. "You'll put a good word in for me, right?"

"Of course," I assured him.

Bradley elbowed him. "Shit, I don't know who's worse. You or Desperate Dan up there."

"Shut up, Brad!" Jeremy glared at his brother.

I smiled as I made my way up the stairs, but my smile quickly dissolved as I glanced into the kitchen. Daniel was sitting at the kitchen table with a mug in front of him. His mother was leaning over him, rubbing his back as she whispered to him.

"I'm going to warm up the car," Dean Grant said.

"He'll be out in a minute," Gwen called out from the kitchen.

Dean Grant helped me put my coat on and then ushered me out the door with him. He opened the front passenger door.

"Shouldn't we let Daniel—"

"He can sit in the back. At this point I think I could throw him in the trunk and he wouldn't notice."

He climbed in and started the car. "I wish you'd told me Daniel was your TA, Aubrey," he said with a sigh.

"He asked me not to. I didn't know what to do. He fenceposted me," I said, hoping he'd understand. "I didn't think it would hurt to come over for dinner. You told me Daniel wouldn't be here."

"I know, but you realize Daniel has to keep his distance from the students in class. That includes you. He has to maintain impartiality and objectivity. Not courting familiarity with students goes with the territory. It's not that he doesn't like you — he can't compromise his academic position. I won't allow it," he added, looking at me almost sternly.

"I understand. I'm sure nothing like this will happen again. Daniel has been nothing but professional for the last month," I told him.

*Up until about twenty minutes ago.*

"That's good to hear. So let's keep this between us and try to forget it ever happened, all right?"

"Yes, of course."

Daniel finally emerged from the house, falling into the back seat with a groan. I kept my eyes trained out the front windows. As Dean Grant drove through the dark streets, Daniel began snoring gently behind us.

"Someone's going to be miserable tomorrow," I said.

Dean Grant smiled and shook his head. "I gather he hasn't eaten much today. It was foolish of him to drink so much."

I looked out the window, watching the city lights go by.

"Oh, and before I forget," he said, "these are for you from Gwen." He handed me two complimentary tickets to the Gardiner Museum.

"Tell her I said thank you, would you?"

"Of course."

A few moments later, we pulled onto Charles Street, and Dean Grant came around to open my door, holding his hand out to help me over the curb and onto the sidewalk.

"Thank you for a lovely evening, sir. Your family is wonderful."

He placed his hands on my shoulders, squeezing gently. "It was our pleasure, Aubrey. Business as usual on Monday, yes?"

"Absolutely."

I watched as he climbed back into the car. Daniel was hunched down in the back seat, arms crossed over his chest, head bobbing.

Adorable.

The car sped off. I walked up the path, prepared to be greeted by my roommates and listen attentively to all their fabulous Reading Week stories, when all I really wanted to do was review the all-important ground rules for playing snooker.

# CHAPTER 15

*Outward Shows*

So may the outward shows be least themselves:
The world is still deceived with ornament.
(*The Merchant of Venice*, Act III, Scene 2)

**B**etween catching up with Matt and Jo and reading ahead for classes, I found plenty of time on Sunday to daydream about firmly grasped pool cues and leg hitches. Even the non-snooker related parts of my trip to the Grant home made me long for a second visit. But that wouldn't be happening. Dean Grant's words rang in my ears like a death knell.

*"It's not that Daniel doesn't like you—he can't compromise his academic position. I won't allow it."*

Dean Grant wouldn't allow it. What about Daniel, though? How did he feel about what had happened?

Dean Grant had advised me not to take Daniel's distance personally, and it occurred to me that Daniel's chilly TA persona was probably a response to his father's guidance. On second thought, *pressure* might have been a better word.

I spent most of Sunday evening worrying about my return to work, unsure what to expect from Dean Grant in the wake of his dire warnings, but everything in the office was normal on Monday morning. He greeted me cheerfully as always, and he mentioned again how much the family had enjoyed my visit. It was as if nothing out of the ordinary had happened, and no more was said about it.

Daniel didn't show up for their routine Monday morning meeting with his father, and Dean Grant didn't leave. I wondered if they needed some time apart after the craziness of the weekend.

Oddly enough, I wasn't dreading seeing Daniel, even though we'd *definitely* crossed a line. The whole crotch-ass rubbing episode — complete with off-the-charts sexual innuendo — had launched us soundly into the dangerous territory that his father would probably refer to as "familiarity."

Euphemism of the year.

There could be no denying the *hard evidence* that Daniel had enjoyed the exchange as much as I had. However, he'd been drunk and was probably horrified once he was in his right mind again and realized that his carefully crafted impartial persona had been completely blown out of the water. As I crossed Queen's Park shortly after eleven thirty, it occurred to me that I was actually looking forward to watching him squirm. Who knew I had such a sadistic streak?

Julie and I sat in our usual seats in the second row, but I wished we were back on the other side across from the front table so that I'd have a clear view of Daniel trying to hold it together. But this wasn't something I could share with Julie, so we remained in our seats by the door.

The class was smaller than usual. Several regulars were conspicuously absent, perhaps needing a vacation from their vacation. Julie could have joined the ones who were dozing. She was tanned and full of exuberant stories about her week, but she was bagged.

When Professor Brown arrived, he was alone. He explained that Daniel wouldn't be joining us and that his Monday tutorial would be canceled since his TA was feeling a little under the weather.

Julie pouted at me, but I shrugged and whispered, "Maybe you'll actually be able to concentrate today." I poked her in the side playfully. My hypocrisy was laughable.

I tried to remain chipper throughout the lecture, but behind my cheerful façade, I was glum. While I knew there would be no public acknowledgment of what had happened between Daniel and me on

Saturday, I still wished we could exchange a secret smile or knowing glance, some small, silent sign to tell me he didn't entirely regret the whole incident. He could hardly deny the chemistry that seemed to be developing between us.

Or could he?

I was also waffling about what to do about Jeremy. Something told me I'd better talk to Daniel first before playing matchmaker between his brother and Julie, so I kept my phone zipped securely in my pocket.

Julie and I left the University College building together after class, but then we went our separate ways. I'd already decided I wanted to make good on my passing comment about visiting the Gardiner Museum, using one of Gwen's tickets which I'd tucked safely in my backpack. I headed straight to the museum where I presented my complimentary ticket and checked my backpack and jacket. I picked up the current guides to the collection, noting the location of the new exhibit that Gwen had been so enthused about on the weekend.

First, however, I wanted to visit my favorite exhibit: the ceramics featuring the Commedia dell'Arte. I made my way to the second floor where the glassed cabinets housing the sculptures of the Italian sixteenth-century street theater scenes were kept. Starting at the beginning of the exhibit, I moved slowly from one display to another, admiring the detail and delicate artistry depicted on the pieces. It was so quiet in the room that I found myself tiptoeing between the displays, as if I might disturb the inert figures on the sculptures if I stepped too loudly.

The silence was broken by a voice behind me.

"Beautiful, aren't they?"

I jumped and spun around, startled. "Daniel! What are you doing here? How did you know I was here? I thought you were sick."

"Hmm. Little white lie, I'm afraid," he said grimly as he walked toward me. "As for what I'm doing here, I was hoping when you told my mother you might come here today after class, you weren't blowing smoke or trying to impress her. I waited outside at one o'clock, hoping to see you."

I gestured around the room. "Well, here I am. What's going on?" I took in his appearance. He seemed tired, but he didn't look ill. In fact, he looked delicious.

"Here, come and sit." He led me to a brown leather bench at the side of the room. "We need to talk. Properly. No mind games and smartass comments."

*Well, can I get an amen!*

I held up my hands in a show of surrender.

A group of four impeccably dressed middle-aged women with matching blond hairdos entered the gallery hall. Daniel nodded at them politely, then pulled his mouth into a tight line.

"Would you be interested in going down to the gallery restaurant to grab a cup of coffee? My treat?"

"That sounds perfect." My heart soared.

I didn't know exactly where this was going, but his demeanor was stripped of its usual bravado and officiousness, and I felt as if I were standing on the brink of a life-altering moment. Daniel led me downstairs to the restaurant, which was clean and spare in its décor; the most impressive feature was the floor-to-ceiling windows spanning three sides of the room.

The host greeted Daniel warmly, shaking his hand. "Mr. Grant, what a pleasure it is to see you. How's your mother?"

"Gwen's well, Michael, thank you. I'd like that table over there by the window, please," he said, his tone confident and commanding.

*Just like Dream Daniel,* I thought gleefully.

"Of course. Janine will take you to your table. Please pass along my best wishes to your parents."

Daniel nodded, and a young woman led us over to the west-facing window. She was about to hand us menus, but he stopped her with a raised hand. "We'll just be having coffee, thank you. Unless you wanted to take a look?" he asked me.

"No, a coffee will be fine."

Daniel sighed deeply, leaned back in his chair, and rested his hands on his thighs.

*Oh, that I were his hands to rest upon those jeans, that I might touch those thighs!* I offered up silent kudos to Master Shakespeare's brilliance. Similar words uttered by Romeo and Juliet in the thrall of their fascination with each other were beginning to make a hell of a lot more sense.

"I don't know where to begin," he confessed.

"Well, how about starting with why you missed class and tutorial today? I don't know how you're feeling, but you look pretty good," I prompted.

"I guess that's as good a place as any," he said, rubbing his chin. "In all honesty, I don't think I could have faced you in that room. My behavior on Saturday was deplorable."

The waitress arrived with our coffees, and we both sat back as she placed the cups on the table and returned to the bar.

"I think you're overreacting," I said. "I had an awesome time. Your family is great. They made me feel so at home."

"I'm glad you like them. That being said, it's pretty clear what my father's hidden agenda was in bringing you over for dinner. My mother quickly got drawn into the plot. I'm sorry you had to go through that."

So Dean Grant *had* invited me over as a prospective suitor for his son, to parade me in front of his wife and seek her approval.

"My father had no idea I'd be there. My plans fell through at the last minute. But you know that," he said, obviously referring to the powder room eavesdropping debacle. "And since you so kindly took my advice about not telling my father you're in Professor Brown's class, he had absolutely no inkling of the prior relationship between us. But you know that, too."

"You don't need to rehash all this, Daniel. It's not a big deal. I explained to your father that I won't tell anyone what happened," I assured him. "And you certainly didn't need to come all the way here to do damage control and bribe me with coffee. I know all about anti-fraternizing rules. You don't have to worry about me compromising your position."

Speaking of compromising positions, I was beginning to wonder if he even remembered his little snooker lesson, but I certainly wasn't about to bring it up.

"What I feel particularly compelled to apologize for is the inappropriateness of my behavior *after* dinner," he said contritely.

*Ah, so he does remember.*

"I don't know. I thought it was pretty amazing," I said, smiling a little cheekily.

"I thought we agreed — no games," he said firmly. "I'm trying to be serious here."

I looked directly into his eyes. "So am I." There was no hint of humor in my voice this time.

Daniel gazed at me for a moment. "I'm sure my actions on Saturday took you by surprise," he said at last.

"A little. You'd been drinking. I figured —"

He shook his head, cutting me off with a look. "My inhibitions may have been lowered, but I would never use alcohol as a way to justify inappropriate behavior. I knew what I was doing."

"Oh." What was he trying to say?

"And what I was doing was inappropriate, Aubrey. I'm your TA."

*Aubrey.* What had happened to "Miss Price"? Not that I was complaining.

"It didn't feel inappropriate. I thought it was pretty wonderful."

I wanted to say more, wanted to spill all of my feelings for him, but without some clear indication of his feelings for me it, seemed unwise to continue.

He cleared his throat and took a deep breath, glancing down at my hands which were clasped on the table, my knuckles turning white as I squeezed my fingers together.

"I do like you, Aubrey," he said.

"I like you, too." I was tempted to laugh at how poorly these insipid words represented my feelings.

"I don't think you understand." He swallowed and looked around hesitantly. "I *really* like you. I shouldn't like you the way I do. It's wrong, and I know it's wrong, but I can't seem to help myself."

Before the angels had made it to the end of the first bar of the Hallelujah chorus, I took a quick breath and leapt in head first. "Does it make me a horrible person if I say I don't care if it's wrong?"

A myriad of emotions crossed his face, relief chief among them. "Then I guess we're both horrible people," he whispered. He unclasped his hands and moved one of them to rest in the middle of the table. I did the same, stretching my fingers toward his. Although our hands were barely touching, my whole body warmed in response to the slight meeting of our fingertips. Any doubt about his feelings for me was obliterated. I hoped he understood that my feelings matched his own.

He quickly withdrew his hand, and I followed suit.

"My father is dean of students at Vic," he said. "The ramifications of this —" he gestured in the air between us " —Aubrey, if I get in trouble, his name would be forever tainted."

"I would never do anything to hurt you or your family, Daniel," I told him. "You can trust me one hundred percent."

"I know that," he said. "My father speaks so highly of you. We talked on the phone yesterday, and he told me you understood Saturday's dinner was an event that wouldn't be repeated, at least not while we're in this current academic situation. He assured me you wouldn't breathe a word of it to anyone. Professor Brown sings your praises highly too, you know. He's very fond of you."

"That's nice to hear," I said. "He gave me a fantastic reference when I applied for the job at Vic."

"It's obvious that his commendations of you are well-founded."

As he looked at me, his face openly betrayed what his heart was feeling. The wall, the bravado, the persona — it was all gone, reduced to rubble at our feet.

"I'd love to spend more time with you and get to know you better, Aubrey."

"I'd like that too," I said, my voice emerging all breathy and whispery.

Either he didn't notice or didn't care. He leaned forward, lowering his tone to match mine.

"I have to be careful. We both do. This position is important to me, and I can't screw up. It's a requirement to complete a certain number of classroom hours. You know I can't treat you differently because I like you. It's already hard to be impartial, and it won't get any easier now that you're aware of my feelings."

"For what it's worth, I think you've done an incredible job in tutorials," I said, eager to set his mind at ease. "You've been professional but friendly with everyone and completely unbiased, at least from what I can see. And there are some challenging characters in this class," I added, thinking of Cara.

He smiled my favorite one-dimpled smile. "'The wheel may be turning but the hamster is dead'? Best. Line. Ever. Bar none," he said.

"You saw that?" I laughed self-consciously.

"The fine art of upside-down reading is my specialty. By the way, that tutorial will go down in history as one of the most simultaneously stimulating and difficult hours of my life."

"Well, suffice it to say that the person we are discussing, who shall remain nameless, has been getting on my fucking nerves for three—count 'em—*three*, long years. I figure if you're going to be that obsequious, you should at least know what the hell the damn word means." I rolled my eyes.

Daniel laughed heartily. "You know what I love about you?" he asked. "You can go from cussing sailor to poet laureate in three seconds without batting an eyelash. It's quite impressive."

My heart lurched. How I wished I could give him the opportunity to love *other* parts of me—parts with *skin*. I sighed rather loudly just thinking about it.

"Well, I'd love to sit here all day because there's so much I want to talk to you about, but I have to meet Jeremy to pick up my car."

I didn't want to leave. I could have sat there all afternoon, staring into his eyes, but Daniel was already on the move. He paid and we left the restaurant. I collected my bag and coat from the front lobby, jamming my gloves into my pockets as we emerged into the bright afternoon sunshine.

"Mind if I walk you back over to Jackman?" he asked.

"You shouldn't. I mean, you don't have to," I said.

"I want to. I still have a few minutes before I have to meet Jer. Besides, I don't think it's a crime for us to walk down the street together."

"All right, if you think it's okay," I said with a small smile.

As we turned the corner onto Charles Street, he looked at me with his eyes narrowed. "So, now that you know how I feel about you, am I going to have to kill you?" he asked, a false tone of menace creeping into his voice.

"Actually, say the magic word, and I'll be as silent as the grave," I whispered.

"Fencepost?" he asked, raising one eyebrow.

"That's the one."

"Honestly, Aubrey, even the fencepost is going to have to be out of the loop on this one." His plaintive expression made my heart hurt.

"Deal," I said, but the thought pained me. I wished I could share my feelings with someone—Julie in particular. "What's going to happen with Jeremy and Julie?" I asked. "He sounded so desperate to hook up with her."

"Did you give her his number?"

"Not yet. I didn't want to say anything before talking to you."

"Thank you for that. I'm glad you haven't mentioned it. I told Jeremy everything yesterday—about how she's in the class as well. I feel bad for him, but I'm not sure what to do. Can you let me think about it?"

I nodded. I guess it was natural for him to feel anxious about more complications. "So, now what?"

We both stopped walking and faced each other. He thrust his hands in his pockets. "When is the final exam for this course?"

"April thirtieth."

"That's about nine weeks. Then I'll have to mark my share of the exams. That'll take a few days. Professor Brown will review them and submit marks to the department. Once the marks are uploaded and accepted, my official duties will come to an end. I guess we need to bide our time."

He looked at me intently, and I nodded in agreement. He smiled, the dimple making an appearance, his eyes wrinkling at the corners.

God, this was too much! Had he actually told me he was interested in pursuing a real relationship with me? My throat was thick with emotion. I swallowed furiously.

We reached my building, and I pulled my keys from my pocket, entering the lobby ahead of him. As much as I wanted to drag him upstairs, taste his lips, run my hands though his hair, and have a clothing-optional repeat performance of the crotch-ass rub, we couldn't. I was determined to prove to him how prepared I was to meet his terms.

"So, I'll see you on Wednesday? In class, of course," I added.

"Absolutely, Miss Price," he said. Then he leaned forward and whispered, "I look forward to it, *Aubrey*," before heading out the door.

He walked out to the sidewalk with a spring in his step I was sure hadn't been there earlier. I tried to take a deep breath, but I couldn't fill my lungs properly. Was I hyperventilating? Dropping my bag on the floor, I leaned against the mailboxes, sliding down the wall until I was sitting on the floor, legs bent up in front of me. I clasped my arms around them and rested my head on my knees.

To my surprise, tears welled up behind my eyes. I was overwhelmed by the events of the day—by Daniel's admission and by the mutual agreement we'd reached about the future course of our relationship. Suddenly the door swung open again, and Daniel was standing in front of me, watching me sob quietly against my knees.

"What the hell happened? Are you all right?" he asked.

"Yeah, I'm fine," I answered, trying to smile while sniffing and wiping at my eyes with the back of my hand. "A bit much to absorb in one day, you know? Why did you come back?"

Please say, *I had to kiss you just once before I left.*

"Is this yours?" he asked, crouching in front of me, dangling a glove in his outstretched hand. I put my hand into my now-empty pocket.

"Crap. I must have dropped it when I took my keys out. Thanks," I said, smiling abashedly.

Apparently there would be no kissing. Not today. Not for weeks. *Oh, Jesus! I can't do this.* His eyes drifted across my face.

"This isn't going to be easy, is it?" he asked.

"Hell, no." I looked from his eyes to his gorgeous lips and then back to his eyes. "*I am as poor as Job, my lord, but not so patient,*" I said, exhaling a shaky breath.

Daniel gently tipped my chin up with his fingers. "He's a wise one, that Falstaff," he said. "How about this for a rebuttal? *'How poor are they that have not patience! What wound did ever heal but by degrees?'*"

"Touché."

He released my chin and stood up. "Nope. Iago," he said, pulling me to my feet.

He reluctantly released me and turned to leave, but this time he swung around to wave. I lifted my own hand, offering a small wave in return.

Daniel Grant wanted me, and I couldn't tell a single soul.

# CHAPTER 16

# Wishing Clocks More Swift

Is whispering nothing?
Is leaning cheek to cheek? Is meeting noses?
…Skulking in corners? Wishing clocks more swift?
(*The Winter's Tale*, Act 1, Scene 2)

I'd avoided self-indulgently lolling about in bed in the morning for months, having very little cause and no time for such decadence. There was always something to be read, something to be written, somewhere to go, or someone demanding my time, energy or attention.

The morning after my coffee date with Daniel, I stayed in bed for ages. I replayed the scene at the Gardiner over and over in my mind, with particular emphasis on Daniel confidently walking me to the restaurant, unburdening his feelings for me, looking into my eyes longingly as he touched my hand, telling me he wanted to spend more time with me, walking me home, tenderly lifting my chin and counseling me to have patience…

The individual vignettes of the afternoon simply didn't lose their luster. The encounter had created havoc with my emotions, but after Daniel had walked away, I'd managed to pull myself together enough not to raise alarm bells with Matt. He'd been a little curious about the motivation behind my sudden decision to make a fabulous risotto for dinner, but I wouldn't be put off. I, of course, was celebrating; he, sadly, wasn't allowed to know that.

My celebration was tempered by an unfortunate caveat. While I was buzzing with the anticipation of a future with Daniel, I was dreading having to wait to pursue a romantic relationship with him. How could I possibly wait nine or ten weeks to touch Daniel again? How could I refrain from kissing those lips and running my hands through his hair, not to mention touching other parts of his body? Keeping my distance from this man who had been making me weak in the knees since I'd first seen his gloriously soulful eyes was not going to be easy.

I finally climbed out of bed and logged onto Facebook before my shower to leave Julie a message. I'd tried to call her several times the night before, eager to talk to her even though I couldn't share my most secret thoughts. I'd finally given up trying to reach her when my call went directly to voice mail for the third time. She was probably recovering from her Reading Week trip.

Several people had posted messages of inquiry on Julie's Facebook wall.

*Where you at?*

*Hey, loser, call me…*

*Helloooo? Is anyone home?*

I added my own message to the collection: *Vacation's over, bunhead. Get your lazy ass out of bed.*

St. Mike's was a mere three minute walk from Jackman Hall, but I would have happily walked for hours. It was a beautiful day. The sun was shining; the flurries of the day before were a distant memory. St. Mike's was quiet for this time on a Tuesday, and of the few people I did see, most looked morose and despondent.

*Snap out of it, people!* I wanted to shout. *Can you not see? It's gorgeous, the birds are singing…love is in the air!* I couldn't help scoffing at my own ridiculousness.

Nothing could ruin my mood as I sat through my children's lit lecture. Even the moribund poetry of Christina Rossetti was powerless against the sheer magnitude of my happiness. At quarter to one, we were dismissed, and I traipsed back to Vic to make it in time for my French lecture. As I walked up the paths, I recalled the day several weeks prior when Daniel had lanced me with an irate glare in this very spot as he'd returned from lunch with his equally angry father. What had been going through his mind? I'd have to ask him about that.

And wonder of wonders, think of the devil — there he was, leaning against the large maple tree in the middle of the Vic quad. One leg was bent, foot planted against the tree trunk, and his hands were in the pockets of a pair of heart-stopping black jeans. To top it all off, between yesterday and today he'd made a trip to the barber. Without an unruly curtain of hair falling across his forehead, his eyes were even more entrancing. In fact, all of his features were somehow sharper. My God, he was *so* gorgeous. Was it really possible that one day in the not-too-terribly-distant-future I was going to get me a piece of that? Be still my ever-loving heart.

As he stepped away from the tree, he held up his hand in greeting. "Good afternoon, Miss Price."

"Good afternoon yourself, Daniel," I said, reining in my urge to leap into his arms and lock my legs around his waist.

He smiled smugly. "What a coincidence it is to see you here."

"Indeed. One might suspect that a certain person's schedule had been examined by someone else with access to said document."

"One *might* think that," he said with mock seriousness. "Or one might discover that this certain someone else never, *ever* forgets important details, like the exact location of the other person on a particular Tuesday several weeks ago, at this precise time, only to hope like hell that this was part of that other person's regular Tuesday afternoon flight path."

I tapped my palm against the side of my head, laughing in complete confusion. "Come again?"

He leaned forward. "Hmm, having not had the immense pleasure of doing so a first time, that request is invalid." A delicious smile played around his lips.

What was that I'd said about no hope of uninhibited flirtation? That was some extremely hot sexual innuendo, and there wasn't a can of Guinness in sight.

"You're not playing fair," I said.

"Sorry, you're right." He bit his lip and shifted his weight, hiking his laptop bag higher on his shoulder, and then resumed a light, conversational tone. "I was taking a chance, though. I remember seeing you walking this way a few weeks ago, and I saw you go into Old Vic at one o'clock. I suspected you might have a class here every Tuesday."

"I do. I actually need to head in," I said, unable to hide my disappointment.

"One hour? Two?" he asked.

"Two. I'll be done about ten to three."

"Okay. And are you free after?"

"As a bird," I confirmed.

"Well, I was wondering if you'd like to meet somewhere to talk about…your *independent study?*" he said. His eyes gleamed.

"Ah, yes, I should start working on that. Would you like to help me?"

"I'd love to," he said, leveling me with his gaze.

"Great." I was having trouble tearing my eyes away from his lips. "Do you want to meet over at Pratt?"

"Prat?" he repeated with a laugh. "What's that?"

"Over there." I pointed to the building on the other side of the quad. "The E.J. Pratt Library."

"What an unfortunate name."

"Why's that?"

"Well, in England, when you call someone a prat, you're essentially calling them a total idiot—a tool."

I laughed. "I've never thought of English as a second language before. I might emerge from this school year tri-lingual. I didn't understand half the things Penny said the other night."

"I admit when I'm with her I tend to fall back into old habits. Sorry about that, poppet," he said smiling.

"Poppet?" I asked, again completely confused.

"Poppet—it's, well—my mother used to call me that. It's like *doll*—or *sweetheart*. Nothing bad," he assured me with a sweet smile. "I'm sorry. I'll try to refrain from relapsing too much."

"No, don't apologize. You go ahead and spend as much time with Penny as is humanly possible. Seriously," I added, blushing wildly.

"Mm-hmm," he said. "I see…" He looked quite pleased with himself.

"Listen, I do have to go." I was cursing my fate and wishing I didn't give a rat's ass about my stupid GPA. "We'll meet over in front of Pratt at three, okay? But can you do me a favor?"

"Of course. Name it."

Oh, the way he said that—like he'd give me the moon if I wanted it. Too bad all I wanted was a snack. "Can you bring me a muffin or something? I'll be starving by then."

"Starbucks?" he asked, one eyebrow raised.

"Mmm, yes, please. A chai latte and maybe a piece of poppy seed loaf?"

"Done," he said. "I'll kill a couple of hours at Chapters. See you around three."

He gazed at me and sighed heavily before taking his leave. I reluctantly headed inside.

I was well-prepared for the lecture and should have been interested and fully engaged, but I wasn't. I'd never fidgeted so much during a class in my life. Would three o'clock never arrive?

After close to two hours of restless tedium, I gathered up my belongings, bounded up the stairs to the main floor, and crashed out of Old Vic's front doors in time to see Daniel rounding the corner at Charles Street and taking the path between Burwash dining hall and the men's residences. He was carrying a take-out tray with two cups in it.

I crossed my arms and leaned against one of Vic's stone pillars. When he caught sight of me standing there, he stopped and stared back at me. Finally, he continued down the opposite path toward the library, looking at me every few seconds. I made my way down the path in front of Old Vic, and we met on the stone walkway that led to the doors of the library.

"For you, *mademoiselle*," he said, handing me a brown paper bag and one of the Starbucks cups.

"Thanks. How much do I owe you?"

"Don't be absurd."

"Well, I didn't want to be presumptuous."

"You're silly," he replied, leading me to one of the benches in front of the library.

We sat while I nibbled on the lemon poppy seed loaf and sipped on the chai latte. He drank his coffee, his arm along the back of the bench behind me. I leaned into him and felt the slight pressure of his arm across my back.

"Is this okay?" I asked him. Were we pushing the envelope?

"We're sitting on a bench drinking coffee, Aubrey. I certainly hope there aren't rules against this, or I've been committing infractions left and right with numerous students over the last three weeks. So how was your class?" he asked.

"Fucking excruciating," I replied, my mouth still full of a cakey blob of poppy seed loaf.

Daniel laughed. "You're a linguistic phenomenon, you know that?"

I gestured toward his grin. "You might want to rein that in a little, sunshine. Major infraction. Dead giveaway."

"You're right." He quickly adopted a serious expression, but slyly winked at me all the same. As I finished off the last of my snack, I pulled my cell phone out.

"Before we go in, I should call Matt and let him know I'm not going to be home for a bit." Daniel looked at my phone, a strange glint in his eyes. "He's very protective. He worries," I explained.

I reached Matt's voice mail and left a message: "Hey, cowboy. I'm at the library doing some research, so don't worry about me, okay? I'll talk to you later. Text me if you want."

I switched the tone to vibrate and stowed my phone in the front pocket of my hoodie before throwing away my cup and paper bag. I gestured to the library doors, but Daniel didn't move.

"Can we stay out here for a minute?" he said.

"Sure." I dropped on the bench beside him again.

"There's actually something pretty important I need to talk to you about. It's got nothing to do with this." He gestured in the air between us, as he'd done the day before at the museum. "I've been trying to sort something out in my head all day. I wasn't sure if I should tell you or wait until Professor Brown announces it to the class. My instinct is that you'd rather know in advance. As much as I wanted to see you, my initial reason for tracking you down today was a little less romantic, I'm afraid."

A quiver of dread ran through my stomach. "You had a class prior to your French lecture, right?" he asked.

"Yes, children's lit."

"You were walking back from St. Mike's. Is that where your class was?"

"Yes..."

"What was it like over there today? Did you hear anything out of the ordinary?"

What a strange question. But now that he'd asked it, I'd definitely noticed a strange tone at St. Mike's today. "It was quiet, I guess. The people I did see were pretty miserable," I admitted.

"Well, it's not surprising that they didn't look too happy. They're probably all reeling," he said. He rested his arm on the back of the bench behind me again. "I received a call from Martin last night — Professor Brown. He'd left a message to let me know something terrible had happened. It turns out one of your peers has been killed in an awful car accident."

He was looking at me intently, observing my reaction.

"Oh my God." I brought my hands up to cover my mouth. "Who was it?" I asked, bracing myself for his answer. All I could see was Julie's Facebook page with her friends' repeated queries. The implications of my inability to get hold of her suddenly gained greater significance. But Julie lived in residence at Trinity, not at St. Mike's.

"It was Mary," he said. "Mary Langford, from your tutorial group."

I gasped, relief and horror mingling in my mind. Julie was all right. But Mary? Poor, lovely, sweet Mary...

"How?" I asked. "What happened?"

"Apparently she was out for the evening with a friend over the break. On their way home on a two-lane road in Guelph, an oncoming car crossed the median. The collision was head-on. Mary was killed instantly. I gather the driver of the other car had been under the influence."

Mary was gone in an instant because of someone else's carelessness. Just like that. I was stunned.

"I'm sorry," he said. "I hate to be the one to tell you."

"No, no, I'm glad you did. I'd rather hear now than in class tomorrow."

"Are you okay?" he asked.

"Yeah. It's — God, it's so awful. She was such a nice girl."

I thought back to the tutorial sessions, remembering how she'd gradually been coming out of her shell. The funny little story she'd told about her uncle rushed back, and tears welled up in my eyes. And she had two little sisters. I covered my face with my hands.

"Aubrey?" Daniel's gentle voice was too much. I couldn't stifle the sob bubbling in my throat. "Damn it." He placed his hand on my back.

"It's okay, please don't," I whispered, flinching away from his touch. I wanted him to touch me, to hold me, but my own needs were overshadowed by my fear of us being seen. Sitting on a bench together was one thing, hugging was something else entirely.

He retrieved his hand and leaned forward, linking his fingers, elbows planted firmly on his knees. "This is so wrong. It shouldn't be a crime for me to comfort you." His voice was tight and weary. "Listen, Aubrey, now might not be the best time for this, but I have a confession to make," he said with a sigh.

"What is it?" I turned to look at him.

"When I got home yesterday, Professor Brown's message was waiting for me on my answering machine. He said it was a young lady from class, but he didn't mention Mary's name. I thought it might be you. It was snowing; you might have gone out for a walk and been hit by a car. Anything was possible. I didn't know how to get hold of you, so I drove back here. A couple of girls let me in. I wandered up and down your hallway, and then I heard Matt calling your name. I stood outside your apartment door, listening to you and Matt talking. I had to make sure you were all right. I thought I'd go crazy waiting for Martin to call me back with the details of the accident, but I didn't need to stand there for as long as I did. I'm sorry I invaded your privacy."

"You don't have to apologize for being worried about me."

"I know, but I felt like I was trespassing on your space. I could hear you talking through the door." Daniel clenched his fists and cracked his knuckles. "You'd made Matt dinner. He'd just had a shower," he said, a muscle in his jaw twitching. "He'd forgotten to take his towel into the bathroom and was calling out to you to bring him one. You were both laughing. You called him 'sweet cheeks,'" he said, shaking his head ruefully.

"Oh, Daniel, don't take any of those nicknames seriously. It doesn't mean anything. It's no different than you calling Penny 'love.'" Okay, here was my chance. If it was confessional time, I certainly had some things to own up to. "I understand how you'd misinterpret my relationship with Matt, though. I did the exact same thing with you and Penny," I admitted, biting tentatively on my thumbnail.

"Penny's engaged to Brad. You've known that all along," he said.

"That's not exactly true."

He leaned back on the bench. "What do you mean?"

I took a deep breath. "After the first lecture, I left the class and was walking behind you when you got a call from Penny. I heard you call her 'love,' and I assumed she was your girlfriend. When you said you'd be taking her out for Valentine's Day, I was convinced of it. Then when I saw the two of you at Canoe, well, I can't even tell you how jealous I was. I didn't recognize myself."

Daniel cocked an eyebrow.

"I wanted to inflict bodily harm on her. With the heel of my shoe. Through her eyeball."

Although he could have taken great offence to this affront to his dear friend, he just laughed.

"Last night I wanted to knock your door down. I would have happily found Matt a towel and then smothered him with it," he admitted.

"So, we're even?" I asked.

"It would seem so," he said. "God, I can't believe you thought I was with Penny. I mean, there's no way. She scares the shit out of me." He laughed again. "And she's definitely not my type. Way too high maintenance."

I smiled and then looked down at my hands with a sigh. It didn't seem right to be smiling and laughing.

"Poor Mary," I said.

"I can't stop thinking about her family," Daniel said. "I can't even fathom what they're going through."

"Life is fragile, isn't it?"

"It certainly is. I've been thinking the same thing non-stop all day."

I nodded quietly, shivering. The raw emotions and the cooling late afternoon air chilled me to my bones.

"We should go inside," he said. "You're freezing."

We grabbed our bags and entered the library together, finding an empty table near the stacks in the corner of the reading room where we sat side by side, facing one of the large windows. I pulled books and papers out of my bag and spread them in front of us.

"Wait, you know I have absolutely no desire to discuss your independent study, right?" he said.

"I don't give a rat's ass about my independent study," I confessed. "This is all for appearances."

"Ah." He chuckled as he draped his jacket on the back of the chair. "You're a master at the art of nefarious activities, I see."

"I'm actually kind of making things up as I go along." I shrugged awkwardly.

Was I trying too hard? The news of Mary's tragic end had settled like a fine dust between us. I struggled to focus on Daniel and live entirely in the moment. If Mary's unfortunate fate had made anything clear, it was that life was way too short.

Suddenly Daniel frowned and asked, "Aubrey, why do you call Matt 'cowboy'? It's a strange nickname."

"I don't know. I'm a bit of an endearment junkie, I'm afraid, sailor." I winked at him and he laughed.

"Hey, now, you can't call *me* 'sailor.' I've called dibs on 'sailor' because of that potty mouth of yours."

"Oh, I don't know. I'm sure you hold your own nicely on that score."

"Okay, so if Matt's the cowboy and I'm the sailor, we just need a police officer, a construction worker, and an Indian Chief, and we can start a Village People tribute band," he said with a smile.

"You don't know how happy it makes me to hear you say that!" I said, laughing loudly, suddenly aware of the stares of people sitting nearby.

"What?" he asked. "You have a burning desire to found a boy band?"

"No, I'm just so relieved. You're *funny!*" I said, still chortling.

A man at a nearby table expelled a sharp, "Shh."

*Yeah, whatever, buddy. You shush me again, and you'll be eating some archives. I'm in serious need of some giggles over here.*

"You're only realizing I'm funny *now?*" Daniel looked hurt.

"Well, not exactly. I knew you were witty and sardonic, and you're kickass with innuendo, but just plain *funny* really floats my boat."

"Seriously?" he asked, leaning his face on his hand. "What else floats your boat?"

"Do you really want to go there, Daniel?"

"All the way," he answered, his voice silky and low. He was devastatingly sexy when he did that. His knee was pushing against mine under the table. I'd never considered my knees to be erogenous zones, but that was clearly an oversight. Daniel was certainly charting undiscovered territory.

"Ahem, well," I said, jiggling my leg and trying not to get flustered. "I'm not sure where to start."

"How about at the beginning?" He looked at me from under his eyelashes, pushing his leg even more firmly against mine.

"I don't know. I thought I'd start at the top," I said, gazing longingly at his hair.

He smiled. "You like my hair?"

"Like? Not exactly the way I'd put it," I admitted. "The haircut, it's—" I shook my head. *Insanely hot and fucktastically sexy* wasn't a description I was prepared to share at that moment.

"Interesting. So what else?" he asked, a vision of smugness. He was having the time of his life.

"If you think I'm gonna sit here and extol your physical attributes until you can't fit your head through the door, you're sadly mistaken."

He smiled and shook his head. "Fair enough. So tell me, when did you, *you know…*" He lifted an eyebrow suggestively.

"What? Decide I wanted to jump your bones?" This time it was his turn to guffaw, drawing angry shushes from several other patrons.

"Next time we meet to discuss your independent study, I think maybe a coffee shop might be a better choice," he whispered.

"You think?" I stifled my giggles with my hand.

"Well?"

He actually wanted an answer? Jeez Louise.

"Um, well, I'd have to say about eleven minutes after you walked into Brown's classroom. Day one."

There. Honesty was the best policy, right?

"Seems you beat me by about twenty-eight minutes. I didn't see you right away, but as soon as you opened your mouth to identify that line from *Hamlet*, and when you looked at me at the end of class…I guess you could say I grew roots. I couldn't think of a reason to stay in the room, but all I wanted to do was stare at you."

"I wondered what you were doing," I admitted. "There's only so much organizing you can do with three pieces of wrinkly paper."

"Pretty lame, huh?"

"Not really. That's very flattering. I didn't realize I'd made such a great first impression. I thought you didn't like me. You gave me such a stink eye the next day when we crossed paths in the quad."

He grimaced at the memory. "My dad had mentioned this girl he wanted me to meet who worked at the office, and how he was so sure we'd hit it off. When he first brought it up, I brushed it off. I'm not prone to taking my dad's advice on relationships. I don't even think I processed your name. But then you told me you worked for him, and I realized you were the one he was talking about. I had visions of him finding out I was your TA and having a shit fit because he'd been trying to play matchmaker."

He rolled his eyes, perhaps imagining having that conversation with his father.

"Anyway, I decided it would be better if he didn't know. When I saw you coming across the quad that day, I pictured you walking up and saying hi or something. I thought if I glared at you, you'd stay away. I guess it worked."

"You confused the shit out of me and ruined the rest of my day, but you certainly stopped me in my tracks," I confessed.

"I'm sorry, poppet. I was a head case that week."

"And that's why you kept me after class the next day and asked me not to tell your dad I knew you?"

He smiled sadly. "You were so pissed off at me. Not my proudest moment."

"I didn't know what was really going on."

"Well, now you know. I have to say, I was impressed with my dad's eye for once. I had this whole scenario hatched where you and I would become great friends during the semester and I'd tell you once the course was over that I'd like to take you out. Then I'd congratulate my dad on his great taste in women, explaining that he was right about you and that we do have a lot in common. Pathetic, right?"

"That's not pathetic, Daniel. It's sweet. At least you didn't have a raunchy dream about me," I said.

Oh, shit. Why'd I have to go and say that?

"Really." He leaned toward me. "Please, tell me all about it. I'm intrigued."

I called to mind the various steamy details of the bookcase dream.

"Wow, that good, was it?" he asked, taking in my flushed face.

"It was pretty incredible. Really vivid," I said. "I remembered it as I was walking down the hall before signing up for the tutorial. When I saw you standing there, I kind of lost the ability to think straight."

He looked at my lips, licking his own as he nodded thoughtfully. "Are there any other secrets you're willing to share, Aubrey?"

I breathed deeply. "No, I think I'm good right now."

"Suit yourself. But it's fair to say you've been pining for me for a solid four weeks, yes?"

"Jesus, would you listen to yourself?" I said, laughing quietly. "Besides, you're the one who camped out to wait for me today. That's pretty desperate if you ask me. I was quite prepared to mind my own business, go to my classes, and see you tomorrow," I said, getting comfortable on my high horse.

"Touché." He smiled as he slid my French novel across the table. "Hey, I love Balzac. Is this what you were studying today?"

"Supposedly, but my prof went on a twenty-minute tangent about this book she'd just read called *Poussière sur la Ville*. It was ridiculous, since none us had read it, and it had nothing to do with nineteenth-century French lit."

"What was the book called again?"

"*Poussière sur la Ville*."

"One more time?" He looked at me strangely.

"What, am I not pronouncing it right?" I said, suddenly feeling like a complete idiot.

"Oh, no, you're saying it perfectly," he said, staring intently at my mouth. "A little too perfectly." He shifted in his seat. "Is it just me, or is getting warm in here?"

I smacked him. "You pervert," I whispered.

He protested and rubbed his arm. We were beginning to draw more and more attention the longer we sat there.

"I think maybe we should go," I said.

"I think maybe you're right."

We put on our coats and grabbed our bags. He started to lead the way to the door when I grabbed his arm to stop him. "You know what? Just a sec."

I made my way toward the stacks, zeroing in on the Canadian poetry section. He followed me, a bemused expression on his face. I stopped in front of the 821s and scanned the shelves.

He came up behind me and whispered, "What are we looking for?"

I froze. *Oh, God. Life imitating dream? Yes, please.*

"Your friend. Mr. E.J. Pratt," I said, looking at him over my shoulder, my face burning with the memory of tightly gripped bookshelves.

"Are you all right?"

*Busted.*

The fiery blush that had started on my neck was creeping to the roots of my hair. I crossed my arms and leaned against the shelves. "There may or may not have been a bookshelf in the dream I had about you," I confessed, sighing heavily.

"Really?" He passed his hand long the spines of the books beside my head. "Fascinating. And what on earth were we doing to this bookshelf?"

"Um…" Oh, what the hell. There was no point stopping now. "Well, I was…using it for…support, I suppose you could say."

"Support? God, this sounds epic. What was I doing that made you require support?" he asked, smiling at me wickedly.

"Well, you were, behind me…you told me I'd better hold on…" I closed my eyes and swallowed. I couldn't finish.

Daniel rested his hand on the shelf and leaned his forehead against his arm. "Are you actually *trying* to kill me, Aubrey?"

"Sorry," I said in a small voice.

"I need some air." He sighed, backing away from me and heading toward the lobby. I abandoned my search for Mr. Pratt and followed him, rushing to match his long strides out of the library.

I had no idea where we were going, but I didn't care as long as we were together. We veered to the right toward the gatehouse. As we approached the archway, he looked around cautiously.

"Come here," he said, grabbing my arm and pulling me into the relative darkness of the bricked gatehouse, dragging my knapsack off my arm and dropping it along with his bag onto the ground.

Suddenly I was in his arms. He was clasping me so forcefully I thought he might crush my chest. I should have resisted, but I couldn't. I stood on my toes and wrapped my arms around his neck, letting my fingers wander upward into his wonderfully soft hair before resting my hands on the smooth nape of his neck.

His face was buried in my hair, his breathing erratic. I settled my face against his neck, breathing in his essence—leather, and that damned sandalwood again. I could have stayed like that forever, feeling the entire length of his body melting into mine, his arms encircling me tightly, protectively. At last he gently nuzzled my ear with his nose, moaning softly before pulling away and looking around guardedly.

"Sorry." He stepped back with a hangdog expression. "I shouldn't have done that."

"I'm so glad you did—you have no idea."

"I may have an inkling," he said with a pained smile. He rubbed his face with his hands, clearly frustrated. "I wish—"

"I know. It's okay."

He stood dejectedly, his hands on his hips. "It's just not fair, you know? I wish I could do something to show you…to let you know…"

"You just did, Daniel. *'Is whispering nothing? Is leaning cheek to cheek? Is meeting noses?'*" I said, quoting from *The Winter's Tale*. Why did I feel that Shakespeare's words spoke more to the heart of every matter than my own ever could?

"Oh," he replied, shaking his head. "You've hit the nail on the head, poppet. The rest of that speech? Do you know it?"

"No, that was the extent of it, I'm afraid."

He took a step toward me, moving me back into the shadows. His voice was soft and beguiling as he repeated the speech to its conclusion. *"'Is whispering nothing? Is leaning cheek to cheek? Is meeting noses? Skulking in corners? Wishing clocks more swift? Hours, minutes? Noon, midnight? And all eyes blind with the pin and web but theirs, theirs only, that would unseen be wicked? Is this nothing? Why, then the world and all that's in't is nothing…'"*

He was gazing at me sadly, but I was enthralled. I hadn't thought it was possible for Daniel to be more alluring, but he'd outdone himself.

"'*Wishing clocks more swift,*'" I said. "That's an understatement."

"Not to mention '*skulking in corners,*'" he said, laughing gently. "But this is all we've got, and we shouldn't even be doing this." He picked up his bag and nodded his head to the side to indicate we ought to leave. "Come on, I sense imminent danger if we don't get a move on here," he said with an apologetic grin.

I grabbed my knapsack, and we emerged from the darkness of the archway into the dim light of late afternoon on the other side of the gatehouse where a row of benches edged the path behind Jackman Hall. We stopped in front of one, and I drew my arms around myself. Daniel noticed me shivering.

"You should head inside and grab a hot bath or something," he said.

"Yeah, you're probably right."

"Before you go, I got you something at the bookstore. It's nothing big, but I thought it was appropriate." He put his laptop bag down on the bench and pulled a plastic shopping bag out of it, folding the end of the bag over the flat object inside. "Open it when you get upstairs. I got one for myself, too."

"Thanks," I said, feeling a little off balance. I hadn't expected him to buy me something.

"No worries. It's nothing, really."

We stood awkwardly, mirroring each other's aimlessness.

"I'm going to say something, and then I promise not to say it again," I blurted.

"Okay," he said. "Shoot."

"This fucking sucks."

He laughed and shook his head. "Not what I was expecting," he said. "But I agree whole-fucking-heartedly. Yesterday, I was so determined to be patient. Today I'm thinking, *screw it*. Life is too damn fragile. Maybe that back there—" He gestured to the darkened gatehouse. "I don't know. I'm all over the place." He rubbed at his face in exasperation.

"Yeah, don't get me started," I said through chattering teeth.

"Look, you really should head in."

I hefted my backpack onto my shoulder. "You're right. I'm frigging frozen. Thanks for coming by. I enjoyed spending time with you."

"Me too, poppet."

"See ya tomorrow, sailor." I backed away slowly.

"Bye." His voice was little more than a whisper.

As he dropped onto the bench, I turned and slowly made my way down the paths behind the men's residence. Looking back, I saw him lean forward, his head in his hands. I willed myself to keep walking.

The apartment was empty. Spared the task of lying about how I'd spent my afternoon, I went straight to my room, crawling into bed and eagerly tearing open the Chapters bag. Inside was a calendar, a large picture of Shakespeare's face on the front cover. Daniel had removed the packaging and clipped a red marker to the top of the calendar. What an interesting gift.

I flipped it open. There was a reproduction of a piece of art on every page with the month's calendar grid below. At the bottom of each page was a quoted reference from a Shakespearean play or poem. Daniel had marked some of the months with Post-it notes.

I turned to February, the first flagged page. Each of the days on the grid, starting with February second, was marked with a large red X. I smiled as understanding dawned on me, and I turned the page to March, which was also flagged. The reproduced art was a painting called *A Dance to The Music of Time*. On the calendar, the squares for Sunday the first and Monday the second each contained a giant red X. Three Shakespearean lines were written beneath the weeks of the calendar. They read:

> *"Let him have time to mark how slow time goes*
> *In time of sorrow, and how swift and short*
> *His folly and his time of sport."*
> *(The Rape of Lucrece)*

Beside the lines, Daniel had written on a Post-it note:

*Fuck! SLOW doesn't even begin to cover it!*

I thought of him sitting at Chapters with his red marker and his Post-it notes. How adorable was he? He had lovely handwriting for a man, too.

I turned the page, excited to see what Shakespeare—and Daniel—would have to say for themselves in April. The painting was an 1885 portrait entitled *Antony and Cleopatra*. The Shakespearean quotation was from the play about the titular passionate lovers:

> *"The April's in her eyes: it is love's spring,*
> *And these the showers to bring it on. Be cheerful."*
> *(Antony and Cleopatra)*

There was another Post-it message from Daniel:

*I'll be fucking cheerful on April 30th, believe me.*

I laughed, absolutely giddy. This had to be the most ridiculous literary analysis he'd ever done. I loved it.

May was a month I was desperately looking forward to. The artwork was Titian's *Venus and Adonis*, and again the Shakespearean quotation related to the figures in the painting:

> *"…kissing speaks with lustful language broken,*
> *'If thou wilt chide, thy lips shall never open.'"*
> *(Venus and Adonis)*

I'd studied *Venus and Adonis* in high school. The painting depicted the section of the poem in which Venus had pulled Adonis down from a horse and was attempting to seduce him as they lay together in the woods.

I turned my attention to the Post-it note beside May's quotation. Daniel had drawn a large red arrow pointing at the painting. Underneath it he had written:

*This will be you and me in fifty-eight days.*
*I don't know about you, Aubrey, but I can't fucking wait.*

## CHAPTER 17

### Light and Lust

This said, he sets his foot upon the light,
For light and lust are deadly enemies…
(*The Rape of Lucrece*)

I lay in bed that night thinking over the events of the day and struggling to reconcile the roller coaster of emotions the afternoon had yielded. Tedium, happiness, grief, contentedness, yearning—the whole gamut. I was completely wiped. As annoying as the situation with Daniel was, it was temporary. In fifty-eight (soon to be fifty-seven) days, he'd be all mine and we'd be in the clear. This was my last thought before I finally drifted off to sleep.

I slept well. Too well—I snoozed straight through my alarm, only to wake and discover that I had twenty-five minutes to get ready for work. I sprang out of bed, dove in and out of the shower, then dashed about trying to find something appropriate to wear. In the end, I panicked and pulled on my black yoga pants and a plain white T-shirt, finishing with a thigh-length black and white belted sweater. It wasn't an outfit I'd normally wear to work, but it would have to do.

I was almost out the door when I remembered I needed to do something of the utmost importance. I tore back to my room and opened my top dresser drawer to find the calendar. Opening it up to March, I took the red pen and drew a large red X through Tuesday, March third. Then I buried the calendar in the bottom of the drawer again before heading off to work.

I was launching into my morning routine and making myself my first cup of coffee when Dean Grant strode stormily out of his office.

"Would you mind pouring me one as well?" he asked. "Then come into my office. We need to talk."

Oh, crap. Here we go.

What had Daniel and I been thinking the day before, gallivanting around the quad, playing kneesies and eye-groping each other in the library, hugging under the gatehouse, all under the potentially watchful eyes of his father? I should have remembered the proximity of the library and Northrop Frye Hall. Which way did Dean Grant's office windows face again? I hadn't even considered that. I was so stupid.

I poured him his coffee and grabbed my own cup, pulling his office door open with my foot. I placed his coffee on the desk blotter, trying to disguise the shaking of my hand.

"Thank you, Aubrey. Have a seat, won't you?" He gestured to the chairs in front of his desk, taking a gulp of his coffee before tossing his reading glasses on the desk and leaning forward to look at me over his clasped hands.

"I'm guessing you don't know why I've called you in here?"

"Um, I'm not entirely sure, sir, no."

This was not sounding good at all.

"Something dreadful was brought to my attention yesterday."

*Brought* to his attention? I looked at the window. It faced south, across Queen's Park. He wouldn't have seen us sitting in front of the library or walking toward the gatehouse. Someone else had reported us!

He sighed deeply and looked at his watch. "The university has experienced the loss of a St. Mike's student over Reading Week."

Wait—what was he saying? Oh my God, he was talking about Mary!

"Yes, I heard about this yesterday." I recovered quickly from my shock. "My morning class is at St. Mike's on Tuesdays. It's all everyone was talking about," I fibbed.

"Oh, so you *do* know?" Dean Grant asked, his eyebrows arching in surprise.

"Yes. Sorry, it didn't occur to me you'd need to talk to me about it. I actually knew Mary. She was in one of my classes—in my tutorial group, in fact. She was a lovely girl." Then, for good measure, I added, "It's Daniel's class."

"Oh, I'm sorry to hear that. This is more than a passing occurrence for you, then. And she was in Daniel's class, you say? I'm surprised he didn't mention it."

"Maybe he doesn't know," I said, fabricating on the spot. "He missed class on Monday. Professor Brown told us he was under the weather." Was it only two days ago that Daniel had met me at the Gardiner? It seemed like eons ago.

"I didn't realize he'd been off on Monday. I haven't spoken to him since the weekend," he said, giving me a pointed look. I tried to maintain a blank expression.

*Nothing to see here, Dean Grant. Move along.*

"I imagine Martin would have contacted him regardless," he said. "Anyway, we don't know how many Victoria students will be impacted by her passing, so would you send an email to the residence dons and student leadership groups to remind them that we have counseling available through Student Services?"

"Of course. I'll get on that right away." I started to stand up.

"And, Aubrey? How is everything going with you?" he asked.

This was a conspicuously vague question.

"Great, sir. Never been better." I smiled confidently, moving toward the door.

"I'm happy to hear that," he replied, a contemplative expression on his face.

I pulled his door closed behind me, leaning against it with an enormous sigh of relief, though I suspected it would be short-lived. How on earth would I make it through the next fifty-seven days in one piece if one day of subterfuge had already made me a nervous wreck?

After work, I headed straight to University College, happy to be early for class so I could secure a seat in the second row on the other side of the room. Students filed in one by one, some looking like they'd heard about Mary, some clearly oblivious.

Julie finally dashed in, moving down the row to sit beside me, her eyebrow raised saucily. "Well, well, well, couldn't stay away from the candy dish, eh?" she asked.

I brushed off her suggestive comment with a quick subject change. "Hey, did you get my messages? Where've you been?"

"Oh, man, I've been so bogged down with school work. I got nothing done over the break. I had to hide in the library and knock off an art history paper. I'm so exhausted." Professor Brown and Daniel's arrival interrupted her complaints. "Holy mofo, check out Mr. Shmexy. He got his hair cut. He's been holding out on us," she whispered in my ear.

She was right. Dr. Hobo, it seemed, was on a sabbatical. Daniel looked spectacular. He was wearing the same black jeans he'd worn the day before, this time pairing them with a fabulously soft-looking tan sweater, a white T-shirt peeking out above the neckline. The kicker though? The footwear. I didn't know a lot about shoes, but I knew what I liked. These shoes — which may have been boots, it was hard to tell — looked to be of the Italian variety and the kind that made a lovely authoritative clipping sound when you walked.

*Authoritative.* Yes, please...

"He shaved too," Julie said. "Man, he cleans up well. He looks fucktacular, don't you think?"

She nudged me.

"Hmm?" I was still imagining the sound of his shoes.

"Daniel! He puts the *edible* in incredible, don't you think?"

"Yes, fine, he looks fine," I stammered, remembering that as far as she knew, I hadn't seen him since before Reading Week.

Daniel took his seat, and Professor Brown quickly called the class to order, casting his eyes around the room somberly. "Ladies and gentlemen, I received some sad news on Monday night."

There were some stunned gasps around the room as he told us about poor Mary. Julie looked at me, shocked. I grabbed her hand and squeezed it.

"Now, I realize some of you may have known Miss Langford quite well, while others may not have," Professor Brown said. "Regardless,

I'm going to afford you the opportunity to grieve appropriately. There will be a memorial service at St. Basil's Church at the corner of Bay and St. Joseph Streets on Friday at eleven thirty. Anyone wishing to attend is more than welcome to do so. My classes and tutorials will be canceled for the remainder of the week. We will reconvene next Monday, but we'll have to double up to stay on course. After we finish our study of *Antony and Cleopatra,* we'll pick up *Othello* on Wednesday."

He then turned to Daniel, inviting him to speak.

"Thank you, Professor Brown," Daniel said, standing but remaining in place behind the table, his eyes flitting briefly across mine. "I apologize for my absence on Monday. Professor Brown tells me he gave you an extension on your *Hamlet* analyses. I'm prepared to accept them any time between now and next Monday. Are there any questions?"

I looked around the room. No one spoke up. Cara was gazing at Daniel appraisingly, though. Apparently Julie and I weren't alone in our appreciation of the *GQ* effect.

"Well, then," Professor Brown said, "if there's nothing else, we'll end there. You're welcome to stay to make plans for Friday and ask us any questions you may have. If you need to speak to someone, you may make appointments at Student Services with the counselors there. I look forward to seeing some, if not all, of you on Friday."

Julie squeezed my hand again. "How awful," she said.

"I know. It's pretty hard to wrap your head around."

"You knew already, I guess?"

"Yes, Dean Grant told me this morning."

At least that one wasn't a total lie. I was starting to despise myself.

"So do you want to go to the memorial service together on Friday?" Julie asked.

"Sounds like a plan."

She stood and slid her books into her bag. "What are you up to now?"

"I think I'll head to the Hart House Library for a bit. I have a lot of reading to catch up on. If I try to do it at home, I'll probably fall asleep. I need to talk to Professor Brown for a minute first, though."

"Okay, no worries. We'll sort out timing for Friday?"

"For sure. I'll be in touch."

I pulled on my jacket and maneuvered out of our spot in the second row. Professor Brown smiled as I approached.

"Professor Brown, Daniel," I said. "I hope this isn't going to sound presumptuous, but I was thinking it might be appropriate to find an alternate venue for the Friday seminar."

"Oh?" Professor Brown looked at me expectantly.

"When I was in the ninth grade, there was a boy in my math class who had leukemia. He stopped attending at the end of October, and he died a month later. For the rest of the term, the tension in the room was unbearable. His empty desk was too awful to look at. There was always this elephant in the room, and that was a classroom of thirty students. I don't know how we'll feel in that small tutorial room looking at Mary's empty seat."

Daniel looked at me with undisguised admiration.

"That's a valid concern, Miss Price," Professor Brown said. "You've always been so intuitive." He turned to Daniel, clasping his shoulder. "What do you think, my boy? Are you up to the challenge of finding an alternate space? You might have luck with some of the small meeting rooms at Hart House."

"Absolutely," Daniel said, smiling warmly at me. "Miss Price is right. I think changing venues is wise. I'll get right on it as soon as we're finished here, sir."

"Okay, well, I guess I'll be heading out then," I said, snagging one last good look at Daniel and his chiseled jawline.

*Shaven or unshaven? This was a tricky one and deserving of some further exploration. With my tongue, of course.*

I slowly walked to the neighboring building, half wondering if Daniel might try to catch up with me. After all, it seemed we were going in the same direction. I peered over my shoulder occasionally as I crossed to Hart House, but he was nowhere to be seen. The thought of not seeing him for two days was depressing.

In the reading room, I claimed the red leather couch facing the bay window. I glanced around as I dug in my bag for my book. Most of the room's occupants were studying, but one guy was curled up on a sofa by the unlit fireplace, snoring softly. I wished I had time to flake out and nap as well.

I was pulled from my reading after about ten minutes by the sound of my phone buzzing in my pocket. My heart thundered as I checked the display. It was a text message from Daniel!

**Have I told you that I love those pants you're wearing, my poppet? -D**

I quickly typed a response.

**How did you get my number? Where are you? -A**

He answered almost immediately.

**Jeremy has his uses from time to time.
Say, that's a sturdy looking bookshelf over there,
don't you think? -D**

Bookshelf? I whirled around. He was here? What the—?

I scanned the room, and there he was, sneaky bastard, sitting in a wing-backed chair facing the side wall, his newly-trimmed locks in plain view above the chair back. His leg was dangling over the left arm of the chair, a sex-boot taunting me shamelessly.

I dropped back onto the couch.

**What are you doing here, sailor? -A**

**Booked that meeting room for tutorial then I thought
I'd swing by the library while I was here.
I overheard you tell Julie you were coming here.
Do me a favor? Lose the sweater and
go look out the window? Please? -D**

I smiled. I knew these pants did great things for my ass!

*Okay. I'll play.* I slowly peeled off my sweater and dropped it on the couch. I stood, pretending to scan the sidewalk outside while stretching my arms above my head. My T-shirt rode up enough to show a little skin. Glancing over my shoulder, I saw him peering around the side of his chair, his gaze intense.

**I want you so badly I can taste it. -D**

My knees jumped, and I instinctively brought my hand to my throat. I was certain everyone in the room must be feeling the raw sexual energy flowing between us, but no one seemed to be paying the slightest bit of attention to us. I stared at my phone for a moment and then started typing, surprising myself with my boldness.

**Tell me, what does want taste like? -A**

He read my message and then looked at me again, his eyes smoldering as they drifted down my body, pausing at my breasts and then slowly scanning my legs. His answer was fast:

**It tastes like the sweetest velvet. -D**

This time my knees buckled, and I had to sit or risk falling over. *Screw you, fifty-seven days!* There was no way. I could feel my cheeks burning. I moved my fingers absently toward my mouth. He quickly typed another message.

**Where your fingers are?**
**I want my tongue right there, RIGHT NOW. -D**

Jesus!

I imagined the way his tongue would feel, dipping between my parted lips. My brain was suffering from lust-induced paralysis, and I couldn't even think of a reply.

He looked around the room to make sure no one was watching, and then he delivered the *coup de grâce*. Leaning on his hand, he subtly placed two of his fingers on either side of his mouth and licked his lips between them, his eyes narrowed seductively as he gazed at me.

If anyone else had done this to me, I might have been offended—disgusted even—but this was *Daniel*. Coming from him, the gesture was undeniably sexy. How often had I read about—and subsequently mocked—swooning women? It always sounded absurd. Well, so much for that. I had officially joined the ranks of the swooners.

I was a puddle.

I closed my eyes, and I'm fairly certain I moaned. When I looked back at him, he was still watching me with unabashed desire. Such brazen lust in both of our eyes, here in the full light of day, surrounded by our unwitting peers.

He typed out another message.

**You look so beautiful. How I wish I could come over there**
**and throw you back on that couch.**
**What I would do to you...-D**

I read his words and then nodded at him, too stunned to respond. We stared at each other without moving for the longest time, and then he held up a piece of folded paper. He placed it on the seat of the chair before pulling on his blazer and throwing his bag over his shoulder, giving me one last look of undisguised longing before striding purposefully out of the library.

Authoritative sex-boot footsteps indeed.

I reached blindly for my sweater. Was I supposed to follow him? My phone buzzed again—one last message from Daniel.

**I'm tied up for the rest of the day with appointments
and office hours, but I had to see you for a few minutes.
Read the note I left you. -D**

Disappointed that he was unavailable but eager to read his note,
I retrieved the paper he'd left and returned to the couch to read it.
It was a typed letter.

Aubrey,

I was up late reading poetry last night. Of course, any
time I sit down to read poetry, I invariably end up rolling
around in the words of our mutual BFF, the Bard. Given
the week we've had and the things we're dealing with,
this sonnet seems to be most topical. I hope you like it
and wonder if you feel, as I do, the weight of that "world
without end hour"...

SONNET 57

Being your slave, what should I do but tend
Upon the hours and times of your desire?
I have no precious time at all to spend,
Nor services to do, till you require.
Nor dare I chide the world-without-end hour
Whilst I, my sovereign, watch the clock for you,
Nor think the bitterness of absence sour
When you have bid your servant once adieu;
Nor dare I question with my jealous thought
Where you may be, or your affairs suppose,
But, like a sad slave, stay and think of nought
Save, where you are how happy you make those.
So true a fool is love that in your will,
Though you do any thing, he thinks no ill.
~ W. Shakespeare

I miss you, Aubrey. I really do watch the clock for you,
wishing away the hours until I'm able to see you again
and dreaming of the day when we can be together.

-D

xoxoxo...

I refolded the paper, pressing it to my lips. How was it possible for someone to be so thoughtful *and* so capable of turning me into a quivering blob of jelly? One thing was for certain: If the next fifty-seven days didn't kill me, the rapture of finally achieving long-delayed gratification in the days and nights that followed very well might.

I packed up my books. How the hell was I supposed to concentrate after that steamy exchange? When my phone vibrated in my pocket as I was making my way down the stairs, I smiled, wondering if Daniel was hoping for a second round of dirty texting. But no, this time he was actually calling.

"Hello?"

"Hi," he said. "I'm so sorry about all that. I don't know what I was thinking."

"I should think so. I've had to pack in my studying. I'm heading home to take a cold shower. Thanks a lot." I laughed.

He didn't laugh with me. "No, that was really inappropriate of me. Can you please delete that conversation?"

"Seriously? I'm not going to show anyone. Don't worry."

"Please? I'd feel a lot better if you'd erase it."

"Well, okay. If it'll make you feel better."

I heard him take a deep breath — presumably a sigh of relief.

"Thank you. So, will I see you at the memorial on Friday?" he asked.

"Of course. I'll go straight after work."

"Perfect. I'll see you then, poppet."

"Sounds good. I'll miss you tomorrow."

"I'll miss you too. See you Friday."

I hung up reluctantly, standing at the bottom of the stairs and taking a moment to reread our exchange. He was being paranoid, but I indulged him, deleting the entire conversation. I supposed he was right. If my phone were to fall into the wrong hands, the consequences could be disastrous. TAs were most likely strongly discouraged from sexting with the students in their classes. This was a most unfortunate rule; Daniel had such a way with words.

# CHAPTER 18

# *One Thread*

...all the shrouds wherewith my life should sail
Are turned to one thread, one little hair;
My heart hath one poor string to stay it by...
(*King John*, Act v, Scene 7)

In the wake of the sexting debacle of Wednesday, I assumed I'd never hear from Daniel via text again. But after a full day of radio silence, he sent me a message which I retrieved at work on Friday morning.

> **Miss Price – Sorry my prior commitments made it impossible for us to get together on Wednesday to discuss your independent study. Perhaps we should try to meet after today's memorial instead? Talk soon. Daniel.**

Daniel was couching his apologies and his hopes in an academic context, but the talk of my independent study had to be a pretense. Sure there were other possible reasons for his coolness, but I quickly cast those aside, sticking with my initial interpretation.

I tidied up the desk, left a few notes for Gisele, and then I sat down to reread the note I hoped to give Daniel today. It was payback of sorts for the lovely note he'd given me on Wednesday.

Daniel,

I don't know if you're familiar with Sarah Waters, but I've been reading her book *The Night Watch*. I came across the most beautiful passage yesterday, in which one character expresses her connection to someone by describing a thread that runs between them and tugs at her heart whenever they're apart.

This metaphor captures perfectly the way I feel. I miss you when we're not together, but I sense somehow that we're connected. I hope you feel the same.

~Your Poppet

xo

I tucked the note into the side pocket of my purse, dreading the walk to St. Basil's church in my heels, but looking forward to seeing Daniel despite the sadness of the upcoming event.

After locking up for the lunch hour, I made my way straight to the church. Julie had promised to save me a seat, but if the service was underway by the time I arrived, I'd have to stay at the back. My concerns were alleviated as soon as I saw the steady stream of people filtering into the church. Relieved that I wasn't late, I waited my turn to enter and then scanned the pews, looking for Julie.

When I spotted her, my eye was immediately drawn to the person she was talking to. *Daniel.* He was standing in the aisle, dressed to the nines in a dark blue suit, his hand in his pocket as he and Julie chatted. I took a deep breath to steel myself before making my way toward them.

*Daniel in a suit and tie. Not a big deal. Yes, he's handsome, and yes, he watches the clock for you and sends you dirty text messages, and when he says your name, it sounds like half a sigh and half a promise, but none of that is important right now.*

*In other words, remember why you're here.*

Julie slipped into the pew just as Daniel looked up and saw me approaching. His smile was subtle, but the warmth in his eyes was enough to put my mind at rest. He was as glad to see me as I was to see him, regardless of the unpleasant circumstances.

"We were starting to worry that my father might have kept you late at work," Daniel said, gesturing to Julie who was slipping off her coat and getting comfortable.

"Not at all. Terrible walking shoes, that's all."

"Aubrey, come sit," Julie said, patting the bench beside her.

I squeezed into the pew, scanning the rows behind us as I removed my coat.

I waved at Shawn and Vince who were sitting a few rows back. Cara and Lindsay were beside them. I held my hand up to greet them as well, but Cara glared at me. Okay, then. I settled into my spot and draped my coat across my lap.

"Great turnout," Daniel said.

"It really is. Not surprising. She was a sweetie," Julie said.

"So, Miss Harper said I could sit here with you," Daniel said, motioning to the sliver of bench beside me. "Do you mind if I squeeze in?"

*Mind? Ha!*

"Of course not," I said. I shifted down to make room for him, although the closer I could be to him, the better.

At the front of the church, a man moved to stand behind the podium, asking everyone to take their seats. I braced myself for what was to come and heard Julie sighing mournfully beside me. Daniel's hand was resting on the bench between us. I casually placed my hand beside his, my coat hiding both of our hands. He reached out to hook his little finger over mine, and I clasped it tightly, trying not to sigh too loudly.

The man at the podium introduced himself as Mary's Uncle Bernard.

"Hey, that must be Banquo-head-wound Uncle Bernard," I whispered to Daniel. "The one who fell in the woodpile at Thanksgiving."

"I think you're right," he whispered back.

How awful. Somehow knowing these little bits of Mary's history increased the pity I felt for her family tenfold. Bernard's role was apparently to introduce the various speakers and the friends of Mary who were reading poems and eulogies. The service was beautiful, the readings emotional and very touching. When her two sisters got up to speak, I squeezed my eyes shut, grateful for the nose-blowing going on around us. I blended in with the snifflers.

From time to time, Daniel's finger would tighten around mine and I would squeeze back, the slight touch enough to console me, though I'd have been even happier if I could have rested my head on his shoulder as he wrapped an arm around me comfortingly.

After a particularly emotional performance of *Do Not Stand at My Grave and Weep* sung by Mary's cousin and the St. Mike's choir, there was no way I could keep the tears in check. I reluctantly let go of Daniel's finger, reaching into my purse for a tissue and retrieving the folded note at the same time, surreptitiously placing it under Daniel's palm. He curled his hand around it and placed the slip of paper in his jacket pocket, waiting for me to finish dabbing at my eyes and my nose with Kleenex and then slipping his finger around mine once more beneath the cover of my coat.

At the front of the church, Bernard wrapped up the service, thanking everyone for coming and making several announcements, one of which was an invitation to a Mothers Against Drunk Driving fundraiser taking place at Brennan Hall the next evening. It was to be a "dry" event, with local bands performing. With the conclusion of this last announcement, the service ended and people began to stand, some hugging their companions, others collecting their belongings, their heads down as they contemplated the terrible reality that Mary was truly gone.

"Lovely service," Daniel said. He gave my finger one last gentle squeeze before reclaiming his hand.

"But so sad," Julie said, blowing her nose soundly.

"Very sad," Daniel said. "She'll be missed." He gestured to the group of professors making their way down the center aisle toward Mary's family and stood up, re-buttoning his suit jacket. "I suppose I should join Professor Brown and offer my condolences to the Langfords. Thanks for letting me sit with you."

"No probs," Julie said.

I nodded my agreement. "Julie and I will leave you to it." I gazed at him wistfully, and he gave me an equally plaintive look. Around us, people were moving to the door. Lingering unnecessarily would seem odd.

We said our goodbyes, and Daniel took his place at the end of the line-up at the front of the church. He turned to sneak another look at me and then slipped his hand into his jacket pocket, pulling out the note I'd given him and dropping his eyes to scan it.

I knew I should move. I *had to*. People were waiting to get out into the aisle and I was in their way, but I couldn't seem to make my legs cooperate. Daniel turned around again and our eyes locked, the truth behind the passage I'd described in the note playing itself out right there before me. It was as if we were attached by an invisible current, dangerously compelling us to move toward each other.

Julie nudged me, bringing me back to my senses. "Aub, are you okay?" she asked. She followed the line of my gaze, and when her eyes reached the spot where Daniel was standing, a confused look crossed her face.

*Oh, shit.*

I moved out into the aisle, quickly sliding the strap of my purse up my arm, looking briefly back at Julie before saying, "Of course I'm fine."

She grabbed my elbow to slow me. "What the hell's going on?"

"What do you mean?" I said, aiming for nonchalance.

"What do you mean, *what do I mean?*" Julie said. "I saw the way you and Daniel were looking at each other! *You*, I get. You've been mooning over him like that for weeks. Hell, so have I! But did you see the way he was looking *back* at you? Jesus H. Christ, do you think he's got a thing for you?" she asked, quiet awe in her voice.

"I don't think you should be using the Lord's name in vain right now, Julie, or giving him a middle initial. This *is* a house of worship." We moved toward the door.

"Very funny. Aubrey, I'm serious."

"I don't know what you're talking about. It was a touching service... he was probably feeling a little emotional and happened to look at me at that moment. No biggie."

She looked at me skeptically. "I don't know..."

"Julie, do you realize how crazy you sound? He's not the slightest bit interested in me, at least not the way you're suggesting."

"I guess," she said. She still wasn't convinced, but thankfully she dropped the subject. We were almost out the door now, stuck behind a bottleneck of people attempting to get outside. "So do you want to grab lunch or something?" she asked.

"I wish I could," I said, which was a bald-faced lie. "I've already made plans for the afternoon." While this was sort of true, I didn't have the first clue what these actual plans were. All I knew was that somehow they involved Daniel.

As the crowd carried us out into the afternoon sunshine, I contemplated hanging back for a bit, wondering if Daniel expected me to wait outside, but I didn't know how to subtly dawdle without arousing Julie's suspicions. Luckily, before we'd moved too far down the sidewalk, Daniel solved the problem for me, emerging hurriedly from a cluster of people.

"Hey, mind if I walk back to Vic with you, ladies?" he asked. He sounded a little winded.

"Fine with me," I said, all calm, cool, and collected, the complete opposite of the way I was feeling. I smiled to myself, cheered by the thought of him running to catch up with us.

"What a great family. I can't imagine what the Langfords must be going through," he said, shaking his head as he fell in step beside us.

"Oh, I know," Julie said. "When you know someone who's been touched personally by drunk driving it hits home, you know?"

"Yes, I know," he said. "Speaking of which, are you planning to attend the MADD fundraiser tomorrow night? It's a worthy cause and a perfect way to honor Mary's memory." He was looking at me pointedly. I was almost afraid to speak, sure I'd inevitably reveal something.

"Are you going?" I asked him.

"I expect so. I'd like to show my support."

"What do you think, Jul? You into it?" I asked her.

"Um, sure. I don't have much going on tomorrow."

I refrained from doing an excited jig. Passing through St. Mike's quad, Daniel walked beside me, occasionally brushing his hand against mine. The brief touches were subtle enough that Julie wouldn't notice, but their subtlety didn't prevent me from experiencing a surge of pleasure with every trace of contact. At the paths to Vic, he stopped and gestured toward Avenue Road.

"I need to go this way to pick up my car," he explained. "I guess I'll see you tomorrow night at the benefit? Maybe we could sit together — if that's not too weird."

"I don't think that would be weird," Julie said, looking at me with a slight flick of her eyebrow. "What do you think, Aubrey?"

"No, I guess not."

"Then, I'll see you there," he said. "Have a good afternoon."

He glanced at me quickly before turning to head off toward the main road. I waved but avoided watching him walk away — no easy task.

"He's in better spirits these days," Julie said. "Maybe Mr. Shmexy just needed a vacation. Gosh, I can't believe we have a date with him tomorrow. I wonder if he's got a thing for threesomes."

"Yeah, that's probably it, Jul. MADD fundraisers are notoriously kinky events."

She laughed and hugged me, and then we parted ways. I sighed, rattled but relieved that she hadn't pursued her suspicions. Daniel and I needed to be more careful. A mere five days in, and things were already getting sketchy.

I stared out at the road for a moment, not sure what I was supposed to do. Assuming Daniel would contact me to clarify what he'd had in mind for the afternoon, I turned and started making my way back to Jackman Hall. As I passed through the quad, it occurred to me that everything at Vic had taken on new significance. The maple tree, the bench in front of the library, the gatehouse — memories of the small romantic moments Daniel and I had exchanged over the past few days permeated everything.

I was passing through the gatehouse, revisiting that fabulous hug we'd shared, when my phone vibrated in my purse. I stopped to dig it out of my bag, my heart galloping as I answered.

"Daniel, where are you?"

"I take it you're alone? Are you home yet?"

"Not exactly." I laughed. "I guess you could say I'm stuck in memory lane."

"I'm almost at the Four Seasons, just north of Bloor. I parked my car in their underground garage. Can you swing by?"

Could I swing by? Would my feet make it all the way to the corner of Bloor and Avenue? Hell, I'd crawl if I had to!

"I can be there in ten minutes."

"Perfect. I'll wait for you in the lobby."

I hurried up Avenue Road as best I could. Crossing Bloor Street, I peered up at the Four Seasons. I'd never seen the inside of the hotel. Yet another place representing how the other half lived. Daniel was apparently a lifetime member of this other half. I experienced a twinge of self-doubt as I contemplated how different our backgrounds were, but I quickly squashed it. Daniel wanted to spend time with me, so why question it?

When I reached the hotel entrance, a doorman ushered me inside. A few people were sitting on the leather couches in the center of the lobby, luggage around their feet. Tourists. My footsteps echoed on the marble floor as I wandered around, peering behind plants and pillars. Daniel was nowhere to be seen. Had I come to the right place?

I was biting my thumbnail hesitantly, considering whether I should ask the concierge if there was another lobby, when I saw some movement out of the corner of my eye. Off to the left of the elevators, a door opened and Daniel looked out, gesturing with his hand for me to join him. I smiled and made my way across the room and through the door. He was leaning against the wall in the stairwell, his coat hanging over the railing.

"Get over here," he whispered, pushing himself off the wall and opening his arms to me. I reached his outstretched hands and folded myself into his embrace. He pulled me close and sighed with pleasure. I responded with a sigh of my own.

Being in his arms was pure, unadulterated joy.

# CHAPTER 19

# Madness

Love is a smoke raised with the fume of sighs;
Being purg'd, a fire sparkling in lovers' eyes;
Being vex'd a sea nourished with lovers' tears:
What is it else? a madness most discreet...
(*Romeo and Juliet*, Act 1, Scene 1)

He held me tightly, the angle of his head forcing me to nuzzle into his neck — right where his cologne lived. His hands wandered under my coat, fingers roaming up and down my back. I willed him to slide his hands underneath my sweater, but he didn't. Instead, he slowly pulled my coat off and tossed it over the stair railing before pulling me back into his arms.

I shivered and slipped my arms inside his suit jacket and around his waist, feeling the warmth of his chest against mine. He didn't object or pull away. In fact, he pulled me against him even more tightly.

"I was so afraid I wouldn't get a chance to do this today," he whispered.

"Mmm, me too."

Who was I kidding? I was afraid I wouldn't get to do this until *May*.

I explored the taut muscles of his back. Humming contentedly, he brought his hands up to cradle my face, caressing my cheeks and gazing into my eyes.

*Daniel, please, kiss me.* I looked at his lips eagerly, but he simply rested his face against mine.

"You have no idea how much I wanted to pull you into my arms as soon as you walked into that church," he murmured against my temple. "You look lovely today."

"You look pretty incredible yourself," I said, shyly smiling, overwhelmed by his complimentary words. "Great suit," I added, running my hands down the lapels of his jacket.

"I'm glad you approve," he said. "I had one hell of a time trying to decide which tie to wear."

He actually blushed. Adorable. I was trying to decide whether this suit surpassed the one he'd worn to Canoe. I hadn't gotten a close-up look at him that night, and this was the first time I'd seen him in a tie. Damn, he wore it well. I pictured him standing in front of his mirror, agonizing over which one worked best with the suit.

I snuggled into him. "You realize we're skulking in a corner again, right?"

"Have I mentioned how much I love skulking with you?" He tucked a wayward lock of hair behind my ear.

"Not yet. Personally, I think I'd prefer not having to skulk."

"All in good time," he said, smiling at me gently.

"Fifty-five days?"

"Ish," he countered.

*Ish?* My eyebrows went up. "Come on, sunshine, fifty-five days is bad enough."

He leaned back against the wall, hands resting on my waist. "Think about how incredible being together will be after having to wait fifty-five-ish days, not to mention the thirty-ish we've already suffered through."

"That's not much comfort," I said, tugging gently on his tie.

"Sorry, Aubrey. We both knew this wasn't going to be easy." His face fell. "Are you hungry?"

"I suppose so. What did you have in mind?"

"You look absolutely ravishing, and we are mere footsteps away from a couple of great restaurants. How about we have lunch? I have to spend some time with you today or I'll go crazy."

"I don't know if that's a good idea, Daniel."

"I happen to know of a discreet little corner in the Avenue Lounge that would be perfect for a leisurely lunch. Besides, the odds of someone we know being here are slim to none. Please say yes." He took my hands in his.

"It's your ass on the line," I said. "I'm trying to give you an out here."

"I don't want an out. I want to treat you to lunch. Please?"

I crumbled when he batted his long eyelashes. "Of course I'd love to have lunch with you." I sighed. "It's your call. If you're fine with it, then I am too."

He smiled and turned to grab our coats. "This way," he said, opening the door and directing me through the lobby.

"Two for lunch?" the hostess asked, looking at Daniel to confirm.

"Yes, please, and I'd like that table by the screen." He pointed to the corner of the restaurant where a table was partially hidden from view by a decorative folding screen and a large plant.

"Of course, sir."

She led us to the table. Daniel pulled out my chair and draped my coat over the seat back before sitting down opposite me. He had a clear view of the restaurant, and he took a minute, eyes narrowed, to scan the other occupants of the room.

"What do you think?" I said.

He relaxed back into his chair and smiled. "The coast is clear."

"Good. So tell me, Mr. Grant, do you come here a lot?"

"This is where I bring all of my unwitting victims, Miss Price," he said, grinning mischievously. I studied his face.

"You looked just like Jeremy for a second. Sometimes I think you're nothing alike, but sometimes when you smile, I can really see the similarities."

Daniel leaned on the table, hands clasped, eyes drifting over my shoulder for a few seconds.

"There's a very good reason why he doesn't look like my brother. You see, he's not."

"He's not? What? I don't understand."

"It's a long story, but oddly relevant given the day we've had." Daniel fiddled idly with his fork. "When we were little, Jeremy's parents — my aunt and uncle — went on a holiday to my family's house in the south of France. Jeremy stayed with us. While they were there, his parents were killed in a car accident. The driver of the other car was impaired."

"God, that's awful."

Daniel nodded. "Brad was five. Jeremy and I were three. He's lived with us ever since. He doesn't remember his own parents."

"Wow. I don't know what to say."

"You don't need to say anything. I just wanted you to know. It's a shitty situation. He has a few issues because of it. He's a nervous driver, and he goes ballistic when he sees people drinking and driving."

"That's understandable."

"He's mellowed a hell of a lot, but he had some problems in high school. He felt as if people didn't understand him. He's never felt sorry for himself or tried to use his predicament to win pity votes or anything, though. He's a phenomenal person." Daniel tapped his index finger on the table. "Anyway, that's why I feel so horrible about this business with Julie, especially now that I've gotten to know her. I'd hate to feel responsible for Jeremy not having a chance to meet a great girl and have some fun."

"Does that mean you *do* want me to give her his number?"

"I don't know. I was thinking maybe he could join us tomorrow night."

"Really?"

Daniel grimaced. "Bad idea?"

"It might be awkward, you know, setting them up while we're hiding behind the TA-student thing. It could be messy, especially after today. Julie saw us looking at each other in the church. She asked me outright what was going on with us, and I had to lie to her. It was awful."

"I can't help it, Aubrey. When we're together, I lose all ability to reason." He moved his leg under the table and pressed his foot against mine as if to make his point clearer. "I shouldn't have looked at your note in the church in front of everyone, but I was dying of curiosity," he admitted sheepishly. "After I'd read your words, it took every ounce of self-control not to run down that aisle, sweep you into my arms, and carry you out the door."

"I'm glad you liked it." I smiled at him. "But we do need to be more careful," I said, aware that having lunch together in a hotel wasn't careful at all.

"I hear you." He scanned the room again, looking back at me and shrugging, satisfied that we were safe in our anonymity. "Let me think a little more about what to do about Julie and Jeremy, okay?"

"Of course. It's your call."

He picked up a menu. "Anyway, enough of all that. Would you like a glass of wine or something? You like red, if I remember correctly?"

I laughed. "I'm surprised you remember *anything* from that night."

"Oh, there are a few choice *ass*pects of that evening that are indelibly imprinted on my memory." Daniel chuckled at his own joke.

"There are a few things I'd be *hard-pressed* to forget as well," I said.

He shifted in his chair and smirked at me. "Very clever. So, anyway, drink?"

"I can't always be responsible for my behavior after a few glasses of red wine."

"Well, that's decided. A bottle of red it is."

He snapped the wine menu closed, and I chuckled. "We can't drink a whole bottle of red wine. You have to drive."

"I know. I'm kidding," he said, before dropping his voice to a lower register and adding, "Sort of."

Noticing our closed menus, the waitress approached. "Are you ready to order?" she asked.

"I'm afraid we haven't even looked yet," Daniel said. "But we'd like some wine. I think we'll go with a half-liter of the Argentinean Malbec."

"Of course," she said, disappearing to place our order.

"So, any menu recommendations?" I asked him.

"Everything's wonderful. You're not a vegetarian, right? You had turkey the other day, but do you eat red meat?"

I couldn't help smiling. We really did have so much to learn about each other. The thrill of a new relationship, the whole process of getting to know someone — it was so exciting.

"I am most definitely *not* a vegetarian, and I'm willing to try anything once."

"That's good to hear," he said with a saucy grin.

I shook my head and looked back down at my menu, pretending exasperation. He really was incorrigible.

"So, I noticed you tossed out the countdown of fifty-five days pretty quickly earlier. I gather you like the calendar?"

"I love it," I said. "I could totally picture you sitting at Starbucks, painstakingly writing out those notes for me."

"So you're saying I'm pussy-whipped?" he asked, furrowing his brows.

"Hell, yeah, I've got you right where I want you."

"I wish I could say the same." He leaned forward and lowered his voice. "Where I *really* want you is upstairs in one of the best suites with a king-sized bed and a Jacuzzi."

"Just say the word." I looked at him steadily.

He leaned back and exhaled heavily before returning my look with an equally unwavering gaze of his own. "As much as it's killing me, you know we can't do that. I'm sorry."

"I guess I can't complain, can I? I knew what I was getting myself into."

He stroked my thumb gently, staring wistfully at my hand. The waitress walked over with a tray, and he straightened up, pulling his hand back calmly. After pouring us each a glass of the wine and placing our waters on the table, she took our orders.

Relieved of our menus, Daniel picked up his glass, tilted it, and swirled the wine around a few times.

"You're not going to take a swig and spit it in the plant, I hope?" I asked him.

He put his glass down and laughed. "I'm actually trying to think of what we can toast to. It seems inappropriate to be happy today."

"It has been a sad day—a sad week. It's important to keep things in perspective, though," I reminded him. "In situations like this, the best thing you can do is honor the person's memory and make the most of each day."

"You're right," he said, smiling at me pensively. "So, what do *you* think we should drink to?"

"To May?" I suggested.

"Hmm, what's happening in May again?" he asked, feigning confusion.

"Absolutely nothing if you don't smarten the fuck up," I said, tapping his shin under the table.

"Ah, yes, it's suddenly all coming back to me. May… *Venus and Adonis*. Tell me, Aubrey, would you say you're anything like Venus in your, um, *passionate tendencies?*"

"Are you asking me if I'd pull you off a horse to seduce you?"

"I suppose that's my question. Would you?"

"You'll have to wait until May to find out," I said with a wink.

He pulled out his phone. "Memo to self," he said, as he typed into it. "Horseback riding with Aubrey on May first. There." He re-pocketed his phone with a smile.

I laughed. "You're adorable."

"Oh, I know," he said, smirking. "I'm also dying to try this wine, so what the hell are we drinking to?"

I picked up my glass. "To Venus," I said decisively.

He clinked his glass against mine. "I'll definitely drink to Venus."

It was delicious. Among many other things, he obviously knew a thing or two about good wines. Which reminded me…

"Can I ask you something kind of personal?"

"That's a loaded question," he said.

"It's nothing major. I was just wondering about your family—how well-off you seem to be…" That sounded awful, even to my own ears.

Oddly enough, he didn't seem upset. He held his hands out. "What do you want to know?"

What *did* I want to know?

"I—I'm not sure. I'm a little intimidated by the house, the private school education, the music lessons, the traveling…"

He leaned forward and took my hand in his. "Money isn't important to me, Aubrey."

"That's easy for you to say because you have plenty," I countered.

"Fair enough, but I don't define myself according to financial criteria, and I don't judge others by their bank accounts. I honestly couldn't care less about money. But like you say, we're comfortable, and I allow myself to enjoy the luxuries money affords."

"Such as?"

"Eating in nice restaurants, going to concerts and enjoying the theater, living in an upscale condo, and splurging on clothes, which might be hard for you to believe, given my horrendous wardrobe over the past few weeks."

"You have made a bit of a, well, transformation. Were all of your decent clothes lost in the move or something?"

"No." He chuckled. "It's kind of silly—my mother suggested I might try to, um, blend in a bit better on campus."

"Then why the makeover?" I asked, gesturing to his suit.

"Well, the suit was for the memorial."

"But you got your hair cut on Tuesday, and you've been looking mighty fine all week."

"I don't know. I went out for a coffee with Jeremy and Penny on Monday afternoon. I think it's the first time Penny's seen me on campus. She told me I looked like I'd been 'shagging in an airing cupboard,'" he said, drawing quotation marks in the air.

"I can imagine Penny saying something like that."

"She wasn't joking. She told me it was a small wonder I didn't have a trail of starry-eyed freshmen following me around. Apparently my efforts to look sloppy and unappealing weren't working. And my unfortunate grooming habits didn't deter you, right?"

"No," I conceded. "I wanted to take you home and give your hair a good wash. Maybe take off all your clothes—so I could iron them, of course. It's fair to say your mom's plan backfired."

"I can't say I'm disappointed. I feel so much more comfortable when I'm not dressed like a homeless person. Anyway, that answers your questions about the wardrobe. Do you have any other concerns? About the money, I mean?"

I shook my head stupidly. I didn't know what to say. He wasn't trying to make me feel like a dolt, but I did anyway.

"So, do you support yourself with the money from being a TA? Or do your parents still look after you?"

"Neither, really. When Jeremy, Brad, and I turned twenty-one, we all received trust fund money from our grandfather's estate," he said matter-of-factly. "He was a wise investor, and he taught my grandmother a lot. She helped us plan our investments. I recently bought the condo, and Penny and Brad have bought a house. It should be ready any day now. Jeremy still lives at home, but he's starting to do well with his freelance work, so I don't imagine he'll stay there much longer. Anything else?"

"No." I grimaced. "I'm sorry; I shouldn't have asked. It's really none of my business, but after seeing your parents' house—I don't know, I felt so out of my league."

He frowned. "I hope no one said or did anything to make you feel that way. We don't intend to be pretentious or snobby. My mother would die if she thought we were coming across that way."

"No, not at all. My upbringing was so different, that's all."

Before I could continue, our food arrived. The waitress placed our dishes in front of us and refilled our wine. Daniel leaned over to take a look at my salad. "That looks good. Is that mango?"

"Yes, I love mango. That smells incredible too," I said, checking out his stir fry. I speared a piece of mango, dipped it in the tandoori dressing, and popped it in my mouth. "Oh, that's divine." I licked my lips.

"Divine? I'd say that's an understatement," Daniel said, staring at my mouth.

I smiled devilishly. "You need to try this." I stabbed another mango slice, but I had a twinge of discomfort as I remembered how Matt and I had fed each other at Canoe.

"I'd love to," he said. "But do me a favor? Lose the fork."

He parted his lips expectantly as I reached across the table to pop the piece of fruit in his open mouth. Before I could pull my hand away, he gently pulled my fingers toward his lips and, after a taking a quick glance over my shoulder, slowly licked the juice from them. When he pulled my fingers into a V and slipped his tongue up and down my index finger, I damn near passed out.

He smiled and released my hand, which would be of no use to me ever again. How could I possibly type, write, do dishes, or complete any other mundane daily task with these fingers, which had just been gloriously serviced by Daniel's hot tongue?

"You really don't play fair," I said, my voice breaking as I touched my fingers to my lips.

"I don't recall ever claiming I'd play fair," he replied.

"No, I suppose you didn't." I thought back to Wednesday's texting session in the Hart House reading room: *I want you so badly I can taste it,* and *It tastes like the sweetest velvet.*

I took a sip of my wine. "Is it my imagination, or are you inordinately fond of the letter V?" He raised an eyebrow. "Or perhaps your fascination is with *words* that start with V. Venus, velvet…" I gazed at the fingers he'd just licked.

He looked at my fingers as well, lips parted slightly and tongue darting between his teeth. "*Velvet*…yes, you're absolutely right." His eyes were smoldering. "I adore velvet. It's one of my favorite things in the world."

I squirmed in my seat, uncrossing and re-crossing my legs. "Okay, I think we need to change the subject…"

"As much as I'm enjoying this one, you may be right." Daniel chuckled.

We turned our attention back to our food, and he quizzed me about my family and upbringing, my hometown and high school. The heat in my face gradually lessened as I talked about my life back in Oakville. I feared I was boring him with my rather run-of-the-mill history, but he listened intently, asking questions the whole time.

I returned the favor, pressing for more information about his family but stopping short of asking him for the details of Penny and Brad's wedding. Might there be a chance that I'd be able to go as Daniel's date? I was afraid to broach the topic. It certainly wasn't my place to say anything, but that didn't stop my imagination from running wild. I tried to imagine possible venues. Wherever it occurred, the wedding was bound to be an epic event. Gwen was probably an extraordinary wedding planner.

We spent a good two hours at lunch, talking, laughing, and flirting shamelessly. After we polished off our meals and wine, we each enjoyed a leisurely cup of cappuccino and shared a plate of biscotti. By three o'clock, Daniel was looking at his watch and lamenting the fact that he had other commitments. As our time together drew to a close, I reflected that even though we still weren't able to "go public," the afternoon had been pretty wonderful.

After paying the bill, Daniel stood up and held my coat for me. He tenderly pulled my ponytail out from under my collar — a small gesture, but one that tugged at my heart with its sweet simplicity. His attentiveness was unparalleled. As we left the restaurant, he looked around, always heedful of his surroundings.

"My car really is down in the underground parking lot," he said as we crossed the lobby. "Do you want me to drive you to Charles Street? Let you out at Bay maybe?"

"That would be great."

We emerged into the underground lot. It was virtually deserted, just a few cars parked here and there. Daniel's BMW was behind a pillar on the other side of the lot. As we walked, he placed his hand on my lower back. How I wished he could do that all the time.

"I really do appreciate this. I don't think I'd make it back to Jackman with both of my feet intact if I had to walk all the way."

"Not comfortable?" he asked, looking at my shoes.

"They're killing me," I said.

"That's unfortunate. I was considering asking you not to take them off ever again. They're incredibly sexy."

After looking around cautiously, he led me behind the pillar and stepped toward me, effectively trapping me against the passenger side door of his car. He clasped both of my hands and brought one of them up to his lips, brushing my knuckles with a gentle kiss. My breath caught in my throat. He leaned toward me, his hips pushing me back into the car door.

Oh my God, what was he doing? There was *nothing* cautious or guarded in his movements. My pulse raced, and I closed my eyes, dropping my head back. He let go of one of my hands and gently pulled my hair free of my ponytail, slipping the elastic hair tie into my pocket before pulling my hair around my face.

"God, you're beautiful," he breathed.

"Daniel, what are you doing?" I asked, licking my lips nervously.

"Do you want me to stop? Should I take you home right now?"

Did he really want an answer? Because there was no way in hell I was prepared to tell him to stop.

"Tell me, Aubrey, is that what you want?" he prodded.

Apparently he *did* want an answer. "Of course that's not what I want, Daniel. What I want is something you're not able to give me right now. I'm not blaming you, I'm really not, but that doesn't make it any easier to deal with."

"I'm sorry." He raked a hand through his hair in frustration. "I know it's not right to do this to you, telling you that we can't be together and then turning around and pawing at you like a horny teenager."

"You don't have to apologize," I said. "I understand. If you're feeling anything like I am right now, your brain is telling you one thing, but your body is telling you something *entirely* different." I took his hand and placed it on my cheek, pressing it there with my palm.

"That's it in a nutshell. I'm at a loss. What do *you* think I should do?" he asked, lightly trailing his fingers across my cheek.

"I really think you should kiss me," I whispered. There was absolutely nothing I wanted more in that moment than for his lips to be against mine. I couldn't allow myself to believe he wasn't going to kiss me until May.

He put his hands on his hips, grimaced, and looked away. "That is the worst possible thing I could do right now."

"Oh, really? How do you figure that?"

He sighed deeply. "You're familiar with the term Achilles' heel?"

"Uh-huh." I ran my fingertips along his jawline.

"Well, let's say the first hint of your tongue against mine, and you'd be over my shoulder and upstairs in one of those king-sized beds faster than you can say 'room service.'"

The mere mention of our tongues touching made me ache.

I moved my hand around to the nape of his neck and leaned forward, running my lips across his cheek. Kissing was his biggest weakness? Good Lord! How hot was that?

"I probably shouldn't have told you that," he said, his breath tickling my cheek.

"Probably not. It's not the best deterrent..."

I parted my lips and darted my tongue gently along his jaw, something I'd wanted to do for a mighty long time. He clasped the frame of the car door behind my shoulders.

"What are you trying to do to me?" he moaned, thrusting his hips forward and rubbing against me firmly.

"I like to think of it as research," I said.

I ran my hands up into his unbelievably soft hair, whimpering as my hands slipped through his locks.

He laughed gently. "I don't know what I'm going to do with you. I think I need to take you home so you can have a cold shower."

I grabbed his belt loops, pulling him against me. What I really wanted to do was grope him through his pants, but through some miracle I restrained myself.

"*Who* needs the cold shower?" I asked huskily, grinding against him.

"Ah, you women, always taking advantage of us poor men and our telltale physiological responses," he said with a strained chuckle.

"I believe I'm having a rather strong physiological response myself," I admitted, a naughty glint in my eye. "Care to do a little research of your own?"

He moaned and leaned down to whisper in my ear, "Fuck, Aubrey, you will definitely be the death of me." Taking a step back, he reached behind me to pinch my ass before pulling open the passenger side door. Cheeky bastard. "In the car, young lady," he ordered.

"Must I?" I pouted.

"Absolutely. If I don't get you home right now, something disastrous is bound to happen."

I looked at him demurely and batted my eyelashes. "Yes, sir."

I climbed into the car, smiling as I saw him adjust himself in his pants before getting in beside me. He started the car and grasped the steering wheel tightly, leaning against the headrest and taking a few deep, shaky breaths.

"This is madness," he said, shaking his head and winking at me. "Come on. Let's get you back."

While he drove, I tried to gain control of my own breathing. Three quick right turns and a mere five minutes later, we were pulling up to the curb on Charles Street. My mood deflated in an instant.

"Is this okay? Not too far to walk?" he asked, looking up the street to the residence buildings two blocks away.

"Sure, this'll be fine. Thanks for lunch, Daniel. I had an amazing afternoon." I didn't want to go. I could quite happily have spent the rest of the day with him, and the night…

He reached over and squeezed my hand. "I did too. And you're welcome. I wish we could spend more time together, but I really need to get some things done, and I meant what I said earlier. The longer we spend together, the weaker my resolve gets. I feel like I need to step away to regain my perspective, you know?"

"I understand completely." Did I ever. His proximity intoxicated me.

"But I'll see you tomorrow night?" he said. "Is it okay if I call you tomorrow so we can sort out plans?"

"Of course it's okay. You don't have to ask permission." I gathered up my purse and pulled on the door handle.

"Sorry I can't walk you there." He glanced out at the people walking by on the sidewalk. "But—"

"No, that's fine. You stay put," I said, opening the door and stepping out. Before I closed the door, I leaned back inside. "About tomorrow, can I make a request?"

"Fire away."

"Can you wear the jeans with the hole in the knee?"

He laughed. "What? Those ratty old things? Are you serious?"

"Completely. Best wardrobe malfunction I've ever seen," I said, staring longingly at his legs.

"If you promise to look at me like that all night, then hell yes." He chuckled, shaking his head.

"Oh, and, Daniel?"

"Yes, Aubrey?"

"Don't shave."

## A Fool for You

Viola: …I am not what I am.
Olivia: I would you were as I would have you be!
Viola: Would it be better, madam, than I am?
I wish it might, for now I am your fool.
(*Twelfth Night*, Act III, Scene 1)

Early Saturday afternoon, Matt and I were having lunch and getting caught up. As we talked, my mind wandered to the events of the previous day. Daniel clutching my pinkie during the memorial service. Daniel licking my fingers at the restaurant. Daniel pushing me against the door of his car…

I tried to concentrate on what Matt was saying and vaguely caught him telling me something about a film he was studying for one of his courses when my phone rang. I leaped up to grab it.

"Hello?"

"Aubrey?"

"Daniel!" I exclaimed.

Matt looked at me curiously. Shit, what was I doing?

"You sound surprised to hear from me. Is this a bad time?" Daniel asked.

"No, of course not. Give me a sec." I turned to Matt and pointed at the dishes on the table. "Leave this stuff, Matt. I'll help you clean up after, okay?" Matt waved me off and continued eating. "I need to grab my notes, Daniel. Hang on," I said, retreating to my room and closing the door behind me.

I breathed deeply, inexplicably winded. Why was I so excited to be talking to him on the phone? It was like I'd been transported back in time to grade ten.

"Hey, now I can talk."

"Are you in the middle of something? Am I interrupting?"

"No, no, Matt and I were having lunch," I explained. "I mentioned my notes because I needed an excuse to get out of the room. I thought that might justify your call, too."

There was a momentary silence. Was he annoyed that I'd blurted his name out?

"I can't believe I let your name slip in front of Matt. I was caught off guard. I'm sorry." I paused, waiting for an answer. "Daniel, are you still there?" I asked.

"Yes, I'm still here," he replied. "No need to apologize for that. I don't think it's a big deal." After a few seconds he sighed, and then his tone changed. "I'm sorry. The thought of you two together over there makes me frigging crazy."

I couldn't believe he was still harping on this.

"You've got to let it go. He's my roommate. End of story. Thinking you don't trust me kind of hurts." I sat on the end of my bed and picked at a piece of lint on my yoga pants.

"It's not you I'm worried about, poppet," he said. "I saw the way he looked at you that night a few weeks ago. I *know* that look, but it's not just that. I wish I could hang out with you all day like he does, doing mundane things like watching TV and eating lunch."

"Are you saying my life is mundane?"

"You know what I mean. Don't be difficult."

"Yes, I know what you mean," I said, flopping onto my back. "Any time you want to invite me over to the condo to watch TV, I'll be there in a heartbeat, you know that. Hell, I'd come over and watch paint dry with you."

"You, young lady, are like a dog with a bone." He laughed.

The tension was broken.

"Wouldn't I be more like a dog *without a bone?*" I joked.

He cleared his throat. "No comment. And wet paint or no, you know I can't have you over here," he said, his tone firm.

Sensible Daniel was back and in full control of the situation once more.

"Yes, dear," I said with an exasperated sigh.

"'Dear'? Oh, fuck. Call me anything, but please don't call me 'dear,'" he said. I could almost hear him cringing. "That's my mom and dad all over."

"Dear" wasn't generally part of my repertoire, but his reaction was enough to make me consider using the term more often just to push his buttons.

"Sorry, sweet knees. I didn't mean to make you feel like an old man," I said innocently. "Sure, you've got years on me and all, but—"

"Hey, easy now," he warned. "Don't be giving me a complex. I already have enough of those." He paused for a second. "Did you call me 'sweet knees'?"

"Oh, come on. You've gotta give me that one."

"It's a little too close to sweet *cheeks* for my liking," he said.

"Dude, let it go, *please*. Now tell me," I said, eager to lighten the tone and move the conversation away from Matt and my pet names for him, "am I going to get a look at one of those sweet knees tonight?"

Daniel sighed again. "Don't worry. Mr. Ratty Pants will be making an appearance this evening."

"Mr. Ratty Pants. I like that." I rolled onto my stomach. "Almost as good as Dr. Hobo."

"Who's Dr. Hobo?"

"You, of course. That's what I started calling you after seeing a few of your wardrobe choices."

He chuckled, which was a relief. I was worried he'd think me a total moron.

"But when you showed up at your parents' place last week, looking like a runway model, I decided to give your non-classroom alter-ego a name, too," I added.

"Huh, a runway model, eh?" he said. "And what, may I ask, was this other name?"

I could hear the smile in his voice; his mood seemed to be lifting.

I cleared my throat. "Um, Mr. *GQ*," I mumbled.

This time he laughed in that uncontrolled giggly way I loved. It was so great to hear him sounding like himself again. "Are you serious?" he said.

"Yeah, well, that's nothing compared to Julie's name for you."

"Oh, please, do tell," he begged, still laughing.

"Don't you dare tell her I told you."

"Scout's honor."

"Well, she calls you…Mr. Shmexy."

"Jesus, do I even want to know what the two of you have been talking about for the last month?"

"Probably not. And even if you did, I don't think I'd tell you. Pretty soon someone's gonna need to take a large hatpin to your over-sized ego," I said.

"Hey, everyone's ego needs stroking once in a while." He was all seriousness now.

"After the week we've had, something else needs some stroking too, don't you think?"

"All right, missy, get your ass over here right now! I'm painting a wall as we speak!" he said, a tone of mock urgency in his voice.

"You keep painting. I'll be there in fifty-four days," I said casually.

"Goddamn that calendar. Maybe it wasn't such a good idea." He sighed.

"Hey, I happen to love that calendar, but I sure wish I knew more about all the artwork inside. I need Julie to explain all the reproductions to me."

"Speaking of Julie…"

"Uh-oh. That sounds ominous."

"Not really. I've been doing some thinking about what you said yesterday—how you wished you didn't have to hide the truth from Julie?" He paused, and I held my breath. "As hard as this is for me, I've got J and Brad and Penny to talk to, but you? You've got nobody. It hardly seems fair. Julie seems to be a great friend, and she'd never do anything to hurt you, right?"

"Right. Absolutely," I said.

He sighed again.

"Telling her about us will make things a little more uncomfortable for me, but I'm willing to take one for the team if that'll make things easier for you — as long as you can guarantee that she can be trusted not to tell anyone. No room for doubt."

"I can't think of another friend I trust more right now, except maybe Matt," I said. Again, his name evoked silence. "Daniel?"

"I'm here," he said flatly.

"Okay, how about we don't talk about *him* anymore. Deal?" I asked.

"Deal," he said. "So, what do you think? Do you want to tell her?"

"That's up to you. The lies are killing me, but I don't think I have any right to make that kind of demand."

"Then it's decided. Tell her tonight. It'll make the outing a hell of a lot less uncomfortable."

"I can see your point there, but I can't just spring it on her at the benefit."

"Why don't you invite her over to your place so you can go over together? Maybe you could soften her up by telling her about Jeremy."

"Are you serious? You want to tell her about that too?"

"The look on his face when I told him I was going out tonight with the two of you? I couldn't continue putting up road blocks. He's definitely interested in joining us."

"Wow. Okay, then. So, when I tell her about us, what am I allowed to share? I don't want to overstep."

"Well, how about telling her we've met outside of class a few times to discuss school issues, found that we get along well and have a lot in common, and we're thinking maybe there could be a future for us…"

He trailed off, and I considered his words. *There could be a future for us.* That could be interpreted in so many ways.

"That's pretty open-ended," I said. "How about I put it this way: Is there anything you *don't* want me to tell her?"

"You can tell her where and when we've gotten together, but could you hold back some of the, um, sordid *details* of our encounters?" he added, chuckling sheepishly.

I could tell he was smiling. I could almost see him shaking his head.

"But I *can* tell her about dinner at your parents' place?" I asked.

"That's a good starting point since that night seems to have been the catalyst, and that's how you met Jeremy," he said.

"Can I say, for the record, I'm so glad your dad invited me to dinner that night?" I said.

Without missing a beat, Daniel replied, "Can *I* say, for the record, I'm so glad my plans in Ottawa fell through that night? I'm especially glad you don't know how to play snooker."

I remembered the way his chin dropped and his eyes became lidded whenever he spoke to me this way. I had a sudden overwhelming urge to be in his arms and felt a physical pang at his distance.

"Hey, sailor?" I whispered.

"Yes, poppet?"

"I miss you," I said.

"Oh, I miss you too," he replied. "My arms miss you. My hands *really* miss you."

Good Lord, where did he come up with this stuff?

"I don't know how much longer I can keep up the pretense, Daniel. It's so hard being near you and seeming indifferent. Tonight's going to be difficult, you know, after yesterday."

"I *do* know, believe me. I was a mess yesterday. Julie wasn't the only one giving us funny looks."

"What do you mean?"

"I think Cara caught me looking at you in the church. She seemed quite interested in the proceedings. She worries me."

"All the more reason for you to behave yourself tonight, mister," I reminded him.

"I could say the same for you. Will you be able to control yourself when you catch sight of my incredibly sweet knee in the ratty pants?"

"You're right." I laughed. "I'll be a puddle, there's no doubt about it. So, um, are you wearing them now?" I asked, closing my eyes to get a visual.

"As a matter of fact, I am," he replied, voice sultry and low.

I sighed, playing along. "What shirt are you wearing?" I prodded.

"A plain black T-shirt."

"Mmm, nice." Now I just needed to complete the picture. "What are you wearing on your feet?"

"My feet? Nothing. I got out of the shower right before I called you."

Daniel, fresh from the shower in the peekaboo-knee jeans with bare feet. Good Lord.

"Aubrey?" he asked. "Are we having phone sex?"

"Don't interrupt. I wasn't finished."

"Okay, sorry." He snickered. "What else do you need to know, to, um, finish?" he asked.

"You didn't shave, right?"

"No, that instruction was perfectly clear."

"Good. And where are you? I mean, are you in your bedroom or living room?" I asked.

"I'm in the living room. I was about to play some guitar," he said.

"You're kidding."

"Nope."

I heard the sound of guitar strings being plucked. I moaned, low and throaty. Although I was kidding around, the visual *was* beginning to make me feel a little overheated.

"Finished?" he asked.

"Yeah, that pushed me over the edge." I let out an exaggerated moan of satisfaction. "For now, at least."

"You crack me up."

"I'm glad I amuse you."

"You do. And I dearly wish you could amuse me all afternoon, but I should get back to marking. I've almost finished these *Hamlet* papers."

"I'll let you go," I said. "I need to finish rereading *Antony and Cleopatra* anyway."

"Shall we meet outside Brennan Hall at eight thirty?" he asked.

"That sounds good," I said. "I'll text you if I need to."

"Sounds like a plan. Good luck with Julie. And sorry about earlier," he added. "Missing you makes me irrational. I can't stand the thought of another man being that close to you when I have to keep my distance. It's so frustrating."

"I can see that, Daniel, but I have a life and friends and other relationships that are important to me."

"I know. Look, I'll see you in a few hours, my sweet. I'm looking forward to it."

"Me too. Bye."

"Bye," he said softly.

And then he was gone. I smiled at my bedroom ceiling, completely overwhelmed by my feelings for him. At the same time, there was a vague apprehension brewing in the back of my mind. Was his overreaction to my relationship with Matt really a result of the imposed restrictions on us, or was he prone to a possessiveness that would threaten my relationships with others? I realized with sudden clarity that my apprehension was coupled with another emotion: Guilt. Here I was, denying any connection to Matt beyond friendship, when no more than three weeks ago I'd been lying on this very bed with Matt's lips and body pressed against mine.

I tossed my phone on the dresser before heading out to the kitchen. Matt was starting to clean up. I helped him bring the last of the dishes to the sink and filled it with hot, sudsy water.

"So, that was your TA, right? Do you make a habit of talking to him on the phone?" he asked.

"Oh, um, not really. We had a meeting scheduled yesterday to talk about my ISU. We canceled because of the memorial I was telling you about, so he called instead."

My face always burned when I lied. I tried to hide my heated blush from Matt by staying intently focused on the plates and cups in the sink.

"He's pretty keen on going out of his way to help you. Driving you home after the play that night, and now phoning you…"

"Yeah, he's a decent guy. My English class is small. He's got a good rapport with everyone."

Matt grunted in reply, seeming to accept my explanation that Daniel wasn't favoring me in any particular way. He continued crashing around in the cupboards putting away pots and pans. I took the opportunity to change the subject.

"So, what are you up to tonight?"

"Shawn called earlier. I'm heading out with him later." He paused in his noisy clean up. "He was talking about you."

"Really?" I looked at him over my shoulder.

"Yeah, he saw you at that service you went to yesterday. Said you looked hot."

"Get out." I flushed again and grimaced as I turned back to the sink. Shawn Ward? He'd never shown me the slightest bit of interest. Why now?

"I'm serious. He even asked me if I thought you'd go with him to the Kap party next Friday—the semi-formal?"

I'd seen flyers for the Kap party. The slogan was:*"It's Friday the 13th— Bad Shit Will Happen—Look Good When It Does. "* I had no plans to go to a semi-formal without Daniel; since his attendance was out of the question, so was mine.

"I don't think I'll be going."

"Why not? You should get out—have some fun. Maybe you'll meet a guy. Or go with Shawn, you know."

He frowned and went back to shoving things into the cabinet. Why was he pushing Shawn on me?

"If the events of the last Friday the thirteenth were an omen, I think it's best if I stay home," I said.

"You puked because you were sick, Aub. That has nothing to do with the date and everything to do with germs," he said, flicking my ass with the dish towel. I grabbed it from him to dry my hands.

"I'll see. Right now I need to call Julie to invite her over before we head to a benefit at Brennan Hall. It's a MADD fundraiser, kind of a tribute to the girl that died."

"Really? What time's she coming over?"

"I was thinking seven o'clock."

"Shit, I'll be gone by then. That's too bad. I haven't seen Jul since last year. Remember when she drank that whole pitcher of mojitos I made? That was a good night."

"I remember some of it." I laughed, tossing the dish towel at him before heading off to my room to phone Julie. As usual she was on the fly, but I managed to convince her to come over around seven before heading to the benefit. As I hung up, I started planning the big reveal. How on earth was I going to tell Julie the truth about Daniel and me?

Without warning, a vision of a guitar-playing, bare-foot, holey-jeans-wearing Daniel distracted me from my agonizing thoughts.

And I was okay with that.

At six thirty, I was ready and waiting for Julie. A note on the counter from Matt told me to look in the fridge for a big surprise. There, in a large glass jug, was a pitcher of mojitos. Maybe some liquid courage would help me tell Julie about me and Daniel.

I grabbed a small glass and conducted a taste-test. Sinfully good—exactly the way I remembered. I couldn't resist pouring myself another, and I'd just knocked it back when the buzzer sounded. I let Julie into the building and waited for her in the apartment's open doorway. As soon as she was close enough, I pulled her into a hug. I squeezed way too hard, anxious about our impending conversation.

"Aubrey, you're crushing me," she gasped. "You been taking lessons from the bruiser? Where is he, anyway?" she asked, looking around the apartment.

"Matt's gone out with Ward."

"That sucks. I was kinda hoping to see the hunk. You know, get one of *his* rib-crushing hugs in person."

"He was hoping to see you too," I said, leading her into the kitchen. "He left you a treat." I opened the fridge and pulled out the pitcher.

"Oh my God! Mint leaves! Is that what I think it is?" she asked, wide-eyed.

"Yep. I had a small glass before you got here to make sure it's fit for company."

I poured out two large glasses, and we clinked before we each took a swig.

"That's divine," she sighed. "He's got a gift, I swear."

"Come on." I grabbed the pitcher in one hand and my glass in the other. "I still have to do my makeup." I led her to my room and turned on my iPod dock. Julie flopped onto the bed as I put on some mascara.

"Aubrey, I don't know what it is, but you're looking super-hot these days," Julie said appreciatively.

"I am?" I looked at myself critically in the mirror. All I saw was the same old me.

"Yeah, you're kind of glowy. And look at your legs and ass in those jeans!" Julie crawled across the bed and knelt behind me.

"You don't think my legs are too skinny?"

"Too skinny? What the hell are you talking about?"

"I don't know. I feel all gangly." An image of Penny and her curves sprang up in my mind's eye.

Julie sighed and moved around to lean on my dresser facing me.

"You have amazing legs. Other women would kill for these gams. And your ass is hot and you know it," she said, looking at me through narrowed eyes.

Yeah, okay, I'd give her that.

"And don't let me hear you complain about your boobs or skin," she warned. "Not to mention your hair, and your eyes. God, listen to me. I sound like I'm about to switch teams!" She laughed.

She was such a great friend. I dreaded having to admit I'd been lying to her.

"Listen," she said. "I think I know what's going on. I'm feeling a little down on myself right now too. I've been so busy with dance that I haven't even bothered with dating, but there's no logical reason why guys aren't falling at *your* feet. Maybe you're giving off bad vibes or something. I bet if you hold your head up high and tell yourself you are *so* worthy of a hot guy's attention, the men will be lining up at your door in no time."

I looked at her, biting my lip. "Well, let's say, theoretically, that there *is* a hot guy I'm interested in, and, for argument's sake, let's say he's interested in me, too."

"What?" she exclaimed. "There *is* a hot guy? Oh my God, I want to hear everything!" She dragged me to the end of my bed.

"I don't know where to start," I said.

"Well, where did you meet him? How long have you known him? What's his name? Did he tell you he likes you?" She didn't give me time to answer in between.

"I met him in a class—"

"Really? So you already have something in common. That's awesome. What's he like?" she prompted.

"Um, well, he's smart, he's kind, he's really funny—"

"Oh, no, this has 'he's got a great personality' written all over it." Julie winced.

"No, no, it's not that at all. He's tall, super-hot, great ass, eyes to die for, incredible hair, and the most amazing jawline—God, there are no words…"

"Oh my gosh! He sounds perfect," she said.

"He's pretty wonderful, but it's not all sunshine and roses. It's actually kind of complicated."

I reached for the pitcher and refilled our glasses. How to proceed? This was all kinds of heinous.

"Complicated? In what way?" she asked.

"Well, we can't *go public*, I guess you'd say." I was choosing my words carefully, trying not to blurt everything out all at once.

"Why not?"

"Um, well, he's a TA, so the whole anti-fraternizing thing, you know — "

I spoke hesitantly, watching Julie's face for signs of comprehension. Suddenly, her eyes widened and her jaw dropped.

She started talking to herself: "What did you say? Tall, great ass, nice eyes, incredible hair, amazing jawline? Holy shit, no way! Oh. My. God! You can't be serious?" Yeah, she'd hit pay dirt. Her eyes shone with amazement.

"Yeah, I am," I said.

She stood up and walked across my room like she was in a daze, then turned and walked back, coming to rest against my dresser with her drink in one hand and her other hand on her hip.

"You know what? I should be in total shock right now. But I'm not. I *knew it*. I even asked you yesterday what was going on between you and Daniel, and you played dumb," she said.

"I know, Jul, I'm sorry."

"How long?"

"Not long. Only a week. Everything happened so fast and totally by accident."

I told her about the dinner at the Grants, and how Daniel had gotten drunk and revealed his feelings for me. I left out the gory details of the snooker lesson, essentially telling her that his guard was down and he told me things he might not otherwise have said.

"So every time I saw you or talked to you this week, you and Daniel were an item? I can't believe you didn't tell me. No, let me rephrase that — I can't believe you *lied* to me!"

"You must get why we're not broadcasting this? He's a TA. There are rules."

"Newsflash, Aubrey—the way you guys were looking at each other yesterday? *Totally* broadcasting. You might as well have been wearing red heart-shaped beacons. Besides, I'm your friend. Don't you trust me?"

"Of course I trust you, Jul."

I reached for her hand, but she snatched her fingers from my grasp as if she'd just touched a hot stove. Her face had turned red. She put her shaking hand on the dresser for support.

"I feel like an idiot. You let me keep rambling on about how hot he is and all the while you two are hooking up? You had a good laugh at this behind my back, huh? Stupid oblivious Julie."

"Not at all. It's not like that—" I reached for her again and she backed up. "Will you just let me explain?"

She put her hand up in front of my face. "I can't talk to you right now." She started crossing the room.

"Julie, you're not going to tell anyone, right?"

She spun around, her eyes blazing. "God, I can't believe you just said that! What kind of person do you think I am?"

I helplessly trailed after her as she rushed out into the living room, slipped her shoes on, and grabbed her coat. She yanked the door open and dashed out to the hallway.

"Julie, please don't go!"

She didn't turn around, pushing her way through the door to the stairwell and disappearing. The door closed with a hollow click. I stood, staring down the empty hallway, before giving a resigned sigh and heading back into the apartment. I grabbed both my phone and my mojito, downing the rest of it before sending Daniel a text message.

**Disaster. Julie just stormed out.**
**She's super pissed at me. -A**

I poured myself another and sat on my bed to wait for a response from Daniel. A couple of minutes later, my phone rang.

"Aubrey?"

"Daniel! Where are you?"

"We're at a pub on Yonge Street. I've just stepped outside. So, things didn't go well?"

"Nope. Not well at all. She is *so* angry."

"Really? I honestly didn't think she'd react that way. She seems pretty even-keeled. What happened?"

"I explained everything like you suggested, left out all the gory details, said we were playing it safe. At first I thought she was okay, but she kind of zeroed in on the lying thing and then took off. I don't think we'll be seeing her tonight."

"Shit, that's not good. You don't think—she wouldn't say anything—"

"Don't even go there, Daniel. I came right out and asked her that, and she flipped her wig. She's mad at me, but she's not vindictive. She won't do anything to hurt you."

"Good. Well, not good that she's mad, but—"

"I know what you mean," I told him. "It's okay. So what now?"

"Well, I guess I'll tell Jeremy he won't be seeing her tonight. He'll be disappointed."

"No offense, but Jeremy is the least of my worries right now."

"Of course. Look, as ugly as this all is, I don't want to cancel our evening. Penny and Brad are here. They decided to join us at the benefit."

"Really? They're all there, and they know we're…kind of involved?"

"They know everything and they think I'm marginally insane, but they'll cover for me with my dad. Don't worry. They've got my back. Yours too."

"Okay. That's good," I said, feeling a bit doubtful.

"Hey, chin up. This'll all work out."

I sighed. "I don't know."

"Don't worry, my love. I know you're upset about Julie, but everything will be fine. She needs a chance to digest everything, that's all. I'll head back inside and finish my drink. Can you meet us in front of Brennan in forty-five minutes?"

The rest of the conversation was a blur. As I hung up the phone, I felt a surge of butterflies in my stomach. Yes, I was worried about Julie, and, no, I wasn't convinced that everything would be fine, but in that moment I was too busy processing the fact that he'd just called me "my love" to think about anything else.

## Satisfaction

What satisfaction canst thou have to-night?
(*Romeo and Juliet*, Act II, Scene 2)

**W**as it wrong that I was excited as I made my way to Brennan Hall forty-five minutes later? My desire to see Daniel completely overshadowed my anxiety over Julie's reaction to the news I'd shared with her. Maybe she was right to question our friendship. I hardly recognized myself.

It was cold out, but I was strangely warm. Heightened anticipation — and three very large mojitos drunk in rapid succession — can do that to a person. As I neared Brennan Hall, I saw Daniel and Jeremy leaning against the wall of the building. Penny was huddled against Brad, her back to his chest as he rubbed her arms to warm her up. A hot flame of envy licked at my stomach. I couldn't wait to behave the same way with Daniel.

Daniel caught sight of me and propelled himself away from the wall with a push of his foot, a casual but incredibly sexy move. In the glow of the floodlights outside the building, I quickly took stock of his appearance. He'd paired the blessed holey jeans with one of his leather jackets and a well-traveled pair of black boots. He looked so hot I actually wanted to cry at the thought of not being able to grab him and kiss him fiercely.

The only disappointing part of his ensemble was the baseball cap which hid his hair and his face, but perhaps the hat had its advantages because he truly looked like a third or fourth year student out for a night of fun. Was this a premeditated decision—an attempt at going out incognito? As I neared him, he sized me up in return, his eyes lingering over my legs. He shook his head and smiled as I stopped in front of him.

"Hey, gorgeous," he said, his voice audible only to me. "If the ratty pants have one-tenth the effect on you as those jeans you're wearing are having on me, we are in *serious* trouble, Miss Price."

"Then we're in big, big trouble," I whispered, winking at him. I took in the whiskers on his chin and along his jawline. Further research was definitely required. Unfortunately, this would have to wait.

"I'm determined to behave myself tonight," he said. "But you seem equally determined to make that difficult, crazy legs." He smiled at me, the dimple making its first appearance of the night.

"Right, you two. Break it up," Penny said, stepping between us. "You're both dreadful at being discreet." She pulled me into a quick hug. "It's so nice to see you again. The playing field's changed a tad since we last met, hasn't it? And I gather everything went a bit pear-shaped this evening?"

I smiled weakly and nodded. "If that means things didn't go smoothly with Julie, then, yes, I suppose you could say that."

"Well, chin up. I'm sure she needs a little time to sort out her feelings. Wounded pride, that's all. I wouldn't start scouting for a new best mate yet." She looked over my shoulder at Daniel. "Oy, you randy bugger, quit ogling her arse and put your tongue back in your mouth."

"Busted, bro," Brad said, laughing at Daniel's sheepish expression.

Jeremy was standing off to one side, looking a little lost.

"Sorry things didn't work out with Julie," I said to him. "I know you were hoping to see her tonight."

"Hey, no biggie. Next time." He stuffed his hands in his pockets and nodded his head toward the doors of the building. "Let's head inside," he suggested. "Penny's freezing."

Penny linked her arm through mine, and we all filed into the vestibule outside the auditorium where a line had formed. From the hall, intermittent guitar chords and drum beats interspersed with sound checks drifted out to the lobby. A table was set up near the double doors to the hall where they were selling the admission tickets.

"I've got this," Daniel said. He walked away to buy the tickets before anyone had a chance to protest.

"Best get used to that, doll. Daniel is generous. Don't ever try to argue with him. He'll get pissy with you," Penny said.

"Thanks for the tip."

Daniel came back and handed us each a ticket, and we lined up together. Jeremy checked phone messages. Brad and Penny were oblivious to their surroundings, but Daniel and I constantly scanned the crowd around us.

Daniel took stock of the line. "Lots of people. This is good. They'll make some decent coin. It must be satisfying to raise money for a good cause."

He began to talk about his mother's volunteer involvement in MADD, explaining the complexities of administration fees for charities. I tried to pay attention, but having such a close-up view of his lips made it difficult to process his words. And he smelled of beer and leather. Delicious.

"You had a pint or two, I gather?" I asked him.

He laughed. "Talk about changing the subject! But, yes, I had a couple."

"What kind?"

"Your favorite." He smirked, turning around to face the doors, his back to Penny and Brad.

"Guinness?" I asked. "You know, that's my favorite as long as *you're* drinking it. In fact, I'm considering buying shares in the company. Say, do you know if there are any pool tables in Brennan Hall?"

"Careful, young lady," he warned, his voice low. "No PDEs tonight, okay?"

"Don't you mean PDA?" I'd heard of public displays of affection referred to as PDAs, but I'd never heard of the acronym "PDE."

"No. While they're inadvisable too, PDEs are *strictly* prohibited this evening."

I frowned. "Public displays of *emotion?*" I whispered.

He shook his head. "No. Think physiological reactions, Miss Price," he said, speaking out of the side of his mouth, his eyes darting down to his crotch.

"Oh, PD*Es!* Gotcha!" I laughed. I was going to have to disagree with him, though. I'd always been quite fond of *those* kinds of displays.

"What are you two nattering on about?" Penny asked, nosily leaning in between us.

"Nothing important," Daniel told her.

"I had a small bone to pick with Daniel, Penny. That's all," I said.

Daniel shook his head. "I guarantee there's nothing small about it," he whispered in my ear before grinning in a self-satisfied way.

*Well, I should certainly hope not.*

The line finally moved, and we were admitted into the hall. As we entered, I stopped to take a look at the MADD display. A large screen showed slides of Mary with her friends and family in various locations and at different events. Off to the side there was a table with fliers and information packages provided by Mothers Against Drunk Driving. Two middle-aged women stood behind the table giving out red ribbons and pamphlets.

"Is this the kind of thing your mom would normally organize?" I asked Daniel.

"No, not usually. She's more involved in the higher-end events," he explained. "Galas and that sort of thing."

"She knows about this fundraiser, though," Penny said. "She was talking about it today. Got a little weepy, bless her. That's how Brad and I found out about it. No thanks to Daniel."

Penny looked at Daniel disapprovingly. He shrugged.

"How was I to know you'd be interested in something like this? It doesn't seem to be your cup of tea, Penn," he said unapologetically. "Anyway, we're here now, so quit bitching and let's grab a table." He led us as far away from the makeshift stage as possible. "You don't mind if we sit at the back, do you?" he asked me.

"No, that's probably a good idea."

We reached a long table against the cushioned benches at the back of the room. An attempt had been made to create an atmosphere. Red tablecloths were placed on all the tables, and a small votive candle glowed in the center of each. Organizers were distributing bowls of chips and pretzels.

"Have you heard from Julie?" Daniel asked as he scanned the room.

I checked my phone for messages. "Nope. Nothing."

"I was hoping she might have texted you by now," he said.

"Daniel, love, you're an eternal optimist," Penny said, rubbing his back affectionately.

Daniel pulled a chair out for me. He and Jeremy moved to the other side of the table, sliding into the padded bench. He unzipped his jacket, shrugging out of both his coat and the dark hoodie he wore underneath. His black T-shirt hugged his chest magnificently and allowed me to see his toned biceps for the first time.

I smiled as I settled in, taking off my own coat and mitts.

"What?" he asked.

"Nothing, it's nothing," I assured him as I tried to tear my eyes away from his arms. "Can you toss these on the bench?" I handed him my gloves, and he tucked them behind him. This was a small thing, like the subtle pressure of his hand on my back when we walked, or the gentle sweeping of my hair from my collar. Nonetheless, it made me feel like we were a couple. I began to realize that in a relationship like ours where discretion was key, the tiniest gestures were going to seem so much more intimate.

Brad sat beside me, and Penny moved around to sit next to Daniel. That struck me as odd. I'd thought for certain Penny would sit with me. Brad leaned on his hand and looked at me. "We're glad you're giving my brother a chance, even though he probably doesn't deserve it and he's got some serious baggage, right, beauty?"

Penny nodded. "He can be a right prat sometimes. But you'll get used to it."

Daniel made a great show of being highly offended. "Hello? I'm right here."

Penny tweaked his chin playfully, but he batted at her hand, moving it away from his face as his eyes locked on the doors across the hall. I turned to follow his intense gaze, and there, inside the doorway, was Julie. She was standing still, her arms crossed as she surveyed the room.

"See?" Daniel said. "She needed some time to think, that's all."

Jeremy sat up a little taller to get a good look at Julie, a small smile tugging at his mouth. Julie's eyes finally landed on us, but she didn't move.

Daniel bobbed his head at me. "I think maybe she's waiting for you to go over there."

"I think you're right." I stood and took a deep breath. "Wow, head rush," I said, feeling woozy all of a sudden. I put my hand on the chair to steady myself.

"You okay?" Daniel asked, leaning forward.

"Yeah, I'm good. I probably stood up too quickly."

*Oh, and have I mentioned I boat-raced three mojitos about thirty minutes ago, handing myself the baton at the end of each round? No? Oops. Small oversight.*

"Wish me luck," I said. Daniel smiled at me encouragingly.

I crossed the room to join Julie. When I approached, she left the hall, indicating that I should go with her. I followed her into the women's washroom. As the door closed softly behind me, she leaned against the counter by the sinks, her arms crossed. She didn't exactly look conciliatory.

"Hey," I said. I didn't move toward her. My legs felt rubbery.

"Hey."

"Did you want to talk?" I asked, prompting her.

"Yes, I did. But now you're here, I'm not sure what to say," she admitted.

"Okay, well, maybe you can let me explain, and then you'll think of something?" I offered.

I took a shaky step toward her. "Julie, not telling you about what happened this week was one of the hardest things I've ever had to do, not just because I was excited and wanted to share, but because you're a great friend and I hated hiding the truth from you. He's not a bad person. This thing between us just kind of happened. It wasn't planned. He never intended to put himself in this kind of compromising situation."

Julie listened intently, not reacting, but at least she was giving me her full attention.

"I *really* like him. He's...well, he's amazing. He pleaded for discretion and asked for my word. I couldn't deny him that. We didn't mean to hurt you, or make a fool of you in any way. I know that's the way it seems, but that was never, ever our intention. Can you forgive me? Forgive us?"

Julie sighed and smiled wistfully. "I already have, Aubrey. I shouldn't have overreacted earlier, but I was hurt. No one likes to be made a fool of or considered untrustworthy."

"I know. I'm so sorry. He needed some time to figure out what to do. I wanted to tell you, but it wasn't my decision to make."

Julie stepped toward me with arms outstretched. I gratefully wrapped mine around her and squeezed hard. Within seconds, we were both crying, and then, just as quickly, laughing at ourselves and our ridiculous sentimentality.

"Sorry," I said, catching my tears to stop the flow of mascara down my face. "I'm a mess."

"Same." She sniffed and pinched some color into her cheeks.

"Let's head inside. His brothers and his best friend are here. They're great. You'll love them. They're all excited to meet you."

*Especially Jeremy.* Julie was in for quite a surprise. Hopefully it would be a better one than the shock I'd dealt her back at Jackman.

"Okay, but promise me we'll make time for some girl talk this week? Just you and me, promise? I mean, you and *Daniel?* I need deets!"

"There honestly aren't many deets to share, but don't worry, we'll figure something out."

We both gave ourselves a quick once-over in the mirror and then headed back into the hall, squeezing past the groups of milling people to our table, where everyone was waiting expectantly for our return. Jeremy looked like he was going to burst with excitement.

"Okay. Julie, this is Brad, Daniel's older brother, and this is Brad's fiancée, Penny. Guys, this is Julie Harper."

Julie gave a little wave to Penny and Brad. They both welcomed her warmly.

"And this," I said, gesturing with a hand, "is Jeremy, Daniel's *younger* brother."

Jeremy stood up, bashful all of a sudden as he reached out to shake her hand.

"It's nice to meet you, Julie," he said. "I was at the indie music revue a few weeks back at the Revival, and I think we stood in line at the bar together. You probably don't remember…" He trailed off awkwardly.

"No, I'm sorry; I don't remember. It *was* pretty crowded."

"Yeah, no worries. It was packed."

Jeremy was being gracious, but I could see that he was disappointed. I gave him a quick reassuring smile.

*Don't give up too easily.*

"Hi, Julie," Daniel said, smiling apologetically. "I'm sorry about all this."

"That's Ms. Harper to you, Daniel," Julie chirped sweetly. "And please don't mention it again. I'll take an A-plus on my first paper and we'll consider it water under the bridge."

Daniel chuckled. "Right. Well, we'll see about that."

"Okay, enough shop talk, and no more bloody drama," Penny said, taking command of the situation. "I've just eaten enough salt to sink a small river barge." She gestured to the pretzels. "I'm going to grab drinks. Jeremy, come with me, love."

Brad started to get up. "I'll grab them with you, beauty."

"No, no, you stay. Jeremy?"

Jeremy stood reluctantly, and he and Penny made their way to the drinks table.

"What's that all about?" Brad asked.

"My guess is she was removing Jeremy for a moment in case there's anything else we need to get Julie up to speed on," Daniel surmised.

"What do you mean?" Julie asked.

"What he means," I said, "is that Jeremy hasn't talked about anything but you since the moment he saw you at the Revival."

"Seriously?" Her eyes widened.

"Seriously," I said. "Smitten kitten, bun-head."

"Huh." She took a quick peek over her shoulder. "He *is* pretty cute."

"Wait until you get to know him, Jul. He's amazing."

Julie turned to look at Daniel. "How do you feel about all this?"

Daniel threw his hands up in the air in mock exasperation. "What the hell. Keeps life interesting, right? But I don't want to hear details if you hit it off. Not from either one of you."

"Dude, they've barely spoken to each other," Brad pointed out.

"I just want to make sure my position's clear from the get-go," Daniel said. "I'm sure you understand my concerns, Julie. This complicates things—that's why I was so reluctant to let Aubrey tell you everything."

"I get it, Daniel. I thought about it and I understand," she assured him. "Man, it's so weird hearing you call me *Julie*. You sound *way* less uptight."

"Well, thank you—I think," Daniel said hesitantly. "Don't blow my cover, though. I kind of like the uptight TA bit."

"Don't worry. Your secret is safe with me." Julie smiled at me wryly. "All of your secrets are safe."

Daniel nodded. "Aubrey trusts you implicitly, and I trust her judgment."

"If there's anything I can do to make things easier or more comfortable, I'll do my best to help." Julie squeezed my hand under the table and smiled at Daniel. "I wasn't joking about the A-plus," she added.

He shook his head and laughed, but then his smile disappeared as he squinted across the room. I looked over my shoulder. Penny and Jeremy were in line for drinks, and Penny was in the midst of an animated conversation with Matt. I'd had no idea Matt was planning to come by.

Brad turned to follow Daniel's dark gaze. "Who the fuck is that?" he asked with a scowl.

"That's Aubrey's *roommate*, Matt Miller. Apparently he made a bit of an impression on Penny when we were at Canoe a few weeks back."

I rolled my eyes at Daniel and looked back to see Penny laughing and touching Matt's arm. My God, she was an outrageous flirt. Matt was lapping it up, smiling widely and leaning in to whisper in her ear. Beside them, Jeremy watched with interest.

"You might want to start advertising for a new roommate, Aubrey, 'cause he's gonna have trouble signing the rent checks with two broken arms," Brad said.

"You want some help?" Daniel said, glowering across the table at his brother.

"Wow, what's with the hate for Matt?" Julie asked me.

"I think they're a wee bit jealous," I whispered, though I knew for a fact that Daniel's jealousy of Matt wasn't exactly *wee*.

"He's looking really good," Julie said, continuing her appraisal of Matt.

"Yeah, he's hitting the gym pretty regularly. You know, boxing, lifting weights, running."

"You know the guy who's with him?" Brad asked.

"Yes, that's Shawn Ward. Completely harmless," Daniel said.

*Oh, the irony.* Daniel was worrying about Matt and discounting Shawn as a threat. Meanwhile, according to Matt, Shawn was considering making a play for me.

"Fuck, give me a break," Daniel muttered, looking contemptuously over Brad's shoulder. I glanced behind me to see Matt helping Penny and Jeremy carry the drinks back to our table.

"Look who I found!" Penny exclaimed as she maneuvered back into her spot on the bench. "Guys, this is Matt, Aubrey's roommate."

Brad muttered an unenthusiastic, "Hey."

"Yes, we've met," Daniel answered cursorily.

Matt seemed oblivious to their disdain. He put the two drinks in front of Penny and said, "Hey, how ya doing?" to no one in particular and then made a beeline for Julie, who jumped up to accept his hug.

"How are ya, dancing queen?" he asked, lifting her at least a foot off the floor.

Julie squealed. "I'm good. How the hell are *you?* You look great!"

Matt stepped back and smiled, shrugging. "I'm hanging in there. You know how it is."

"Do you want to join us?" Julie offered.

Matt looked around the table. Daniel and Brad were still frowning.

"Thanks, but Shawn and I are meeting some people at the Brunswick House in a bit. We just came by 'cause Shawn wanted to show his support. I should head back. But let's get together soon, okay? Get Aubrey to set something up." He ruffled my hair affectionately as he spoke. Daniel wasn't impressed. Matt wasn't helping my case in the slightest.

"Okay. We'll have to do something soon," she said.

"Absolutely. Okay, have a good night. Penny, guys, nice to meet you. Aubs, see you for pancakes at eleven."

*Oh God, Matt. Shut up!*

"Cheers, love." Penny flashed him a beautiful smile.

Matt turned and made his way through the crowd, rejoining Shawn on the other side of the hall. Once Matt had disappeared from view, Daniel relaxed his shoulders.

"Bloody hell, that young man is serious VFM," Penny said with a cheeky smile.

"What's that?" Julie whispered to me.

"No frigging clue. I didn't bring my Penny-as-a-second-language dictionary," I said, looking around the table helplessly.

"VFM is 'value for money,'" Daniel clarified, his tone cool. "Penny happens to think Mr. Miller delivers a lot of bang for the buck."

"I don't see the big deal," Brad complained.

"Well, I'm only making an observation. Don't get your knickers in a twist. It's not like I fancy him or anything, darling." Penny winked at him and blew him a little air kiss. He appeared mildly placated.

I wondered if Daniel found Penny and Brad's affectionate gestures contagious because I know I certainly did. I longed to join in. I tried to catch his eye, but he was looking around the room, avoiding my gaze entirely.

"Besides, I'm not into cradle robbing," Penny said. "How old is he anyway, Aubrey?" she asked.

"He's twenty-two," I said.

"Good Christ, I have socks older than him." Penny laughed.

"Oh, sure, beauty, you're ancient. I should consider trading you in for a younger model," Brad joked, turning and making a big show of scanning the room for potential candidates.

Penny joined him in perusing the crowd. "Nope. Sorry, love, I don't see the perfect woman anywhere." She looked around the table with a cheeky smile. "You all know Brad's ideal woman is three feet tall, with no teeth, and a flat head for him to put his beer on?"

We all collapsed into laughter. She was an absolute wing nut. I was grateful for her joke, though, because Matt was seemingly forgotten, at least for now.

Brad rolled his eyes. "Okay, okay, very funny. Look, speaking of drinks, are you going to share or what?" He pointed to the collection of cups in front of Penny.

"I grabbed everyone a Coke. Hope that's okay?" Penny passed the drinks around. "Too bad there's no rum or rye in them. What's with the lack of booze?"

"Penny, this is a fundraiser for Mothers Against Drunk Driving," Daniel pointed out.

"Well, it's not called Mothers Against Drunken *Stumbling*. We took a cab," Penny said defensively. "And they'd make a hell of a lot more money if it was a licensed event."

"I'm sure they're satisfied with the turn out," Daniel said. "They'll do well off the proceeds from the door."

"Regardless of what we're drinking, we need a toast. We're celebrating," she announced.

Jeremy leaned forward to look at Penny. "What exactly are we celebrating?"

Penny and Brad looked at each other conspiratorially. Penny nodded to him. "It so happens, that in three days, we'll officially be homeowners," he said.

"I knew it was soon, but I had no idea it was that soon," Daniel said, reaching across the table to high-five Brad.

"I know. We're so bloody excited," Penny said. "We're picking up the keys on Wednesday. We couldn't wait to tell you all."

Penny held up her glass. Brad took his cue. "A toast to Grandpa Wright — one hell of an investor. And to Patty for being so nosy and paying such close attention to everything Gramps did so she could teach us all his tricks."

We all lifted our cups and everyone took a drink.

"Aubrey, wait until you meet Patty. She's an absolute corker," Penny said.

"Is that a good thing?"

"It's a very good thing," Daniel assured me. "Henrietta Wright is an amazing woman. You'll love her."

"In that case, I can't wait," I replied.

Julie leaned forward in her chair. "Wait, how do you get *Patty* from *Henrietta?* That makes no sense."

Brad laughed. "When Daniel was little she used to play patty-cake with him. He couldn't get enough. He used to run around after her yelling, 'Patty! Patty!' Eventually he just started calling her 'Patty,' and it sort of stuck. Now everyone calls her that."

I looked at Daniel across the table. "Is that true? That's adorable."

"Yes, it's true," Daniel sighed. "Thanks, Brad, I owe you one."

"Hey, gotta keep it real, bro. A relationship's supposed to be based on honesty, right, Aubrey?" he turned to me with a smile.

"Absolutely," I replied. "Gosh, I guess I better start working on my hand-clap games. I'm a little rusty."

"Very funny," Daniel said as he threw a pretzel at me.

Everyone laughed at Daniel's expense. He shook his head and smiled helplessly. "Okay, fuck off, the lot of you." He took a swig of his drink, eyes dancing as he gazed at me over the lip of the cup.

Beside him, Penny was less-than-subtly examining Julie. Daniel's turn in the hot seat was over. Julie was up. "So, Julie, Aubrey tells us you're a dancer. Are you bendy?" she asked.

Julie looked confused. "I think she wants to know if you're *flexible*," Jeremy explained.

Brad snorted and shook his head.

"Ah, I see," Julie said. She locked eyes with Penny and grinned wickedly. "I'm *extremely* bendy."

"Excellent!" Penny exclaimed, clapping her hands gleefully.

"Hey, are those real?" Julie asked, pointing to Penny's long red nails.

"God, no. Acrylic, darling."

"What about those?" Julie asked, gesturing to her boobs.

Daniel dropped his head into his hands, seemingly mortified, but the exchange was highly entertaining. Penny had met her match.

"They're one hundred percent real, courtesy of my mum," Penny said proudly, jiggling for effect. Brad smiled broadly.

"I don't suppose I need to ask you the same question?" Penny dropped her eyes to Julie's rather flat chest.

"Jesus, Penny, what the hell?" Jeremy interjected. He cast Julie an apologetic look.

"That's okay," Julie said, reaching over to pat Jeremy's hand. "You're right, Penny. I suppose I am a little under-endowed, but what is it they say? More than a handful's too much, and more than a mouthful? Well, that's just a waste, isn't it?"

Julie now looked at Penny, an eyebrow raised in challenge. Jeremy continued to gaze at Julie as if the sun rose and set on her. He was too cute for words.

"That's an interesting way of looking at it, I suppose," Penny mused. "And tell me, how would you describe your philosophy? Are you a *dance like nobody's watching* kind of girl?"

"Actually, I prefer to dance until everyone *is* watching," Julie countered.

Jeremy raised his hand. "Seen that with my own eyes. Believe me, everyone watches."

Penny winked at Jeremy and then leaned over the table with her cup. "Well played, dolly." She and Julie clinked cups and smiled at each other before taking a drink.

Julie squeezed my hand under the table and looked at me as if to say, "Jesus Christ, what just happened?"

Suddenly, Daniel interrupted the lighthearted banter. "Fuck, here we go. Two o'clock, Penny."

"Brad, darling," Penny said, one eyebrow cocked.

I felt Brad's arm slide around my back, his hand landing casually on my left shoulder. Penny ran her fingers through Daniel's hair and then linked hands with him possessively. What the—? Had someone slipped something into my drink? Daniel winked at me. The next thing I knew, Cara and Lindsay were slinking past the table, and everything fell into place. Penny and Brad were in wingman mode. That explained the seating arrangement.

Cara tossed her head haughtily, gave me a withering look designed to kill on the spot, and continued past us to a table on the other side of the hall, dragging a confused-looking Lindsay behind her. What the hell?

"Well, then," Penny said, rolling her eyes. "Someone needs to tell those ladies that having big knockers isn't a license to go around looking like a slapper."

"Um, can we please stop talking about boobs?" Daniel asked.

"What? Getting squeamish all of a sudden? That's not like you," Penny said, nudging him with her elbow.

"I think Daniel's suddenly realized he's an ass man." Brad leaned toward me suggestively.

"For Christ's sake, Brad," Daniel complained, apparently not interested in discussing his penchant for either boobs or asses.

Jeremy came to Daniel's rescue. "Hey, looks like things are getting started," he said, gesturing to the front of the hall where the temporary stage was set up. I turned in my chair and Julie moved her seat around to the end of the table, which gave her a better view of the stage and also happened to position her closer to Jeremy. He smiled like he'd just won the lottery.

On the stage, Mary's Uncle Bernard was holding the microphone. He thanked everyone for coming and introduced the first act. Mary's cousin, Rebecca, the same one who'd sung at the memorial service, was settling onto a stool with a guitar.

She sang several songs, her airy voice commanding the attention of everyone in the room. From time to time, I'd feel Daniel's foot tapping mine under the table. I'd turn to smile at him and he'd smile back, sometimes winking furtively. How I wished I could sit beside him and hold his hand. I tried to content myself with playing footsies and being in his company.

As Rebecca played the closing chords of her third song, the crowd applauded politely and three guys took her place, one plugging a guitar into an amp and another settling in behind a drum kit. After messing around with wires and cables for a few minutes, the singer introduced the band, and they embarked on their set. There was no denying their talent, but by the second song, my head started to throb. I needed a break from the incessant pounding of the bass drum.

"I'll be back in a minute," I said, having to shout to be heard. I pushed my chair back and Daniel frowned up at me.

I smiled at him encouragingly before escaping through the crowd to the washroom where I peered at myself in the mirror. I was definitely a little pasty. As I was running my hands under the cold water, the door flew open.

"Hey," I said, turning to find Penny and Julie behind me. "Checking up on me?"

"Yes, we're checking up on you," Penny said. She took a moment to scan the stalls for other occupants. Satisfied that we were alone, she stood against a sink, handing me a paper towel. "Daniel was concerned. He said he thought you seemed out of sorts."

"Yeah, I've got a bit of a headache starting."

"Well, *someone* won't be pleased to hear that." Penny grinned.

"How many mojitos did you have?" Julie asked.

"Three large ones. Right after I finished two small ones."

"Aubrey, you have no idea how much booze was in those drinks."

"Oh, I know, believe me. I think I've gone straight from the drinking to the hangover without the fun buzz in between."

Julie rubbed my arm. "When we get back inside, you should grab a glass of water. I'm sure that'll help."

"I don't think I can go back in there. That drummer is too fond of his bass pedal."

"Maybe you should go home," Penny suggested.

"I don't want to leave."

"Listen, if you're worried about leaving your other half behind, I can guarantee he'll be right behind you as soon as you walk out the door. And I bet I know where he'll be looking, too," Penny said, patting me on the butt.

"I don't want to miss any fun."

"We'll be really boring, won't we, Julie?" Penny said.

Julie nodded. "Dull as dirt."

Penny laughed. "I don't know if I'd go *that* far."

"Good point," Julie conceded. "I'm sure there's never a dull moment when you're around, Penny."

"Oh, you know I'm harmless, right? I hope I didn't frighten you earlier. I'm always game for a bit of fun, that's all, and you two are right up my alley."

"You didn't give *me* the gears like that," I said.

"Oh, I seem to remember making you squirm a little," she claimed. "I was particularly interested in your relationship with a certain hunky fella you happen to live with."

"Ah, yes, you're right," I said.

"So, honestly now, there's nothing between you and Matt?" she asked.

I had no doubt that whatever I said would get back to Daniel. Her loyalties were abundantly clear. This was my chance to put his mind to rest.

"Listen, Penny, I won't deny that we're close. We'd do anything for each other. There's definitely affection, but certainly nothing *close* to what Daniel seems to think is going on."

*With the exception of Valentine's Day when he slipped me the tongue and attacked my hip with his hard-on. Yep, we're just really good friends.*

"Don't take my nosiness the wrong way, Aubrey. I just don't want him to get hurt. He's such a fantastic bloke."

"I have no intention of hurting him, Penny. You have my word on that."

"Good. Let's go back in, and then you can get a move on if you want. I'm sure Daniel won't mind. If Julie's okay with being left with us, that is. I know Jeremy would be thrilled."

"No kidding," I said, grinning at Julie. "He's so into you."

"He talks about me all the time, you said?" Julie asked.

"Non-stop," Penny confirmed.

"I *suppose* I could stick around for a while," Julie said with a coy smile.

Penny laughed as she pulled open the door. There was no need to return to the table. Daniel was standing against the wall outside the washroom, already wearing his coat, his ball cap pulled low over his eyes, my coat in his hands.

"Hey, you okay? You weren't looking well there a few minutes ago. I thought maybe you'd want to bail," he said.

"Would you mind?" I asked as I pulled my coat on.

"Not at all. You go on out and wait for me. I'll be there in a couple of minutes." He didn't want to be seen leaving with me. That was understandable.

I hugged Penny and Julie. "Say goodbye to Brad and Jeremy for me," I said.

"I'll call you tomorrow," Julie assured me.

I squeezed her arm and gave Daniel a quick smile before making my exit. I pulled my hood up and waited for him at the far corner of the building. A few moments later, he pushed his way through the doors and scanned the deserted street. We met at the pathway leading to Vic's quad and walked along quickly and quietly, staying a safe distance apart.

The weather was brutal—cold and a bit drizzly—not exactly conducive to moonlight strolls. The upside of the nasty weather was the fact that we didn't see a single person on our trek.

We passed the men's residences and were about to turn a corner when I impulsively grabbed his arm and pulled him into the recessed entryway of Burwash Hall, pushing him toward the large oak door and leaning into him so I could rest my forehead against his shoulder.

"I need a hug, Daniel," I pleaded.

"Are you all right, poppet?" He lowered my hood and looked at me, genuine concern in his eyes.

"I'm okay. But a hug would make me feel better."

"I think I can manage that." He wrapped his arms around me tightly. His jacket was cold and damp, not the best conditions for a warm and comforting hug, but it would have to suffice.

"Better?" he asked.

"Not really. Honestly? I don't want you to go home."

"We can't stay out here. It's freezing. I should get you home and find myself a cab."

"Can't I come with you?" I hated the neediness in my voice.

He sighed and jammed his hands into his pockets.

"I just want to see where you live," I said. *Liar. More like I just want to see your bed. And lie in it. Naked. With you.* "Let me come with you in a cab and then you can send me right back home, I promise." I *had* to spend some time with him alone. Somewhere warmer than this.

He scanned my face, the muscle in his jaw twitching crazily. He pulled my hood up, tucking my hair inside the fur, then pulled his hoodie up over top of his ball cap.

"Something tells me I'm going to regret this, but—okay, let's make a run for it. Bay Street. You ready?" he asked, a glimmer of anticipation in his eyes.

"Absolutely." My heart was racing—I was actually terrified.

We dashed out onto the sidewalk and started jogging. It was freezing, and the drizzling rain made it feel colder. God, I was in terrible shape. I berated myself for being such a couch potato. After one block, I started to get a stitch in my side, and I couldn't see where I was going with my hood in the way and rain hitting my face as I ran.

"Can we slow down?" I asked, panting a little. "Your legs are like three feet longer than mine."

We slowed to a speed walk. The anticipation of getting into the back seat of a taxi with him was eclipsed by the pain in my side and all the blood in my body surging through my temples.

"Okay, here we are," Daniel said, coming to an abrupt halt and pulling me to his side at the corner of Bay Street. He waved his arm at an approaching taxi. When it stopped at the curb, Daniel opened the back door and ushered me inside.

"Mill Street in the Distillery District please."

The cabbie set the fare and pulled out. I pushed my hood back, afraid to think what I must look like. Daniel reached over and ran his thumbs under my eyes.

"Is my makeup running?" I asked. I was gradually regaining my breathing.

"A bit," he said, gently rubbing my cheeks again. "There, that's better." He took my hands and kissed my fingers gently, sending a thrill straight through me. "Your fingers are freezing!" he exclaimed, breathing on them to warm them up.

"I know. I had gloves earlier. You must have left them on the bench at Brennan Hall."

"Oh, shit, I did. I'm sorry."

"Don't worry. They weren't expensive. I'm terrible with gloves anyway. I'm always losing them," I admitted sheepishly.

"I do seem to recall another glove losing incident not that long ago." He looked at me with a secretive smile.

"Oh, please don't remind me. I can't believe you caught me crying. I felt like such an idiot."

"Hey," he said softly, "don't say that." He pulled me into his arms and tucked my face into his wonderful-smelling neck. I sighed contentedly. "I didn't think you were an idiot. I thought you were amazing. I still think you're amazing," he whispered.

Unable to find the right words to return his sentiments, I snuggled in even closer, sighing happily. Loosening the zipper on his jacket and hoodie, I ran my hand across his chest. "I love this T-shirt on you. Smells good, too."

A gentle laugh rumbled in his chest. "I guess that's a compliment," he said as he trailed his fingers tenderly through my hair.

"Definitely. You know what? I'd love one of your shirts. I'd sleep in it. If I can't have you in bed with me, I need something that feels and smells like you."

"That's a bizarre request."

"I don't think so," I said defensively. "You don't understand women at all, do you?"

He looked at me somberly. "I guess maybe I'm out of practice," he admitted. Suddenly he looked like an adolescent boy, opening his heart to a girl for the first time.

"We'll have to work on that, then, won't we?" I whispered.

I trailed soft kisses along his jawline, moving gradually toward his chin. His head fell back against the seat, and he sighed. Was this my chance to snag a kiss? His lips were slightly parted. It would be so easy. But then he rolled his head to the side, lips out of reach. I kissed my way back along his jaw to his ear and nibbled on his earlobe. My hand on his chest registered the quickening beat of his heart. I breathed gently in his ear, and heard his sharp intake of breath.

"Daniel?"

He moaned quietly.

I spoke softly into his neck, "I want you so badly. I don't think I can wait. I'm not just saying that. I mean, I *really* don't think I can wait."

He lifted his head and shifted in the seat, frowning as he looked at me. "Maybe we need to stop doing this to each other. It's obviously getting difficult for both of us."

Well, shit. This was definitely *not* the answer I was hoping for. I wanted him to crumble. We were on our way to his apartment. No one needed to know. Again, I tried to avoid sounding desperate.

"'*O, wilt thou leave me so unsatisfied?*'" I said, resorting to the safety of Shakespeare's words.

He smiled. "'*What satisfaction canst thou have tonight,*' crazy legs?"

"If you need to ask, then you *are* out of practice," I said. "And it's kind of ironic that I'm quoting Romeo and you're quoting Juliet. Aren't you supposed to be the one who can't control himself while I frantically fight off your advances?" I was trying to keep the tone light, but I was genuinely amazed at his self-control. Any other guy would be ripping my clothes off by now, back seat of a taxi or no.

"Don't fool yourself into thinking I'm a paragon of virtue, Aubrey. I'm not. And *please* don't question how desirable you are. You know how much I want you. You also know why we have to wait." He sighed in exasperation. "I don't want to rehash this."

I extricated myself from his arms and settled back against my seat, not only frustrated but also irritated by the whole situation. Daniel rubbed his face, equally aggravated.

"I don't know what to say anymore, Aubrey. I'm sorry you're annoyed. I thought the night was going well. We were having fun, and you get along so well with everyone. Things worked out with Julie and Jeremy. That's truly all I was hoping for this evening. I'm sorry if you thought there were other things on the agenda."

I looked at him in disbelief. "Well, that makes me sound like some sort of a sex-obsessed freak. Thanks a lot."

"Come on, that's not what I meant. It's just that we can't keep pushing the envelope like this. It's not fair to either one of us. I genuinely *did* try to behave tonight. I think we need to rein things in a little. Don't you agree?"

I avoided his question. "Are we nearly there?" I needed him to get out of the car. I was afraid I was going to say something I'd regret.

"Yes, a couple more minutes," he said.

"Good." I resolutely kept my mouth closed.

"Aubrey, please don't be like this."

"Don't be like what?"

"Unreasonable," he said.

I bit my tongue. Counted to ten. Tried not to fly off the handle.

"Maybe I am. Maybe I'm not cut out for this. I warned you I wasn't a patient person, and now you see for yourself what I meant. I'm sorry to have disappointed you so thoroughly."

He sighed and shook his head. "I don't know what the fuck is going on here. What just happened?"

"I don't know. Maybe we both need some time to think." I had nothing more to say. I was hurt and wanted to go home to lick my wounds in private. He remained silent and unmoving.

Apparently we'd reached our destination because the taxi was now parked against the curb. The driver turned in his seat, awaiting payment. I didn't bother looking out the window, no longer interested in seeing Daniel's condo. I kept my arms crossed and my eyes facing forward. Daniel gave the driver money with instructions to take me back to Charles Street.

He opened the door and climbed out, ducking his head back inside. "Can I call you tomorrow?"

"Whatever."

"Whatever? That's nice."

He slammed the door and disappeared behind the cab.

I didn't even watch him walk away.

# CHAPTER 22

## *Pride*

All pride is willing pride, and yours is so.
(*Love's Labour's Lost*, Act II, Scene I)

Back in the apartment, I went straight to my room. I doubted Joanna would be home at all that night, but I didn't want to cross paths with Matt if he came home early.

After changing into PJs I flopped onto the bed. While the pain in my head had lessened to a slight throb, my heart was aching and I was stewing in shame. I stared at my phone, sliding my thumb back and forth across the display. The best course of action would be to text Daniel or, better yet, phone him to apologize. But the prospect was terrifying. He'd been so disenchanted when he'd slammed the door of that cab. What if he'd decided in the last hour that I wasn't worth the trouble? Right now I could hang on to the hope that he'd forgive me. If I were to call and face a dismissive answer, that would be the end of it. I wasn't ready to deal with that possibility.

What had possessed me to behave so foolishly? Daniel was right. I'd been unreasonable. It was wrong of me to treat his feelings so lightly. I'd snapped and behaved like a sullen child. Was I entirely at fault, though? He'd been the one to initiate all of our flirtations — the hugs, the texting, the innuendo — always pulling back when *he* decided things had gone far enough. He'd been getting me going for *days*. This time I'd been the instigator, and he'd shut me down immediately. This wasn't fair of him either.

I was so confused. In my heart I felt that I owed him an apology, if for no other reason than for reacting so petulantly when he'd rejected my advances, but I wasn't prepared to shoulder all of the responsibility for our squabble. The whole situation sucked.

Shivering, I crawled into bed with my phone, setting the ring tone volume to its highest level on the off chance that he'd call or text me in the night. After what felt like hours of tossing and turning, I finally slept, phone tightly clutched in my hand.

I awoke at nine o'clock the next morning. On the one hand, this was a good thing because it meant I'd had a decent sleep. On the other hand, there had been no chiming of my phone to rouse me—definitely a bad thing.

Where *was* my phone? I felt around on the bed, looked under the covers, and lifted the pillow. Nothing. Dragging myself to the side of my bed, I peered over the edge and saw my phone on the floor, red message light flashing. I grabbed it with shaking hands. A Facebook alert. Someone had commented on a picture I'd posted the week before. Damn. Nothing from Daniel.

He hadn't called.

He hadn't sent a text.

What did that mean? Was he upset? Was he angry? Was he as remorseful as I was? Afraid to take the chance to call or too proud to do so?

I spent the next half hour curled in bed, rereading the sonnet he'd written out for me, remembering the day we'd texted each other in the Hart House library and how he'd made my knees weak without laying a single finger on me. He was so incredibly sexy. No, I simply couldn't be held responsible for wanting him so much. What woman in her right mind could resist him?

I tormented myself further by flipping through my calendar to gaze wistfully at Daniel's hand-written Post-it notes. April's note, which had made me so giddy only days ago, now made me want to cry. I methodically marked a red X through Saturday, March seventh.

Fifty-three days. That's how much longer we had to wait—no—that's how much longer we *would* have to wait if we were still a couple. Acknowledging that awful condition brought me to tears, and several wet splotches fell onto the calendar page, smudging the red ink.

I dabbed at the page with a tissue, but then I blew my nose and rubbed my eyes, taking myself to task. Crying wasn't going to solve anything. If I wanted to fix the situation, I'd have to *do* something. I stared at my phone indecisively. A light tapping on the door interrupted my waffling.

"Um, give me a minute," I called.

"No problem. Just wanted to see if you were up," Matt said through the door. "You want some French toast?"

After quickly checking my face for stray makeup smudges, I slipped the calendar back in the drawer and opened the door.

"Hey," I said, trying to put on a convincing smile. "French toast sounds great. You want some help?"

"No, that's cool; I can do it. Hey, you sick? Your nose is kinda red."

"Yeah, I think I might have a head cold coming on or something. It was pretty gross out last night."

"No kidding." He hesitated. "So, that was an interesting group of people you were with." He crossed his arms and leaned against the door frame. He was aiming for a casual tone, but his question had "fishing for info" written all over it.

"You think?" I said, striving to be equally casual and no doubt failing as thoroughly as he was.

"Well, hanging out socially with your TA and his family? That's a little strange."

"I guess it does seem odd, but Daniel wanted to go to support the Langfords, and his family has affiliations with Mothers Against Drunk Driving, so that's why his brothers and Penny were there. When he found out Julie and I were planning to attend, we decided to all sit together. No biggie."

I was impressed with myself. This story sounded pretty damned good.

"Huh. That's cool, I guess. So, the angry dark-haired dude you were sitting beside?"

"That's Daniel's older brother."

I smiled at his description. Matt had truly brought out the worst in Brad.

"Right," he said, pursing his lips and nodding. "And are you two, you know…?"

He lifted a brow. The wingman act designed to throw Cara off course would probably work just as well for Matt, but I simply couldn't lie to him again.

"No, he's a good guy, but there's nothing going on with us," I assured him.

Matt nodded. "Look, I should tell you, Shawn didn't have the guts to come over and say hi. All of a sudden he's turned into this ridiculous adolescent when he talks about you. What should I tell him?"

"His interest is flattering, Matt, but I wouldn't want him to get his hopes up. He's a nice guy, but I'm not on the lookout for anything right now."

"Fair enough. Well, listen, I'm gonna get started on breakfast. You can grab a shower if you want."

I took him up on his offer while he cooked. It was completely ridiculous, but I took my phone into the bathroom with me, anxious about missing a potential call or text from Daniel.

He didn't call while I was showering. He didn't call while Matt and I ate brunch, nor was there a peep out of him while I did the dishes. By noon I was getting antsy. I was settling in to do some French homework when my phone finally rang. I looked at the display, praying I'd see "D. Grant." I didn't — it was just a number.

"Hello?"

"Aubrey? Is that you, lovey?"

Oh my God! It was Penny!

"Yes, it's me. How are you?"

"I'm fine. I hope you don't mind, but I got your number from Jeremy. I'm calling to see how you're feeling. You really didn't seem well when you left last night."

"I'm surviving," I said. *Just barely.* "Did you guys stay late?"

"No, we were in a taxi ourselves by half past ten."

"So what did you think of Julie?" I asked, skirting around the only topic I was really interested in discussing.

"Oh, she's absolutely brill. A real gem. She and Jeremy seemed to get on well after you left. I think he even managed to wangle a date out of her for this evening."

I tried to allow my excitement for Julie to overrule the distress I felt about my situation with Daniel. "They seem like a good match. I'm really happy for them."

"Me too. You two must come round once we're settled. We'll figure something out before I head off back home. A girls' night in or something."

"What? Home, as in *England* home? You're leaving?"

"Only for a fortnight. I've left my poor mum and my friend Veronica making all the wedding arrangements. It's all getting to be a bit much for Mum. She's probably going off her nut."

The other shoe dropped.

"Wait, you're getting married in England?"

"Yes, darling, didn't Daniel tell you?"

"No, it didn't come up, I guess."

"How disappointing. You don't spend all of your stolen moments together talking about me?" She laughed. "But, yes, I'm being a bit daft about it actually. I can't bear the thought of not having my family and friends around when I get married, and they're not in a position to afford a trip to Canada, so we're going back there instead."

"And Daniel's family is joining you?"

"Yes, the whole lot. Even Patty. She'll be a riot on the plane. Brad's convinced she'll be knocking on the cockpit door to tell the pilot to hurry up if he's not on schedule. Brad does the best Patty impersonation. Nearly makes me wee laughing."

I smiled at the thought of Brad impersonating his grandmother. I imagined Brad and Penny laughed a hell of a lot together. If only Daniel and I could have as much fun. I braced myself and carefully broached the topic.

"So have you spoken to Daniel this morning?" I asked.

"Are you joking? He knows better than to call me when *Coronation Street* is on." I laughed, and she groaned with embarrassment. "I know it's terrible. It's my guilty pleasure. Always makes me feel like my life is totally sorted when I see that lot buggering everything up."

"I don't know, Penny. I wouldn't think you'd need to compare your life to a soap opera to know things are going pretty damn well for you right now. Brad's awesome, you're about to move into a new house, planning the wedding…"

I was rambling. I didn't know what to say. She hadn't spoken to Daniel, so she had no clue that we'd had a disagreement. Should I tell her or gloss it over? I remembered my words to her from the night before.

*I have no intention of hurting him, Penny. You have my word on that.*

Nope. There was no way I was mentioning our argument.

"Well, listen," she said. "I didn't call to natter on at you. I wanted to make sure you were all right. Hopefully we'll see you again soon?"

"I hope so," I said.

I didn't have the heart to tell her I wasn't sure if I'd ever see her again. I couldn't bear to admit the fact to myself. Not only was I becoming emotionally tied to Daniel, I was also getting seriously attached to his family.

We hung up, and I continued my internal debate. Every time I considered phoning Daniel, I'd see his hurt and angry expression and hear him saying, "Whatever? That's nice." A complete coward, I dreaded facing his antipathy. There would be no avoiding him on Monday. I would wait to see what the next day would bring.

Instead I called Julie, flopping on my bed and listening to her rave about Jeremy. Despite my misery, I responded to her stories enthusiastically.

"I told you he was awesome, Jul. You really like him?"

"He's so cute. We seem to have a lot of common interests. Music, art…he's a graphic designer. How cool is that?"

"Sounds like someone's smitten."

"I only talked to him for a couple of hours. I'll update you after our date tonight."

"So you *do* have a date already? You get him, babe."

"Aubrey, darling, I don't chase. I *replace*. I'm letting him do the chasing."

"Well said, girlfriend."

Very well said. In fact, I wished she'd shared this nugget of wisdom with me before I'd been so pushy with Daniel in the back of that cab. I would've saved myself a whole lot of grief.

When the conversation turned to me and Daniel, I quickly decided against sharing the details of our squabble. As far as Julie was concerned, Daniel and I hadn't ventured into any sort of romantic territory yet. How would I explain that I'd been pissed off because he wouldn't take me home for a tumble between the sheets? Plus, Daniel would be angry if he knew I was airing the personal details of our relationship. So once again I resorted to half-truths, and once again, I hated myself for it.

Before hanging up we made plans to go out for dinner on Tuesday night at the Madison House, an opportunity to have some time to talk properly. Maybe by then Daniel and I would have everything resolved so I could go back to giggling and swooning over his beautiful eyes and fabulous ass.

Going to work on Monday morning should have provided a welcome distraction from my incessant thoughts about Daniel, but every time I looked at Dean Grant's face I remembered Daniel's wounded expression and sad eyes. No, my job was officially the least effective diversion. At nine o'clock, Dean Grant left for his weekly coffee meeting with his son. As for me, I wouldn't see Daniel until noon—three more hours of uncertainty.

When he returned a little after nine thirty, Dean Grant headed straight for his office, and I went about my work, trying not to obsess about the upheaval the afternoon might bring. At eleven o'clock, the interoffice mailman arrived with the Vic mailbag. He hefted it onto the front counter.

"Good morning, Aubrey. Here you go. It's a heavy one today."

"Thanks, Ned. Have a good day!" I called after him as he turned and pushed the door open with a parting wave.

I separated the mail into piles. When I reached the bottom of the bag, I came a across a package—a padded manila envelope with a typed label on the front: AUBREY PRICE - PERSONAL AND CONFIDENTIAL. I quickly tore open the sealed envelope and peered inside to find a note typed on plain white paper. I sat down at my desk to read it.

Aubrey,

We need to talk. I've been thinking a lot, and not just because of what happened on Saturday. We have some important things to discuss. Today is a write-off, and tonight I have a faculty event to attend. I know you have classes most of the day tomorrow. Can we meet after your French lecture? I hope we can find time to get together. I'd rather not discuss these issues on the phone.

As for what's enclosed, I was careless and I lost your gloves. I'm sorry. I've replaced them. I'm hoping you'll have an easier time keeping track of these ones! Unfortunately I worry that more than your gloves was lost on Saturday, and I fear we won't be able to rectify that loss quite as easily. As for the other item I've included, I don't know if you still want it. It didn't seem to bring me much luck on Saturday. Your choice. I hope you'll spare me a few moments of your time this afternoon to arrange a meeting. ~D

I dug around inside the envelope and pulled out a soft pair of chenille gloves. They were striped in multiple bright colors — loud, but cute. Daniel was right. They would be difficult to overlook. I slipped them on. They were very cozy. I was in the midst of rereading the note when Dean Grant strode out of his office to refill his coffee cup. He looked at me, sitting at my desk, wearing the outlandish striped gloves, and clutching the piece of paper.

"Cold?" he asked, chuckling.

I smiled and took the gloves off, folded the note, and placed it casually back inside the envelope with the gloves.

"They're a gift from a friend. It's a long story."

"They go perfectly with your outfit," he joked. "I have some calls to make, and I know you're off shortly. Lock up for lunch, and I'll see you on Wednesday, all right?"

He returned to his office and closed the door behind him. I scanned the note again, trying to gauge the tone. It wasn't particularly warm. In fact, the more I read over his words, the more ominous they sounded. Reading between the lines, the words "break-up" came into focus. There was no indication of affection — no endearments. There wasn't even an XO at the end.

I took a deep breath and reached into the envelope to look at the other item he'd mentioned. It was his black T-shirt. I closed my eyes and held the shirt to my face, a thousand thoughts and feelings rushing through me as I took in Daniel's essence—man and soap and cologne. Sandalwood.

*Daniel.*

Surely this was a good sign. If he wanted to cut ties, would he have given me something as intimate as a piece of clothing? That was doubtful. So, what did he want to talk about? Perhaps he wanted to clarify how things needed to be from now on? That I could handle. Even if he chastised me for being immature, I could cope. I would defend myself and call attention to the unfairness of his own inconsistent behavior, but I could certainly be big enough to apologize for speaking impulsively and hurting him in the process.

If he was still interested in pursuing something, perhaps I ought to make some conditions of my own. Maybe it would be a good idea to pull back a little. It was too difficult to have the carrot dangled in front of me, just out of reach. I was only human, after all—a human who was simply not strong enough to resist the charms of Daniel Grant.

When I arrived in the classroom, Julie was already in our spot in the second row, rapidly texting someone. I settled into my chair, peering nosily at the tiny screen.

"Things went well with Jeremy last night, I see?"

"Amazing," she said, smiling and continuing to tap at her phone.

"You know, this blossoming relationship with Jeremy is going to have serious health implications. I hope you've read up on carpal tunnel syndrome because you are headed down that path, young lady," I scolded her.

She puckered her lips. "Zip it, Aubrey," she said, not missing a beat in her rapid-fire text conversation.

"What happened to 'I don't chase, I replace'?" I asked.

She shrugged. "Now that I'm getting to know him better, I realized I'm full of shit."

I stifled a laugh and she rolled her eyes, finishing her last message and pocketing her phone.

"Hey, those are awesome gloves! They'd go well with this," she said, pulling her rainbow-colored hat out of her sleeve.

"Well, you can't have them. They were a *gift* from someone special," I said coyly, clutching them tightly against my chest. I was aiming for playful nonchalance, but I knew Daniel was going to walk through the door any moment, and I was a bundle of nerves. I stuffed the gloves securely in my backpack. I'd be damned if I was going to lose them.

"I *see*," she said, tapping her chin with her pen.

When Daniel and Professor Brown arrived, Daniel sat in his usual spot. He was tired and scruffy-looking, almost as unkempt as he'd been at the beginning of the semester. My heart went out to him. Was he suffering as much as I was?

Professor Brown waited for everyone to settle and then launched into his lecture, repeating his instructions to have *Othello* read for Wednesday. A few groans and grumbles erupted around the room. I tried to catch Daniel's eye, but he didn't look up. In fact, he was wholly preoccupied. He appeared to be doodling, of all things.

I was distracted for the better part of the hour as well, frequently losing my focus to glance at Daniel. At one point, I saw him staring at someone on the other side of the room. I followed his gaze and caught Shawn looking at me. Shawn blushed when our eyes met, then he cleared his throat and made a great show of turning the page in his notebook. Daniel then glanced at me, face impassive, almost vacant. I gave him a small smile, but instead of returning the gesture, he dropped his eyes to his notepad and resumed scribbling.

Things were not boding well.

As Professor Brown concluded the lecture forty-five agonizing minutes later, he turned to see if Daniel had anything he wanted to say. Daniel stood and pulled a pile of papers from his bag.

"I have the *Hamlet* papers for those of you who completed the comparative analysis of the text and the live performance. If any of you have questions, feel free to make an appointment since I have to head off to tutorial in a few moments. I'll leave them here. That's all for me for today."

Daniel fanned out the assignments on the front table, and Professor Brown waved and left the room. Everyone dispersed, many picking up their papers before heading for the door. Daniel stepped off the platform and walked toward us, nodding briefly at Julie before turning to look at me.

"Miss Price, if you could spare a moment, we should talk briefly about that issue you've been struggling with," he said coolly.

"Of course," I replied, trying to mimic his calmness.

He returned to the table to collect his things. Cara and Lindsay moved down the aisle to head for the door, but before leaving, Cara looked back at me over her shoulder with a knowing expression.

Julie turned to me anxiously. "What was that all about?" she whispered, gesturing to the departing pinheads.

"I don't know. The girl is a frigging nut job. Don't worry about it. Listen, things are crazy for me the next couple of days, so you might not hear from me, but we'll meet at the Maddy at six thirty tomorrow night, okay? Say hi to Jeremy for me."

"I will. See you tomorrow." She squeezed my hand briefly. "Have a nice *chat*," she added, smiling conspiratorially before leaving.

A *nice chat?* That was looking doubtful.

There were still a few people milling around, reading over their essays, presumably trying to determine if they had anything they wanted to ask questions about, but I approached the front table anyway. Daniel assessed me, his face an indecipherable mask. I met his gaze levelly, trying to maintain an equally impassive expression.

Look at the two of us, trying to one-up each other with our indifference. What was that old saying? "*Pride goeth before the fall.*" The only point of contention was which one of us was going to hit the ground first. As the silence stretched out before us, I realized someone was going to have to buckle. I decided to take the plunge.

"How are you, Daniel?"

"I've been better, Miss Price," he replied, pulling himself up to his full height and jamming his hands in his jeans pockets.

"Right. Well, um, I appreciate your willingness to work through those difficulties you mentioned," I said, aware that we had an audience.

"Yes, I think I have some ideas about how the problem can be resolved." He was being equally obscure. "Unfortunately, today is completely spoken for. How's tomorrow, say, after three o'clock?"

I was about to answer when my two remaining classmates moved past the desk.

"Thanks, Daniel. This is all good. See you on Wednesday," the dark-haired guy said as he ambled past the podium and out the door. Now we were alone.

I turned back to look at Daniel.

"Sorry, Daniel, I have a study meeting with some people from my French class. We have a group presentation to plan. I have no idea how long it will take."

He frowned. I got the distinct impression he thought I was lying, trying to put off our meeting. Nothing could have been farther from the truth.

"What about in the evening? Maybe after dinner? I'm sorry to push this, Aubrey, but we need to talk. I don't want to protract this, and I *really* don't want to do this over the phone."

Protract *what?* Do *what* over the phone? This was sounding bad.

"Yes, I know, you indicated as much in your note," I said.

"Oh, good, you got the package? I wasn't sure I'd gotten it into the courier on time this morning, and I wanted you to have those gloves before you walked over from Vic."

I imagined him rushing to the campus mail room first thing this morning to have the envelope deposited into the Vic mailbag and was touched by his thoughtfulness. My icy wall crumbled.

"Thanks for the gloves. You didn't have to do that. It was as much my fault as yours that they got left behind on Saturday, but I appreciate it. And thanks for the T-shirt, too." I smiled at him sadly, and this time he returned my smile with a wistful one of his own.

"Well, regardless of everything else, I still wanted you to have it," he admitted, his tone softening slightly as well.

*Regardless of everything else?*

"So, tomorrow evening you don't have a night class if I remember correctly. Can you spare an hour or so to talk then?"

"Julie and I are going out for dinner. There's no way I'm canceling after the argument we had on Saturday. That would be adding insult to injury, don't you think?"

"No, you're right. I wouldn't ask that of you." He glanced at his watch, clearly agitated. "Listen, I have to get downstairs. Walk with me?"

We headed to the hall, and he locked the classroom door behind us. He stopped at the top of the stairs, speaking in a low voice.

"What about after your dinner with Julie? Do you think you'll be finished by eight thirty or nine? I could pick you up. We could go for a drive…or something," he said.

"That might work. We're going to the Madison House. I could text you when we're almost done."

"That sounds perfect. I'll go to Robarts Library, do some work, and then come get you. I'll wait in the car for you."

"I think that's a great idea," I said, grappling with my coat as we made our way down the stairs.

"Do you need some help?" he asked.

"No, I've got it." I slid my hand ineffectually up and down the lining of my coat several times.

"Here." He stopped on the bottom stair and grabbed the side of my coat while gently guiding my arm into the sleeve.

His voice, now so warm, his touch, so tender, almost brought tears to my eyes. He stepped off the bottom stair and turned to look at me, our faces level.

"I've made an important decision, Aubrey," he said, almost inaudibly. "It'll be good to talk this all through."

Panic coiled in my stomach, but I tried to remain calm.

"I feel terrible about what happened on Saturday, but it crystallized some things in my mind, too. We have a lot to talk about."

He searched my face for a moment, and then he sighed. "I have to go."

"Of course. You've got a room full of people waiting for you."

I needed him to go. If he kept standing there I'd be in his arms, begging him not to leave. I was beyond desperate for resolution. I had to know, one way or another, what the hell was going on with us.

"Okay. Well, have a good couple of days," he said at last.

"I'll try. You too."

My hand itched to move toward his. I made myself remain still as he slowly turned and retreated, jamming both hands in his pockets as he rounded the corner. I had to take a few deep breaths to calm myself. When my phone buzzed in my coat pocket, I thought it might be a text from Daniel, typed quickly as he'd walked to the seminar room—some word of affection, some sign of hope.

It wasn't. It was a text from Julie.

**It was strange seeing all of his casual, uninterested
glances now that I know everything.
So weird having inside scoop. Ttyl gf. -J**

I grimaced. While she might have been right about Daniel's
demeanor in the past weeks, today I didn't know how much effort
was actually required for him to look indifferent. I carefully typed
in a vague response.

**I know...so crazy right? c u at 6:30 tomorrow. -A**

I sighed, convinced I was going to drive myself insane trying to
make sense of everything. I simply needed to bide my time until the
next day. One way or another, I would soon know whether Daniel
and I had a chance at a future together.

# CHAPTER 23

## An Impediment

This forenamed maid hath yet in her the continuance
of her first affection: his unjust unkindness, that
in all reason should have quenched her love, hath,
like an impediment in the current, made it more
violent and unruly.
(*Measure for Measure*, Act III, Scene I)

was a wreck by Tuesday afternoon. After barely sleeping Monday
night, I dozed through my four hours of classes on Tuesday and
fumbled my way through my meeting with my classmates from my
French course, overcompensating for my lack of attention during our
session by offering to take on way too many responsibilities.

Returning home at the end of the meeting, I panicked as I realized the implications of volunteering to create an entire PowerPoint
presentation with content they would email me over the next few
days. What had I been thinking? I was more wordsmith than techie,
but for some stupid reason I'd stepped up, and now I felt compelled
to follow through.

I showered in a desperate bid to wake myself up. By six o'clock,
I was presentable and absolutely starving. Certain I wouldn't be able

to wait an hour to eat, I headed to the kitchen for a snack. Matt was at the table eating a plate of spaghetti and meatballs.

"Did you use up all the hot water, or did you actually leave a couple of minutes' worth for me?" he asked.

"Huh, I didn't think you used hot water, horn dog," I retorted, flicking his ear. I watched him shovel a few mouthfuls of pasta into his mouth. "Feel free to chew."

"Don't have time," he explained through a mouthful of noodles. "Heading to the Kap house at six thirty. I want to make sure I get my share of the keg."

"Need I remind you it's a Tuesday night, dude? You have classes tomorrow."

"Oh, quit being so sensible. Besides, I don't know if you've noticed, but our carefree-student days are numbered. Not much longer and I'll be joining the world of the working stiff, falling asleep on the couch at eight o'clock every night. Gotta have fun while I still can."

I smiled. Funny how time meant such different things to different people.

"Yeah, I guess so, but at the rate you're going, you might as well throw your liver in a jar with some dill pickles."

"Damn it, Aubrey, if you're gonna nag me like a girlfriend, I should at least get some of the fringe benefits."

He wiggled his eyebrows at me, smiling while stuffing his face.

"No comment," I said, kicking his chair leg. "While we're on the topic of nagging, though, you know what's been kinda bugging me since Saturday? You acting like Molly Matchmaker for Ward. What's up with that, anyway?"

He dropped his fork onto his plate and looked at me thoughtfully while he finished chewing.

"You want it straight?" he asked, adopting a serious tone.

"Of course." I pulled out a chair to sit opposite him.

"Shawn's a good guy. He likes you. I guess I hate the thought of you wasting your time on someone who's not available. Shawn would treat you well; you know he would."

I froze. *Someone who's not available? He can't possibly be talking about Daniel, can he?* I feigned confusion. "You lost me, dude. We both agreed our friendship is too important to risk, and I'm totally cool with that. If you think I'm still—"

"I'm not talking about you and me."

*Shit, I take it back. No cards on the table. Fuckity fuck, are we really going there? I'm not prepared for this.*

"Sorry, cowboy. I'm not sure what you mean."

"Look, I don't want you to think I'm getting into your business. I just think it's a bad idea to avoid a relationship with someone who's available because you're stuck on someone who's not. So if me helping you see Shawn as a potential catch helps you get over whatshisname, then slap my ass and call me Molly."

Was Daniel "whatshisname"? Could Matt really be that astute? Or was I simply that transparent? Or maybe he was fishing—throwing out a line to see if I'd bite?

I went with the latter, floundering as I tried to bring the conversation to a close.

"Wow, you've been watching too many movies. I appreciate you looking out for me and all, but you're barking up the wrong tree, my friend."

I grabbed a granola bar from the cupboard. I had to get out of that kitchen. I was simply no match for Matt and his insightful observations. If he *was* referring to Daniel, he was a little off the mark, perhaps assuming I was pining for someone who was, as far as he knew, attached to the beautiful Penny. But he wasn't far off, and that scared me.

"Okay, whatever you say, Aub. I'm not gonna force the issue. I'm here if you ever want to talk about anything."

I squeezed his shoulder and looked at him with perplexed amusement. "Well, thanks, *Dad*. I'll remember that. Listen, I'm heading out. Have fun tonight, okay?"

"Yeah, you too," he said, picking up his fork again. "Where you off to, anyway?"

"The Madison House. Grabbing dinner with Julie," I said.

"Cool. I haven't been there in ages. You'll be careful out there, right?"

"Yes, dear," I joked, escaping into the hall. I pulled on my coat and checked my pockets for my gloves. I wanted Daniel to see me wearing them when he picked me up.

*Daniel.* In a few hours we'd be alone in his car, finally hashing everything out. I couldn't let my nervousness ruin my dinner with Julie, though. I was bound and determined to enjoy our girl-time.

At six thirty-five sharp, Julie and I were tucked away at a table in the corner. I told Julie that Daniel and I were hoping to get together later for a coffee, and we ordered right away. By seven thirty, we were on our second drink and working our way through three platters of salty, greasy pub fare.

I scooped up a large dollop of guacamole with a nacho. "I'm surprised to see you eating this crap, Jul. What would your dance instructor say?"

"Oh, don't remind me," she groaned. "Sometimes you have to live a little, you know? I have to buckle down hard for the next five weeks anyway. I've got that huge showcase running from the end of April to early May. You know the one at Ryerson? You're coming, right?"

"Of course. Make sure you put a ticket aside for me," I said.

"For sure." She smiled down at her chicken strip. "Maybe you can sit with Jeremy."

"Oh, I see how it is. Making long-term plans now, are we?"

"He's so amazing, Aubrey. I know I probably sound ridiculous after only a couple of dates, but man, I can't help it. I could seriously fall for him so hard. As soon as I mentioned the showcase, he was all over it."

She was dissecting her chicken strip, pulling off most of the breading before biting into the chicken. This was Julie's version of *living a little*. She was a riot.

"When I met him at Daniel's parents' place during Reading Week, he was *so* sweet. He couldn't wait to call you. It was adorable."

"Yeah, he told me all about how he'd begged Daniel to let you tell me about him."

"You made quite the impression on him at the Revival that night, I guess. And you look great together."

She smiled, nibbling on the celery from her Caesar. I was making short work of several potato skins.

"Same with you and Daniel," she said. "And you have so much in common. You think there's a future for you guys?"

Oh, God, what could I say to that? "I don't know. There are all these limitations on us right now. We can't be ourselves. Things are always kind of tense."

"That's understandable. Jesus, that must be so hard. I don't know how you can keep your hands off him," she said with a compassionate sigh.

*Well, actually I've been pretty restrained with the hands. The tongue? Not so much.*

"It's not easy."

"What's he like when you're alone? Is he completely different?" she asked conspiratorially, leaning over the table.

This was painful. How could I talk about Daniel in the present tense when our relationship could potentially be over already? I chose my words carefully.

"He's a lot more relaxed outside of the academic setting, that's for sure."

"I almost dropped my teeth when I heard him throw down the F-bomb. Who would've guessed that Mr. Shmexy swears like a trucker? What else?"

"I don't know. He has a really cute nickname for me," I said, offering up one of the few details I was comfortable sharing.

"Really? What is it?"

Julie's enthusiasm was so heartwarming. This was what I'd been yearning for all week. I hadn't even realized how much I was missing out on by not being able to talk about my feelings for Daniel.

"He calls me 'poppet,'" I said, smiling shyly, but at the same time feeling somewhat wistful. Would I ever hear him call me that again?

"Oh, that's so sweet." She leaned on her hand, looking at me dreamily. "He does seem to be the romantic type." She sighed. "And he's got it bad for you. You should have seen his face when Matt ruffled your hair on Saturday. He looked like he might have an aneurism."

"You noticed that, eh? Yeah, he's got blinders on where Matt's concerned. It drives him crazy that we're so close."

"That's kind of sweet. It must be hard for him. What an awkward position to be in. Trying to get closer to you but knowing he can't get too close."

Julie wiped her hands on a napkin and pushed her plate away. It seemed to me as if she'd hardly eaten anything, but apparently she was already full.

"You know what, though?" she said. "Maybe it's good that you're being forced to take things slowly. You've got weeks to really get to know each other before shmexy times complicate things. As hard as it is to keep your hands off him, I think it's an ideal situation. I can't tell you how many times I've regretted getting too serious with a guy too quickly. Once you've gone all the way, you can't go back."

I mulled over Julie's warning. Maybe I'd been looking at this from the wrong angle all along. Was the delay a blessing rather than a curse? Was there even any point in contemplating the issue? I snuck a look at my phone. It was quarter to eight. I still had some time.

"So, does that mean you're planning to take your time with Jeremy?" I asked her.

"He kissed me the other night after our date, but he was cool about stopping there. Not that we have anywhere private to go." She laughed.

"Sounds like you need a back seat. Maybe you should suggest car shopping to him."

"I don't know. That's a tough sell. You know his background, right?"

"I do. Daniel told me all about his parents' accident. Crazy, huh?"

"He takes public transport everywhere, and I completely understand that. I'd never pressure him to buy a car."

I stole another peek at my phone. This time Julie caught me.

"Whenever you need to go, I understand," she said. "I don't want what happened on Saturday to make you think that I'm not going to support you through this." She reached over to squeeze my hand.

"I know, Jul. You're a great friend. The best. I wish things hadn't gotten so messed up last week. I felt completely out of control of the situation."

"It wasn't your choice to make. Shit happens. I'm glad it's all worked out now."

How I wished that were true. Something told me we wouldn't be enjoying any back seat time in his car tonight.

"Oh my gosh, do you see that girl over there?" Julie asked, looking over my shoulder and squinting into the crowd. "The one in the green T-shirt?" I craned my neck and spotted the dark-haired girl she was referring to.

"Yeah, what about her?"

"That's Hilary Walker. I went to high school with her. Do you mind if I pop over to talk to her? You can come with me if you want."

"No, that's cool. You go ahead. I'll grab a bottle of water, and then I have to head out."

My mouth had become dry as the anticipation of seeing Daniel began to transform into dread. What if this was the end? What if an hour from now there was no more hope for a future for us? The thought made me queasy.

"I'll be right back, okay?" Julie bobbed away excitedly toward her friend.

I typed out a brief text message to Daniel, trying to keep the tone light:

**Hey there. At the Madison. Almost done.
Will let you know when we're finished. -A**

I headed over to the bar, trying to squeeze into an opening. I ended up near the stairs beside the front door, waiting as the bartenders poured pint after pint of draft. I perched on the edge of a barstool, cursing the stream of people whose entrances and exits through the front door were allowing frosty air to pour in and assault my legs. When that stupid groundhog had predicted another six weeks of winter, he hadn't been whistling Dixie.

I tapped my fingers impatiently. I hated waiting to order drinks at a bar. Women with their boobs spilling all over the place always seemed to get such prompt service. My boobs were currently well-contained in my modest, long-sleeved T-shirt. I took a look at my phone. No answer from Daniel. Not that I was expecting one; he hadn't texted me since the Hart House sextathon. He'd most likely wait to hear from me again.

I was tapping my fingers on the bar in irritation when Julie reappeared beside me, excited.

"Aubrey, there's three other people here from my high school. Hilary's gonna take me upstairs for a sec to find them. You want to come?"

"No, you go ahead. I'll track you down in a minute."

"Okay. Hilary said they're hanging out near the dart boards," Julie said.

She turned, and I watched her push her way back through the crowd to reconnect with Hilary. I looked out at the crowd, wondering if I should abandon my quest for water and head upstairs when suddenly the door swung open and someone was lurching toward me. Jesus — it was Matt, and he was drunk as a skunk.

"Aubsss," he slurred, taking the six or seven shaky steps from the door to the bar and falling against me, almost knocking me on my ass.

"Matt, you're frigging wasted," I said, pushing him back against the bar to steady him. How on earth had he remembered where I'd be tonight given the condition he was in? I maneuvered a barstool behind him and settled him onto it. He sat unsteadily and held the bar railing for support.

"What the hell have you been doing? Well, that's a stupid question."

"Sarah," he said. "It's Sarah. She's got a new boyfriend. I saw her. At the Kap house. Kissing him. I'm so drunk. Fuckin' tequila."

"Uh, yeah, I can see that."

This was not good. He must have had a hell of a lot in a short time to get this drunk so quickly. He teetered, and I had visions of him falling sideways like a sack of potatoes. I propped my foot up on the crossbar of his stool to trap his leg and stop him from sliding off the seat and grabbed his shoulders firmly. Jesus, how was I going to get him home? I'd have to get him into a cab, but I was going to need help.

He fell forward, his head hitting my shoulder, and then he wrapped his arms around my waist. I couldn't figure out if he was seeking comfort or hanging on for dear life. I tried to push him upright, but he was dead weight.

"Matt," I said, putting my arms on his shoulders. "Can you sit up? You're going to knock me over."

*Please don't puke on me*, I silently begged. He mumbled and buried his head in my neck.

"What's that?" I said, trying to make sense of what he was saying.

"She's so over me," he slurred, his voice cracking.

My heart broke for him. I cradled his head on my shoulder and stroked his hair, rubbing his back with my other hand.

"Oh, Matt. I'm so sorry."

He clutched me more tightly and mumbled into my neck. I couldn't understand what he was saying. It didn't matter. He needed comfort, and I tried to do my best to provide it. The door flew open again and more cold air rushed in. I braced myself, using Matt's body to shield myself from the arctic blast.

*Why wasn't the damn door closing?*

I looked over my shoulder in irritation, hoping to send a message to the dink providing off-season air-conditioning.

And there he was.

Daniel.

He was standing in the open doorway, gaping at me—at Matt and me—a look of complete shock and disgust on his face as he took in the sight before him: Matt's arms around my waist and his face buried in my neck. My arms around Matt's neck, my leg hitched up beside his hip, and my body pressed close to his. Taking two unsteady steps backward, Daniel shook his head. And then he was gone.

"No, Daniel! Wait!" I called.

I was trapped in a bad dream. I wanted to move, but I couldn't. Everything was going in slow motion. I dared not let go of Matt, but I had to. I had to reach Daniel. I had to stop him and explain that what he'd seen was not at all what he *thought* he'd seen.

I turned to the guy standing beside me at the bar.

"Excuse me, can you do me a favor? Make sure my friend doesn't fall over?" I begged, removing Matt's arms from my waist and untangling my legs from his.

The stranger at the bar looked at me like my hair was on fire, but as I stepped away and Matt started to topple, he grabbed Matt and leaned him up against the bar. I didn't stick around to see what happened next, instead running out the door. Daniel was a half a block away, striding purposefully to his car.

I ran after him and called his name, but he didn't hesitate or turn around. Instead he climbed into the car and left, careening around a corner, tires screeching as he sped away into the dark night.

# Daniel

# CHAPTER 24

## *Confusion*

I am out of breath;
Confusion's near; I cannot speak.
(*Coriolanus*, Act III, Scene 1)

I sped away from the Madison House in a fury. If I'd stuck around, I wouldn't have been able control myself. I'd never felt such an overwhelming desire to hurt someone in my whole life, but I had to avoid making a scene. How the hell would I explain punching Matt Miller in the face? My hands shook as I clung to the steering wheel.

Driving blindly, I somehow arrived home alive, a scorching ball of jealousy churning in my gut and a horrible feeling spreading through my chest. This was not heartache. An ache is a dull pain, and there was nothing dull about this; shards of glass were being repeatedly thrust into my heart, twisted, and then violently pulled out. By the time I reached my condo, my breathing was labored and I realized with horror that I was on the cusp of another anxiety attack.

Once inside, I dropped onto the couch, head between my knees, breathing deeply and regularly and massaging my shoulder. Twice in the last few weeks these symptoms—which, for months, had been a distant memory—had resurfaced. Both times they were inspired by this ill-conceived relationship with Aubrey Price. When the first resurgence of anxiety had happened in the quad, mere moments after I'd told Aubrey how I felt for her, I'd been startled by the surge of panic, but not necessarily surprised. After all, I'd just openly confessed to having feelings for one of the students in Martin Brown's class. Talk about stupid.

I'd managed to avert a full-blown attack that day by talking myself through the clutching pain around my heart. I did the same thing now, counting to ten with each breath until the stabbing in my shoulder blade slowly receded.

Though I was gradually mastering the immediate physical effects of Aubrey's betrayal, my mind was a mass of contradictions. How could she do this? How could she so easily throw away what had the potential to be an amazing relationship? And wouldn't you know it — the guy she'd turned to had been Matt.

I reeled with shock as I tried to fathom how she could do something so completely out of character. Then, almost simultaneously, something else dawned on me: Did I really know her? She'd captured my interest with her wit and intelligence, bowling me over with her understated beauty and assertiveness, but I'd made a blind leap of faith little more than a week ago.

Fuck, talk about rushing headlong into something. I should have heeded my instincts. I'd known Matt wanted her, sensed all along that he was watching for a tiny chink in her armor so he could weasel his way in. The expression on his face when he'd looked at her on Saturday, the way he'd affectionately caressed her hair — these were not the actions of someone who was content to simply be a friend. I'd heard them flirting and frolicking behind their closed apartment door the week before, but I'd allowed Aubrey to convince me to dismiss their obvious domestic bliss. What a fool I'd been.

If there was one thing I couldn't abide, it was having my intelligence insulted. Now I felt like the butt of a cruel joke. I had another surge of panic as I wondered whether or not she'd pull the rug out from under me entirely and tell someone about our relationship and the advances I'd made. But surely she wouldn't do that. Regardless of what had happened to turn her feelings against me, there's no way she would want to hurt me that badly. Would she? She'd chosen Matt, but she still had to care for me, at least a little. But enough to protect me?

I needed a drink.

I rummaged through the unpacked boxes stacked against the living room wall until I found the bottles which would eventually fill my liquor cabinet. I poured myself a generous glass of scotch, knocked back a few mouthfuls, and shuddered deeply as the alcohol burned through the bitter lump in the back of my throat.

Thinking back to my conversation with Aubrey from the day before, I tried to puzzle out whether I'd missed something. Should I have known she'd decided to call it quits? It was hard to believe our ridiculous fight on Saturday had impacted her feelings so significantly. Sure, the way we'd parted in the taxi was unpleasant, but with a little effort, we could have easily gotten things back on track.

After class, I'd left Aubrey, thinking she was looking forward to talking and clearing the air, but hadn't she claimed that something had crystallized in her mind as she agreed we had a lot to talk about? Perhaps she'd been intending to tell me she wasn't interested in continuing our forbidden romance and that a relationship with Matt was easier and more satisfying. Then I'd screwed up her plan by walking into the bar unannounced, catching her red-handed.

Dinner with Julie. That must have been a ruse. Julie hadn't even been there. If I hadn't surprised Aubrey by heading into the Madison to get her, I'd have been none the wiser. She would have met me at my car, told me she'd decided she didn't want to pursue our relationship, and then possibly gone back inside to continue her evening with Matt.

The memory of them clinging to one another—their bodies pressed together while she ran her hands all over his back—nauseated me. I spiraled from jealousy, to rage, and then to complete self-loathing before settling into a state of utter despondency.

She didn't want me.

I drank glass after glass of scotch, pacing back and forth in front of the floor-to-ceiling windows in the living room and stopping occasionally to lean against the cool glass. The bright city lights mocked me. Knowing Aubrey was somewhere with Matt, possibly experiencing the satisfaction I was currently incapable of offering her, ate away at me.

And the lengths I'd considered—what I'd been prepared to do to hold onto her—what a complete fool I'd been.

I woke up the next morning on the sofa, roused by the sunlight streaming through the windows. I sat up slowly, the pounding in my temples rivaled by the churning rot in my stomach. I was still fully dressed, and my teeth felt like little cashmere sweaters had been knitted over them in the night. Revolting. Standing unsteadily, I staggered to the bathroom to brush my teeth.

Getting up was my first mistake. Walking was my second.

As soon as I started to move, my stomach lurched into my throat. Making it to the washroom with seconds to spare, I puked myself dry. But there's one good thing about being bent over a toilet chucking up your guts: when you're in the midst of it, that's really all you can think about. It wasn't until I was in the shower, leaning weakly against the tiles as the hot spray beat down on me, that I contemplated my day. It was Wednesday. I had to go to Martin's class and then run a tutorial. The thought of calling Martin to tell him I was ill crossed my mind, but what was the point? I'd have to face Aubrey eventually.

After my shower, I gathered my notes and looked them over while I ate a couple of pieces of dry toast. Monday's tutorial had gone well. I could muddle through again today. As for Friday? Well, that would be a different story.

Retreating to my office, I turned on some music in the hopes of quieting the sound of my inner monologue. Instead, I felt worse as one song after another reminded me of Aubrey and of what we could have had if she'd been patient—if she'd given me a chance to prove I was worth waiting for.

But was I worth waiting for? I couldn't even be sure. Maybe I was too cynical and too prone to jealousy. Had I pushed her into Matt's arms with my distrust? Or was my indecisiveness the final straw? Were my mixed messages and on-again off-again advances too much for her to tolerate? Was *I* the one being unreasonable? Fuck, I needed to talk to someone.

I tracked down my cell phone, sighing as I scrolled through my unread text messages. There were three from Aubrey. The first one had been sent shortly after I'd left the Madison House the night before:

**Would you please come back so I can explain? -A**

Another had followed about fifteen minutes later:

**I'm heading home. We need to talk. Please answer me. -A**

At nine thirty, she'd sent her final message:

**I'm home now. I won't bother texting again. I was going to call, but you'll probably ignore that too. Very mature. -A**

Shit. Now what was I supposed to do? I wasn't about to reply, providing proof of our connection in black and white. I wasn't prepared to phone her, either. What did she think I'd want to hear? She'd made a choice. Did I need to hear why I'd been found inferior? I'd swallowed my pride on Monday, giving her those gloves and my shirt—writing that note. She couldn't have been under any misapprehension about my feelings for her, and yet she was still prepared to throw everything away.

I started dialing Penny's number and then quickly abandoned the idea. Today was Wednesday. She and Brad were picking up the keys to their new house. The last thing she needed was me crapping on her happiness with my misery. I couldn't even call Jeremy. His relationship with Julie would complicate things.

Shit, this was going to be messy.

I gritted my teeth as I let myself into Martin's class room. I was early, my plan already formulated. I'd lose myself in my notes and ignore the students as they entered. That way I could avoid looking at Aubrey entirely.

As it turned out, my strategy wasn't necessary. The students filed in, and while a few came over to chat about the upcoming test, Aubrey didn't arrive. Neither did Julie. Were they together? Was Aubrey ashamed or too embarrassed to face me?

Regardless of what had inspired her absence, I was grateful as hell and made it through the lecture and tutorial in one piece. After meeting with Martin about the following week's test, I escaped to the sanctuary of my condo, relieved.

I knew I was going to have to face Aubrey eventually and make an effort to clear the air. Having a romantic relationship was inappropriate for a TA and student, but so was harboring grudges about personal conflicts. I couldn't bring myself to deal with the situation, though. I had this vague uneasiness lurking in the back of my mind—a strange feeling that I wasn't allowing myself to acknowledge.

To deter my wayward thoughts, I kept busy. Order—that's what I needed. Unpacking would fit the bill perfectly. It took me three hours to unpack and break down the remaining boxes. I was gripped by a sort of mania, not stopping until I was completely finished. Drained, I finally allowed myself to relax, ordering a pizza and then cracking open a beer, my morning hangover long forgotten.

# *Cold-Hearted*

Cleopatra: Not know me yet?
Antony: Cold-hearted toward me?
(*Antony and Cleopatra*, Act III, Scene 11)

When I arrived on campus Friday morning, I picked up the key to the Committees Room from the Hart House porter, ready for the afternoon tutorial and its new venue. I settled into my spot at the front of Martin's classroom, keeping my eyes fixed on my notes and books, just as I'd done on Wednesday.

Students arrived individually and in small groups. A couple of minutes before twelve o'clock, Aubrey and Julie walked in right on Martin's heels, claiming two spots near the door where they'd sat earlier in the semester. I stole a quick look at Aubrey, enough to confirm that she was as unwilling to make eye contact as I was. I feigned disinterest as I'd done so often in this room.

As Martin lectured about *Othello*, my mind wandered—pure self-preservation. I wouldn't be able to check out during the upcoming tutorial; I'd simply have to put on my game face and prove that I could maintain a professional demeanor.

GEORGINA GUTHRIE

With the class winding down, Martin reminded students of
the upcoming test and notified my seminar group of the change of
location for their tutorial. I quickly packed up my bag and dashed
out of the class. I had to get over to Hart House first so I could have
a few moments to breathe before everyone arrived.

The second-floor meeting room at Hart House was a hell of a
lot less claustrophobic, partly due to its size, but also thanks to the
three large windows which lined one wall. The tables were set up
in a square U-shape. I took a seat at a corner where two tables met,
angling myself so I'd have the best vantage point.

As the students filtered in and gradually filled the tables, I tried
to measure the tone. Despite the change in location, Mary probably
wasn't far from everyone's thoughts. There was definitely a different
vibe, and I'd have my work cut out for me today.

By the time Aubrey arrived with Julie, there were six seats left,
three of them in a row along the side of the table nearest me. Aubrey
chose the farthest seat, and Julie took a seat between us. I couldn't
bear to look at Aubrey or permit myself to acknowledge the pain her
presence aroused in me. I had to stay focused on my job.

I was about to begin when Neil Hammond, a shy young man
with chronic acne, rushed in and sat beside me. I assumed that would
be it for today. Cara and Lindsay had been notably absent from class.

While everyone unpacked their books and settled in, I took a
moment to try to make sense of my papers which were a chaotic
mess, mirroring my brain perfectly. I assumed a business-like tone
and launched into the day's topic.

"Welcome back. Today we have to try to squeeze in a quick discussion of both *Antony and Cleopatra* and *Othello*, so let's get started.
Based on Professor Brown's lectures this week or thinking about your
own reaction to the play, what did you learn from reading *Antony
and Cleopatra*?" I asked, trying to open general discussion.

I was met with silence; the only sounds were some throat clearing and paper shuffling.

*Come on. Someone say something.*

"Life's a bitch and then you die?" Shawn said, laughing softly.

This was a classic knee-jerk reaction to the uncomfortable atmosphere and undoubtedly a reference to Antony and Cleopatra's tragic
story, but it was also an unfortunate reminder of Mary's absence.

"And if you're dating a bitch, you'll want to die sooner," Vince added.

The two of them looked at each other and chortled.

"Well, that's not the most critical literary analysis of the play I've ever heard," I said dryly.

I wasn't sure how to proceed. I didn't want to be too heavy-handed on the first tutorial since Mary had passed; by the same token, I didn't want the session to be reduced to a three-ringed circus, either. The space around Aubrey was virtually crackling with tension. Even Julie seemed completely on edge. Was it safe to assume she knew what had happened? I hadn't talked to Jeremy so it was difficult to know for sure.

Whereas in the past I'd always counted on Aubrey and Julie to have something intelligent to say, I concluded that neither one of them was going to do anything to save my ass today.

But I was wrong. Sort of.

Aubrey looked across at Vince. In a weary monotone, she said, "The nineteen fifties called, Vince. They want their uninformed, narrow-minded views back."

"Wow, Aubrey, settle down," Vince said.

She looked at him disparagingly. I couldn't blame her. His comment had been pretty asinine.

"Don't talk to me like I'm a frigging five-year-old. And for the record, just because Cleopatra is strong and powerful, that doesn't make her a bitch." She looked vacantly up at the windows on the opposite wall, crossing her arms in front of her.

Shawn and Vince exchanged a look that said, "Who the hell pissed in her cornflakes?"

Julie glanced at her sympathetically. People shifted uncomfortably in their seats. Would it be inappropriate to dismiss the tutorial after only five minutes? I had to do something and quickly.

"Well, I may not agree with the word choice used to voice the opinion, but I'd echo Miss Price's sentiments," I said, trying to elevate the tone of the discussion. "A few weeks ago, we broached the topic of misogyny, and as it turns out, Miss Price is pursuing that topic with her independent study."

Simply saying those words called to mind our so-called meeting to discuss her topic at the Pratt Library. Aubrey raised her eyes to mine, and I felt like she could see right through me and knew exactly where my mind had wandered. Her lips were pursed, and her jaw was tense and set. I couldn't understand where she got off looking at me as if *I'd* been to one to rip her heart out. I took a deep breath and broke eye contact.

"I don't necessarily agree that Shakespeare is being misogynistic in *Antony and Cleopatra*," I continued. "Some critics argue that Shakespeare was modeling Cleopatra on Queen Elizabeth. Cleopatra's expertise in guile and seduction make the male characters around her uneasy, but ask yourselves if it necessarily follows that Shakespeare intended this portrayal as a negative one. You'd all do well to think about that. Always consider context when assuming a theoretical or critical lens in textual analysis."

Shawn interjected, attempting to give credence to Vince's ridiculous analysis. "Maybe what Vince's saying is that Antony was a total mess because of Cleopatra. She totally screwed with his head. He lost everything because of her."

Trina, a slight girl whose hair color seemed to change weekly and who often seemed surly and reluctant to share her opinions, put up her hand. I was open to any contributions today, and Trina's *Hamlet* paper had been good. She was no slouch intellectually.

"Miss Collins?"

"Cleopatra didn't hold a gun to Antony's head," she said. "He followed her ships and lost the battle at sea because of a poor military decision. Even Enobarbus said Antony's affection beat his captainship. That's not Cleopatra's fault."

I held my tongue, waiting to see if Shawn would respond.

He leaned forward. "But later she totally manipulated him. Like, when she sent word that she was dead when she really wasn't? That's mind games, pure and simple. Right, Daniel?"

All eyes turned to me, expecting me to mediate. It was time to fall back on my lecture notes. I looked at the collection of papers in front of me and immediately realized I wasn't going to be able to make sense of them. Instead, I tossed my pen on the table and rubbed my temples, hoping I could patch together a coherent response.

"It's not surprising that there's such a varied reaction to the play and differing opinions about who is most deserving of pathos," I argued. "The psychology of the characters is central to the plot, but we don't get a clear idea of what's going on in their minds because of the lack of soliloquy."

"Oh, yeah. I never really noticed that," Neil mused.

"We don't have the same benefit of constant dramatic irony that we have when reading *Hamlet* or *Macbeth*, for instance," I said. "You may *think* you understand a character's thoughts and motivations, but you can't always be entirely sure. We can either assume the characters' words are true, or constantly distrust their veracity, which isn't a pleasant notion. This, of course, is the way relationships work in life."

Aubrey held up her hand as if she were flagging down a taxi.

"Let me understand this, Daniel. You're basically saying that in life we should give people the benefit of the doubt, because otherwise we'd all be going around mistrusting everyone all the time. Am I following?"

*Holy fuck. Is she serious? If I survive this hour, it'll be an act of God.* I picked up my pen and tapped it thoughtfully on my notepad.

"I suppose that's a valid interpretation, Miss Price. Unfortunately, sometimes people do things to make it quite clear that they haven't been deserving of that leap of faith. I'm reminded of your words earlier in the semester about King Duncan. Look what happened to him."

She expelled her breath in a huff, muttered something to Julie, and crossed her arms in irritation. I was fairly certain the whispered comment had been about me, but I couldn't let that distract me. Around the room, her peers were beginning to look at her with confused expressions. Did she have no regard for the fact that we were in a room full of other people? I forced the discussion back to the play.

"Anyway, our interpretation is bound to be based on our prior experiences. I find that with a play like this, my understanding of the theme differs every time I read it, depending on the frame of mind I'm in."

"But you're on Antony's side, right?" Shawn asked.

"Well, I don't know if it's as easy as taking sides, but I can understand his predicament," I clarified. "Here's a man caught between doing his duty and devoting himself to a woman. It's an age-old dilemma." I glanced at Aubrey. "He seems to know that being with her will bring him grief—"

"But he can't stay away from her. He loves her too much," piped up Neil. "There's that line he says—I don't remember it. She's, like, fishing for a compliment or something, and he says something. It's near the beginning. Daniel? Do you know what I mean?"

"Yes, I think I know exactly what you mean. Give me a second." I turned quickly to the first scene. "Ah, here it is. Cleopatra asks for an assurance of how much he loves her, and he says, '*There's beggary in the love that can be reckoned.*' Is that the one you meant?" I asked.

Neil nodded, but seemed disinclined to comment further.

"That's a significant line, I have to admit. Anyone have any thoughts?" I asked, looking around the room.

Julie's hand flicked up. "Well, he's saying that love that can be calculated or quantified is meaningless or lacking true value," she said in a sad voice. "Essentially, he's telling her that his love for her is so great that it defies measurement."

"Precisely," I said. "He can't even articulate the depth of his feelings for her. So we shouldn't be surprised that he's prepared to sacrifice everything. And incidentally, that's not a flippant decision for someone whose honor and reputation mean everything to him. This, essentially, is Antony's psychological conflict. Cleopatra distracts him from his duties, and yet he's unable to give her up. He simply can't reconcile his clashing values."

*And, fuck me, do I ever identify with that feeling.*

Across the table Shawn was frowning.

"You disagree, Mr. Ward?" I asked.

"No, I wouldn't say that, but it seems like a hell of a lot to give up for a woman's love."

"Again, it's all about what we bring to the table. A reader who's been prepared to make enormous sacrifices to secure someone's love would not find his actions incomprehensible," I pointed out.

Aubrey expelled another loud sigh. Against my better judgment, I decided to call her on it. "Something to add, Miss Price?"

She narrowed her eyes. I could almost see her synapses firing.

"Well, a minute ago, you said you weren't taking sides. But that was fairly undisguised admiration for Antony as far as I can tell." She sat upright in her chair and crossed her hands in front of her. "Do you think Cleopatra really loved him?"

I wasn't sure if she was baiting me, but I carefully kept my comments within the scope of the play. "I don't deny her feelings for him, but I can see how readers might second guess her motivations. The way she handles Antony involves a degree of changeability and opportunism which may make her seem capable of betraying him."

All eyes were on us again. As we bandied ideas back and forth, I was reminded how much I loved intellectually sparring with her. Even in a state of conflict, we seemed to be connected by an invisible current. Everyone else in the room faded into the background.

Not surprisingly, Aubrey had a rebuttal at the ready. "Personally, I think she adores him," she claimed. "After he's died in her arms and she says, '*The odds is gone, and there is nothing left remarkable beneath the visiting moon*,' well, to me, that exemplifies the depth of her love."

She never ceased to amaze me, again quoting directly from the play without even looking at her book. And she was right. That was one of the most heart-wrenching lines in the play. I wanted to shake her, rail at her for giving up on me. And in that moment, my heart betrayed me. *I* actually felt sorry for *her*.

She seemed to have talked herself out. After holding my gaze for a moment, she lowered her eyes. I'd lost the thread of the discussion entirely, staring down the table stupidly. Luckily, Julie stepped in to fill the silence. "It was such a waste," she observed. "You have to wonder what possessed either of them to behave the way they did."

I recovered my equilibrium and picked up on her comment. "That's part of Shakespeare's genius. Here we have characters, like people, acting in response to a multitude of motivations. Readers might not be able to discern the reason for their behavior. What I find myself doing is wondering whether the characters themselves even understand why they're behaving the way they are. Their psychological crises make them seem most human."

"Well, they both frustrate me," Julie said, looking at me boldly. "I'd like to take their heads and bash them together to knock some sense into them."

Was it possible that Julie had now moved beyond the printed page and started talking about real life as well? If so, that meant she knew exactly what was going on between Aubrey and me. I had to bring this to a close. Comments were beginning to cut a little too close to the bone for my liking.

"Again, that's the mark of a great writer, I suppose—to be able to elicit that reaction from you." I collected my papers and flipped through to find my *Othello* notes. "I sense we've only skimmed the surface on these issues. I'll be sure to tell Professor Brown what kinds of questions and themes have come up, and perhaps he'll be good enough to include some of these relevant quotations on next Friday's identification test. Now, sorry to rush things along, but we should spend some time discussing *Othello* before you go."

Out of the corner of my eye, I saw Aubrey move, packing up her bag. She whispered something to Julie, grabbed her things and made a speedy departure, mumbling something about an appointment. I didn't buy it, but I wasn't about to stop her. Shawn Ward waved and smiled. She didn't acknowledge him. As she closed the door soundly behind her, another uneasy silence settled over the room.

"Well, let's turn to page three-forty-six in our anthologies and rake our friend Othello over the coals, shall we?" I said with a grim smile.

The sound of rustling pages broke the tension, and little conversations broke out around the room. Shawn and Vince debated the reason for Aubrey's sudden departure. Vince proposed that she might be getting her hair done in preparation for some event later tonight. Shawn didn't look convinced, claiming he wasn't surprised to see Cara and Lindsay away, assuming they'd probably gone to a day spa, but that he didn't think Aubrey was the type.

I feigned interest in my notes, letting them ramble on for a couple of minutes, eavesdropping shamelessly and wondering if Julie would offer them—and me, for that matter—an explanation. She didn't, which left me wondering what event was taking place that would require an appointment at a hairdresser's. Was Aubrey going to this event with Matt? Envy burned through my chest, but it was neither the time nor the place to indulge jealous preoccupations.

I pulled myself together and launched into *Othello*. We spent the next twenty minutes trying to figure out why Iago was such an ass and why Othello had been so quick to believe his lies about Desdemona. More people contributed to the discussion this time, but Julie remained silent throughout, deep in thought. I avoided making eye contact with her and almost leapt out of my seat with joy when I saw that it was time to wrap up for the day. How many more Friday tutorials were there? Five? Six? Surely this would get easier with time.

Barely holding myself together, I collected my things and waited for the room to empty. My mouth was dry, and my heart was hammering. Keeping control of that tutorial had been one of the most taxing challenges of my job thus far as TA, and I wasn't convinced I'd done a terribly effective job at that.

My bag packed, I glanced up to see Julie still standing by the end of the table, watching me pull on my coat. She looked as though she had something to say. I gazed at her, waiting for her to speak.

"Aubrey wanted you to have this," she said. She dropped a plastic bag on the table, and then she quickly turned and walked out of the room.

I rubbed my face in frustration. Yep, she knew. How was I going to make it through the rest of the term? Grimacing, I headed for the door, picking up the bag and jamming it in the side pocket of my laptop bag. I dared not look inside now.

I took the stairs two at a time and raced out the front doors of Hart House, trying to shake off the anxious tension the last two hours had provoked. Could Aubrey have been any more pointed with her comments? Why did she have to be so goddamned sharp? I thought I had the ability to mind-fuck people, but today I'd met my match. God only knew what would have happened if she'd stayed for the discussion of *Othello*.

I reached the crest of Hart House Circle, nearing my car which was parked in its usual spot in front of University College. As I topped the hill, I realized I had company.

Matthew Miller.

What was he doing here? And why the fuck was he leaning on my car?

## Then Shall He Mourn

Then shall he mourn,
If ever love had interest in his liver,
And wish he had not so accused her,
No, though he thought his accusation true.
(*Much Ado About Nothing*, Act IV, Scene 1)

Matt glared at me as I stopped in front of him.

"Matt. To what do I owe the pleasure?"

"Oh, I just thought I'd come and pay you a little visit," he said. "I knew Aubrey had a one o'clock tutorial with you over here. I was going to try to track you down, but then I saw your shiny ol' Beemer and figured I'd wait here for you instead."

He smacked the side of my car with the palm of his hand as he spoke, and I seriously considered doing the same to his head.

"Mind telling me what this is about? I'm assuming you didn't come all the way here to clean my car door with your ass?"

"Oh, I have no desire to clean your car, but I *am* tempted to clean your fucking clock," he said, taking a menacing step forward and clenching his fists at his sides. I dropped my bag on the ground with a thud, adrenaline ripping through my veins.

GEORGINA GUTHRIE

"Well, how incredibly *junior high* of you, Mr. Miller. Are we waiting for some of your pals to show up to cheer you on?"

"Don't talk down to me, Grant. If you've got any sense in that thick skull of yours, you'll listen to what I have to say and drop the pompous act."

"I'm all ears. Go ahead," I said, crossing my arms. It took every ounce of self-control not to grab him and smash his head through the windshield. I wasn't accustomed to such primal anger.

"I came to tell you that if you hurt Aubrey again, I'll fucking kill you. No questions asked," he said levelly.

"Now that is *quite* a threat. Why on earth would I hurt Miss Price? I have no idea what you're talking about." I was trying to remain nonchalant.

"Oh, I think you know exactly what I'm talking about," he said, voice dangerously low.

I sighed. "Listen, why don't you quit playing games and tell me what this is about, because I assure you I have no clue what you're trying to say."

He crossed his arms, his posture mirroring mine. "All right. No games." He narrowed his eyes. "I happen to know that you and Aubrey are close. Probably closer than a TA and student are supposed to be."

I flinched internally but tried not to betray my panic. Had Aubrey sold me out? Fuck, this was not good. What this guy could do with that kind of information! I could be on my way to being well and truly screwed.

"And before you jump to conclusions, Grant, she didn't volunteer this information. I practically had to wring the truth out of her. She was having a weak moment. Otherwise I'm sure she wouldn't have said anything. But really? I didn't need her to confirm it. I'm not stupid. It wasn't hard to figure out. I've been piecing this whole thing together for a while now."

I swallowed dryly but said nothing. Did he honestly know everything, or was he bluffing? And if he did know, was he now playing the part of the jealous new boyfriend, threatening me to stay away from his girl? Is that what this was about?

"Don't feel like you have to confirm or deny anything. That's not why I'm here," he said. "And for the record? I don't give a good goddamn whether or not you're supposed to be together or what the rules are. It's none of my business. I don't even think it's all that big of a deal.

You might think you're all important with your fancy car and your arrogant airs, but you're not a prof. You're just a TA for Christ's sake."

*You don't understand*, I wanted to say. *If only you knew what was at stake here.* But no, I hadn't even told Aubrey the precariousness of my position. Of all people in the world to confide in, Matt was not the one. I did my best to remain non-committal. "Go on. I'm listening," I said.

"I don't care about the lines you've crossed or whatever. If I did, I'd be at the English Department offices right now instead of standing here talking to you. What I *do* care about is Aubrey. She's been a mess since Tuesday, and she'll probably kill me for coming here and telling you this, but I've never seen her so messed up over a guy. She's a strong girl — not a crier. But this week? Not good, man." He looked at me quizzically. "I have no clue what she sees in you, but she must see something 'cause you completely knocked her on her ass with your fuckery."

Another unwelcome flicker of sympathy licked at my conscience. I wanted to continue feeling hurt by Aubrey's betrayal, but his account of how she'd struggled through the last few days rattled my cage. How in the hell did he think he had the right to call me out for *my* so-called "fuckery," though? I was the victim here, wasn't I? I wasn't the one who'd been dry humping someone else in a bar.

Did I dare speak frankly to him?

"Listen. I'm not going to pretend I'm comfortable talking to you about all this, but I see there's no point in continuing to deny that Aubrey and I are...*were*...close friends," I said, selecting my words with infinite care. "She trusts you. She cares about you. I know your loyalties rest with her. But after what I saw you two doing on Tuesday, I don't see how you think you can come here and try to make me feel like shit. Does she expect me to turn a blind eye to her conduct?"

"Her *conduct?*" Matt snorted. "You're talking about what you thought you saw happening at the Madison? I don't remember much — I was wasted. I showed up there, and Aubrey had to take care of me. Apparently she had to hold me up. If she hadn't, I would've ended up on my ass. So when you arrived, that's what you saw. And she tried to follow you, and then she tried to text you — wanted to explain what had happened — but you ignored her. And you know what? As usual, she didn't take anything out on me. Somehow she and Julie got me home in a cab. I could barely stand up, never mind walk."

I stared at him dumbly. I couldn't reconcile what he was saying with what I'd seen: The two of them tangled together, his arms around her, his face buried in her neck, her leg between his knees, one hand in his hair, the other caressing his back. And Julie *had* been there?

"You have no idea how much I want to believe you, Miller, but what I saw was way more than Aubrey propping you up, man."

He laughed cynically. "You know what you saw, Grant? I'd just seen my ex making out with another guy, and I was spinning. I'm sure even *you* can understand that. Aubrey was there for me, as always. She was *consoling* me. If someone needs her, she's there. If that threatens you, man, you'd better walk away right now."

"Are you telling me *nothing* happened between you two on Tuesday night?"

"Nothing but Aubrey being a great friend. If you think there's more to it than that, you've hatched it in your own fucked-up imagination."

The truth behind his words struck me with a suddenness that took my breath away as the details of his story clicked into place. I sighed heavily, rubbing my face roughly.

"Ah, fuck. I can't believe this!"

"Try harder," he said dryly.

"Christ, she must hate me." I sighed. "She does, doesn't she?"

"*Hate* is a strong word. She's ticked that you assumed the worst and wouldn't give her a chance to explain herself, but I don't think she hates you. I wouldn't say you're out of the game just yet."

I put my hands on my hips and stared at him helplessly. "Why *are* you telling me all this? Honestly."

He clenched and unclenched his jaw a few times. "Because Aubrey cares about you. Because you wouldn't listen to her when she tried to get through to you, and because she's too proud to keep trying. Aubrey's one of the most independent and strong-willed women I know. She might have moped for a day or two, but she's not gonna wallow forever."

He seemed to be right on the money. During the tutorial today, she'd been nursing what could only be described as a deep-seated anger.

"You want a chance with her?" Matt said. "You'd better give your arrogant head a shake and make the first move, because she's convinced you think she can't be trusted."

I weighed my options, trying to decide how to proceed. While I had Matt in front of me and he seemed prepared to speak frankly, I was sorely tempted to ask the question I'd wanted to ask Aubrey since that fateful night we'd seen *Hamlet* together. After a moment's deliberation, I decided to give it a go.

"Can I ask you something and request the courtesy of an honest answer?"

"You can try," he said. "I'm not making any promises."

"Okay. Has there *ever* been anything between you two?" There. I'd asked. Now it was up to him to man up and tell me the truth.

He smiled and looked away. "Don't you think that's something you should ask Aubrey?"

"Well, I'm asking you, aren't I?" I said, trying to goad him into responding.

"Aubrey and I are great friends," he said. "Do I love her? You bet your ass. If I didn't, I wouldn't be here talking to you right now. Am I *in love* with her?" He paused and shook his head. "No. I can't speak for Aubrey's feelings. You want more information than that, you'll have to ask the lady."

That wasn't exactly a comforting answer. But he wouldn't be here telling me all of this if he wanted her for himself. So he was intervening because he loved Aubrey enough to want her to be happy, even though he disliked me? Could I allow myself to believe him? I wanted to — so badly!

"I appreciate your candor." I rubbed the back of my neck. "So now what do I do? She left tutorial early. Should I call her? Try to get her to meet me somewhere?"

Something in my expression must have reached him because he took two steps toward me and sighed. He almost looked like he felt sorry for me. *Almost.*

"Listen, I'm gonna to tell you this because, for some reason, Aubrey believes you might be able to make her happy. Frankly, I couldn't care less if you dropped off the face of the earth right now, but I'm trying to think of someone other than myself. You might want to try that some time," he said.

He paused, and for a second, I thought he might have changed his mind, but then he continued, speaking as if he were sharing top secret government information.

"A few of us are having dinner out later. Then there's a semi-formal party at the Kap house at eight o'clock. I can tell you right now that she is gonna look kick-ass hot. I've seen her in the dress she plans to wear, and it's smokin'. I suggest you eat a hearty slice of humble pie, try to rein in your gargantuan ego, and do something tonight to fix what you've totally fucked up. If you don't? You could lose her once and for all. I happen to know there's someone who's gonna be there tonight who's mighty interested in, I don't know, *picking up the pieces,* shall we say."

"But this person is not you?" I asked.

"Nope," he said.

So, now I had new competition? Could this get any worse?

"Well, thanks for the info. And for what it's worth, I do appreciate you coming here today to set things straight. Aubrey is lucky to have you as a friend," I added as sincerely as I could.

"Damn straight she is," he said.

"But you know I can't go to that party, right? I don't expect you to believe this, but we've been trying to keep a low profile. Given my position, going to a frat party is out of the question," I explained.

"So, get there close to eight and hang tight outside. I'll watch for you. I'll do what I can. But let me make one thing absolutely clear: I meant what I said earlier." He pointed a finger at me. "If you and Aubrey manage to mend your fences, you'd better not hurt her again. If you do, you'll have me to answer to."

"Duly noted."

He jammed his hands in his pockets, and after one last warning look, he walked off toward the paths leading to Queen's Park.

I didn't waste any time. I threw my things onto the passenger seat and hopped in the car. I was about to pull out when I remembered the bag Julie had given me. I pulled it out of my laptop bag. A folded piece of paper was stapled to the outside of the plastic. I gently pried the sheet free. On it was Aubrey's handwriting, but Ophelia's words:

"...remembrances of yours
That I have longed long to re-deliver.
I pray you, now receive them."

Jesus. A series of flashbacks unfolded before me: Sitting beside Aubrey at the Hart House Theatre as Hamlet and Ophelia's shocking break-up scene played out on the stage; the intoxicating feeling of being so close to her in the confines of the theater and wanting to lean over to kiss her; later, knowing she was ill and that I was powerless to help her; and the desperate envy I'd felt when Matt had appeared to escort her upstairs to their apartment. It was then that the seed of my jealousy — apparently an unsubstantiated one at that — had taken root, only to grow insidiously in my heart over the course of the past three weeks.

I shook my head to clear the painful images from my mind before reaching into the bag. *The calendar.* Aubrey had given it back. I opened it up to March — she'd stopped counting down. Monday March ninth bore the last red X. I closed the calendar with a dejected sigh and placed it on the seat beside me.

I reached into the bag again and pulled out my black T-shirt. I unrolled it, and the striped gloves fell out. I held the T-shirt to my face and breathed deeply. I could still smell my cologne, but Aubrey's unmistakable fragrance was there as well — the fruity soap or perfume she used. So she had worn it, then? Perhaps on Monday night, before the emotional upheaval of Tuesday? But now she wanted nothing else in her possession that would remind her of our brief relationship.

Tossing the shirt and gloves on the passenger seat, I took one last look inside the bag. There was a piece of paper at the bottom — a page torn from her *Norton Anthology.* It was from Act III of *Othello,* and one of Iago's lines had been highlighted:

> *"Trifles light as air*
> *Are to the jealous confirmations strong*
> *As proofs of holy writ."*

In the margin, Aubrey had written:

You're an intelligent man, Daniel.
I trust you'll be able to figure this out.

I collapsed back into my seat. Holy Christ. Those words on the page — Iago's — pointed out how easy it is to find proof on which to base accusations when one's suspicions completely overtake all rational thoughts.

What had I done? I thought I might actually be ill.

Fuck, fuck, fuck. Matt was right. I'd screwed up — badly. How the hell was I going to redeem myself? Was it too late? I peeled out of my parking spot. I had a million things to do, and I needed to get started. Now.

As I drove, I frantically planned my route home, working in a trip to the dry cleaners to pick up my suit. Then I dropped in to the barber for a trim. Before heading home, I stopped for gas, tacking on a car wash.

My thoughts swam in circles as I contemplated Matt's visit. After hating him so unequivocally for so many weeks, it was hard to come to terms with his actions today. He'd been harboring as much animosity for me as I'd had for him, yet he'd come to see me specifically to plead Aubrey's case. That took an enormous amount of selflessness. His generosity shamed me. He'd completely shown me up — proven he was the better man. How could I possibly rise above that?

The answer loomed before me, as obvious as it was inevitable. I needed to tell Aubrey the truth.

All of it.

Getting ready to head over to the Kap house later that evening, I stared at my reflection in the mirror, wondering whether or not I should shave. Normally I did when I wore a suit, but Aubrey seemed to have a thing for whiskers, and I needed every brownie point I could scrape together. I decided against both shaving and a tie, leaving my white collared shirt open at the neck.

I smiled as I put on cologne, remembering how she'd licked my jaw on Friday after we'd gone out for lunch. Such a turn-on. What was it about this woman that made me so insane and inspired me to behave so irrationally? I'd never considered myself a jealous person, and I had certainly never been particularly violent. I'd run the gamut of extreme emotions this week.

Was it foolish to hope that I'd be able to cap the night off with extreme relief? After her behavior today and now that she'd returned everything I'd given her, would she even consider giving me a second chance? I closed my eyes, trying to remember exactly what Matt had said.

*I don't think you're out of the game just yet.*

Jesus, I hoped he was right.

I collected everything I'd need for the evening, pocketing my phone, my iPod, my wallet, and keys. I pulled on my suit jacket and overcoat, and then I was off to the Kap house to try to fix the spectacular mess I'd made. I willed myself to drive calmly and be patient—I'd always been intolerant of crappy driving, but it seemed that Toronto's worst drivers were on the street tonight.

At ten past eight, I pulled up to the curb about half a block away from the frat house. True to his word, Matt was out front, talking to another guy who was alternately taking drags from a cigarette and chugging from a plastic beer cup. I called out to him, and he sauntered down the pathway to join me.

"Daniel," he said, nodding curtly.

"She's in there, Matt?"

"Yep."

"How is she?"

"She's doing okay. You'd better brace yourself. She looks fierce. I'll try to get her out here."

"Okay, I'll wait here. And thanks, man." I grabbed his arm as he turned. "No, really, Matt. Thanks. I mean it."

He shrugged out of my grasp. "Don't thank me yet."

He disappeared inside the house, and I paced back and forth as the minutes ticked by. I was just beginning to think Matt wouldn't be able to get her outside when finally he reappeared at the door with Aubrey trailing behind him. Even from this distance, she looked phenomenal. Matt pointed down the road to where I stood. I raised my hand to her—a quiet greeting.

She shook her head vehemently, stepping back through the door. Matt grabbed her by the shoulders and seemed to be trying to reason with her. He steered her down the steps and took off his suit jacket, draping it around her. She walked reluctantly down the pathway, pushing her arms into the sleeves before crossing them tightly across her chest.

*Well, thank you again, Matthew Miller.*

Sure enough, once she was standing before me, I had no words. She looked so beautiful, delicate, and strong at the same time.

"Hi," I said, my voice tinny in my ears.

"What is it, Daniel?" She sounded emotionally drained.

"Can we talk?"

"You're a piece of work, you know that?" She looked at me in utter disbelief.

"I know you're angry with me. I don't blame you. But I'd appreciate it if you'd hear me out."

Her look of disbelief transformed — her jaw set and her eyes narrowed dangerously. "I asked you to hear me out on Tuesday, but you ignored me. Why does everything have to be on *your* terms all the time?"

I was at a loss for what to say because she was absolutely right. I hadn't responded to her when she'd needed to talk, and now here I was, expecting her to drop everything to listen to me. I was giving all new meaning to the term "double-standard."

"And in case you hadn't noticed, I'm actually busy right now. Tuesday night I was *all yours.* One hundred percent committed to being with you. You saw something you chose to misinterpret and wouldn't let me explain. Now you'll have to deal with the outcome of that decision."

I hadn't thought this would be easy, but I'd flattered myself into believing she might listen to what I had to say. Clearly I'd overplayed my hand.

"You're absolutely right. I — I'm sorry. I'll let you get back to your evening. I shouldn't have come. I thought that if — "

"What? You thought that if *what? That* if you came here to *surprise me* — all dressed to the nines, looking hotter than hell with your hair cut and your sexy whiskers — that you could charm me senseless? Did you think I'd fall all over you and forget everything? This isn't a movie, Daniel."

Fuck, she had my number. "Well, yeah, something like that, to be honest. Hey, a guy can hope, right?"

She sighed in exasperation, seemingly torn. Her teeth were chattering. She was totally underdressed for the weather. I pushed aside my selfish desire for resolution.

"Go back inside. You'll catch your death. I'm sorry I interrupted your evening. I'm a little late coming to the table, and you have every right to be pissed with me. We'll talk on your terms — you say the word and I'm there, okay?" I started to turn away.

"Ten minutes," she blurted. "I'll give you ten minutes."

I looked back at her gratefully. She shivered and wrapped her arms around herself. "Let me go grab my coat."

Air rushed out of my lungs. "Thank you, Aubrey. My car is down the block. It'll be warmer than talking out here. I'll wait for you."

As I said those words, I realized I meant them in more ways than she could possibly imagine. If she needed time to forgive me, to sort out her feelings, to consider her options, well, I would wait for her. As long as necessary.

She disappeared, and I returned to the car, tossing my coat in the back seat and blasting the heat. A few minutes later, she reappeared and eased herself into the passenger seat. She crossed her legs and turned to look at me steadily.

"Talk."

# CHAPTER 27

## Love Cries

Oft our displeasures, to ourselves unjust,
Destroy our friends and after weep their dust
Our own love waking cries to see what's done,
While shameful hate sleeps out the afternoon.
(*All's Well That Ends Well*, Act v, Scene 3)

I didn't know where to start, but I had to think of something — and fast. I saw no better approach than to be honest. What had Matt said? Something about eating a slice of humble pie? It was officially time to start chewing.

"Aubrey, I don't know how to tell you how sorry I am about what happened on Tuesday. I fucked up. Badly."

"Yes. Yes you did." She looked at me disapprovingly, but she motioned for me to continue.

"I don't know what came over me. Of course there's nothing going on between you and Matt. I let myself believe something that was a figment of my own imagination. I don't know what else to say, other than I hope you can find it in your heart to give me another chance, to let me prove I'm worthy…"

I trailed off. She was staring at me, eyes narrowed.

"Wait a minute—what the hell? Where is this all coming from? One minute you think I'm messing around with Matt and you don't answer my texts when I'm begging you to let me explain, and then today in tutorial you implied that I'd made you regret having faith in me. Now, all of a sudden, you realize you created the whole thing and you're *sorry*? Help me out here, Daniel, because this does not fucking add up."

I couldn't fault her. I'd done a complete one-eighty in the space of six hours.

"You want to know what happened? Someone took me down a few pegs. That's what happened."

"I have absolutely no idea what you're talking about," she said.

"I had a little chat with someone this afternoon after class. Someone who set the record straight for me."

She shook her head, frowning, trying to piece together what I was saying. "A chat? Oh, crap. Was it Julie? It was, wasn't it? She wasn't supposed to say anything. I asked her to give you back your stuff. I knew she wouldn't be able to resist getting into it with you. Shit." She crossed her arms in a huff.

"Hang on, now. It wasn't Julie. She did exactly what you asked of her. Much to my displeasure, I might add." Thinking about how I'd felt going through that bag inspired a painful spasm in my gut.

"Well, if it wasn't Julie then who—?" She looked at me again, her eyebrows furrowed. "No one else—" Her mouth popped open, and her eyebrows rose as the truth came into focus.

"Matt," I confirmed.

"You're kidding me. Tell me you're not serious!" she hissed.

I nodded.

"Jesus. What the hell did he tell you?"

"He told me about the brutal week you've had. He explained what happened on Tuesday. He told me enough to make it perfectly clear that I've been a complete asshole."

She turned and reached for the door handle.

"What are you doing?" I asked her.

"I'm going to give him royal shit. That was *not* his information to share," she said, voice shaking.

I grabbed her arm. "Damn it, Aubrey, don't. Please don't go."

"Let go of my arm, Daniel."

"Just — can you please wait a minute before you go and tear a strip off him? I'm so glad he came to talk some sense into me. I can't tell you how much I respect him for what he did today."

"What, so now you're best friends?" she asked incredulously.

"No, of course not. Frankly, I think he hates my guts. But seeing you suffer was making him crazy. He cares about you. He was trying to knock some sense into me."

She kept her arms crossed but looked as though she'd given up wanting to take out Matt, opting to stay and fight with me instead.

"Look, I'm not sure what the deal is here tonight — who you've left in there — " I gestured back toward the Kap house. "Maybe you've got a date waiting for you. I don't know. But in all honesty, I don't think ten minutes is going to cut it, and I'm *really* not comfortable sitting here in the middle of fraternity row. I'd love to get the hell out of here and sort all this shit out with you, but if you want to go back inside, I understand."

I was being as gracious as I could manage; it would have gutted me to watch her go back, but I was in no position to make demands of her.

"Where did you want to go?" Her tone was noncommittal.

"Nowhere in particular. Anywhere off campus."

"Jesus…" She sighed deeply. "Okay — just give me a sec." She reached into her pocket and took out her cell phone. "I'm going to text Matt to tell him I'm leaving, *if that's okay with you.*"

I rolled my eyes. "Of course that's okay. I'm not a monster. Please don't make me feel like one."

While she was busy texting, I took the opportunity to pull out of my parking spot. I didn't want her to change her mind, and I figured she couldn't escape as long as the car was moving. I had no clue where we were going so I drove south, trying to put as much distance between us and the Kap house as possible. I glanced over as she slipped her phone into her purse.

"All done?" I asked.

"Yes, thank you," she replied with forced politeness.

I tried to split my attention between her and the road.

"You look gorgeous, by the way. The dress, your hair — you look stunning."

"Thank you," she said crisply. "Joanna did it for me."

"Joanna?"

"My roommate. My *other* roommate. I guess I haven't told you about her. She's not around much. But don't worry; I'm not sleeping with *her* either."

"I wasn't…" I didn't even know what to say. Was she even going to give me a chance? Or was I bashing my head against a brick wall? I sighed, exasperated.

"And in case you're thinking I told her about us, I didn't, so please don't—"

"That didn't even occur to me." I glanced at her quickly. "I trust you."

"Ha!" She shook her head and turned to look out the window. "That's rich."

Oh, shit. This was not going well. I could feel my blood pressure rising.

"Daniel, would you slow down?" she asked, her voice tight.

Crap—I was going seventy-five in a fifty zone. The last thing I needed was a speeding ticket. I brought my speed more in line with the legal limit and then was forced to come to a screeching stop. Up ahead, the traffic lights at College Street shone green, but for some reason cars in front of me weren't moving.

"Jesus Christ, is there a particular *shade* of green you're waiting for, assholes?" I growled.

Aubrey was grasping the arm rest tightly. "If you're gonna drive like a maniac, you can let me out. I've had a bad week, but I'm not frigging suicidal."

I forced myself to breathe, and as the car in front of us moved forward, I proceeded slowly, maintaining a safe following distance.

"There, is that better?" I asked.

She let go of the arm rest and clasped her hands in her lap. "Much. Thank you."

"Here." I handed her my iPod and plugged it into the stereo. "Why don't you find some music? We'd better save the talking until I can pull over somewhere."

We reached College Street, and she scrolled through my playlists. Instinctively I wanted to turn left toward my condo, but I turned right instead, still having no earthly clue where I was going. I should have planned this more carefully. I glanced at Aubrey again. She was examining my iPod with interest.

"See if you can find my UK playlist. Look for a song called 'The Weight of My Words,'" I suggested.

"Yeah, it's here."

"Okay, throw that on," I said.

I turned up the volume, hoping against hope that the song's lyrics might soften her up. It would be easy for me to tell her that I was at a loss to properly communicate my feelings, but I decided to let the song speak for me—at least for now.

She peeked at me out of my peripheral vision. "Daniel," she said. Her tone was heart-wrenching.

"Shh. Listen."

I tried to keep my attention focused on the road, battling with my frayed emotions. Aubrey was wringing her hands, staring out the passenger window, perhaps as wrecked as me.

Somehow we'd arrived at Lakeshore Boulevard. I turned right, continuing to move away from the city center. Traffic was light, and now that I no longer wanted to punch out every driver on the road, I focused on finding a quiet place to stop.

I scanned the parking lots at the side of the boulevard, then I remembered the Palais Royale was a little farther along, just past the Boulevard Club. The perfect spot to talk. I smiled, wondering if Aubrey had ever been there. Probably not. Now I was excited—eager to share this wonderful place with her. How quickly I'd forgotten that I had a hell of a lot of work to do before I could count on her wanting to share *anything* with me.

I stole another quick look at her. The song was drawing to a close, and she was nibbling at her thumbnail. As the final note rang through the speakers, I reached over and turned off the stereo. There was no way I could cope with the next song. Up ahead, the Palais Royale lit up the darkened boulevard. I pulled into the busy parking lot, maneuvering into a spot and turning off the engine.

*Now what?*

"That was a nice song," she said, her voice a strained whisper.

"I listened to it on Wednesday, and it damn near killed me," I admitted.

She didn't respond, instead training her eyes out the front window where the lake was shimmering, the lights from the boardwalk lamp posts reflecting across the waves. The gulf between us seemed insurmountable. Regardless, I had to try.

"Aubrey, how did this happen?" I struggled to maintain a deferential tone. I didn't want her to think I was accusing her of anything.

"I hope that's a rhetorical question," she said, her expression weary.

I gazed out at the lake for a moment before looking back at her. "I'm not sure that it is."

"So you want an answer?"

"I think it's about time I gave you the opportunity to say what you wanted to tell me on Tuesday. I'm sure I'm not going to like what I'm about to hear, but that doesn't mean you shouldn't have a chance to say it. I promise to listen rationally if you promise to allow me the chance to explain myself, too."

"All right. Well, you handled things extremely poorly this week, Daniel."

"Tell me what I should have done. I've obviously got some learning to do."

"'To teach a teacher ill beseemeth me.'"

I smiled grimly. "Your uncanny ability to come up with some sort of Shakespearean comeback is impressive, but I think you already outdid yourself on that score today. I want *you* to talk to me tonight, Aubrey, not Ophelia, not Cleopatra, not Desdemona, and not the Princess of France. *You.*"

"I don't even know where to start." She shook her head. "How could you assume I'd betrayed you with Matt after the time we spent together last week? Do you honestly have so little faith in me? That hurt. A lot."

I'd jumped to conclusions; I knew that now. I also knew with unshakeable certainty that she deserved the truth. She needed to know why I'd been so confused—that it hadn't been a reflection of her character, but rather my own hang-ups and fears. Christ, how to start?

"Aubrey?" I reached over to hold her hand.

"Please don't. Not now, Daniel. I can't right now."

I sighed, disheartened and desperate to connect with her.

"I handled things poorly on Tuesday. Our argument on the weekend threw me for a loop. Everything that happened this week goes back to that damn cab ride."

THE WEIGHT OF WORDS

"So you're saying it's all my fault for coming on too strong?"

"No, that's not what I mean at all. Do you have any idea how much I wanted to take you home with me? I came so close, and that really scared me. I know we've already crossed a line, Aubrey. We can't go back. But the thought of taking things further made me hate myself. I couldn't do it. But God, I wanted to. I really wanted to."

I impulsively reached out to her again, and this time she let me take her hand in both of mine. I rubbed my thumb across her knuckles, looking down at our joined hands before meeting her eyes again.

"Instead I rejected you, and I'm sorry for that. The look on your face when I pushed you away—it tortured me. You're so beautiful, Aubrey. I imagine you spending time with single guys like Matt, and I can't believe they don't want to be with you. I was terrified that I'd lose you to someone else because I couldn't move forward with you."

"That's crazy. I don't want anyone else."

I nodded, ashamed of my insecurities.

"It might seem crazy to you," I said, "but trust me, it all made perfect sense to me on Saturday night. I did a lot of thinking the next day and came to an important decision—one that would allow me to be with you. I went shopping and bought you those gloves and packaged them up with my T-shirt and that note. I couldn't wait to tell you what I'd decided. I convinced myself you'd be so happy that you'd forgive me for sending you mixed messages. But then we couldn't seem to find a time to get together—I was even tempted to cancel my tutorial so we could get the hell out of there and talk."

She looked at me expectantly. "What was it that you were so desperate to tell me?"

"I'd decided to withdraw from my position in Martin's class. That's how badly I wanted you. I was prepared to give up my position for you, Aubrey. For us."

My heart pounded as I waited for her to react to my words.

"Daniel, that is *hands down* one of the most ridiculous things you've ever said."

The blood drained from my face. *Ridiculous?*

"I thought you'd be happy..." I faltered.

She sighed and shifted in her seat. "For an intelligent guy, you say and do some *really* stupid things sometimes." She shook her head in exasperation.

I was completely dumbfounded.

"I thought you'd be thrilled when you heard I'd be willing to make that sacrifice for you."

"Are you kidding me?" She flopped her head back against her seat, beyond irritated. What the hell? "Look, can we get out—go for a walk or something?" she said. "Something about us trying to have discussions in cars—I don't know. It doesn't work."

She opened her door before I had a chance to respond. I climbed out, pulling on my overcoat and buttoning it up as I led her toward the sidewalk, instinctively reaching for her hand and threading it through the crook of my arm.

"Okay," I said. "Why the hell was my decision so stupid?"

She stopped and put both of her hands in her pockets. It was like I'd been cut adrift and needed to grab on to her to keep me grounded. She was obviously pulling away for a reason, so I put my hands in my pockets too, trying to avoid appearing as uncomfortable as I felt. She gazed up at me earnestly.

"Think about it, Daniel. You love being Professor Brown's TA. You should see yourself in tutorial. You become so, I don't know, passionate—professorial—I don't even know how to explain it. It's obvious that you love it. You do, don't you?" she asked.

"Yes, of course I love it. But isn't that even more of a reason to appreciate what I was willing to give up to make things work? To not have to sneak around anymore? To not have to wait?"

"Maybe in theory, but do you think I want to be responsible for you giving up something that means so much to you?"

My heartbeat quickened as her face softened, her intensity gradually giving way to tenderness. How on earth could she possibly be so intuitive? I didn't want to give up this position. It *did* mean a lot to me. But at what cost?

"Do you see what I mean now?" she said.

"I swear you understand me better than I understand myself sometimes."

I thought about the strange niggling feelings I'd been having over the last few days—the hazy unformed thoughts hovering on the edges of my mind. Of course. That's why I was so quick to assume she was messing around with Matt. I'd been considering dropping out of Martin's class, but deep down, I wasn't happy with the decision.

Believing Aubrey had chosen another guy over me was merely my subconscious kicking in, fabricating a scenario that would give me another out. How could it have taken me a whole damn week to understand what she'd figured out in five minutes?

"So you're not going to quit, right?" she pressed. "Promise?"

"I won't. I promise. And God knows I don't deserve you, but there's no way in hell I'm going to give you up without a fight, either." I stroked her cheek with the back of my hand. "Tell me you forgive me. Tell me I haven't ruined everything with my pride and stupidity." She looked up at me, her chin trembling. "Please say something. You're killing me."

And then she smiled—a small, reluctant upturn of her beautiful lips.

"I thought I'd never get to have a conversation with you where I wasn't 'Miss Price' ever again," she said, her voice wavering. She struggled to keep her emotions in check, and my heart clenched.

"I hate myself for what I've done to you this week. And today—you were so angry. Knowing I'm the one who's responsible for that? I'm a prick."

Aubrey nodded, and I couldn't blame her. "I hate how emotional I've been this week. I'm not usually like this," she said.

"You don't have to beat yourself up for having feelings," I assured her. "Believe me. I've had my fair share of ups and downs this week as well."

She looked at me grimly. "So now what?"

I shoved my hands into my pockets again. "Well, I'm determined not to take you home until we've figured out where we go from here."

"Literally or figuratively?" She turned to look at the two paths ahead of us which veered off in opposite directions. "I don't think I'm up for a stroll on the beach. What's that building over there?" she asked.

"Well, I kind of pulled into this lot on purpose. This is the Palais Royale. I'd love to take you inside and show you around. It's beautiful. There are a couple of quiet spots where we could sit and talk. You game?"

"We definitely have lots to talk about."

"Before we go in, can I do something?"

"Um, okay."

"Can you please hold out your hands?" I waited for her to comply, her expression wary. I pulled her rainbow gloves out of my pocket. She smiled contritely and offered me a hand. I pushed a glove onto her left hand, followed suit with the right, and then clasped her fingers tightly. "I know these gloves are crazy and probably not what you would have picked out for yourself, but as soon as I saw them I couldn't resist. You *do* want to keep them, I hope?"

"Yes, Daniel. I want to keep them. They may be crazy, but I love them. They're perfect."

"And you'll try not to lose them?"

"I'm not going to let them out of my sight," she whispered.

She glanced down at our joined hands before looking back up at me.

"Daniel—"

I didn't wait to hear what she had to say. I pulled her against me tightly, encircling her with my arms, a surge of relief washing over me when her hands moved up to my shoulders. A familiar flicker of desire stirred within me when she snuggled into my neck, her warm breath tickling my throat.

How could I have failed to notice before how perfectly she fit there?

# Aubrey

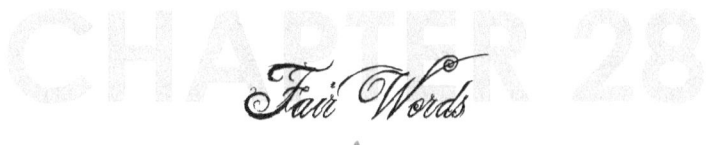

## Fair Words

Speak, fair; but speak fair words, or else be mute:
Give me one kiss, I'll give it thee again,
And one for interest, if thou wilt have twain.
(*Venus and Adonis*)

**M**y resolve went completely down the drain. It was next to impossible to stay angry with him. He was so apologetic, so remorseful. And that damn song we'd heard in the car — how could I not react emotionally to that? How could I think straight with his arms around me and his whiskery cologne-scented jaw intoxicating me? Surely I couldn't be faulted for wavering.

"You'll never believe how much I've missed you," Daniel whispered.

Yep. That did it. I was toast. "I missed you too," I said, my face still buried in his neck.

He squeezed me tightly. "Mmm. It feels so good to hear you say that." He pulled back to look at me. "You really do look beautiful tonight."

"You look amazing too. Great suit." I raised an eyebrow. "And, uh, nice hair."

"I got it cut for you."

"I knew this whole get-up was premeditated, Mr. *GQ*."

He grinned broadly, his eyes sparkling. "Come on. Let's get inside so I can have a good look at you."

He took my hand, leading me down the pathway. As we neared the building, I heard music drifting out into the night. It wasn't contemporary music, though. It sounded like—well, it sounded a lot like something from a nineteen forties movie.

"Is this a banquet hall?" I asked him.

"The Palais Royale? It's a dance hall—a ballroom. There's a live orchestra, and they play standards and jazz, big band tunes, that sort of thing."

We entered the building together, the sound of band music traveling into the lobby from behind a pair of double glass doors. A young woman stood behind a long counter beside a cloakroom, and she smiled as we approached.

Before Daniel had a chance to speak to her, I grasped his elbow. "I'm just going to use the washroom first."

"Of course. It's over there, to the left." He pointed to the other end of the lobby.

"I'll be right back."

Inside the washroom, I unbelted my coat and dropped it on one of the two white leather chairs flanking the wall by the door. I was instantly reminded of the lush restroom at Canoe.

A month.

That's how long it had been since my night out with Matt. My stomach clenched with guilt. I'd raked Daniel over the coals for accusing me of being involved with Matt, and yet he *did* have some cause for assuming that Matt and I had more than just a close friendship. I shook my head to wipe out the memory of Matt's tongue exploring my mouth.

*No, no, no. This is not what I need to be thinking about right now.*

I finished up in the washroom, checking the hair clips to make sure they were still holding my curls in place. Joanna really had done a great job. Satisfied, I grabbed my coat and headed back out to the lobby. At the counter, Daniel was chatting with the girl who'd greeted us.

"I'm sure that can be arranged," I heard her say as I neared the counter. When she saw me approaching, she cleared her throat conspicuously.

"Oh, Aubrey, here, let me take your coat," Daniel said, holding out his hand.

The counter-girl hung it up and then grabbed a set of keys from a drawer, telling us to follow her. I eyed Daniel curiously as we crossed the lobby, but he just took my hand and winked at me. Sexy bastard. The girl opened the door at the far end of the room and ushered us inside.

"Good luck," she whispered to Daniel as she pulled the door closed.

"What was that all about?" I asked.

"I told her I'm in the dog house and I'd be forever indebted if she could arrange for us to have a quiet half hour in here."

"In other words, you charmed her pants off?"

"I did what was necessary to secure some privacy. Anyway, never mind tactics, let me look at you." He made a clicking noise in his cheek. "You look absolutely stunning. Beyond gorgeous, poppet, really."

Okay. He was killing me. Talk? Did I say I wanted to *talk?* Talking was suddenly highly overrated.

"Listen, mister. Quit trying to distract me," I said, scrambling to get back on track.

"You're right. I'm sorry. I'll try to behave. Come on over and sit."

He led me to the cream-colored leather sofa. I settled into one of the cushions and took in the rest of the room. Plush red draperies hung beside the French doors which led to an outdoor deck or patio of some sort. A cherry-wood bar stretched the width of one of the walls. Delicate orchids in an elegant long-necked vase adorned the side table along the opposite wall beside another set of curtained French doors. The room was beautiful.

Daniel unbuttoned his blazer and sat beside me, his arm resting along the cushions behind me. I crossed my legs and noticed his eyes travel appreciatively from my thighs down to my ankles. I quite enjoyed having the upper hand for once.

"So, you said we have lots to discuss. What's first?" he prompted ed me.

"I don't know where to start. There's so much we need to talk about. It's a little daunting."

"Would you mind if I asked you a question?" he said, absently twirling my hair around his fingers. "On Monday, you said you had something you wanted to tell me. If we'd had a chance to talk on Tuesday night as we'd originally planned, what would you have said?"

I sighed, reaching for his hand which he eagerly offered.

"I was going to tell you that we needed to take some time apart. After last Saturday, I couldn't stand the thought of being so close to you without really being *with* you. It seemed like it might be a good idea to suggest backing off, not spending time alone together until May."

He squeezed my hand and smiled ruefully. "Huh, we couldn't have been in more entirely different mindsets if we'd tried. Why didn't you call to talk about this on Sunday?" he asked.

"I was afraid to. I thought you'd suggest a *permanent* break."

"Oh, my lovely, how could you possibly think that?" he asked, bringing my hand to his lips.

"I couldn't help it. You should have seen your face when you got out of that taxi, Daniel. You were so angry. I thought I'd blown it," I admitted.

"People in relationships are allowed to be angry with each other sometimes. It doesn't mean they hate each other. Having said that, I do have one small request. In the cab, you said a word I'd rather you didn't say to me again, at least not the way you said it."

I sighed as shame coursed through me. I knew exactly what he was talking about.

"When I asked you if I could call you and you said 'whatever,' I heard, 'I don't give a fuck what you do.' I know you were hurt, but I can't stand that word. It haunted me all night. Even if you're pissed off at me, I want you to tell me what I'm doing wrong. At least then I'll know you care enough to address the problem. I don't ever want to feel like you don't give a flying fuck what I do. Deal?"

"Deal," I said quietly. "And you have to promise not to ignore my texts like that. Even if you're too paranoid to text me back, at least call me."

"I promise. You know, I didn't even get your texts until Wednesday morning, and by then I'd convinced myself you'd moved on. I couldn't bear to hear you tell me why you didn't want to be with me."

"Wow, that's nuts," I said, leaning against him and twirling my fingers through the sprinkling of hairs peeping out of his open collar. "But I guess I was pretty irrational myself the last few days. Thank

God for Matt and Julie. Poor Matt. He wanted to call you to explain everything. I threatened him with a covert attack on his testicles if he did. I can't believe he went to see you anyway. I wish I'd been a fly on the wall when you guys were talking. You know I didn't set out to tell him everything, right?"

"He suggested that he practically had to torture the truth out of you."

"It was impossible to keep lying. I couldn't cover up any more. He won't say anything, Daniel. I'm not trying to upset you by saying this, but I'd trust Matt with my life."

"That doesn't upset me, although it does make me feel completely unworthy. As for being able to trust him, if he wanted to screw me over, I'm sure I'd be twisting in the wind right now instead of sitting here with you."

He pulled my head down to rest on his chest, and I placed my hand over his heart, feeling its steady beat under my palm.

"So, where do we go from here?" he asked. "Do you still want to take a break from things until May?"

I tried to imagine not spending time with him alone, not talking to him on the phone, not being able to have moments like this for another month and a half.

"Aubrey?"

"Sorry. I'm thinking."

"And?"

"I don't know. How do you feel about everything?"

"All I can think about is what a mess I've been the last few days without you. If you want to step away—temporarily, I'd hope—I can't force you to change your mind. But right now, I want to be with you more than ever."

"I want that too."

He looked at me warily. "But?"

I sighed, sitting up and turning to face him. "It's not really a *but*. It's just…well, Julie and I had a great talk on Tuesday. She put things in a different light."

He looked at me curiously.

"I told her we were being completely hands off, as you'd suggested. She thinks it's great that we can't be together because it forces us to get to know each other. After what happened with Matt, I think I agree. If you truly knew me, you'd never believe I was capable of that sort of calculated betrayal."

"So you *do* want to pull back? Take a break from seeing each other?"

"Not exactly. I still want to spend time with you, but I'm going to do my best to stop fixating on the things we can't do. If we were dating under normal circumstances, I'm sure we wouldn't be having this conversation. I don't think I'd have made it past that little texting session in the Hart House Library. I'd have tackled you as you tried to walk out the door."

He smiled, and his eyes had a faraway look. "That *was* pretty hot."

"*Anyway*," I said, trying to get us back on track, "my point is, instead of seeing the limitations of our relationship as being imposed on us, why don't we *choose* not to cross those boundaries and focus on learning about each other? I know it sounds old-fashioned, but is it really so bad to take things slowly and not leap head first into a physical relationship? Let's start at the beginning, not at the end. Am I making any sense?"

"You're making perfect sense. I know for a fact that I can't promise to stop doing this, though," he said, pulling me close again and hugging me tightly. "I swear, when I thought I'd never get to hold you again—well, let's say it drove me to drink."

"What is it with you men drinking when you're upset?" I said, leaning back to look at his face.

"Classic avoidance, I believe. An inability to deal with emotions. We're pathetic."

"I'll say." I smiled gently as I gazed up at him. "Wow, doesn't it feel good to finally be on the same page?"

He squeezed my hand, sighing deeply and closing his eyes.

"What is it?"

"I don't think we're on exactly the same page just yet. There's something else we need to talk about before we go any further."

The suddenly somber tone of his voice and his stony expression made my heart thump double time.

"Okay. Go ahead."

He frowned, pursing his lips as if bracing himself.

"What I have to tell you isn't easy for me to share, and you have to keep this to yourself. No one can know. Not Matt, not Julie, *no one*."

"God, Daniel, you're scaring me," I said, trying to read his expression.

"I'm not trying to scare you, but I do need your word. It's very important."

"Of course you have my word."

"Okay. Good," he said, lifting his eyes to look at me. "Did you know that this is actually my second teaching assistant assignment?"

"Really? Why didn't you mention it before? I'm surprised your father hasn't talked about it."

"That's not surprising at all, actually. I had a bit of an unfortunate experience last year. At Oxford."

"Unfortunate experience? What happened?" I wondered if this had to do with the file folder with Daniel's name on it that I'd seen in Dean Grant's drawer.

"Well," he said, huffing out a breath, "I was working with a first-year class. A great group of young people, seventeen, eighteen years of age. It was a Renaissance lit class."

He paused, his eyes drifting past my face and over my shoulder, as if he was conjuring up a memory.

"There was a girl in the class called Nicola. She was one of those students who managed to rise to the top at her little hometown school," he said, his eyes flitting back to mine. "Her family didn't have much money, but she got some small bursaries and a loan and muddled through somehow. Turns out the leap from secondary school to undergraduate academia at Oxford was more than she could handle. She had a part-time job, and it interfered with her school work. She had trouble completing essays on time, and her analysis was generally shallow and unoriginal."

I was losing the thread. Where was all of this going? I didn't interrupt, though. I simply sat and waited as his eyes flickered over my shoulder again.

"I tried to help her. She came to me for guidance many times, but nothing seemed to work. She failed one essay after another. I would try to squeak out extra marks for her on the assignments I assessed, but even then, she generally couldn't do better than a D plus."

He stopped and took another deep breath.

"One day she came to see me during my office hours and begged me to secretly let her rewrite a term essay that she'd bombed. The prof would never have approved a rewrite, and I wasn't about to let her do it on the sly. She started crying and saying she'd lose her scholarship for the coming year and not be able to continue her studies. She begged me to help her. I told her I'd help her as much as I could on upcoming assignments, but I wasn't prepared to do something underhanded."

He frowned, his eyes hardening.

"Once she stopped crying, her face completely changed. She said she'd give me 'one last chance' to change my mind. I told her there was nothing I could do to help her beyond what I was already doing. She collected her things and got up to leave. As she stopped at the door, just before opening it, she turned and said, 'I think you might regret that decision.'"

His story was making my heart race. I realized I was grasping his fingers tightly, but he didn't seem to care.

"The next day, I was called to the head of department's office. The proverbial shit had hit the fan," he said with a pained smile. "Nicola had gone to the dean's office to level a complaint against me." He paused, licking his lips and rubbing his eyebrow and temple with his index finger.

"What was it?" I asked, my voice low, matching his.

"It wasn't as much a complaint as an accusation, really," he said. "Three little words from her, and my life blew up in my face. I've spent the last ten years of my life studying words — marveling in their power, their weight. Never once in all those years did I have an inkling that the weight of so few words could be so crushing," he said, chuckling darkly.

"Daniel, what did she say?"

He looked at me uncomfortably and said through gritted teeth, "'He molested me' were her exact words, I believe."

I slowly fell back against the sofa, feeling as if I'd been punched in the stomach.

"She claimed I'd locked my office door and tried to have my way with her," Daniel said. "She alleged that the reason I was giving her poor marks came down to her refusal to…shall we say…*reciprocate* my advances."

He went silent, waiting for my reaction, but I was too stunned to speak. A series of epiphanies collided in my brain, the events of the past six weeks making so much more sense. Daniel insisting on conducting office hours in busy public places, never allowing himself to be alone with a girl in a class room with the door closed, keeping us all at a safe distance, using only our last names, frantically trying to remain objective. This was more than a newbie TA being extra cautious. This was someone doing his best to cover his ass.

Dean Grant's shock that night at their house—when he realized Daniel was the TA of the course I was taking—now made perfect sense. He'd been innocently trying to set up a match between Daniel and me and must have been horror-stricken when he thought about the implications of his actions.

Then I remembered Brad's question—what he'd asked his brother as we'd flirted at the pool table. *"Are you trying to teach her to play pool or are you molesting the poor girl?"* he'd said. Something spoken in jest, that one word, "molesting," had brought Daniel back to reality. He must have realized he'd given me enough rope to hang him with if I cared to use it.

"Quite the story, huh?" Daniel said, now prompting me to respond.

"I, uh, my God, I don't even know what to say. What happened then?"

"There was an inquiry. I was pulled from my position, and my PhD candidacy was revoked pending investigation. My parents were devastated. They flew over to try to help me. It looked like I might even have to go to court to deal with a sexual harassment charge."

The file folder in Dean Grant's drawer had been labeled *Daniel's Court Case—Oxford.* Of course...

"My dad worked tirelessly to get to the bottom of things," Daniel said. "He visited Nicola's parents, and it seemed they got a sense of the, well, let's say, the financial benefits inherent in Nicola withdrawing her accusation. She recanted, and there was an out of court settlement. I still don't know what it cost my parents. The worst part is the element of doubt the episode raised about my conduct. I'd been so mindful of being professional and doing all the right things, and it didn't make one iota of difference. To this day, I wonder if my parents believe me entirely, especially my dad. It's a constant source of conflict between us. It makes my mother crazy."

I shook my head slowly. "So, when your dad didn't want her to know about me being in your class when I was over at your house for dinner that night—"

"He was trying to avoid an ugly scene. He told her everything when he got home. She was upset, but she could see how the misunderstanding had occurred. Truthfully, I think she was disappointed. She likes you," he said. "You already know how much my father likes you. Now you know why he was so insistent on us not being friends."

"It made sense to me then, but yes, it makes even more sense now."

"He's been freaking out since the day I started in Martin's class. U of T admin knows what happened last year. There's a letter in my file. Even though Nicola's handling of the whole situation calls her claims into question, the university is being extra careful. I'm lucky to have my dad's influence behind me, but even he won't be able to help me if things go wrong again. If he knew you and I were involved..."

As he trailed off, he searched my face while I tried to work through everything he'd told me. What a mess. How I wish I'd known about this all along. I'd spent the first four weeks of the semester mooning over him like a love-struck adolescent, cursing his mood swings and obsessing over his coolness. Then, once he'd shared his feelings for me, I'd sulked and given him grief because he wouldn't throw himself wholeheartedly into our forbidden relationship. How juvenile I'd been.

"What are you thinking?" he asked me. "You must think I'm an absolute idiot for allowing this to happen between us when there's so much at stake."

"I don't think you're an idiot. How can you even say that? I'm the one who feels like an idiot. I've been so pushy and demanding. I wish I'd known."

"Believe me, I thought about telling you every time we were alone together, but something held me back every time. Nicola made me feel like a monster. I spent a hellish year convincing myself I wasn't one, and then I met you, and you made me smile and laugh. You seemed to like me. You helped me like myself again. I tried to keep my distance from you, but when I discovered you had feelings for me, I couldn't push you away any more." He shook his head mournfully. "After spending the last year wondering if everyone I know is questioning what really happened, I didn't want to risk falling from your good graces."

"Did you molest that girl, Daniel?"

"God, of course I didn't," he said, his eyes flashing with anger.

"I'm sorry." I squeezed his hand comfortingly. "Don't be mad. I had to ask. I thought you might like to see what it feels like to be asked the question by someone who'd believe your answer unequivocally."

"Thank you," he said, closing his eyes and leaning forward, resting his forehead against mine. "You have no idea how it feels to hear you say that."

"I'm glad you told me."

"You deserve to know the truth. Even if you want to run screaming in the opposite direction, at least you understand why I've been so hot and cold. This has been such a confusing month for me. Last week, when Brad said I had a ton of baggage, he wasn't joking. None of the craziness that happened this week is your fault, Aubrey. It's not you. It's all me. I'm so sorry."

I launched myself at him, wrapping my arms around him tightly and rubbing my cheek against his. Daniel hummed against my hair, his arms circling my body, keeping me close. "Does this mean you're not going to run screaming?" he asked.

I pulled away and glanced down at my feet. "I'm not running anywhere, especially in these shoes."

#

# CHAPTER 29

Your love and pity doth the impression fill
Which vulgar scandal stamp'd upon my brow;
For what care I who calls me well or ill,
So you o'er-green my bad, my good allow?
(*Sonnet 112*)

He smiled at me, his eyes darting from my eyes to my lips and back again. "So that's it?" he said. "You're honestly okay with all this? We'll keep the status quo?"

"I can't fathom walking away from you now. If you're okay with what we've decided, then so am I. Absolutely status quo."

Albeit a much better informed status quo. I still wanted to shake a bookshelf or two with him, but there was no way I'd be forcing the issue. We'd crossed a line and broken so many rules, but if things were to continue with us, the last thing I wanted was to be responsible for ruining Daniel's second chance. From here on in, I was even more determined to follow his lead.

"Telling you everything went so much better than I thought it would," he said, his face showing a slightly puzzled expression.

"You thought I'd cut and run?"

"I wasn't sure what to think. I called Penny and Brad earlier this evening to tell them I was considering telling you about Nicola. Penny said she was sure you'd stick by me. She really likes you."

"I like her, too. I like your whole family."

"That makes me really happy. You have no idea."

His eyes roamed across my face for a few seconds, and then he slipped his sleeve up, sighing as he checked his watch. "I don't mean to rush things, but we should probably head out soon. Did you want to take a peek inside before we go? The ballroom is just on the other side of those French doors."

"Do you think that's a good idea?"

"You can't be here and not check out the band. They're really something. Come on."

He led me across the room and opened the door a crack. I poked my head through.

"There's one of those Japanese folding screens in the way. I can't see a thing. Can I go in?" I asked.

"Of course."

He urged me forward, and I stepped through the door and popped my head around the decorative screen. The ballroom featured a hardwood dance floor with tables around the perimeter. A glittering ball cast flecks of sparkly light across the floor and walls. While the room was beautiful, it was nothing you wouldn't see at an upscale wedding reception. What took my breath away was the orchestra—like something from another era—a group of men in tuxedoes sitting on tiered levels on the stage, the back row currently standing with their instruments raised high.

On the floor, at least fifty couples twirled in spectacular unison with the music. I felt Daniel's presence behind me. Safely hidden behind the screen, he stepped close to me and wrapped his hands around my waist, leaning down.

"Well, what do you think? Impressive, right?" he whispered.

"It's amazing."

I placed my hands over top of Daniel's and watched the orchestra as the bandleader brought the song to a close. The dancing couples turned to applaud the band, and the conductor put down his baton and leaned forward to speak into a microphone.

"Ladies and gentlemen, we'll be taking a ten minute break before we get to our final few songs of the night," he announced.

He left the stage, and several of the musicians followed suit. Piped in music began to play from the speakers, and many of the couples on the dance floor resumed dancing.

"Hey, I think I know this song," I said. "Isn't it called 'At Last'?"

"That's right. Etta James. Very romantic." He pulled me back against him and rested his chin on my head. Mesmerized, I gaped at the dancing couples. I wished I could dance like that. And as I watched, it occurred to me that there was no one on the dance floor our age, or even our parents' age.

"Daniel, is it my imagination, or is everyone here kind of old?"

"Apparently the second Friday of every month is seniors' night. So, tell me—do you like to dance?"

"I do, but I could certainly never pull *that* off," I said, gesturing to the dance floor.

"I could teach you—I mean, if you want. It's not as hard as it looks."

"What, you can dance like *that*? You've got to be kidding me."

Jesus, was there anything he couldn't do?

"My mother forced us all to take lessons in high school."

"Even Brad?"

"Yep, even Brad. He's brutal. Awesome football player. Terrible ballroom dancer."

"I can imagine." I was getting a clear visual. I laughed, and Daniel nuzzled my hair, embracing me tightly.

"I'd give anything to take you over there and dance with you right now," he said.

"Daniel, there's no way I'm going out onto that dance floor with you."

"I know. I'm not saying we can. I'm just saying I wish we could."

He kissed the top of my head, and I smiled to myself as I watched the dancing couples. The Etta James song came to an end, and a new song started. I recognized it as Michael Bublé's rendition of "The Way You Look Tonight."

Daniel slowly turned me around in his arms. "I love this song. Listen to that saxophone. Now *that* is one sexy instrument. This is actually a perfect song for tonight."

He sang softly in my ear, his breath tickling my neck and making me shiver. I looked up at him. "What are you trying to do to me?"

He smiled. "I believe I'm renewing my efforts to woo you, Miss Price. Am I having any luck?"

Luck? Good Lord! Luck had nothing to do with it!

"Maybe." I batted my eyelashes. He laughed and took my hands again, leading me back into the other room but leaving the door open.

"Come on, dance with me. I can't think of a more appropriate song for our first dance."

He took my hand and held it over his heart, placing his other hand on my back and pulling me close. Frigging hell, he could write a book. I figured it would be called *The TA's Guide to Making Up with the Girl You're Not Really Allowed to Be with but Refuse to Give Up On.* He never ceased to overwhelm me. As usual, I retreated into the safety of humor.

"You know, I'm only well-versed in one particular dance."

"And what's that?" he said, coaxing me into moving to the music.

"I believe it's most frequently referred to as the *Grade Nine Grope.*"

He smiled down at me. "I'm not sure I'm familiar with that one, but it sounds intriguing. Tell me about it."

"Well, you're supposed to start with both of your hands here."

"How's that?" he asked, his hands encircling my waist.

"Perfect. Then, I put my hands here." I placed my hands on his shoulders. "And my face here." I snuggled into his neck. "And then you pretend you're in grade nine. You know, follow your instincts," I murmured against his Adam's apple, watching it bob as he swallowed.

"Now, let me clarify a point or two," he said. "Is it appropriate during this dance to attempt to steal a kiss from your partner?"

My heart skidded to a halt. *Steal a kiss?* I tried to remain calm.

"That depends," I said coyly.

"On...?"

"Well, you need to make sure the principal's not paying attention."

"Right. That seems to be a running theme, doesn't it?" He made a show of looking around the room. "I'd say we're alone. Does that give me the green light?"

I shrugged and smiled softly.

"You know what? This one time, I think I'm going to take my chances," he said.

I realized we'd stopped dancing. He moved his hand from my waist to gently cradle my cheek. I held my breath as he slowly leaned down to brush the gentlest whisper of a kiss on my lips. And then, because we'd obviously done something to offend the god of fucktastic first kisses, someone knocked on the door. My eyes flew open, and I stumbled backward guiltily.

"You've got to be kidding me," Daniel said, closing his eyes as his jaw jumped with frustration. "Wait here. And hold that thought."

He crossed to open the door. The coat-check girl was standing outside holding two champagne glasses. She handed over the glasses and then listened to Daniel whisper something. After a few more quiet words, Daniel nodded and thanked her as he pushed the door closed with his foot. He made his way back over to me, holding out one of the glasses.

"Compliments of the manager," he said. "Obviously a man who knows a thing or two about being in the dog house."

"And a man who has appalling timing," I pointed out.

Seriously. The *worst* timing ever. The song had ended. The wonderful moment had passed, and with it my chance of a hot first kiss with the man of my dreams.

"You're right about that," Daniel said. "But it seems a shame to waste perfectly good champagne. Mind if I make a toast?"

"Be my guest."

"To our anniversary," he said, eyes sparkling.

"Our anniversary?" I raised an eyebrow.

"One month ago today we had our first date."

"We did?"

"*Hamlet*? February the thirteenth?" he said.

"You consider that our first *date?*" I laughed.

"Don't you?"

"Seriously? Vomiting in the washroom while the hot guy you're trying to impress paces outside waiting for you? Not my idea of a great first date. Plus, you were still Miss Price-ing me that night. It wasn't a date."

"Funny how different things stand out for different people," he said.

"Why? What do you remember?"

"Well, for starters, I remember you swearing. I think that was the first time I heard you say 'fuck.'"

"Ah, yes, that's terribly romantic."

He smiled. "Then you elbowed me in the ribs."

"Again, just a little something I do to turn guys on," I added.

He took a step closer to me. "Then once the play started, I remember whispering something to you, and you had the most delicious expression on your face. I came close to kissing you right there and then."

I racked my brain for a witty comeback, but I couldn't pull anything together. He had that lidded-eyes-dropped-chin thing going on. He ruined me with that every time.

"So, yes, I'm going with that as our anniversary," he said, tipping his hand forward and clinking my glass with his. We both took a sip of champagne.

"Okay, you win. Happy anniversary, sailor."

"Happy anniversary, poppet," he said, stroking my cheek. Then he sighed and shook his head. "Now, this sucks, but unfortunately we have to go. Tiffany gave me fair warning that the parking lot is about to get crazy. She said everyone tends to pour out at quarter to ten. I'm not concerned about the rush, but I would like to make an inconspicuous exit. We should probably leave."

Of course. Right when things were getting good. But our actions were being guided by the need for discretion, and I couldn't complain. At least not out loud.

"Okay." I took another swig of my champagne.

We left our glasses on the coffee table, and Daniel led me out to the lobby, helping me with my coat and gathering my hair up to gently pull it free of my collar. I remembered him doing something similar the week before at the Four Seasons. Was this a trademark move? I sincerely hoped so.

Then we were out the doors and into the cold night air. Daniel took a cursory glance around the parking lot as we walked. I found myself doing the same, on high alert now, even more paranoid than I'd been the week before, though the odds of running into anyone we knew at the Palais Royale certainly seemed slim. Daniel was steering me toward his car when a blue sedan came to a quick halt beside us. The passenger window rolled down, and a voice echoed through the night air.

"Daniel? Is that you?"

## Compromise

And now the matter grows to compromise…
(*King Henry VI, Part 1*, Act v, Scene 4)

Daniel took a step toward the car while I tried to stay out of sight behind him, deciding if I should make a run for it.

"Patty?"

*Patty?* Not Daniel's grandmother? Holy crap—we were screwed.

"What are you doing here?" he asked. It sounded like he was trying to keep his voice light and conversational.

"Having a night on the town, of course," she said. "I could ask you the same question—this is seniors' night. They aren't supposed to let in the riffraff." Daniel laughed. "Open my door, Daniel."

He opened the door and helped her climb out. I hung back, hoping she had bad eyesight, but was unable to resist checking out this woman who'd been described as a "corker" by Penny. So this was Granny Wright. She was wiry and silver-haired with sparkling eyes and coral lip-sticked lips. She was wearing a knee-length fur coat. I had no clue whether the fur was real or faux, but if it was real, it had to have been hellishly expensive.

"Now give me a hug," she ordered him. He did as he was told.

"So, you've been here all night?" Daniel asked her.

"Yes, of course. Gerald and I come here every month."

"Gerald?"

"Yes, Gerald. And if you tell your parents about this I'll disinherit you." Patty was scowling and wagging her finger at her grandson. "The last thing I need is them prying into my personal life."

Daniel leaned into the passenger side window. "Hello, Gerald," he said, reaching in to shake the hand of his grandmother's beau.

"Gerald, this is my grandson, Daniel," his grandmother said, poking her head in the window.

Gerald's jovial voice rang out clearly, "Well, it's about time I met one of the boys. I've been doubting your existence. Nice to meet you, Daniel. Henny speaks highly of you."

"Well, thank you, sir." Daniel stood up and turned to me, pulling me forward.

"There's actually someone I'd like you to meet as well, Patty. Aubrey Price, this is my grandmother, Henrietta Wright. Patty, this is Aubrey, a very good friend of mine."

What in the living hell was he doing? Had he lost his frigging mind?

"Well, Aubrey, what a delight to meet you." She shook my hand, her inquisitive eyes piercing my soul. Very unnerving. I stood there, smiling stupidly. "How lovely. Daniel, you've been holding out on me," she chided him.

"Sorry, Patty. We're not quite ready to go public. Mom and Dad don't know. Not up to dealing with the Spanish Inquisition yet. You understand, right? I'll keep your secret if you keep mine?"

"I see." Granny Wright's eyes flickered over to me briefly. "I understand perfectly. You know me. I'll take your secret to the grave if that's what you'd like me to do. Speaking of which, when are you coming for dinner? I'm not going to live forever, you know."

"Oh, I don't know. I'm sure you'll give it your best shot. If only to piss a few people off."

Daniel's grandmother chuckled. "You're right. That's my strongest motivation to stay healthy — to drive your father mad."

"Well, name the time and I'll be there," Daniel said. "Apparently we've got lots to get caught up on."

"I'm an old lady, dear boy. Long range plans are inadvisable. How's this Sunday?"

"This Sunday's perfect," Daniel said. "Will you be inviting Mom and Dad?"

"Oh, heavens no. I'd actually like to have a nice time." She scowled at him while she winked at me. Amusement nudged at the corner of Daniel's mouth. "I'll expect you at five o'clock," his grandmother said, a tone of finality in her voice.

"Sounds wonderful. What can I bring?"

"A bottle of red wine. Not one of those skinny little things either. Don't be a cheapskate like your father."

Daniel laughed. "Deal."

"And bring your young lady, too. I'd say she needs some feeding."

Daniel looked at me and smiled. I felt like I'd stumbled into an episode of *The Twilight Zone*.

"Open my door, Daniel."

Patty was finished. Her word, it seemed, was law.

Daniel did as he was told, holding her hand while she backed herself into the car and swung her legs in. "Gerald, it was nice meeting you," Daniel said, closing the door carefully.

Patty peered out the window and held up a warning finger. "Fencepost, Daniel."

"Fencepost, Patty."

"Give my love to your brothers and tell them to call me if they know what's good for them. And get your young lady there some food."

"I'll get right on it." He took her gloved hand and kissed it. "Love you, Patty."

"I love you too, my boy. Now move out of the way. It's past my bedtime. I need my beauty sleep."

She closed her window, and we stepped back. As Gerald drove off, Daniel raised his hand to wave at the retreating vehicle. Then he turned to look at me, a goofy grin on his face.

"Are you out of your freaking mind?" I asked him.

"What?"

"What do you mean *what*? You just told your grandmother my name, and now we're going there for dinner on Sunday? Are you high?"

He steered me down the path toward the car. "I know what you're thinking, but it's not a problem. Patty meant what she said. She won't tell my parents a thing. Plus, I've got something on her, too. She doesn't want my folks knowing about Gerald."

"Are you sure?"

"I'm one hundred percent sure. I'm her favorite." He winked at me. "She won't breathe a word of this to my father. Wow, I can't believe she was here all night."

"I know. What are the odds? Do you think we're being punk'd?"

Daniel laughed, opening my door and waiting for me to get settled before closing it. When he climbed in and started the car, I was still shaking my head in disbelief. Daniel tried to comfort me.

"Do I look worried? Believe me, if there was something to worry about, you'd know." He turned the heat on high. "Listen, if it was anyone else, you can bet your sweet ass I'd be having a frigging cow right now. But it's not. It's Patty. Trust me. Everything's going to be fine, okay?"

I sighed and nodded, trying to shake off my uneasiness. He seemed completely unfazed. "Hey, she fenceposted you."

"And I returned the favor," he said, grinning at me. "You know what that means. In my family, a fencepost is an unbreakable bond." He turned the heat down a notch; the air was gradually warming up. "I'm sorry if you felt railroaded, though. Are you sure you're free to come with me on Sunday?"

"Of course. If you think it's okay for me to go, then I'd love to join you."

He smiled and grabbed my hand, pulling it onto his thigh as he pulled out of the lot and onto the road.

"So, what did your grandmother mean when she said she wasn't inviting your mom and dad because she wanted to have a good time?"

"Patty and my father haven't always seen eye to eye. My grandmother finds my dad a little, uh, *rigid*, shall we say? She's a firm believer in seizing the day, and my dad's morals are so firmly entrenched. He can't do anything without dragging his principles along for the ride."

This was an interesting analysis. I'd always admired Dean Grant so much. But perhaps living with someone who always took the high road would get a bit wearing after a while.

"I can't believe I'm going to dinner at your grandmother's," I said. "It's kind of nerve-racking. What if she doesn't like me? What should I wear?"

"I guarantee she'll love you. And wear something comfortable. Some nice pants and a sweater or something."

"Okay." I settled back again. Hell, if he was totally cool with it, who was I to worry?

He glanced at me from time to time as he drove, his face brighter than I'd seen it in a long time.

"I'm so glad we talked. Now there're no more secrets. It's very liberating."

No more secrets? Well, shit. Maybe as far as Daniel was concerned that was true, but a little gnawing voice reminded me that I hadn't been completely honest with him. Not telling him the truth about Matt was eating me alive. Did I dare take the risk? And hadn't Daniel just taken a huge chance by sharing his Oxford story? He'd finally opened up to me completely. I owed him the same courtesy.

"Um, Daniel, there is *one* other thing that I need to tell you. You might not like it. Actually, you probably won't like it at all. You might want to pull over."

He looked at me worriedly. "Well, that doesn't sound good."

He pulled into the right lane and turned into the next parking lot. It was a picnic area, dark and deserted at this time of night. We parked in a corner, and he looked at me, brows furrowed.

"What is it?"

"I wasn't going to tell you this because I knew you'd probably take it the wrong way, but I feel like it needs to be said, and you've shared everything with me. I don't want there to be any secrets between us, either, but promise me you won't freak out?"

"I'll do my best. Go ahead."

"Okay. Since we got together, you've been worried about Matt, assuming something was going on with us. There's honestly nothing—and I mean *nothing*—but friendship between us. The only thing I can compare it to is your relationship with Penny. But to be truthful, there was a time when we did sort of toy with the idea of possibly getting together."

He closed his eyes and swallowed. "When was this, Aubrey?"

"In first year, we kissed at a party, but it didn't go beyond that. We both realized it wasn't meant to be."

"So you kissed him four years ago?"

"Yes."

"The idea of you *ever* kissing him doesn't necessarily thrill me, but I think I can cope with that."

"Yes, but that's not all," I said.

Daniel grimaced.

I took a deep breath to steady my nerves. "On Valentine's Day, we went to Canoe for dinner, as you know."

"Right."

"We were honestly there as friends, but then I saw you with Penny, and I thought you were together. I was so jealous, and I'd had a few drinks. I guess I kind of lost my mind, and we sort of, well, no, *not* sort of, we kissed—a few times."

"What kind of a kisses?" His voice was tight.

"*Real* kisses."

"By real, I take it you mean passionate—intimate?"

"I guess you could say that. At least I think they were *supposed* to be. But it didn't feel right to me." I grabbed his hand again. He looked down at our entwined fingers contemplatively. "I knew it was wrong, Daniel, because the whole time I was thinking of *you*, imagining what it would be like if it was you, *wishing* it was you kissing me instead of Matt. That's all that happened. We both knew it was a mistake and decided nothing like that would ever happen again. He was rebounding, and I was trying to soothe my ego. It was a bad scene."

He looked at me, not speaking. I didn't know what to do, or if I should say something else. But then, out of nowhere, he pulled his hand from mine, climbed out of the car and slammed the door. He was running away again? Couldn't he ever deal with anything maturely? In the time it took me to begin contemplating whether or not to follow him, I realized he wasn't running away. He was coming around to my side of the car. He opened my door.

"Could you step out for a minute?" he asked, offering me his hand.

I undid my seat belt and climbed out of the car with a sigh. *Now what?*

He sat in my vacated passenger seat and fiddled with his iPod. The opening notes of Michael Bublé's "The Way you Look Tonight," the same song we'd heard no more than half an hour ago in the Palais Royale, filled the car. He got out, leaving the engine running and the door wide open so that we could still hear the song. He pulled me toward him, settling one hand on the small of my back and bringing the other to rest over his heart as he'd done earlier.

"Thank you for being honest with me. I'm sure that wasn't easy, given the way I've been acting this week," he said softly.

"So, you're not mad?" I asked.

"No, I'm not mad, my angel."

I looked at him in amazement. Would I ever understand the way his mind worked?

He smiled. "Not the reaction you were expecting, I guess? Forget all that for a minute. I was so disappointed earlier when Tiffany knocked on that bloody door. Don't get me wrong, I enjoyed the champagne, but I'd have more than gladly traded the glass of bubbly for a few more quiet moments with you. Maybe it's silly of me, but I love this song, and I was hoping it would provide the backdrop for more than just our first dance. I know the setting isn't ideal, but at least I've got the mood music, right?"

I nodded and watched his lips, transfixed.

"You said when Matt was kissing you that you were imagining what it would be like if it was me instead?" He looked steadily into my eyes. "To hell with imagination."

My heart was pounding so hard I was sure he could hear it. I bit my lip and looked at him longingly. "What about Oxford?" I whispered.

"Screw Oxford."

He cradled my face, his lips inches away. I closed my eyes, waiting for the moment of contact, and when his lips finally touched mine, they were warm and soft. Twice, three times, he kissed me tenderly. I leaned into him, reveling in the feeling of his hands moving down to my waist to pull me close and his teeth gently biting my lower lip. At last he turned his face and nudged my nose softly with his before claiming my mouth and teasing my lips open with his tongue. Slowly, torturously, his tongue slid against mine again and again, making me dizzy with desire. An involuntary sound—half moan, half whimper—betrayed how badly I wanted him.

After a few moments, he pulled away. My eyes fluttered open, and Daniel was watching, his eyes lidded, the corner of his mouth turned up.

"Are you all right?" he asked.

"I'm better than all right," I whispered. "How's your Achilles' heel?"

"I'll be making an appointment for physiotherapy first thing in the morning."

"Maybe I'll come with you. I seem to be having a little issue with a weak sensation in my knees."

"Hmm. Well, in the absence of a suitable bookshelf to support you, why don't you hold on right here?"

He took my hands and curled my fingers around the lapels of his suit jacket. Then he spun me around, trapping me against the car as he pressed his lips against mine. The kiss deepened, becoming increasingly passionate, almost frantic, as weeks of unrequited longing tore through us.

My hands tangled in his newly trimmed locks. His lips broke from mine briefly, tracing fiery kisses along my jaw. He tickled me with his stubble as he slowly moved toward my ear, where he paused for a moment to whisper, "I was right. You do taste amazing—the champagne chaser is definitely a bonus."

My God, he was so sexy! I kissed him feverishly, desperately, both of us now moaning into each other's mouths. He reached down to undo my coat and quickly unbuttoned his suit jacket before pressing his body flush against mine. With nothing but thin layers of fabric keeping us apart, my head spun.

I let my head drop back as he lowered his face to kiss and nuzzle my neck, awakening sensations I hadn't felt in well over a year. His hands snuck inside my coat to grasp my hips, his hands traveling lower, cupping my buttocks as he ground his hips against me.

"God, you've got the greatest ass," he groaned.

I was vaguely aware that I was gasping like I'd just run around the block several times. "Daniel," I breathed.

"Yes." He sighed and nibbled on my ear lobe, sending delicious shivers through my stomach to the center of my body where a tense spring of desire waited to uncoil.

If I allowed things to continue, I had no doubt his hands would be traveling under the hem of my dress any minute, and we'd be in the back seat in a heartbeat. That was mighty tempting, but what had I said to him an hour ago? *"Let's start at the beginning, not at the end."* I didn't want to be the one sending mixed messages now. Regardless of how badly I wanted him to touch me—everywhere, and right now—I wasn't prepared to have sex with Daniel in the back seat of his car, at least not tonight. I wanted our first time to be romantic, not cheap and tawdry.

Our second time? Now *that* could be cheap and tawdry.

"Daniel, we should stop," I panted, trying to pull away.

"No, not yet," he pleaded, tenderly kissing me again with measured control, his tongue moving deliberately against mine. Gradually he loosened his grasp, slowly pushing me back, kissing me sweetly, calming the stormy passion that was raging through me.

"Stop—please," I sighed between kisses.

He leaned back to look at me, running his thumb across my lower lip. "You're trembling all over."

"Not to question your ability to make me quiver with desire, but I'm actually freezing."

He looked at me in stunned silence for a second or two. "Crap, of course you are. I'm such a moron." He kissed me once more and groaned with frustration. "Come on. Let's get you back into the car where it's warm."

He helped me in, closing the door behind me. I turned the heat on full blast and held my hands over the vent to warm them, quietly chanting, "Thank you, God. Thank you, God," while beaming my stupid ass off.

If his incredible kisses were any indication of the hot times in store for me, the future was looking mighty bright indeed, since what I'd just experienced in mere moments showed that Daniel was capable of extreme tenderness as well as pure, unadulterated lust.

I peered out the front window. He was standing off to the side of the car, his hands clasped on top of his head, a look of what can only be described as agony on his face. What the hell was he doing? I leaned over the driver's seat to watch him as he dropped one hand to his hip and rubbed his face roughly with the other, pacing back and forth a few times. After another moment or two, he strode to the car and climbed in.

"Are you okay?" I asked.

"Yes, I needed a minute to pull myself together. Jesus Christ."

"Sorry."

"Don't be silly. If this is how it's got to be, then so be it. I need to learn to deal with it until — well, you know."

I smiled and nodded. "Okay, no more apologies. I don't want you to be angry with me, that's all."

"I'm not angry with you. I knew our first kiss would blow my mind. I warned you."

"Yes, you did."

"Are you feeling warmer?"

"I'm fine now, thanks," I said, pushing myself upright and crossing my legs.

"God, give me strength," he muttered, his eyes darting down to my legs as he turned the stereo off.

"Blew your mind, huh?" I asked.

"Don't pretend you don't know what you do to me," he said, lacing his fingers in mine and resting our joined hands on his thigh again.

*God, while you're giving him strength, toss a little my way too.*

He looked over at me. "What are you thinking?"

I laughed. "Not telling."

"You're not having regrets, I hope?"

"What, about kissing you? Lord, no. Don't even go there. I'm just kind of impressed with my self-control."

"Well, I'm glad you had your wits about you. I was *this close* to tossing you in the back seat."

"Yeah, I had a feeling I'd better put a stop to things or you'd be teaching me the naked mambo any minute."

He laughed in an I've-been-drinking-Guinness-all-night kind of way.

"Aubrey, where do you come up with this stuff? You crack me up, I swear."

"And you're not mad at me? About — Matt?"

"Let me ask you something. When we were kissing, who were you thinking about?"

"Well, obviously I was thinking about you. I was thinking about how I wanted to rip your clothes off." I laughed. "I just want *you*, sailor."

"See?" He smiled. "That's all I need to know. All this business with Matt? I'm over it. We have enough other crap to deal with. But for the record, I wanted you to rip my clothes off, too."

He brought my hand to his lips, eyes sparkling as he brushed a kiss across my knuckles. I couldn't believe how well he'd taken my news. Something had changed in the course of the last few days, maybe even the last few hours. He seemed prepared to take my words at face value and believe that what I was saying was the absolute truth.

"This has been one of the most insane days of my life," he said.

"Ditto."

"I'm happy with the compromise we've reached, but before I take you home, we do have one other piece of unfinished business."

He leaned back and pulled a plastic bag through the space between the seats. It was the bag I'd asked Julie to give him.

"Oh, crap. How much did you hate me when you opened that?"

"I didn't hate you, poppet. I was gutted."

"Is the T-shirt in there?"

"Yes. The calendar, too. You want them back?"

"Of course I do."

"Wait, there's something we have to do first," he said, pulling the calendar out and turning the page to March. "Where's the pen?"

I rummaged in the bag and uncapped the marker. He wrapped his fingers around mine and together we put an X through Tuesday, following suit with Wednesday and Thursday.

"What do you think?" he asked. "Is today over?"

"Close enough."

We filled the box for the thirteenth with an X, then he took the pen, and with a soft chuckle, Daniel traced a big red heart around the thirteen.

"After all, it *is* our anniversary," he said with mock earnestness.

"Oh, of course," I said. He was adorable.

"I'm not completely ignoring what you said earlier, by the way. Maybe you won't even be ready to — you know — move forward when the semester's over, but that doesn't mean I'm going to stop counting down. If nothing else, I know that in forty-seven days I can take you to Tim Horton's and hold your hand in public while we sit at a table, drinking coffee and eating Timbits."

It was ridiculous how wonderful that sounded. He pushed the calendar and pen back into the bag.

"There. Done and dusted. Right, then, let's get you home. Do you still have your gloves?"

I checked my pockets and pulled them out. "Ta da! Both of them."

"Excellent. And tonight, will you sleep in my shirt?"

"You know it."

"How about tomorrow? Can I call you?"

"I'm counting on it, sweet knees."

"*That's* what I like to hear." He looked at my lips. "And right now—may I steal another kiss?"

I grinned at him. "Is it still stealing if I agree?"

I eagerly leaned across the center console.

And he moved forward as well, meeting me in the middle.

# *Acknowledgments*

Over the past four years, I have been blessed with the opportunity to share my writing online with thousands of people who were more than just readers to me: they were coaches, cheerleaders, mentors and in many cases, they became friends. I want to take this opportunity to recognize those who read, and in many cases, reviewed, blogged and Tweeted their enthusiastic responses to my first draft of *The Weight of Words*. Your kindness and support motivated me to continue writing, and ultimately gave me the courage to publish this novel. Thank you.

Special thanks to Nora, LS, Christina G and Christina D, whose feedback and assistance at various points in the initial writing process was invaluable. To Dee, I cannot thank you enough for your years of pre-reading and support (you have the loveliest green pom-poms in town). More importantly, though, I'm grateful for your kind spirit and your friendship. To Jen, your enthusiasm and ingenuity have inspired me and fed both my spirit and my mojo. Thank you for always having my back.

To everyone who created beautiful artwork inspired by my words, thank you for sharing the fruits of your creativity with me. I must thank Michelle, in particular, for making me feel as if my every word counted for something. Michelle, your art is beautiful, and so are you.

I also owe a debt of gratitude to SR who has graciously mentored and encouraged me over the past few years, always offering words of advice and reassurance. I feel lucky to know you, sir. And to Neens, thank you for believing in me and for teaching me all about acronyms (UST FOREVER!) and word-grunt hybrids (UNF). Knowing you're just a flaily email away is more comforting than you could possibly know.

To the team at Omnific — thank you for your taking a chance on me. This has been such a wonderful learning experience.

Of course, this story would not exist without the Bard's words which have enthralled me since, as a starry-eyed adolescent, I opened the pages of *A Midsummer Night's Dream*. In *Hamlet*, Shakespeare's Gertrude tells us that "all that lives must die." Happily, this has not been true of the Bard's words, and I have to give credit to Master Shakespeare for the immense inspiration his stories have provided.

Finally, the deepest gratitude goes out to my husband and my family. You allowed me the time to pursue my dreams, and you understood when I "left the room," even if I was still sitting beside you on the couch. I will be forever grateful for your unconditional love.

# About the Author

Georgina Guthrie has been a self-professed book hugger for as long as she can remember. An avid reader and compulsive diarist, she is thrilled to be taking the leap into the world of publishing. GG resides in Toronto, Canada, but she still considers herself a Brit through and through and can often be found roaming the aisles of her favorite British import shop.

A graduate of the University of Toronto where she studied English literature, GG is happy to fill her hours reading and writing, but she's just as likely to be found enjoying a good film with her husband, dancing around the kitchen with her daughter, or hanging out with friends and family, almost certainly with a glass of red wine in one hand a bag of cheese and onion crisps in the other.

## Young Adult

The Ember Series: *Ember* & *Iridescent* by Carol Oates
*Breaking Point* by Jess Bowen
*Life, Liberty, and Pursuit* by Susan Kaye Quinn
The Embrace Series: *Embrace* & *Hold Tight* by Cherie Colyer
*Destiny's Fire* by Trisha Wolfe
*Reaping Me Softly* & *UnReap My Heart* by Kate Evangelista

## Erotic Romance

The Keyhole Series: *Becoming sage (book one)* by Kasi Alexander
The Keyhole Series: *Saving sunni (book two)* by Kasi & Reggie Alexander
The Winemaker's Dinner: *Appetizers* & *Entrée* by Dr. Ivan Rusilko &
Everly Drummond
The Winemaker's Dinner: *Dessert* by Dr. Ivan Rusilko

## Paranormal Romance

The Light Series: *Seers of Light, Whisper of Light,* & *Circle of Light*
by Jennifer DeLucy
The Hanaford Park Series: *Eve of Samhain* & *Pleasures Untold* by Lisa Sanchez
*Immortal Awakening* by KC Randall
*Crushed Seraphim* & *Bittersweet Seraphim* by Debra Anastasia
*The Guardian's Wild Child* by Feather Stone
*Grave Refrain* by Sarah M. Glover
*Divinity* by Patricia Leever
*Blood Vine* & *Blood Entangled* by Amber Belldene
*Divine Temptation* by Nicki Elson
*Love in the Time of the Dead* by Tera Shanley

## Romantic Suspense

*Whirlwind* by Robin DeJarnett
The CONduct Series: *With Good Behavior* & *Bad Behavior* & *On Best Behavior*
by Jennifer Lane
*Indivisible* by Jessica McQuinn
*Between the Lies* by Alison Oburia